Archangel's Heart

A GUILD HUNTER NOVEL

NALINI SINGH

First published in Great Britain in 2016 by Gollancz
an imprint of the Orion Publishing Group Ltd
Carmelite House, 50 Victoria Embankment
London EC4Y 0DZ

An Hachette UK Company

1 3 5 7 9 10 8 6 4 2

Copyright © Nalini Singh 2016

The moral right of Nalini Singh to be identified as
the author of this work has been asserted in accordance
with the Copyright, Designs and Patents Act of 1988.

All rights reserved. No part of this publication may be
reproduced, stored in a retrieval system, or transmitted
in any form or by any means, electronic, mechanical,
photocopying, recording, or otherwise, without the
prior permission of both the copyright owner and the
above publisher of this book.

All the characters in this book are fictitious, and any resemblance
to actual persons, living or dead, is purely coincidental.

A CIP catalogue record for this book is
available from the British Library.

ISBN 978 1 473 21749 2

Rotherham MBC	
B54 015 604 1	
Askews & Holts	07-Nov-2016
AF	£8.99
CLS	

Hide

She was tired.

Not old in years. Just tired. While her vocation called to her as powerfully as it had always done, the reality was a relentless workload that offered little time for the life of study and reflection that she craved.

But this was the life the Lord wished for her and so this was the life she would live.

The worn black fabric of her habit brushed the wooden floor as she walked down the aisle, checking the pews for items left behind by the faithful. Father Pierre was getting on in years so, though he always offered to close up the church, Constance was the one who did it every night. At least she didn't have to deal with the homeless. Her closest friend in the order, Maria, who was in a house of worship in a more derelict part of town, often had to nudge out those unfortunates.

It made her question her faith on a daily basis.

"Should we not provide sanctuary, Sister Constance?" she'd ask when they gathered at the order's simple house for their late dinner meal. "And yet I must push them out into the dark and the cold because, elsewise, they defile the church.

Why, the other day, I found a vampire feeding from a drug-addled young man right out in the open."

Constance had no answers for Maria, but she'd volunteered to take charge of that church next year, to help balance the load. For they must all do their duty.

Ah, it looked like someone had left behind a coat.

They would surely return for it, she thought as she moved down the pew.

Then the coat moved. Heart thumping, she stopped . . . and realized that while the pale blue fabric *was* of a coat, that coat was on a person. A small person. A child.

Close enough now to see the peacefully sleeping child's golden-skinned face and soft hair so pale it was almost white, she looked down and saw the child wore a dress of soft pink broderie anglaise. The stockings on her little legs were white with blue butterflies along the sides, her shoes a shiny black.

This was a child who was loved, who'd been dressed with care.

A little bag sat next to her, printed with the image of a storybook princess.

Constance whispered a prayer and looked around in case she had somehow missed one of the faithful, but no, she was alone in the church but for this beautiful child, who couldn't have been more than five years of age. Not knowing quite what to do but aware she couldn't let the child sleep on the hard wood of the pew, she bent to lift her into her arms.

The child awoke. "*Maman?*"

It was a hopeful word but the little girl's lower lip trembled.

Constance replied in the same tongue. It was not her own, but she'd lived for many years in this land of corner bakeries and stylishly dressed people and hidden avenues cloaked in darkness. "Your mother is not here yet." She held out a hand. "Come, we will go have hot chocolate and cookies while we wait for her."

"I have toys," the child said, picking up the princess bag before slipping her tiny hand into Constance's with the sweet trust of a being who had never been hurt, who knew only love. As she walked the child to the back room, where she and Father Pierre often did the paperwork of an afternoon, she caught sight of a stark white envelope in the child's coat pocket.

She didn't reach for it until her small guest had taken off her coat and was happily eating a cookie, Constance having made her a hot chocolate in a chipped but pretty red cup she thought a child would like.

The envelope proved to be the size of a photograph. That was what lay within it, along with a letter written in a lovely hand:

> *To the sister and the father who care for this church—you don't know me, but you were so kind to me when I first arrived in this distant land that was not my home but that became my sanctuary.*
>
> *I know your souls are full of light.*
>
> *Please watch over my Marguerite and keep this photograph of us together for her. I will return for her within the week. She is the very beat of my heart. If I don't return . . . then I am dead and Marguerite is an orphan. Call her that if the worst happens, but please, please do not ever say that she was abandoned. Do not ever let her believe anything but that she was my greatest treasure.*
>
> *The only reason I won't return for her is if there is no life left in my body. Even then, you must never allow her to become suspicious and search for the truth—that way lies only horror and death. I would have my baby live her life free of the shadow of fear.*
>
> *Tell her I love her.*

The child looked at Constance with eyes of silvery gray, a smudge of chocolate on the edge of her lips. "Will *Maman* be here soon?"

Constance swallowed, touched trembling fingers to that hair so delicately pretty. "Your mother loves you very much."

And the child smiled, as if that was a simple fact of life.

1

Two years had passed.

Two years since Alexander woke.

Two years since the last confirmed sighting of Zhou Lijuan.

Two years since Illium threatened to burn up in a catastrophic explosion of power.

Two years while the Cascade seemed to hit Pause.

Elena was fucking over waiting for the other shoe to drop.

"Come on already," she muttered up at the sky, Manhattan a toy borough hundreds of feet below the edge of the railing-free Tower balcony on which she stood.

"Speaking to your ancestors, Elena-mine?" The voice came from behind her, familiar and imbued with a power so violently deep that the mere sound of it engendered fear in the hearts of mortals and immortals alike.

It made Elena's own heart ache, the love she felt for her archangel a painful, terrifying thing in these times of uncertainty. If she lost him . . . No, she couldn't think that way. Even if that damn other shoe was still smirking at her, just waiting to thunk down on top of her head when she least expected it.

"Whoever or whatever it is that controls the Cascade, that's who I'm talking to." She leaned back into Raphael. The position trapped her wings in between, but with Raphael, she could be vulnerable, she could be weaponless, and still be safe. Not that she wasn't armed to the teeth, but that was habit and none of it would ever be turned against Raphael except when they sparred—or when he pushed her buttons a little too hard.

Her archangel hadn't quite got the hang of the fact he wasn't lord and master over his consort. He tried but a thousand-five-hundred-years-plus of power had a way of messing with his attempts at seeing his once-mortal lover as an equal when it came to their personal relationship.

Elena cut him some slack every so often. "Some" being the operative word.

Today, he wrapped his arms around her shoulders from behind, his jaw brushing her hair as the two of them looked out over their city from their vantage point on the cloud-piercing form of Archangel Tower. New York. Brash and messy and noisy and full of color and energy and life. *So much* life. Elena could hear it on the busy streets far, far below, sense it with every beat of her heart, taste it in the myriad scents that clashed and fought and yet somehow made their peace.

Her blood hummed in awareness.

"I have news," Raphael murmured. "It may inject a little excitement into your currently mundane life."

Elena snorted. "I don't need any more excitement. I just need the damn Cascade off Pause so we can get it done." Her hand twitched to go for the lightweight crossbow strapped to her thigh.

Unfortunately, she didn't have anyone or anything to shoot at right now.

Raphael's chuckle vibrated against her. "You sound a little tense, Consort."

Elena would've elbowed him if her wings hadn't been in the way. "Why are you in such a good mood?" The past two years had been as tautly tense for him as they'd been for her. All the archangels had stayed within the borders of their own territories—but for a few secret trips here and there—in preparation for further Cascade madness.

Only the unpredictable worldwide phenomenon that caused dangerous power fluctuations in the archangels as well as some angels, along with tumult across the earth in the form of storms, quakes, and floods, seemed to have decided it was finished. But of course, they all knew it wasn't. Not by a long shot. Even Elena could feel the thunderous portent in the air, just hanging there, waiting to unleash itself.

"My good mood is because something has at last broken the stalemate of the past two years."

"I'm not going to like this, am I?" Elena said darkly.

"Such a suspicious mind."

"Yes. It keeps me alive." She watched an angel with wings of an astonishing, haunting blue edged with silver rise up over a skyscraper in the distance, Illium's physical strength back to what it should be for his age and development. There had been no other vicious and possibly deadly surges that threatened to tear his body apart from the inside out.

Even better, he was laughing again, was once more the playful angel who'd become her first friend in this immortal world. "Bluebell's about to do a dive," she predicted from the way Illium was soaring up into the crystalline sky.

And then he was turning and falling, a sleek bullet whose laughter she could almost hear.

"I bet you he's planning to go low enough to freak out the pedestrians." New Yorkers were used to angels in their city, turned up their noses at the tourists who gawped up at the sky, but angelic acrobatics could still make them jump. Especially acrobatics done by an angel as fast and as quick to maneuver as Illium.

"That is no bet," Raphael answered. "He's been playing such tricks as long as I've known him."

And Raphael, Elena thought, had known Illium since the other angel was a child.

She reached up to close her hands over the arms he'd wrapped around her. Illium meant a great deal to her archangel; that was a truth most people didn't comprehend. All of Raphael's Seven meant far more to him than simply the positions they filled in his Tower or in his Refuge stronghold.

They weren't just his most trusted warriors—the Seven were family.

Rubbing his jaw against her temple in a silent response to her touch, he said, "We are about to leave New York."

Elena blinked; she couldn't have been more surprised if he'd told her he wanted her to strip naked then and there and start chanting to invisible sky gods. "What happened to batten down the hatches and watch for an attack? All our enemies are still out there."

"The Cadre has been called to meet."

Rubbing at her face, Elena turned and took a step back so she could face Raphael, her wings a familiar weight at her back and the wind tugging lightly at her feathers as if in invitation for flight. The almost cruel masculine beauty of his face hit her hard, as it sometimes did when she looked at him after glancing away. All clean lines and skin brushed with finest gold, he had eyes so shatteringly blue they had no equal on this earth, his hair a black beyond midnight and his lips shaped with a sensuality that hinted at passion and power both, wings of white gold arching over his shoulders.

Already, he'd been magnificent, but the Legion mark on his right temple—the violent, vivid blue and hidden white fire of it shaped like the primal manifestation of a dragon—added a wildness to his beauty that made him beyond beautiful, beyond magnificent. He was Raphael, Archangel of New York, and the man she loved so much that sometimes she couldn't breathe from the force of it.

And he loved her.

That truth she could never doubt, no matter if, at times, he crossed lines in their relationship that made her threaten to pull out a blade. Even if the Cascade messed with everything else, this one thing no one and nothing could ever mess up.

Lifting his hand, he cupped her cheek, brushed the pad of his thumb over her cheekbone. "Your eyes are even more luminous today."

Elena scowled. "I don't want luminous eyes," she said. "I want normal gray eyes that let me blend in, not silver eyes that make it obvious I'm an immortal."

Raphael's lips curved. "A pity about the wings then."

"Ha ha." Putting her hands on her hips, she turned her head to press a kiss to his palm before facing him once more. "Which one of the archangels called for the meet?" It would tell her which ones were likely to go—and which ones would be salivating at the opportunity to attack other territories while the archangels to whom those territories belonged were occupied elsewhere.

"None."

The single word fell like a gunshot between them.

Shaking her head, Elena reached up to tuck back a strand of hair that had whipped across her face. She'd left the near-white stuff unbound today since she wasn't on a hunt and had been planning to hang out close to the Tower and the Legion skyscraper.

"I know I've only been an immortal a zillionth of a second according to angelic time," she said dryly, "but I'm pretty sure there's no one more powerful than an archangel. Unless it's one of those Ancestor creatures Naasir told me about." She'd taken those Sleeping beings to be myth, but maybe not.

"There is no one more powerful than the Cadre," Raphael confirmed. "However, in one situation and one situation *only*, another group can call the Cadre to a meeting. Attendance is mandatory—anyone who does not attend can have their territory divided with the might of all angelkind standing behind those who are given the resulting pieces."

Elena whistled. "Sounds like an invitation to war." Especially since angelkind wasn't exactly united right now.

"Yes—which is why no one refuses an invitation. It's not worth the aggravation when all possible threats will be at the meeting with you." Raphael nodded to behind her. "Aodhan is dodging crossbow bolts."

Swiveling on her heel, Elena spotted the angel who seemed created of pieces of light, a thousand rays of sunshine sparking off the filaments of his wings, the glittering strands of his hair; he was darting this way and that while an entire squadron shot at him. The members of the squadron were wearing wraparound sunglasses in an effort to track the piercing blaze of him in the sky.

Aodhan, meanwhile, dropped and dodged with uncanny skill.

"And the prize for most bored goes to . . ."

Raphael moved forward to stand beside her, his wing sliding over her own. "He's just staying in shape for the battle to come."

Unfortunately, that was true. The battle *would* come and that damn shoe *would* drop. "This group that has the power to force the Cadre to meet, what's it called?"

"The members call themselves the Luminata. They are a spiritual sect—not religious in the human sense." He paused, as if thinking of the right words to describe them. "The closest mortal analog is likely the Buddhist search for enlightenment. The Luminata seek to understand themselves individually and angelkind as a whole; their self-imposed task is to discover who and what we are in the greater scheme of the universe, and to accept whatever answer may come. They call it a search for luminescence."

Spreading his wings, he folded them back in a susurration of sound she'd never associate with anyone but her archangel. "Many mortals believe in gods, but when death is but a faint glimmer on a distant horizon that may never be breached, such beliefs fade into confusion. The Luminata attempt to find luminescence in the now, rather than hoping for it on the other side of that distant horizon."

"I met a holy man once during a hunt in India," Elena found herself saying. "He lived as a hermit, had nothing to his name but the clothes on his back, but his eyes . . . such peace, Raphael. I think he's the most peaceful being I've ever met. Even Keir doesn't have such a well of peace inside him." And the revered angelic healer had lived thousands of years.

"From what I know, this is what the Luminata search for." Raphael continued to watch Aodhan's movements in the sky ahead of them. "A purity of soul that leaves them with no earthly questions or concerns."

"Have they had any success in their quest?"

"The only Luminata I've ever met are those who have been asked to leave the sect, and the once-novices—those who walked away from the life after a short attempt. So I have no basis to judge the luminescence of those who follow the path."

Elena raised an eyebrow, but kept silent, interested in this sect that could call a Cadre of archangels to order.

"At some point in our past," Raphael told her, "a point so far back that no one remembers—"

"Did you ask the Legion? Their memories of the past are fading but they're not totally gone."

"I did." Raphael's eyes went to a nearby high-rise, one that had a shape unlike any other in the city, and that was covered in the fresh green of living things, a building that was designed to *be* a living thing. For the Legion were of the earth and it was in earth, in growth, that they thrived. "But those memories, if they existed, are gone. The Legion know the Luminata only from more recent times."

"Recent" being a relative term, Elena thought. "So a long time ago in a land far away, the Luminata . . ." she prompted.

Raphael's laughter was a caress of sunkissed waves over her senses, the power of him no threat but a promise. "I wonder what the sect will make of you, Elena." Love surrounded her, so deep that she felt it in her bones. "As you say, long ago the Luminata were entrusted with a certain task. This task was given to them because it was—and is—believed that they are the only group that can be trusted to be impartial with it."

He raised one hand to stroke it over the arch of her wing, the touch an intimate one between lovers, as, not far in the distance, Aodhan took a crossbow bolt in the thigh. Pulling it out, he threw it back and kept dodging. *Yeah*, Elena thought, *he might be training to stay in shape, but he was also bored. So was Illium, if the screams floating up from the city streets were any indication.*

He'd clearly kept up the dive bombing.

"I think," Raphael said, "I must tell your Bluebell to stop scaring our citizens."

Illium appeared in view a few seconds later, a grin on his almost too handsome face that Elena could see from here. Dipping his wings toward the Tower in acknowledgment of Raphael's order, he joined Aodhan's "dodge the bolts" game.

One bolt went crazily wild at nearly the same instant, heading straight for Elena.

Snatching it from the air with a single hand, Raphael passed it to her. "Whoever this is needs further training."

Elena recognized the markings on the shaft, grinned. "Izzy." The young angel was still a baby in angelic terms. "You have to admit, he's brilliant for his age."

"Galen wouldn't have recommended him for a Tower apprenticeship elsewise," Raphael said before continuing to speak about the Luminata. "By dint of their spiritual quest, the Luminata have no earthly ties and no loyalties beyond that to their quest for luminescence. They take no lovers, participate in no wars, and when they become Luminata, they sever all blood ties."

"A perfect neutral body."

"Yes. Such neutrality is a necessity because the task with which they're entrusted is to call a meeting of the Cadre should a certain span of time pass with no sighting of an archangel."

Elena nodded slowly. "A safety measure of sorts." It made sense given the staggering impact the archangels had on the world. "Though," she said with a frown, "two years isn't that long in immortal terms."

"The period of time that must pass before a meeting is called has never been specified," Raphael said, his eyes on Aodhan even as he spoke to her. "As a result, at some point— and weighing up all available knowledge on the situation—the Luminata must make a judgment call." Taking the crossbow bolt from her, he threw it with archangelic strength. Aodhan barely avoided it before the bolt fell victim to gravity, to be intercepted by the squadron tasked with making sure none fell to skewer the mortals below.

The squadron had been intelligent enough to set up nets to catch the spent projectiles.

"The purpose of the meeting," Raphael said as Aodhan and Illium began to dodge bolts in tandem, "is to determine if the missing archangel is dead or has gone into Sleep. If so, the archangel's territory must be divided, archangelic borders redrawn."

Elena now understood why Raphael had never met a practicing Luminata. After Uram's death, the Cadre had apparently met within months to divide up his territory. Even when Alexander went to Sleep and his son attempted to take over the territory by hiding his father's withdrawal from the world, she'd learned the Cadre had rectified the situation within a relatively short period of time.

Yet it had been two years since Zhou Lijuan, Archangel of China and Goddess of Death, disappeared from sight.

2

"We all know Her Creepiness isn't dead." Elena's lip curled at the thought of the archangel who'd sought to rain death on New York, and whose reborn were shambling mockeries of life. "That would be too easy."

"Regardless, something must be done." Raphael's face was all brutally clean lines, his expression that of a being who was one of the most powerful in the world. "Xi is keeping Lijuan's territory in check, the vampires under control, but for all his strength, he is no archangel. China is beginning to fray at the edges."

Elena had no need to ask him how he knew—Jason was the best spymaster in the Cadre and he called Raphael sire. "You're worried about bloodlust?" Powerful vampires like Raphael's second, Dmitri, had iron control over their urge to feed, but the newer, younger vamps? Control was a gossamer-thin thread held in place by fear of the archangels.

Elena's mother and two older sisters were dead because a vampire had broken the leash and turned into a ravening monster.

Belle would never again throw a baseball because of Slater Patalis. Ari would never again scold then kiss Elena when she ran so fast that she fell and bloodied her knee.

And Marguerite Deveraux would never again laugh with her husband.

A husband who had died the day Marguerite took her life and who was now a man Elena barely recognized. Jeffrey might be walking and breathing, might even have another beautiful, intelligent wife, but he was no longer the man Marguerite had known, no longer the father Elena had loved before it all went so horribly wrong. Elena's two much younger half sisters knew a stern, unsmiling, and distant father when Elena had known a father who'd once blown soap bubbles with her for an hour just because it made her happy.

I see memories in your eyes, Elena.

Raphael's voice was the crash of the sea, the crisp bite of the wind in her mind.

They're part of me. She'd accepted that, no longer fought them when they surfaced. And in return, the nightmares came less and less. Some nights, she still heard the blood dripping to the floor, still felt terror clutch her in a clawed fist until she woke sweat-soaked with her heart a painful drum in her chest, but other nights, she dreamed of racing through the house to hide behind her mother after Belle found her in her room.

"I was a bratty little sister sometimes," she told the man who was her eternity. "I just wanted so much to be like my sisters that I'd sneak into their rooms and try on their shoes, their clothes, even if they didn't fit."

Raphael touched the back of his hand to her cheek. "Such is the way of younger siblings everywhere, is it not?"

"Yeah, I guess." Her lips kicked up, though sadness was an iron hammer on her soul. "Belle was so hot-tempered. She'd threaten me with all sorts of things . . . then she'd take my hand and lead me to her room and do my nails or brush my hair." Her oldest sister had possessed a wildly generous heart under the temper.

"I didn't bother Ariel as much," Elena added. "She was calmer, quieter, but she had this mischievous sense of humor only people who really knew her ever saw." Memories cascaded through her, of helping Ari pull pranks, of sitting close to her sister's warmth while she read a story aloud, of the stunning turquoise of Ari's eyes.

Smile deepening as the wind rippled through her hair, she

took a breath, released it. "I wish I could talk to Jeffrey some-times," she admitted. "He has so many of the same memories, things Beth wasn't old enough to remember." Her younger sister had been only five when Slater Patalis murdered Belle and Ari, and mortally wounded Marguerite's soul.

He'd tortured her, too, but it was being made helpless while her daughters were brutalized that had broken Elena's mother. "It'd be nice just to sit and talk about our family." Instead, all they had between them were broken shards of grief and guilt and loss.

The blue of Raphael's eyes turned dangerous. "He doesn't deserve to carry the title of father."

"Ah but we don't choose our parents, do we, Archangel?" If anyone understood the complex emotions that tied her to her father, it was Raphael. His own mother had gone insane, mur-dered thousands, then risen over a millennia later apparently sane—and full of love for the child she'd once left shattered and bleeding in a remote field distant from any civilization.

"No," Raphael admitted. "And I have promised not to kill Jeffrey, so let's talk about something else before I forget my vow."

"Fair enough." At times, thinking of her father was enough to turn Elena homicidal, too. "Getting back to Lijuan—whether she's dead or not matters less than the fact she's van-ished from sight?"

A short nod. "Bloodlust has already begun to rise, though only in isolated patches. According to the report Jason sent in an hour ago, a small kiss of vampires massacred an entire vil-lage four days past."

Elena's spine went stiff. "Xi have the kiss under control?" The angel was Lijuan's most trusted general and a power in his own right—though he was nowhere near as powerful on his own as he was when Lijuan was feeding him energy. "Shit. Is Xi displaying signs of being cut off from Lijuan?"

"Jason has been unable to confirm either way, but Xi did eliminate the kiss very quickly." Raphael's tone cooled. "He can't keep it up, however. No one who is not Cadre can. And these incidents are only the start—let it go and the vampires will swarm a blood red infestation across China." His voice was so cold that she found herself running her hand firmly down the edge of his wing in a silent reminder that he wasn't only an archangel, distant and lethal; he was her lover, the man who owned her heart and whose own belonged to her.

Raphael's expression didn't change, his voice still chilly, but he moved his wing so she could caress more of it. "If Lijuan rises again, new decisions will be made, but for the time being, we must work on the assumption that she overextended her new abilities to the point that she caused herself significant damage." He nodded in greeting at a passing squadron. "I do not believe her dead any more than you do, but I do think she may have chosen to Sleep."

And when an angel chose to Sleep, it could be centuries or millennia before they awoke. Caliane had Slept for more than a thousand years, and that was barely a drop in the ocean. "I guess I better pack for the Refuge then." Raphael's earlier words had made it clear he wouldn't be asking her to remain behind in New York, as he had more than once before.

At first, she'd fought the restraint, frustratingly conscious that he wanted her safe within the borders of his territory rather than in danger by his side. Later, she'd come to understand that, at certain times, Raphael needed his consort to be visible in the heart of his territory while he was gone. It settled people, because surely no archangel would leave his consort behind were the storm clouds of war gathering on the horizon?

"It'll be nice to see Jessamy and Galen again," she said. "Naasir and Andi, too." Venom was also still at the Refuge, but Elena didn't know the snake-eyed vampire as well as she did the others.

Raphael's response was unexpected. "I'm afraid we will have to wait to see our people at the Refuge. This meeting will be held on neutral ground, with no access to any strongholds or armies. Each archangel can bring their consort should they have one, plus one other."

Elena felt like she was racing to catch up. "I didn't know there *was* any other neutral ground." The world was sharply delineated into areas of archangelic control. The Refuge alone stood separate.

"There are a rare few small areas," Raphael told her. "Mere acres in each case. In this particular circumstance, it is the land that was given over to the Luminata so long ago that no one knows the names of those on the Cadre that made the decree."

"Where?"

"Lumia, the Luminata stronghold, stands in the land your grandmother called home."

"Morocco?" Delight kicked her bloodstream. "I love Morocco!" Though she had no ties there, she'd passed through the country during her days as a single hunter, felt its heartbeat sync with her own, as if her blood recognized the hot, desert land filled with a stark, golden beauty.

"From the covert flyover I did when I was a youth," Raphael told her with a smile, "Lumia is located on a hilly rise, an elegant stronghold that has stood for eons. There are no roads to break up the wilderness that surrounds it—to visit Lumia, you must have wings or you must brave a harsh trek made no less difficult by the high walls on the very edges of their land."

Elena was about to ask him to tell her more when her brain finally clicked. "Hold on," she said with a scowl, placing her hands on her hips again. "Yeah, people can't bring armies but Charisemnon's will be closer than anyone else's." The disease-causing and cowardly bastard responsible for the horror of the Falling, an event that had seen New York's angels plummet to the earth in an agony of fear and suffering and death, was the Archangel of Northern Africa.

"Unfortunately, yes." Raphael's own anger was frost in the air. "But Titus will no doubt mass his army on Charisemnon's border when he leaves for the meeting, forcing Charisemnon to do the same or leave his border open to Titus."

"I always knew I liked Titus." Elena bared her teeth. "When do we leave?"

"Unless one of the Cadre refuses to attend, we go on the dawn."

Implicit were the words that if someone did say no, it could set in motion a chain of immortal violence that would end with a devastated world. Because when archangels fought, people died and cities fell.

Two hours later, in the library of Elena and Raphael's Enclave home, that danger was no longer a concern. According to Jessamy, who was in touch with the Luminata in her role as the angelic Historian, every single archangel had RSVP'd to the meeting. "Except Lijuan, of course," Jessamy corrected, the other woman's fine-boned face up on the screen placed on one wall of the library.

Elena's blood began to pump a little faster. "That settles it then—we'll be on the plane tomorrow morning."

Raphael had already told their pilot to be on standby.

Had he been going alone, he would've probably flown on the wing, but Elena wasn't strong enough or fast enough to do that over such a long distance. She was getting there, could now achieve a vertical takeoff nine times out of ten—though it always cost her. Her body simply wasn't "old" enough in immortal terms, to have grown the necessary muscle strength. So when she forced a vertical takeoff, she did so knowing she'd have a shorter time in the air and could possibly rupture a tendon and be grounded until it healed.

In most cases, it made more sense for her to climb up someplace and take off from there, but at least she no longer faced being trapped on the ground if she couldn't find a handy launching spot. And once in the air, she had far greater endurance than when she'd first woken up with wings. Though that wasn't saying much, since she'd been about as graceful as a baby chicken on awakening.

"Has there been any word from Lijuan's court at all?"

The Historian—and Elena's friend—nodded at Raphael's question, her features lit by the delicate golden light thrown by the old-fashioned blown glass lamp on her desk, the Refuge yet swathed in the deep blackness of very early morning. "Xi confirmed receipt of the Luminata's request."

Had it been any other man or woman, Elena had the feeling the rest of the Cadre would've already acted. However, the general was so utterly devoted to his "goddess" that no one had any fear he'd forget who and what he was and give in to delusions of power he simply did not possess. Xi wanted only to hold the territory for Lijuan.

The thought of the archangel who considered herself evolved beyond even the Ancients triggered another thought. Glancing at Raphael, she said, "Did the Luminata invite Alexander and Caliane as well?"

Alexander had quickly become an active member of the Cadre, while Caliane preferred to keep to her small territory, but both were Ancients who should've never been awake, should've never been in the Cadre during this time.

The Cascade, however, had other ideas.

"Yes," Raphael answered.

"And," Jessamy added, "since saying no to the Luminata is unacceptable, both will be attending the meeting." The beautiful burnt sienna of her eyes lit with quiet humor. "I think Caliane might have a few words to say to *the* Luminata."

Elena caught the emphasis. "Head guy?"

A nod from the other woman. "The members of the sect do have names, but the leader is referred to as the Luminata as a gesture of respect. In direct speech, archangels use the Luminata's name—and so should you as consort."

"Because an archangel will only bend so far," Elena said dryly.

Similar to a guild hunter I know.

Grinning at the mental comment, one made in a very "Archangel of New York" tone, Elena leaned against Raphael's side. "So, it looks like it's going to be an unhappy reunion of the Cadre." She whistled at the implications of that. "Holy hell. Is Michaela coming, too?"

Jessamy's nod was quick, her eyes bright.

"That should be interesting." Unlike Lijuan, the most beautiful archangel in the world hadn't done a disappearing act, but she'd become far less visible for the span of an entire year before returning once more to the limelight—though still nowhere near at the level she'd been at before her strangely reclusive year.

Because Michaela loved attention and the media loved her.

To say that Michaela was beautiful was an understatement. With skin the shade of finest milk chocolate and wings of delicate bronze, her hair a waist-length tumble of brown and gold, and her eyes a hypnotic green, she was the definition of breathtaking. Throw in a body that turned mortals and immortals alike into slaves and it hadn't surprised Elena to learn that Michaela had been the muse of artists and emperors through the ages.

The artists were mostly alive, since Michaela liked those who paid homage to her beauty—no, that was bitchy. The truth was that Michaela did have a reputation as a generous patroness of the arts. But the emperors and other powerful men who'd been her lovers, well, they were pretty much all dead as doornails. The second-to-last one had died at Raphael's hands in an exchange of angelfire above New York that had left Elena broken and on the cusp of her own death.

It kind of pissed Elena off that Michaela had been partially responsible for her meeting Raphael right back at the start. Without the other archangel's poisonous encouragement, her lover would've never turned into an insane serial-killing nightmare. One who'd ended up ripping out Michaela's heart and replacing it with a glowing red fireball that may well have fouled her bloodstream with a noxious poison.

"Our pregnancy theory," Elena said to Jessamy, concerned what the poison, if it did lurk within Michaela, would've done to a child in the archangel's womb. "You heard anything to confirm that?"

"Nothing," Jessamy replied, then bit her lower lip. "I shouldn't gossip, but I so want to know." Switching her attention to Raphael, the other woman asked if Jason had discovered anything.

"There is not even a faint whisper of an angelic babe in Michaela's territory. Though that doesn't mean anything—Michaela has properties hidden in multiple difficult-to-reach locations."

"If there is a child, I hope he or she is safe and healthy." With those gentle words, Jessamy went to sign off. "I just heard Galen land. He's been out for hours with the current batch of trainees—I want to make sure he gets something hot into him."

Saying good-bye to the kindest angel she knew, Elena waited until the screen turned black before heading out of the library and toward her greenhouse, Raphael by her side. Licked by the rich sunlight of late afternoon, the glass shimmered in welcome.

"Dahariel must know if Michaela gave birth." Astaad's second was no longer Michaela's lover, but he had been at the critical time.

"Not necessarily." Raphael's answer had her frowning. "It's the archangel who makes all the decisions when the other parent is not their official consort."

"Not exactly fair."

"No, but archangels have enemies." Raphael's voice turned to midnight, his eyes dark. "Given the current state of the world, I wouldn't blame Michaela if she didn't trust anyone with the safety of her child, even the father of that child."

"He is a cruel bastard," Elena admitted grimly, well aware of Dahariel's penchant for torture. "I wouldn't trust him with my baby, either—if I had a baby. Which won't be for many, many, many, *many* moons."

The white gold of his wings shimmering in the sunshine, Raphael opened the greenhouse door for her. "Your body is not yet strong enough to bear an immortal child. In our terms, you are a baby and I am robbing the cradle."

Elena stepped into the humid warmth of one of her favorite places on the earth. "Rob away, Archangel." She was painfully glad she couldn't physically have a child for decades at least— according to Keir, it was more apt to be a hundred years. Terror gripped her when she thought of trying to keep a child safe, of protecting that vulnerable life from harm.

If she ever had to watch her child be hurt, ever had to bury a tiny innocent who'd looked to her for love and protection . . .

She swallowed.

At times like this, she understood why her father was the way he was; not only had he lost his hunter mother to violence, but he'd then had to bury two beloved daughters and an equally cherished wife. It had killed something vital in him. What had been left hadn't been enough to love a daughter who walked into possible death every time she went to do her job. He'd been fine with her younger sister, Beth—maybe not the father he'd once been, but not awful, either.

It was only with Elena that he'd become so . . . hard. The daughter who lived with danger on a daily basis instead of staying safe, staying protected.

Yes, sometimes she understood Jeffrey.

"The memories haunt you today."

Elena began to snip off the spent blooms on a cheerful pot of daisies that had been a gift from Illium. "I guess it's probably because I'm thinking about Morocco." Putting the neatly snipped off blooms in the hand her archangel held out, she showed him where to drop them so they'd return to the earth.

Only the dry, brown flowers uncurled the instant they touched his palm, gaining color and softness until he held a palmful of bright yellow daisies.

3

"Well," he said, "this is interesting."

Elena's lips twitched, the ache of memory retreating under the brilliant life of today. "Give those to me and touch the dried flowers I haven't yet cut off."

Nothing happened.

And the next time she put dried up blooms in his hand, they stayed dry. It wasn't a surprise—from what they'd been able to gather, all the Cascade-born abilities seemed to come and go without warning, like a signal that only transmitted in intermittent bursts. Even Elijah couldn't always call animals, though the ones with whom he'd already bonded tended to hang around even when he couldn't "speak" to them.

"Ah well," she said with a sigh. "You'll be useful again one day."

Flexing his hand after dropping the dry blooms in a garden she'd created in one corner of the greenhouse, Raphael made a blue flame dance on his palm. "As always, I am glad to be of some use to my consort."

Elena grinned. "Maybe while you're meeting with the Cadre," she said, "I can do some research on my roots." She shrugged. "I don't have much to go on, but there can't be too

many local families with this"—she gestured to herself—
"combination of hair and skin, right?"

Her mother's coloring had been very similar; she'd told
Elena once that the near-white of her hair as well as the dark
gold of Elena's skin came from her grandmother. The memory
unfurled like a film reel inside her mind . . .

"I had a photograph of my *maman*." Marguerite cut up
fabric for a sparkly black skirt Belle wanted. "The nun who
helped me in the first days after my mother died had saved it,
kept it in a secret place, only giving it to me when I was
eighteen and no longer a foster child."

A sadness to her face that made Elena reach out to her. Her
mother was a butterfly, colorful and bright and happy. She
smelled like flowers. She didn't get sad, didn't cry.

Smiling, her mother leaned in to kiss Elena's cheek, the
familiar scent of gardenias swirling around her. "Ah, *chérie*,
you and your sisters make my life a joy."

The tight thing inside Elena's chest melted away. "Why did
the nun keep your photo?"

"She knew that such treasures get lost when a child is
passed from hand to hand." Marguerite paused. "Sister Constance, she had kind eyes—I think she would've raised me as
her own if only she was able. But she watched over me from a
distance, and found me the day I moved into my own tiny
apartment, gave me that photo and another one that she'd
taken the day I saw my mother for the last time."

A smile. "I was wearing such a pretty dress and coat, and
clean, shining shoes. Sister Constance told me I had a bag of
snacks and toys with me." Laughing, she added, "I was maybe
a little spoiled, I think, but sweet girls should be spoiled, *non?*"

"That was the day your mama died?" Elena didn't like
thinking about that, didn't like to imagine that maybe, one
day, her mother would die, too.

"*Oui*," Marguerite said, her attention on the pattern for
Belle's skirt. "She asked Sister Constance to watch me while
she went out of town for a work interview, but her bus, it
crashed off a jagged ravine. Sister Constance did not know

anything about us except that we lived in Paris, were alone in the world but for one another, and came often to her church."

Elena's mother looked up when Elena didn't respond.

Touching her hand to Elena's hair, she shook her head. "My strong baby, with such a heart. Do not be sad—it was so long ago, in another life." Marguerite gave Elena a piece of the sparkly fabric to touch. "My mother's eyes were the same color as Ariel's and her skin was darker than yours—like she had soaked in more of the sun, but other than that, you are a pretty little copy of her."

"That's why my name is Elena." It wasn't her real name, but it was the name she liked best other than Ellie. Elieanora was so long and complicated.

"Yes, just like my *maman*. Elena was her home name, too." Lines forming between her eyebrows, Marguerite said, "I know it was not her true name, but I cannot remember people calling her anything but Elena." A smile, a shake of her shoulders. "No *bébé* knows her mama's true name."

"Beth is too small but I know. It's Marguerite Deveraux," Elena said proudly from where she sat atop the bench attached to the old-fashioned sewing machine her mother preferred over the new one Elena's father wanted to buy her; she kicked her legs as she watched her mother while Beth played with her toys on the blanket Marguerite had spread out on the floor.

Belle and Ariel were at school but Elena had been allowed to stay home because she had a cough. Actually, she could've gone to school, but Marguerite had smiled and cuddled her and said, "So, my *chérie* wants her *maman* today. We will be naughty and let you play hooky, *oui?*"

Elena loved her mother's accent, loved the lyrical beauty of it, loved how gentle Marguerite always sounded. She tried to speak that way sometimes, but her accent was plain old American, her voice that of a child, not Marguerite's husky gentleness. Now her mother laughed. "You are smart, my baby."

Smiles filled her insides. "Can I see the photo?" Elena asked, excited to know something about her grandmother.

Marguerite's smile was soft, a little sad again. "It was lost in a fire that burned my apartment building not long before I met your papa." She moved the scissors with a graceful hand, the fabric falling cleanly away on either side.

Belle was going to wear the skirt with a white shirt she'd got for Christmas. Elena had helped pick the shirt and her papa had bought it. It made her happy her big sister liked it so much.

"Oh," she said, really sad for her mama that she didn't have a picture of her own mama. "Do you remember the photo?"

"*Oui*, of course." Sparkly eyes met Elena's, so much delight in them that she felt as if the bubbles of happiness would lift her right up.

Her mother was full of sparkles, full of happiness. When Elena was around her, she just wanted to dance, wanted to laugh. Clapping her hands today, she held out her arms. Marguerite laughed and came over to lift her up and smack a kiss on her mouth. "You are a petite monkey, Elena," she said when Elena wrapped her arms and legs around her and refused to let go.

Then Beth got up on her plump little legs, held up her own arms.

"I think this little *bébé* wants a kiss, too." Going down to the blanket after Elena released her, Marguerite picked up Beth and sat with her in her lap.

Elena took a cross-legged position across from her and made funny faces at Beth.

Her baby sister giggled, tiny hands pressed to her mouth.

"When I see you, Elena, I see my mother," Marguerite said. "The same hair"—she ran the strands through the fingers of one hand—"the same kind of bones in the face, the same smile." A deep smile of her own, though the sparkles were gone. "You carry my Jeffrey in you, too. His expression, so serious at times."

Laughter again, bubbling out of Marguerite as if it simply could not be contained. "I had to teach your papa to laugh, *chérie*. He was such a solemn man when I met him—but I could see the goodness in his heart, and I knew he was mine, this quiet American who sat in one corner of the café where I waitressed."

A secret light in her face that made Elena want to smile, too, this story one of her favorites to hear her mother tell. "He never ordered anything until I came to take his order, your papa. It used to annoy the other waitstaff until they decided to find it romantic, and then of course, it was all right. A man can be foolish in Paris if he is being romantic also."

Elena didn't quite understand all of what her mother was telling her, but she could feel the joy radiating through her mother's words and that was enough. "What did Papa order?"

"Always the same." Marguerite shook her head, putting Beth back down on the blanket when she started to wriggle. "A black coffee and toast." She threw up her hands. "I started ignoring him and bringing him whatever I felt like. Croissants fresh from the oven, eggs so exquisitely flavored, bacon smoked with apples, special cereals that we created fresh every morning. And he ate each thing."

Marguerite laughed. "Until one day, he ordered for two— black coffee and a frothy chocolat with hazelnut. My favorite, you see."

Her mother cupped Elena's face in her hands, her expression oddly solemn all at once. "I remember—in the photograph, my mother is holding me and I'm a *bébé* wrapped up in a soft blanket." A sudden frown between her eyebrows. "There was a mark on one edge, *azeeztee*. A monogram it is called in English, I think: *M.E.*" A sudden smile. "So perhaps my last name was an *E* word."

They'd had so much fun coming up with possible last names that started with *E*. At the time, Elena had thought it the best day ever, but there had been other days as wonderful.

Marguerite had been a dazzling butterfly who loved pretty clothes, coffee dates with friends, and going out to dance with her husband, but she'd also been an affectionate, loving mother. For all her interests and wide circle of friends, her husband and children had been the center of her existence.

"M.E.," she murmured to Raphael, her heart trying to hold on to the echo of those bubbles of joy. "I have initials to explore as well as just the unique nature of my grandmother's looks."

"You may be in luck," her archangel said. "The Luminata, when they aren't engaged in the quest for luminescence, seek to gather wisdom, so you may discover something in their archives. And your bloodline does have a vampire in it some-where. Perhaps it was in the time of your grandmother."

It still sent a shiver up Elena's spine to know she had a vampire relative; Raphael had scented power in the blood that had soaked into the quilt Marguerite had lovingly sewn for her daughter, the kind of power that wasn't a mortal thing. That blood had been mere drops from where her mother had pricked herself while sewing, but it had carried enough strength to hum to Raphael's senses.

"Weird to think that one of my ancestors might still be out there, living their life."

Raphael shook his head. "A vampire strong enough to have sired a bloodline that carried a certain level of power through time wouldn't normally drop all contact with those he sired. But of course, there are always exceptions."

And vampires, Elena knew too well, weren't true immortals. They could die. "I know my vamp great-grandma or -grandpops is probably long dead, but still, it'd satisfy my curiosity to un-earth the truth."

A sudden chill shook her, her skin pebbling.

"Elena?"

Shaking her head, she joined Raphael at the door, the two of them due at the Tower for a meeting with Dmitri. "Nothing. Just someone walking over my grave."

She and Raphael flew to the Tower without playing in the sky today. When they landed on a high balcony, the wind lifted up Raphael's hair like a lover that couldn't stay away. She didn't blame it. Some nights, she just lay there and played with the midnight silk of it, her wing draped over him with unhidden possessiveness.

"Come, *hbeebti*," he said, folding back his wings. "Let us speak to Dmitri, then return home. Montgomery may stop feeding us if we keep sleeping in the Tower."

They'd only done that the past week because Dmitri had been out of state, having taken Honor to their private cabin for a break. He'd returned today, ready once more to take up his responsibilities as Raphael's second.

Slipping her hand into Raphael's, Elena walked with him

into the Tower. Her lips tugged up at the contact, the eerie chill having faded during the flight over the red-gold waters of the Hudson, the first edge of sunset spectacular today.

Raphael caught the change in her mood, glanced over. "What amuses you?"

"Why do you sound so suspicious?"

"Because your favorite things are sharp and draw blood."

"Funny, Archangel." Laughing because he was guilty of feeding her addiction to the most beautiful blades, she said, "We're holding hands. I never held hands with anyone before you, and when we first got together, I never thought we ever would." He'd been so hard, so dangerous.

"In this, Elena, I, too, was a virgin." His fingers tightened on hers, his wings outlined with a glow that would've terrified her once.

And she realized he was exactly as hard and even deadlier than he'd been when he made her close her hand over a blade, when he made her bleed—but she was no longer a mortal hunter meeting one of the Cadre. Nor was she the new consort still learning the man she loved beyond life, beyond reason. Oh, he'd keep surprising her for centuries, millennia, of that she had no doubt. But the one thing she no longer had any question about was that they were an impregnable unit.

The world might attempt to tear them apart, but the only way it would ever succeed would be through death.

If this is death, Guild Hunter, then I will see you on the other side.

Her heart squeezed.

No, not even death would separate them. "I like holding hands," she declared, moving their clasped hands slightly back and forth as they walked down the wide hallway in which Dmitri had his office, the walls newly painted an elegant gray, the thick carpet beneath their feet a darker gray.

Raphael's response was silent, his wing brushing hers as he . . .

"Raphael!"

The damn archangel had dusted her.

Glittering, sparkly stuff stuck to her, delicious beyond compare when she parted her mouth and it licked onto her tongue. Her thighs clenched. "This is not funny!" She glared at him even as arousal flooded her system, but he was laughing too hard to care.

Her heart, it just stopped.

Even now, the Archangel of New York rarely laughed and never like this. Until she could see the youth he must've once been, with eyes of a wild, astonishing blue that asked a woman to laugh with him. She'd never before seen him as truly young. How could she? He had so much *power* that it pulsed in his every touch, burned in his skin.

Hauling him close to her with her hands fisted in the cream linen of his shirt, she took a kiss, took him. He sank into her, his wings sweeping up to wrap around her until all she could sense was Raphael, all she could taste was him. And angel dust. The special blend he'd created just for her.

He pushed one hand into her hair, fisting it as he wrapped his other arm around her waist and backed her up against a wall. Something fell with a dull thud. Maybe the vivid painting of wildflowers that had just been put up, all the art having been taken down during the repainting.

Elena loved that simple piece Honor had found in a thrift shop, but right now, it could've been a priceless artwork by the Hummingbird and she wouldn't have cared. She was far too happy to be pressed up against the hard warmth of her archangel tip to toe after spending the previous night on watch. No time for shenanigans with Dmitri away and Illium off-shift, Aodhan assigned to patrol the sea border, and Raphael dealing with the overall security situation.

She'd flown a proper defense grid, both to stay in practice and because none of them could afford to be blasé with the Cascade an unpredictable foe that could unleash itself at any moment, smashing the world back into chaos and, possibly, war.

Today, however, the others were on-shift and she could kiss her lover. He burned hot, Raphael, but he was a crashing sea in her mind, a tumultuous, passionate storm that swept her up and thundered through her veins.

We can talk to Dmitri later, she sent to Raphael, sliding her hands up the ridges and valleys of his chest. *Let's go upstairs to our suite.*

"A-hem."

She tried to ignore that pointed cough that held a biting amusement.

Raphael's lips smiled against hers. *I think my second has other ideas.* Pulling away with a kiss that promised more to come, he folded back his wings to reveal the vampire who leaned against the wall about ten feet down the corridor, beside an open door.

Dmitri was dressed in black jeans and a black T-shirt, his arms crossed to reveal well-defined biceps. His only ornamentation was the gold wedding band on his left ring finger; he never took off that ring, no matter what. And sometimes, Elena almost liked him because of that. The rest of the time, she thought him a pain in the ass—especially as he still liked to jerk her chain with his scent games.

Hunter-born were highly sensitive to scents, particularly vampiric scents; that was what made them such good trackers. The flip side was a vulnerability to those same scents that certain vampires could exploit. Just her damn luck that Raphael's second was one of them.

Now the vampire, his sensually handsome face carved in strong lines overlaid with skin of bronze, his eyes a rich brown, and his natural scent as darkly seductive as chocolate and champagne and all things sinful, raised an eyebrow. "I knew she was going to be a bad influence from the first."

Elena gave him the finger.

He grinned, and suddenly, she was drowning in the chocolate and champagne of him while fur rubbed over her skin. Gritting her teeth, she'd pulled a blade from her forearm sheath and thrown it at him before she consciously thought about what she was going to do.

4

Dmitri moved just barely in time.

The blade thudded home in the wall on which he'd been leaning, would've pinned his ear to it if he hadn't shifted. As it was, he rubbed his jaw, then reached up to remove the blade and throw it back to her in an easy spin she caught without issue. "You're faster."

Raphael nodded. "Yes." He moved down the corridor until they were about fifteen feet apart. "Throw blades at me," he said. "As fast as you can."

Elena didn't hesitate—Raphael was more than strong enough that even if he didn't dodge in time, he'd heal from a knife wound in a heartbeat. But she didn't think he wouldn't be able to dodge. She'd sparred with him enough to know he moved like lightning. The only angel who was faster was Illium.

Bluebell could outdodge even his sire's blades if he tried hard enough.

She threw every one of her blades one after the other in a blur of metal, aware of Dmitri watching with dark-eyed focus as Raphael dodged or simply caught the weapons in the air.

Honor poked out her head from her office across from Dmitri's, realized what was going on, and stayed safely out of the line of fire. She, too, would heal from a knife wound, but she was a baby vampire. It would take time—though not as much as it should.

At Dmitri's request, Raphael was the angel who'd Made Honor. She had the blood of an archangel running through her veins, just enough to make her stronger and more advanced in vampiric terms than she should've been for her age as an almost-immortal. Not that it had changed her except on the surface, honing her beauty to a luminous edge.

No, Honor was still Honor: a woman full of heart who loved history and languages and who was a hunter to the core. A number of former street kids owed their bright new futures to Honor's deep capacity for love—and the other woman wasn't resting on her laurels. She continued to work to save children who were lost and alone.

"Whoa!" Honor cried out as one of Elena's blades almost clipped Raphael's temple.

Elena grinned and spun out another blade before he could recover from his harsh swerve, but he was still too fast. He caught her final blade, spun it over, and threw it back. She slid it into her thigh sheath, then put away the others as he threw them back to her one by one. Several had embedded into the carpet and the walls after he moved out of the way, and Elena wondered what the Tower repair crew would make of the random knife holes that had appeared in this newly renovated hallway.

Probably shrug and mutter, "Business as usual."

"So?" she asked as she sheathed the last of the blades, her heart thumping with the exhilaration and pure fun of what they'd just done.

Surprisingly, it was Honor who answered. "You're faster," she said definitively. "I remember watching you practice in the Guild ring a year ago, and while you were dangerously good, you could've never come that close to actually hitting Raphael."

Dmitri's gaze had softened when it landed on his wife, but by the time he returned his attention to Elena, those dark irises gleamed once again with taunting amusement. "It appears the Tower's resident baby is now a toddler."

"I'm going to carve out your heart one day, fry it with salsa sauce, then feed it to the crows," Elena said conversationally. "Don't worry, Honor. It'll grow back. Unfortunately."

Shaking her head, Honor walked over to stand beside her husband. He immediately put his arm around her shoulders. Unlike her usual casual office wear, Honor was dressed in hunting clothes today—leather pants, boots, a simple T-shirt, and a leather jacket that would protect against knife strikes or claws.

"You on a hunt?" Elena asked.

"Just got back," Honor said with a roll of dramatic green eyes tilted up at the corners and set against skin of warm honey brushed with a shimmer of gold, the soft ebony of her curls pulled back in a ponytail. "A spoiled and frankly idiotic vampire decided to take off after a fight with his angelic master—who also happens to be his lover."

She threw up her hands. "I mean, who thought that was a good idea? I found him 'hiding out' in a fancy hotel drinking expensive room-service blood, hauled him home, and left vampire and angel both looking at each other with equally sulky, pouty faces."

Adding her own eye roll to Honor's because, seriously, people were stupid sometimes. Even people who'd lived for centuries. "A job's a job I guess—and we have to stay sharp."

"That's what I figured." Honor shrugged. "But forget about me. When are you two going to be friends?" A pointed glance from Dmitri to Elena and back.

"Never," Elena and Dmitri said in concert, then scowled at each other for that unintended agreement.

Honor laughed and reached up to run her lips over the hard line of Dmitri's jaw, while Raphael's amusement was quieter but no less potent.

"Nice of you to dress up for me, though," Dmitri said to Elena.

"What?"

"You're sparkling."

"Oh, bite me," she said, realizing her mistake a second too late.

The damn vampire bared his teeth, fangs flashing. But before he could say something designed to aggravate her, Honor pressed a finger over his lips. "Dmitri only bites his wife now," she said before pointing at Elena. "Shoo. Go home so we can get some work done. Or my husband will spend all his time having fun by irritating you."

Raphael was already by Elena's side, his wing overlapping hers, his feathers a shimmering white gold against the midnight and dawn of her own. "I give the Tower and my territory into your keeping, Dmitri. Not simply for tonight, but until I return from Lumia."

Dmitri straightened, his expression wiped of all humor and his skin taut over the bones of his face. "They've called a meeting?"

"Yes. We leave on the dawn."

Suddenly, Dmitri wasn't the infuriating vampire who messed with Elena just because he could, but very much Raphael's second, his own strength such that certain angels had been known to warn Raphael to be careful, that he couldn't trust a man with that much personal power. Those angels didn't understand the bond between the two men. They weren't simply sire and second. They were friends as close as brothers.

Dmitri would die for Raphael.

And difficult as it was for outsiders to understand, he would die for Elena, too.

Because you are his heart, Elena. A man with his heart torn out is a broken creature. I know.

Words he'd spoken to her once, when they'd been alone on a balcony one quiet midnight long before he'd found Honor. He'd made no attempt to hide the scars on him when he looked at her. And not for the first time, she'd realized that Dmitri had had a life before he became a vampire. A life that had involved a wife and children.

"Sire, you must take care." The vampire's body was all hard lines. "The rules have been—*are*—being broken. I don't trust the others not to strike even within the sacrosanct halls of the Luminata's innermost sanctum."

"Have no fear, Dmitri. I have no intention of lowering my guard." Raphael paused. "I thought to take Aodhan as our escort. He will enjoy seeing the art that is meant to line the walls of Lumia, and he is powerful enough that no one will consider him an easy mark."

"But not as powerful as Illium." Dmitri's eyes narrowed before he nodded, his arm still around a silent Honor. "Illium might be seen as too confrontational. Of course, Aodhan doesn't exactly blend in, so you'll still be making a point."

The point being that Raphael's Seven was made up of extra-ordinary men; Elena had come to realize the oldest three could've *all* been an archangel's second. Each and every one was strong, intelligent, and honed enough to hold a position at an archangel's side. Yet they chose to serve one archangel, chose to work with one another instead of in competition.

"Can I take my Guard?" Elena asked, wanting to give Raphael as much firepower as he was "legally" permitted.

While she still wasn't really sure what to do with the Guard she'd somehow acquired, they were all capable fighters. A couple of them—namely Ashwini and Janvier—were also excellent at being smartly sneaky, using that to offset the disadvantage of their relatively young ages.

But Raphael shook his head. "In this situation, you are coming as my consort, and as such, if you take your Guard, it would be seen as an admission that I don't believe I can protect you."

"I hate angelic politics." She ran a hand through her hair. "So, it'll be me, you, and Aodhan. Dmitri and Illium will watch the city?" The two could definitely handle it, but it'd be hard going with little time for rest.

"Venom will be back in New York in the next twenty-four hours. Galen has authorized his return." He spoke to her and Dmitri both. "Naasir and Galen will hold the Refuge territory safe, while Jason will do what he does."

In other words, she thought as the two of them flew off the Tower after a short good-bye, Jason would provide any and all intel the others needed to do their jobs. Elena's Guard, mean-while, would be co-opted by Dmitri. It was how they'd set it up. Those in her Guard were being trained under Dmitri's guidance because, while she could say many things about Raphael's second, the one thing she couldn't say was that he was bad at his job.

The setup worked for all of them—Elena wasn't yet ready to take full control of her Guard, not when she was still learning herself. She'd only ended up with a Guard by accident anyway. It was Elijah's consort, Hannah, who'd convinced her to give it serious attention.

"As you grow in power and age," the other consort had said, "you'll come to be seen less as a curiosity and more as a threat." Hannah's dark eyes had held a quiet wisdom, her ebony skin exquisitely without flaw and her jet-black curls woven into an intricate knot at her nape, her wings a lush and luxuriant cream with a caress of peach on the primaries. "Never forget that while archangels are extremely difficult to kill, consorts like you and I aren't so difficult."

Savaging the archangel's heart in the process.

"And," Hannah had said with a smile, "now is the best time to build your Guard, when you are at the same level as your people. They will become strong by your side, your friendships forged into iron over time. It will be far more difficult to gather people you trust once you *are* influential in any sense— then you'll first wonder if they are truly loyal to you, or if they hunger to be attached to a woman with power."

Elena knew she already had a certain level of power by dint of being Raphael's consort, but she also knew that mattered little to the people in her Guard. Ashwini had been a trusted fellow hunter and friend for years. Her mate, Janvier, adored Ash with such open delight that Elena knew he'd never betray anyone Ash called a friend—quite aside from the fact that Janvier was also fiercely loyal to Raphael.

Izak was . . . well, he was adorable.

She wanted to smile every time she thought of the young angel who had such a big crush on her. His soul was honest and sweet and out there for the world to see.

As for Vivek, he'd saved her life so many times that she'd lost count. The Guild's former head of intelligence was now a vampire but he was still Vivek, as acerbic and as cuttingly intelligent as always. Placed on the Tower's intelligence team after his Making, he'd proved so capable that he'd become Jason's right-hand man when it came to intelligence gathering.

Not that the Vivek whom Elena had always known wasn't
a little different these days. She'd become friends with a brilliant hunter-born man who'd been paralyzed below the shoulders in a childhood accident. But while Vivek remained in a
wheelchair, he'd regained feeling above the waist, had full
control of his arms and torso.

*Vivek's probably going to leave my Guard and his position
in the Tower at some point*, she said to Raphael as they swept
through the darkening sky above a city ramping up for the
night to come.

He flew beside her, his wings glowing in the faint, last rays
of the sunset—but they were solid. The wings of rippling
white fire she'd seen the day he rescued Illium—when the
other angel suffered a catastrophic incident in the sky—hadn't
reappeared since; all she'd caught in the past two years had
been rare flickers of that pristine flame, flickers that disappeared as quickly as they appeared.

Yes, Raphael answered. *Vivek Kapur was forced into certain choices because of his accident. He will need to explore
in freedom before he decides if he wants to return to the life
and the work he has made for himself.*

It's going to happen sooner than anyone predicted.
Vivek was healing at a speed even Keir hadn't foreseen—
likely because Vivek had been Made a vampire by Aodhan, with
Keir's assistance. *He's still going to be under Contract.* A hundred years to serve in return for the gift of near-
immortality.

*Elena, you know he is yours. I will not hold him to the
Contract.* Eyes of searing blue meeting her gaze. *But you
should—he is your friend but he will still be a young vampire
with violently strong urges. He must have a firm hand on him
until he regains his human control once more.*

The idea of restraining Vivek in any way was abhorrent to
Elena, though she knew Raphael was right. *Maybe I can
ask Jason to oversee him.* She'd never thought to witness
Vivek in awe of anyone but he was definitely in awe of
Raphael's spymaster. *I think he'd listen to Jason in a way he'd
never listen to me. I'm pretty sure he wants to be Jason when
he grows up.* She and Vivek were contemporaries, equals,

while Jason occupied a whole different category. *What do you think?*

I think you know your Guard well. Raphael's wings glinted as he swept down to glide over wings of silver blue.

Illium immediately changed direction to fall in line with Raphael.

I'm not ready to go.

I'm not ready for you to go.

Memories of the awful day when Illium had threatened to burn up alive, power cracking him open from the inside, awoke without warning at the sight of the two of them flying so close. If Raphael and Dmitri were friends before being sire and second, Raphael and Illium's relationship was more the latter—but with a familial element. Illium had sounded so young that day when everyone had believed he might be ascending to archangelic power.

Had it been true, he'd have had to leave Raphael's territory.

He was too young for that, and when the blue-winged angel had told Raphael he didn't want to go, Elena had seen a shaken youth asking for reassurance from someone he respected and trusted.

Naasir treated Dmitri like a father.

It was only in that moment when Illium said he wasn't ready to leave that Elena realized Illium saw Raphael in the same light. Not quite, not exactly, but close enough.

Elena had never asked what had happened to Illium's actual father. She could have—Illium remained her closest immortal friend—but his face was so sad when he talked about his mother, the broken Hummingbird, that she couldn't bring herself to do it. Instinct told her there was a reason the Hummingbird was the way she was, and there was a good chance it was tied to Illium's father.

Raphael would've told her, too, but it felt dishonest to go behind Illium's back. If Illium ever wanted to talk about his family, he would. Right now, he was back to his usual form, his spirit irrepressible.

No one knew what would happen when the Cascade kicked back into gear but Illium wasn't allowing that uncertainty to dictate his choices. "I'll worry about that when it happens," he'd said to her. "I'm not going to waste a minute when I can be me free from any Cascade effects."

Today, he dropped below Raphael, circled, then came to where Elena had been riding lazily along their wake. His hair, that astonishing black tipped with blue, was longer than usual and fell forward when he shifted to line up with her. "Ellie," he called out after pushing back the strands to reveal eyes the color of newly minted gold coins, "want to race?"

She thought about it. When they raced, he gave her a considerable head start as a handicap and it was fun to try to push past her best. "Not today," she said at last. "I don't want to accidentally strain a muscle or tendon." She needed to be at peak strength when they reached Lumia.

Flipping over onto his back, Illium dropped before twisting around to return to her. Raphael, meanwhile, had swept up and over them, his shadow a kiss against Elena's senses. *Is Illium coming to dinner with us?* she asked.

I thought you'd wish to see your Bluebell before we leave. Sparkle will join us, too.

Lips twitching, Elena said, *You know Aodhan hates that nickname.*

Ah, but it is so appropriate. Raphael dropped down beside her just as Illium spoke from her other side.

"Um, Ellie. You're shimmering."

She pointed a finger at the blue-winged angel with the wickedly dancing eyes. "Be quiet." Turning to a Raphael who wasn't doing much to hide his amusement, she tapped a mirror-shiny blade on her nose before angling it in his direction. "I'm going to get you for that. Right when you think you're safe, boom, you'll be covered in whipped cream . . . or tomato sauce if I'm feeling extra evil."

"I am forewarned." He dipped his wing, nodded at Illium. "First to the Enclave. Go."

Whooping, Illium turned into a sleek bullet as he dived to build up speed for the race. Raphael stayed high but he was as fast, even though it didn't appear his wings were beating with any more momentum. Elena enjoyed watching him move—he was magnificent in flight. So she had her eyes on him when his wings turned aflame, and suddenly, even sleek, fast Bluebell didn't stand a chance of defeating him.

Her stomach clenched.

The other shoe had dropped.

The Cascade was no longer on Pause.

5

Raphael and Illium landed on the lawn of the Enclave home just in front of Elena. The two had come back to ensure she wasn't alone in the sky. On their faces, she saw the same realization she'd just reached.

Illium had parted his lips to speak when the earth began to shake under their feet.

Illium and Raphael both lifted off instinctively. Elena couldn't react that fast, her ability to pull off a vertical takeoff not a thing of speed. But in this case, that didn't matter. Raphael had taken one of her arms, Illium the other, raising her off the ground with them as it bucked and rolled. Below the cliffs of the Enclave, the river churned, waves smashing against those cliffs with brutal force.

When she turned to look at Manhattan over her shoulder, she saw the buildings swaying in the smudged post-sunset light. Her gut twisted. There were so many people in those buildings, so many of her friends.

But even as her heart was wrenching itself into a tangled knot, the Hudson calmed, the shaking over as abruptly as it had begun. Releasing the breath locked tight in her lungs, she said, "We have to go back, survey the damage."

"Illium."

Illium released his grip on her and then Raphael had her in his arms and was winging up high. He had no need to tell her what to do. She folded in her wings to reduce drag until they were high enough up that he could release her. Spreading out her wings as she fell, she swept out and toward Manhattan at a lower elevation than her archangel, Illium already a blue dot far in the distance.

Don't land, Elena, Raphael told her. *Dmitri has people out checking for land damage. We must do an aerial survey.*

Got it. She went left as he went right, fellow angels doing sweeps in other areas of the city. *No collapsed buildings on this side, a couple of shattered windows.*

I have the same.

They flew for an hour, found their city had weathered the quake with only minor damage. A few fender-benders, more smashed windows, but no buildings had collapsed, no trains derailed. The worst damage appeared to be to a large ship in port that had smashed into the side of its mooring. Raphael had also received similar reports of minor-damage-only from other parts of the territory.

But, of course, it wasn't about harm to property.

Elena had managed to send a one-word text to Sara while in the air—*OK?*—received a message that her best friend and her family, as well as all hunters in the area, were safe. Beth called right as Elena was about to call her. She was hyperventilating.

"Shh, Bethie," Elena said, so much love and pain inside her. "I'm fine." She knew it was what Beth needed to hear— her baby sister had such a sunny personality, but of late, she tended to panic when she couldn't get hold of Elena, the nightmare of their past rising up to suffocate her without warning.

As if with the birth of her daughter had come a fear Beth couldn't shake.

Calming once she knew Elena was all right, Beth told her that she hadn't heard from Jeffrey yet, but that everyone else in their family was fine.

Elena hung up to see Raphael dropping to fly at her wing.

"No reports of fatalities," he told her, easing her concern about Jeffrey.

Elena and her father might have a broken relationship, but

he would always be her father. "Does the quake change our plans for tomorrow?"

"It would take a major disaster to cause the Luminata to call off a meeting. We cannot know until we hear what has happened in other parts of the world."

Because, with the Cascade in full effect, the New York quake was highly unlikely to have been an isolated incident.

"Homeward, then?" Dmitri appeared to have the situation under control here, and if there was a chance of a dawn departure for Lumia, the two of them had to rest up.

Nodding, Raphael did a wide turn so she'd have more room to maneuver, and they flew back in a straight line across the river rippling quietly under the first edge of night. Montgomery was waiting for them, the butler's black suit and white shirt as pristine as always and his features quietly handsome. "Sire." He inclined his head in a respectful bow. "Dmitri is on the device in the library."

The "device in the library" was a wall screen. Elena sometimes forgot Montgomery was a vampire centuries old, then he'd slip up and use terms like that and the facts would snap sharply back into focus: though vampirism had effectively frozen his body and face in time—his appearance that of a man in his early thirties—he'd lived for far longer.

"Thank you, Montgomery," Raphael said. "Illium and Aodhan will be joining us for dinner."

"I will prepare." Montgomery melted away, no doubt to inform the chef, Sivya—who also happened to be his wife. The two had married in a quiet, beautiful ceremony a year earlier.

"Dmitri," Raphael said as they walked into the library. "What have you learned?"

Looking up from something he was reading on a handheld screen, his expression devoid of anything but hard-eyed concentration, Dmitri said, "I heard from Dahariel."

Elena wasn't surprised at the news. Dahariel might be a cruel bastard with inexplicable taste in women, but he was also an experienced second whom Dmitri respected as a peer.

"Astaad's territory experienced a number of small tidal waves triggered by undersea quakes," Dmitri told them. "Minor damage only." He motioned with the handheld. "The media's confirmed quakes around the world, but so far, there are no reports of any significant damage except to buildings that were already weak for other reasons."

Elena's phone buzzed.

Stepping away from the screen when she saw Sara's name flash up, she walked outside onto the lawn so her conversation wouldn't overlap Raphael's. "Sara," she said. "What's happened? Did someone in the Guild get hurt after all?"

"No, but I just heard that your dad was in a town car that got hit by a truck."

Elena's hand clenched tight on her phone, her stomach tensing. "Injuries?" She knew her best friend would've made sure to get that information for her.

"Jeffrey's got a broken arm but is otherwise fine. Not a scratch on either driver." Sara told her the name of the hospital where her father was being treated. "I know you two don't have a warm and fuzzy relationship but I figured you'd want to know."

"Thanks, Sara." Staring out toward the glittering skyline of Manhattan, thousands of tiny windows lit up against the night, Elena wondered what Jeffrey Deveraux was thinking at this moment, knew she could never predict his thoughts or actions.

"Damn it," Sara muttered. "That's another idiot."

Elena knew exactly what had her friend—and head of the Hunters Guild—so hot under the collar. It was a welcome distraction from thinking about a father who would never again be the papa she'd so adored. "How many vamps decided to make a break for it in the confusion after the quake?" That was why the Guild existed—because not every vampire wanted to fulfill his or her hundred-year Contract.

Elena had heard all the sob stories, but fact was fact: to become a vampire, you had to agree to serve a hundred years under the angels. And it wasn't as if the angels made any effort whatsoever to hide that such service could involve pain and torture and treatment so harsh it might break you. Not all angels were brutal, but enough had been jaded by centuries or millennia of life to the point that sadistic and often sexual punishments were a source of sick pleasure.

Vivek hadn't wanted to become a vampire for that very reason, even knowing that vampirism would eventually heal his spinal cord.

"A hundred years of slavery to have the use of my body," he'd whispered. "A hundred years at the mercy of some random immortal who might decide to treat me like a pet dog."

Elena had promised him that he wouldn't ever be under the command of a "random immortal," that he'd be overseen by whichever of the Seven was in charge of the Tower at the time.

Quite aside from that, Raphael was smart: he'd never waste Vivek's skills by assigning him to a menial task.

As to Vivek's Contract—while he might be permitted more flexibility because of his friendship with Elena and his unique circumstances, her fellow hunter was adamant about completing his hundred years of service. "I *want* to pay my way," he'd told her, his jaw set. "As far as I'm concerned, the century of service is fair payment for the permanent medical treatment that is vampirism."

That was truer in Vivek's case than in others—but all vampires gained the potential for millennia of life on becoming near-immortal. As more than one hunter had been known to point out to a whining vamp who'd breached his or her Contract, there was no point crying over it after you'd already accepted the gift with open eyes. Not like you could give it back.

"I try to tell myself I should be glad," Sara responded in a jaundiced tone. "Because as long as there are idiots, there will be a Guild, but honestly, the recent crop of rabbits doesn't seem to have a single complete brain between them." She blew out a breath. "I better go. Got reports coming in of collars."

Elena had barely hung up when her phone rang again. This time, it was Marcia Blue, the chief operating officer of Blood-for-Less. It had begun with one small blood café and was now a thriving chain of three across the city. And Elena was the official CEO. That cracked her up every single time.

Ransom and Demarco found it so funny that they'd printed out glossy black business cards for her with *Elena Deveraux, Guild Hunter Angel CEO* on the front and a silhouette of a suit-wearing, crossbow-wielding female angel on the back.

Smart asses.

"Hey, Marcia," she said. "Our businesses still standing?"

The once-timid vampire responded in a warm but efficient voice and they talked over a number of matters, including plans for expansion. "I'm heading out of town," Elena said after listening to what Marcia had to say, "but talk to Jonas, hammer out the finances." Jonas was a vampire and Elena's financial manager. "I'll make a final call once he gives me all the numbers."

"Oh, sure." Marcia's enthusiasm bubbled over. "Jonas is great to work with."

Elena's eyes widened. *Hmm . . .* "I have to go now, Marcia," she said as Raphael stepped out to join her, "but we'll talk when I get back."

"Okay, sure. Good night."

Hanging up, Elena slid away her phone. "Archangel, I think my business partner and my financial manager might have zing between them."

"Zing?"

Turning, she touched her finger to his chest, felt the spark ignite, her belly heating. "Zing."

Raphael closed his hand over hers. "That's excellent. Perhaps Marcia can steal Jonas totally away from the angel to whom he is loyal so I can then steal him from you and Marcia."

"Hey, no industrial espionage while I'm setting up my conglomerate." Elena gave him her best scowl before returning to the matter at hand. "What else did Dmitri have to tell you?"

When the heartbreaking blue of Raphael's eyes went metallic in its chill, she knew the news wasn't going to be good.

6

"He received a report from Jason while we were speaking," Raphael told his consort, anger ice in his veins at the possible implications of Jason's information. "The tremors in Lijuan's territory were similar to what we felt. But Xi didn't send out extra troops to check the damage."

"As if he needs those troops to stay somewhere else? Guard his crazy mistress maybe?" Elena folded her arms, feet set widely apart.

"Or to give that impression." If Lijuan had told Xi to cover her absence long past the time when she was safe in her place of Sleep, then she'd deliberately set up her territory for bloody anarchy.

The other option was that the Archangel of China *had* only recently gone into Sleep, but that she'd been in trouble for a long time beforehand after overextending her Cascade-given abilities. Of course, there was a third option. "Lijuan could be playing a lethal game, hoping to get the Cadre in one place at one time for purposes of her own."

Narrowing her eyes, Elena nodded. "It doesn't really matter, does it? Not when nonattendance at the meeting could lead to war."

"No—we must go to Lumia." Raphael settled his wings, which were once more solid. "Whatever happens, we'll have an answer after that meeting. Lijuan may mount a siege. If she doesn't, but she isn't in Sleep, then she won't permit her lands to be divided and thrown into war as Xi attempts to hold the territory against the might of the rest of the Cadre."

"Yeah. She's psycho but she takes the goddess-over-her-people thing seriously."

"Yes." It hadn't stopped his fellow archangel from turning many of her people into the shambling reborn, a mockery of life stinking of death, but the idea of anyone else taking control of what was hers? No, that she would not permit.

"You think the Cadre will also discuss the whole Alexander-Favashi thing?"

"The question is moot if Lijuan has retreated from the world." Alexander, the former Archangel of Persia, had risen unexpectedly and, as an Ancient, had far more power and influence than Favashi, the archangel who'd been the Archangel of Persia on his waking.

As a result, Persia had been divided in two.

Alexander retained the title, while Favashi was now the Archangel of Sumeria. Relations seemed calm between the two, but Raphael knew neither was satisfied, tensions simmering beneath the surface that would eventually explode into war. Alexander wanted all of his lands back, and Favashi was furious at what she saw as a demotion.

"Right," Elena murmured. "You'll be a Cadre of Ten again, enough territories to go around with no two archangels on top of one another."

"That would be the best-case scenario; the current situation is dangerously unstable." Because if Lijuan *was* alive and awake, there were *eleven* active archangels in the world. There had never been more than ten at any one time. Less, yes, but never more. It had shaken the critical balance that kept the most powerful beings in the world from killing one another.

"I can see why it's a great idea to put all these parties who hate each other in a small area together." His consort's tone was acerbic. "And forget about a siege—Lijuan's probably creeping around in her noncorporeal form ready to drop one of her black poison bombs down on the rest of you."

Raphael leaned forward to surround her with his wings.
"Ah, but she is a goddess, Guild Hunter, and as such, needs
someone to worship her. And she wants tribute from some of
her fellow archangels at least." The Archangel of China
wanted to be a goddess to her fellow archangels, too, to be the
Queen of Queens.

"Right, how could I forget?" Wrapping her arms around
him, his hunter pressed her cheek to his chest, the wings of a
warrior arching over her shoulders. "Don't get dead, Raphael,
or I swear I'll hunt you down in the afterlife."

"I would not dare, Elena-mine." Life held too much
promise—never could he become jaded with Elena's fierce
honesty and wildfire spirit in his life. "Now"—he fisted one
hand in her hair, his jaw against her temple—"tell me why
your spine is so stiff and your eyes haunted."

Tone flat, she shared the news of her father's injury, but no
matter how hard she tried, she couldn't conceal the raw emotions that still tied her to Jeffrey Deveraux. Raphael knew too
well that the love of a child for a parent who'd once been all a
parent should be couldn't be erased—he'd tried to hate his
mother after her atrocities; he'd failed.

So, despite his disdain for her father, he said nothing, just
held his strong consort with her mortal heart that felt so
deeply.

They stood wrapped up in one another as the final hints of
twilight faded to true dark, Archangel Tower a spear of light
that dominated the sky. Illium landed in a showy flash not
long afterward, Aodhan following far more sedately. But Illium's closest friend drew attention whether he wanted to or not.

Every filament of his wings and each strand of his hair
seemed to be coated with crushed jewels that refracted the
light, while his skin was white marble. Not cold, however. No,
it was warm, invited touch—the one thing the gifted and
powerful angel couldn't stand. Only Illium had the freedom
to touch Aodhan as he wished, though Aodhan had healed
enough to accept a small amount of contact with a limited
number of others.

Including from the warrior in Raphael's arms.

Who drew back then, old pain held deep within her, and

her smile glorious. "Come on in, let's go see what Sivya's cooked up for us."

Raphael sat beside Elena at the table in the library, where they had most of their meals, the formal dining room used only when many more of his Seven and/or her Guard were present, or if they had other guests. At this instant, his consort was laughing with one of his Seven who sat across from her.

It was Illium, of course, her favorite.

Another man might have been jealous of their relationship, might've stewed in a bitterness that destroyed all the bonds that tied each one of them to the other. Raphael, however, had watched the blue-winged angel grow up, seen his power and his personality develop; he knew he had Illium's unflinching loyalty.

Bluebell would cut off his own wings rather than consider duplicity of any kind.

And Elena. His hunter had no concept of betrayal. When Elena loved, it was with every fiber of her being. She would walk with him into death without hesitation, his fiery consort.

Her eyes met his at that instant, the silvery sheen in them a physical sign of her growing immortality. *You're too ridiculously good looking.* A scowl. *Stop it.*

He felt his lips curve. *Your Bluebell would disagree.*

Yes, he's pretty. So is Aodhan. But you're you. She was music in his head, sharp and clean and like a perfectly balanced blade.

He wondered if she realized her mental voice was gaining in strength. His consort was maturing—in terms of her immortality—far quicker than anyone had expected. Yet there was only so far her once-mortal body could go in the time that had passed; she remained a newborn angel, so much easier to hurt than him or any of his Seven.

And you, Elena, are you. A warrior to the bone. His warrior.

"Sire, is there anything I should know before we leave?" Aodhan's voice was deep, quiet, but today, it held the faint touch of a faraway land where he'd spent part of his youth.

He'd been in Raphael's employ at the time, had gone to Ireland to study under a master artist. Because Raphael had always understood that, for Aodhan, creating art was life, was breathing.

For ten long years after they rescued him from hell, Aodhan had created no art and Raphael had thought they'd lost him forever. Until Illium accidentally spotted his friend by a river near the Refuge. Aodhan was gone by the time Illium returned from his task as a courier, but in his friend's place, he'd found a delicate stack of stones that cast an astonishingly intricate shadow—a stack placed so it would be washed away when the river next rose.

Raphael could still remember Illium's tear-wet eyes, his trembling voice when he reported his find. "Aodhan's not gone." A husky rasp. "He's still alive inside. We just have to wait for him to find his way back to us."

Tonight, Raphael glimpsed faint flecks of yellow and blue paint in Aodhan's hair. "I think you can guess the knives that will be out," he said in response to the angel's question, "all of them ready to stab us in our backs." He sipped from his wine, nodding in thanks at Montgomery, who'd come in to top up their glasses. "This is a meeting of vipers, Aodhan. Your task will be to keep Elena safe."

Elena threw a roll at Raphael's head.

He caught it, startled. "Elena, did you just throw a bread roll at the Archangel of New York?"

"I felt like throwing my biggest blade but I restrained myself," was the response. "Aren't you proud of me?" A saccharine sweet smile.

Illium choked on his laughter, while Aodhan managed to keep his face expressionless, the shattered mirrors of his eyes suddenly deeply interested in the small centerpiece on the table. Montgomery had been about to leave the library, hesitated, then gave in to his better nature and training, and slipped out.

Switching to private mental speech after putting down the offending roll, Raphael said, *You have to be aware you need protection. Michaela will likely bring Riker as her escort just to spite you.* And the twisted vampire male wanted a piece of Elena.

The fact Raphael had torn Riker's heart out of his chest, punching a bare hand through Riker's ribcage to grip the pulsating organ, might hold him back—or it might not. Because Riker wasn't quite sane after so long in Michaela's service. Not after the things she'd done—and who he'd been before he became her pet vampire.

I can take that asshole. Elena stabbed at her meal with her fork.

There'll be others, you know that.

She looked up, her eyes holding not fury or even aggravation but something else, something deeper, more important. *Of course I know that, Archangel. I've been your consort for more than three years, and during that time, many people have tried to tear off my head, rip me limb from limb, stab me, you get the drift.*

His blood iced, his anger directed not at Elena, but at those who had attempted to harm her. Most of them were dead. *I do get the drift, Consort*, he said to Elena when she raised an eyebrow.

Her lips kicked up at his edgy tone but her eyes remained serious. *I also know you'll concentrate better in the meeting if Aodhan is with me. I like Sparkle. I don't mind hanging with him while you're wheeling and dealing in the Cadre.*

As Elena had been Consort for several years, Raphael had been an archangel with a consort. So he knew that, right now, he was being called to account. *Perhaps I should ask Illium and Aodhan to leave.* The two members of his Seven were chatting quietly to each other, totally at ease despite the jagged sparks in the air . . . because this was their home, too.

It had become so after Elena became Raphael's. His Seven had always come and gone from the Enclave house, had stayed here at times, but never had they been so at home here. It was his hunter who'd made that happen—and it wasn't only the Seven she'd affected. It wasn't chance that Montgomery had begun to court Sivya only after Elena had been living here for some time.

She'd brought life with her, brought heart.

They can stay. Elena took a sip of her wine. *I'm not going to go for your throat—not until after dessert anyway. Montgomery took over the kitchen with Sivya's permission and made some kind of thing called a pavlova that looks like a cloud with strawberries on it and I really want to eat it.*

Shoulders unknotting and the strain easing from wing muscles tensed in readiness for a private battle, Raphael leaned back against his chair, his wingtips lying against the thick carpet. *So, if you understand the need, then why did you assault me with baked goods?*

Can I have that back, by the way? I really like Sivya's rolls.

Lobbing it over to her, Raphael watched her catch it with effortless ease. *Thanks.* She made a stern face at Illium when her Bluebell said, "Have you two finished your discussion?"

"Shh, the grownups are talking."

The blue-winged angel grinned. "Can you finish before dessert? I don't want a side dish of anxiety with my dessert."

"Eat your entrée," Elena ordered before looking back at Raphael, her eyes luminous. *Here's the thing, Raphael. Past couple of years, while we all waited for the shit to hit the fan, things have been fairly peaceful—this is the first time we're going back into danger.*

Raphael inclined his head in a silent agreement.

That's why I'm cutting you some slack. She took another sip of her wine, her slender throat moving as she swallowed. *You've lacked positive reinforcement on how to thrash out such issues with your consort.*

Raphael drank some of his own wine. *I believe my consort is now amused.*

Just a little. Her smile deepened. *Remember our first disagreement? It involved my blood in case you've forgotten.*

It involved a woman with endless courage.

Putting down her wineglass, that same woman locked gazes with him once more, as courageous and as fearless as ever. *You default to thinking me weak and in need of protection. Instead of recognizing that I'm not mortal now. I was never a normal mortal anyway.*

No, she was hunter-born. Stronger, faster, deadlier. Putting down his own wine, he offered her a blade he carried on himself because Elena had given it to him after a fight months ago. *Your consort accepts his mistake, Guild Hunter. I should not have stated things as I did—I shouldn't, in fact, have thought in such a pattern.*

Elena took his peace offering, slid it away with a smile. *Don't sweat it. You are kind of old.*

Very funny, Elena. In immortal terms, he was young, the youngest angel ever to become an archangel.

Come on, you set yourself up for it, she said with a laugh.

And that laugh, it was wildfire in his blood. Was life. "Aodhan, you will be with Elena during the Cadre meetings. I'll leave it to the two of you to decide how best to utilize your resources."

Elena's eyes widened. Placing her hand on his thigh under the table, she said, *Hey, I didn't want a public statement. I know it's important the Seven see you as their sire.*

Yes, his hunter still had that mortal heart that loved him when it wasn't the least bit to her advantage. She'd be far safer had she never met him. But Elena had never lived a safe life. *That won't change if they see me accepting my consort's point. I'd be a stupid archangel if I didn't value my greatest treasure.*

Expression soft in a way that was for him alone, Elena lifted her wineglass. *Knhebek, Archangel.*

7

Elena spoke the words of love in her grandmother's language, felt Raphael's response in the look he gave her. It was blue fire and it was furious tenderness.

When she turned back to face Illium and Aodhan, she caught the sorrow in Illium's eyes. It was old, that sorrow, came from the loss of the mortal he'd once loved, a woman for whom he'd lost his feathers in punishment and whom he mourned to this day.

Then Aodhan leaned in to murmur something against his ear. Face lighting up at whatever it was his best friend had said, Illium chuckled.

"Sire," the light-shattered angel said afterward, his profile a purity of clean lines. "I have been doing further research on the Luminata."

Intrigued, Elena focused on the angel who was more luminous than any of these Luminata could possibly be.

"Their leader, Gian," Aodhan continued, "has held his position for four centuries—this is unusual among the Luminata. They are meant to rotate the leadership through their membership every five decades to ensure that politics and power do not distract from or corrupt a member's search for luminescence."

Raphael, who had gone motionless beside Elena, now said, "How do you know this, Aodhan?"

"Yes." Illium's tone was as hard as stone. "The Luminata don't exactly advertise their internal workings."

Elena realized she was missing something, so much withheld aggression in the air that she could've cut it with a knife.

Aodhan broke eye contact with Raphael to meet Illium's gaze. The words he spoke were edgier than she'd ever heard Aodhan sound. "I'm no longer a broken doll who needs to be protected from those who might play roughly with me."

Flinching as if he'd been slapped, Illium shoved back his chair and left the library through the doors that stood open to the lawn.

Elena.

She was already moving. *I've got it.* If she hadn't heard that tone in Aodhan's voice before, she hadn't seen that expression on Illium's face, either. So furiously angry and yet hurt. Deeply hurt.

Following the angel outside, she hoped he hadn't taken off—because if Illium wanted to outpace her, she had no chance in hell of catching up to him. But he was standing on the very edge of the property, on the cliffs that looked down on the dark waters of the Hudson, the Manhattan skyline in the distance. Angels landed on Tower balconies as she watched, but today, even that sight didn't have the power to hold her attention.

Walking to stand beside Illium, she very deliberately slid her wing over his tightly held ones; a touch that told him he wasn't alone but that made no demands. Words weren't always easy when things mattered.

The wind was quiet against her face tonight. It pushed Illium's hair back gently from his face, those black strands dipped in blue that simply grew that way, to reveal the lines of a face that held a pure masculine beauty. But beautiful though he was, it hadn't been his looks but the playful wickedness in Illium that had drawn Elena—that light in him, it was a bright, joyful candle against the dark.

Today, the light was snuffed out, his golden eyes strangely flat—as if he was holding himself in such fierce check that he'd buried the best part of himself. Elena couldn't stand it.

She took his hand, wove her fingers through his. He didn't respond for a second, two . . . then, at last, his fingers curled around hers.

His skin grew warm in the minutes that followed, the horrible flatness retreating from his gaze.

"Do you know how badly hurt Aodhan was when we found him?" The words trembled. "His wings were all but rotted away, mere strings of tendons, and bone as soft as unfired clay all that remained. All his beautiful feathers gone, the webbing in shreds, his strength stolen and his body encrusted in dirt."

Horror clawed Elena's gut at the grim recitation. She knew something terrible had happened to Aodhan, bad enough that it had made him retreat from life for two hundred years. He'd imprisoned himself in the Refuge, had refused physical contact with anyone, hadn't laughed, hadn't interacted with the people who loved him.

It was Illium who'd reached him, Illium who was his best and closest friend.

"He was so *hurt*, Ellie," Illium continued without waiting for an answer. "Not just on the outside." He slapped his free hand against his heart. "This, the part that makes Aodhan who he is, it was so badly damaged that I thought I'd lost my friend forever." Tears glittered in his eyes.

Glancing away, he stared at Manhattan with such harsh focus that she knew he was fighting those tears. His throat moved, his jaw a brutal line.

It hit her hard, because beauty and playfulness aside, Illium was one of the toughest fighters among Raphael's people. He gave no quarter, was a warrior who'd fly headlong into an enemy squadron if a pitiless charge was what was required.

"Hey." She flexed her fingers around his, tugging lightly until he turned to face her. "I can take it, Bluebell. Whatever you want to unload." She smiled. "It can't be any worse than Ransom's love life before Nyree took pity on him."

The bleak despair that gripped him seemed as if it would defeat the bonds of their friendship, but then his lips tugged up a little. Lifting their clasped hands, he pressed a kiss to her knuckles. And he was her Bluebell again, beautiful and wild and with power humming in his veins. So *much* power.

She sucked in a breath, suddenly realizing she could see

every vein in Illium's body—on his neck, down his arms, across his face. They glowed, as if his blood was molten gold. Her heart slammed into her ribcage, propelled by memories of the blazing light that had shoved out of him two years ago.

He'd almost died that day.

"Illium."

"It's nothing dangerous. Comes and goes." A shrug. "There's no attendant surge of power." A sudden grin. "I'm just glow-in-the-dark for a minute or two." The smile faded as quickly as it had come, along with the golden light in his veins.

Consciously taking a deep breath, then another, Elena lifted a hand to brush his hair off his forehead. Her heart was a racehorse in her chest, but this wasn't about her. "Aodhan hurt you."

"It's more that he's hurting himself." He looked out at Manhattan again, but he was no longer holding his wings to his back with unforgiving tightness. Opening them a fraction, he allowed his feathers to slide against hers.

Many people would see that and think it an intimacy. It was. One between friends. Raphael called Illium her favorite. That was true, too. But he wasn't her lover, would never hold that position—that part of Elena belonged always to her arch-angel. That was why she could hold his hand, why she could slide her wing over his, why he could kiss her knuckles.

"During his recovery," Illium said into the quiet, "right at the start, when Keir was basically trying to put him back to-gether, Aodhan didn't speak, didn't meet anyone's eyes." Such pain in his voice. "He'd just stare at whatever nightmares existed in his mind, a broken doll."

The use of those words, Elena grasped, had been deliberate on Aodhan's part.

"The person who described him that way was an angel named Remus." Illium's hand clenched around Elena's with such strength that her bones hurt.

She said nothing, just listened.

"Remus was Keir's assistant at the time." He released a breath, eased his grip. "I'm sorry, Ellie."

"I'm hunter-born, Bluebell. A little squeeze won't do me any harm."

Chest rising and falling in an uneven rhythm, Illium said,

"Remus was a failed member of the Luminata." He shifted to walk in the direction of her greenhouse, tugging her along with him.

She went, the glass structure a beacon of light on that side of the yard. It was the heat lamps within, the ones that nurtured her plans. "Did Remus get kicked out of Lumia?"

Illium's satisfaction was in his voice when he answered. "I always thought he must've been kicked out, too, but Remus insisted he'd left because he realized he hadn't finished living his life in the outside world yet. He implied that he'd be able to walk back into Lumia at any point in time."

"This Remus guy, he's not Keir's assistant any longer."

"No." A word so razor-edged the air bled. "Remus had no business being in a healer's employ." Coming to a standstill beside the greenhouse, Illium looked back toward the open doors to the library. "He spent a lot of time with Aodhan while Aodhan was in the Medica. I was there, too, as were the others of us who were with Raphael at that time, as well as Raphael himself. My mother. His parents."

He swallowed audibly. "I would've lived at the Medica had Keir allowed it—I couldn't bear to have Aodhan out of my sight after what had happened." Wings shifting restlessly, his fingers clenching down on hers again. "But every so often, Remus would tell us that as a healer's apprentice, he could see Aodhan was growing strained at the constant companionship, that he needed a little time to find his own peace. We didn't want to hurt him—we *never* wanted to hurt him—so we'd leave."

Hairs rose on the back of Elena's neck, an ugly feeling in her gut. "And this Remus dude would be alone with him?"

Illium nodded. "I came back early one day. I planned to sit outside Aodhan's room until Remus said it was okay to go in again." He broke their handclasp to spin away, a sound of raw rage erupting from his throat. "But the door was partially open," he said without turning back. "Because it was, I went closer in case Remus had cleared visitors . . . and I heard someone whispering in there. It was Remus. He was telling Aodhan he was a broken doll and that broken dolls needed masters."

Elena's eyes grew hot with fury. "Bastard."

"I didn't need to hear anything else. It was obvious Remus was using his position to abuse Aodhan, break down anything that remained inside him so Remus could 'own' him." Rage and tears vied for space in Illium's voice. "Everyone wants to own Aodhan. He's a beautiful jewel and the world can't bear just to look at him and wonder at his beauty. They want to break him, cage him."

"What did you do to Remus?"

"I threw him out of the room then proceeded to attempt to beat him to death," Illium responded in a tone so cold it caused goose bumps over her skin. "I would've succeeded if Aodhan hadn't spoken at last. It was so quiet, so soft, but I heard him. He said, *Bluebell*." Illium blew out a harsh breath. "It was like a gunshot going off inside my head. I dropped the bag of broken bones that was Remus and rushed into Aodhan's room—"

He cut off his words, as if the memory of that moment was too much to bear.

Shifting to stand beside him once more, Elena ran her hand gently over his wing, his feathers silky and warm under her palm. In profile, against the light of the greenhouse, he was a granite statue, his jaw clenched with agonizing force.

When he spoke, each word was a jagged chip of flint. "Remus was lying bleeding and broken outside when Raphael came. He didn't ask me anything at that time, just threw Remus in a treatment room and alerted Keir that one of his people needed his assistance."

"He knew you must've had good reason."

"When I was finally calm enough to speak, after Aodhan fell into a natural sleep, I told him what I'd overheard." He thrust a hand through his hair. "To this day, I don't know what Raphael said to Keir, but Remus was banished from the Medica for the duration of his immortal life. If he's ever injured, he must wait outside and hope someone comes to assist him."

Elena thought back to her time in the Refuge, came up blank. "I've never heard of him."

"He's an outcast." Harsh satisfaction ran through Illium's voice. "People respect Keir no matter their political affiliation. That he banished Remus was enough for most to shun him; none of us ever spoke publicly about the reason he'd been banished." Shoving back his hair again, his hand rough, he said, "We refused to give that bastard the satisfaction of having others look on Aodhan with pity. He survived hell, Ellie. He deserved nothing but accolades for his courage. *Never* pity."

Elena connected the dots, hissed out a breath. "Shit. Aodhan's obviously been speaking to him again." She could see why both Illium and Raphael had reacted so badly to the idea. "You're not worried that Remus was successful in brainwashing him, are you?"

An immediate shake of Illium's head. "That day, when Aodhan first woke, he told me that Remus was nothing, a worm. Aodhan had blanked him out the same way he'd done the rest of the world until he heard me in a rage, beating Remus to death."

Illium's voice broke. "Aodhan was worried about me. He was shattered, his body and soul wounded to the breaking point, and he was worried about *me*. That's what brought him back to us, his worry about me. And he kicks at me because I'm worried about him now?"

His hurt was so deep and so violent that Elena felt her own heart ache. "He's waking up more and more," she said, fighting her own angry response to the idea of Aodhan exposing himself to harm. "It's been a long process for him." The angel had been locked inside himself for an eternity before he decided to come to New York, spread his wings again. "He's going to react badly to anyone questioning his ability to look after himself."

Illium's jaw worked. "So I'm not allowed to worry about my friend?" His wing sliding away as he turned to face her, he shook his head again. "Do you know what it did to me when we lost him? The nearly two years he was gone?"

Not saying another word, he spread his wings and took off in a harsh gust of wind that whipped Elena's hair across her face. So fast and high that all she could do was watch him disappear into the stars.

8

Raphael, Bluebell is in the sky—I think we need to let him go.
He was in no mood to listen to anyone right now.

I'll warn Dmitri to keep a watch for him.

Returning to the house, Elena stepped inside the library to find Aodhan still in his seat. He didn't appear to have eaten anything in the time she'd been gone, and when she walked in, his eyes went immediately to behind her. "Where is he?" he asked the instant he became aware Illium wasn't about to appear.

Elena shrugged and pointed up.

Jaw going taut, Aodhan stared at his plate. "Is he all right?" The question sounded like it had been torn out of him.

Elena decided to be honest. "Angry and hurt in equal measures."

Face flushing, Aodhan pushed back his own chair. "Sire, I will take my leave."

"I will see you on the dawn, Aodhan. Thank you for the information on the Luminata."

A quick nod later, Aodhan was gone in a cascade of light sparking off his feathers. So extraordinary, so beautiful.

Everyone wants to own Aodhan. He's a beautiful jewel and

the world can't bear just to look at him and wonder at his beauty. They want to break him, cage him.

Taking her seat as Illium's passionate words echoed through her mind, Elena threw back half a glass of wine before angling her body to face Raphael. "Illium told me about Remus." She had to fight to keep her voice even. "I can see why you both reacted badly to the realization Aodhan must've been speaking to him. Why didn't you kill the bastard at the time?"

Wings sweeping to the floor in a white gold fall, her archangel leaned back in his chair, his eyes difficult to read. "It would've raised too many questions about exactly what he'd done to deserve such a final punishment."

Exposing what the asshole had tried to do to Aodhan.

"Aodhan was correct," Raphael added after a long pause. "He is no longer who he once was, who we have so long been accustomed to thinking of him as. He did what was necessary in his capacity as the warrior who will accompany us to the Luminata's inner sanctum."

Elena frowned. "Why did you choose Aodhan for the trip to Lumia? You had to know it would bring up a bad time of his life."

"I'm afraid your consort's memories let him down," Raphael said, a darkness in his expression that she could read very well; it was old, aged anger. "Prior to that moment when Remus rose to the forefront of my mind, I saw Aodhan only as he is now—a powerful member of my Seven who fought to save my city and who makes art full of quiet wonder. Remus was dealt with centuries ago—I had long forgotten him."

Elena nodded. "Yeah, I can see that. Aodhan's been so strong—he recovered from his battle injuries faster than anyone expected and he's far more sociable these days." Not in comparison to most people, but for Aodhan. "No wonder you forgot."

Drinking the last of the wine in his glass, Raphael placed the glass back on the table. "While you were outside, Aodhan told me that he was pleased to get the assignment, pleased at the silent acknowledgment that I didn't see him as too damaged to take on this task."

"Ah." Aodhan's coldly furious response to Raphael and Illium suddenly made even more sense. "Then you two spoiled it by bringing up his past." She shook her head. "How'd you fix that?"

"I'm not sure I did." Raphael rose. "Walk with me, Elena-mine."

Getting up, she slipped her hand into his. "Aodhan's still coming with us, right?"

"Of course. I made an error of judgment in questioning him, but I wouldn't compound it by changing his assignment when he remains more than equal to it."

"Good. Then we'll figure things out during the trip." Aodhan might be angry right now, but he was one of the most even-tempered of the Seven. He'd calm down . . . but then again, Elena hadn't known Aodhan before he was hurt, so she suddenly realized she might have no idea what she was talking about.

"Did he have a temper before he was taken?" While she didn't know exactly what had happened to him, she'd picked up enough to know he'd been kidnapped, held in captivity. The rest, as with Illium and his father, she had no right to know unless Aodhan chose to tell her.

Raphael's chuckle was a warm, rich sound in the night darkness. "He is a gifted artist, Elena, one of the greatest in angelkind, though he does not like it when we say thus."

"Artistic temperament? Okay, yeah, that I didn't figure."

"He rarely gives in to it. Illium was always the more volatile of the two, but Aodhan had his moments."

Elena worked through the idea of a hot-tempered Aodhan, began to smile. "Well, he might be pissed, but you know what?"

"What?"

"It means Sparkle really is coming back." Artistic temper and all.

"Yes," Raphael said with a slow smile, "you are right. Our Sparkle is indeed coming back to us." He raised his head to look up at the stars. "I wonder how long it will take your Blue-bell to understand that?"

Artistic moodiness or not, Aodhan was in an even temper in the gray predawn light the next morning when he met Elena and Raphael for the flight to the plane that'd take them to

Morocco. The baggage had already been sent forward, with Montgomery having taken full charge of that task.

"You will need gowns," the butler had told Elena. "The Luminata would be insulted if you stalked through their hallways in hunter gear."

Elena had scowled so hard her mother would've no doubt warned her that her face would freeze into that expression if she wasn't careful. "I am who I am."

"Even archangels respect the ways of the Luminata."

Well, that had shut her up. Who the hell was she to disregard rules the Cadre itself respected? "Damn it, what the heck do I pack?"

The butler's expression had been as restrained as usual, but she'd caught a glint of hidden laughter. "I will take care of it, Guild Hunter. I will also ensure that you have a gown on the plane that you can change into before you head for Lumia."

Elena had no idea what she'd do without Montgomery. Probably insult everyone around her without realizing it. "You have to wear formal gear, too?" she asked Aodhan now.

The other angel was currently dressed in warrior leathers of a beaten gold that suited his coloring so beautifully, she knew those leathers had been made for him and him alone. "Once we get to Lumia, I mean." Right now, she was in jeans, boots, a tee, and a thin sweater with leather straps that crisscrossed her torso.

"I am your escort," he responded. "I'm expected to be in leathers or other clothing suitable to a warrior."

"I hate you," Elena said without heat.

His eyes, those strange, hauntingly beautiful eyes of crystalline blue-green shards shattered outward from an obsidian pupil, warmed. "I'll let you hold my swords if you're nice."

"Very funny, Sparkle."

His eyebrows drew together over his eyes at her reference to the nickname he was trying to stamp out of existence. "I'm going to kill Illium," he said, not for the first time. But his eyes, they looked up, as if searching the skies for wings of blue and silver.

Those wings hadn't appeared by the time they took off from the Enclave. And despite Aodhan's teasing, Elena did have all her weapons. Raphael had told her that as a warrior-consort, she was expected to have weapons on her. "If Hannah turned up armed to the teeth, that would raise some eyebrows, but everyone is aware of the fact that my consort was and is a hunter."

That had cheered her up. Especially since Montgomery had made it a point to come out and tell her that the gowns he'd packed were such that she wouldn't be hindered in a fight should such a fight become necessary.

It was a good thing she'd made herself practice in gowns over the past two years. Her hunter friends found it a hoot to spar with her while she was glammed up, but the lunatics had helped her refine her technique. It was Ransom with his skin of copper gold, eyes of Irish green, and skill as a streetfighter who'd given her a tiny switchblade. "Even if you can't wear any other blade openly, you can hide this somewhere, use it to cut slits in your dress so you can run, find a weapon."

Elena had shown the dangerous weapon to Raphael. "Don't get worked up about another man giving me a blade," she'd ordered. "Ransom is very happily married, and I like this beauty."

Her archangel had said nothing—but Ransom's switchblade had disappeared mysteriously two days later, to be replaced by an even deadlier version.

Her archangel really didn't like it when anyone but him gave her a blade, she thought with a grin as all three of them lifted off, Elena flying off the cliff and down to the Hudson before sweeping up to join Aodhan and Raphael.

Waving to Montgomery when she saw the butler standing perfectly suited on the lush green of the lawn, she luxuriated in the cool air that ran over her wings and tugged at the small strands of hair that had escaped her tight braid. Aodhan had gone high, as he preferred, but Raphael was flying nearby. And his wings, they were dangerous white fire.

He could've outpaced her in a heartbeat, but he stayed on the same drafts, and when she looked over to him, he glanced back with a smile that was for her alone. They didn't speak; there was no need for it, the two of them in perfect harmony as they dipped and angled and rode along the winds. It felt as if they arrived at the airport far too fast.

Landing first, Raphael waited for her to join him, then the

two of them watched Aodhan descend. He was a fracture of light, so bright even in the pale dawn sunshine that Elena had to slide on sunglasses to continue to watch. Every part of him seemed to shimmer as he landed in front of her and folded back his wings.

The captain descended the steps of the plane at that instant. "Sire." The vampire inclined his head.

Elena had been around the Tower long enough to have caught on to the subtleties in the greetings Raphael received. Dmitri never bowed his head, his and Raphael's friendship far too deep, their trust too cemented to need it. As slight a bow as the captain had offered meant the other man was a powerful vampire who held Raphael's trust and respect.

Elena smiled at the medium height male built like a tank, all muscle and power. "Hey, Mack."

Dougal Mackenzie gave her a quelling look. "Consort."

He was such a stick in the mud. It put paid to all her ideas about Scottish lairds. Okay, fine, she hadn't actually had any ideas about Scottish lairds before meeting Dougal, but it just seemed wrong that he was so by-the-book. Maybe he was still sore that his clan had said he couldn't be laird for any longer than the span of a natural human life. Not fair to the coming generations to have a vampire laird who could live for thousands of years.

Of course, she was just speculating since Dougal had never deigned to satisfy her curiosity. Today, he met Raphael's eyes, said, "We're ready to take off on your word."

Dougal headed back inside after Raphael acknowledged the statement, while Elena raised her eyes to the sky once more. *Come on, Bluebell. You know he needs you.* Aodhan might be getting ever stronger, but he still permitted only Illium to touch him freely.

He wouldn't shrug off Elena's touch or Raphael's, but he wouldn't welcome it, either. It was more that he'd learned to bear it—no, that wasn't right. He'd held on to her hand when she needed it, given her comfort. It was better to say he could break through his trauma to make contact. Only with Illium was that barrier nonexistent.

That told Elena a lot about how far Aodhan still had to go. "Raphael, you know what happened with those two last night?" she asked when the other angel removed his dual swords and harness and took them to store inside the plane, where they would be within arm's reach.

Raphael shook his head. "Dmitri told me both were missing all night, that is all."

"From the way Aodhan looked at the sky before he went into the plane," Elena said, her own eyes lifting up once again, "I have a feeling he didn't find Illium. You think . . ."

"I do not know if your Bluebell will come here," Raphael said. "Illium rarely takes offense—and when he does, it is often over in a flash. He forgives more generously than any other angel I know."

That fit with everything Elena understood about Illium herself. "Then why?"

"Because this, *hbeebti*, isn't only about anger."

She thought of how Illium had fought not to cry, his body rigid. "He was really hurt." Looking over her shoulder as Aodhan came back out to stand beside the plane, she switched to mental speech. *Can we wait a little longer?*

Eyes of heartbreaking blue landed on the angel who shone like a star under the sunlight. *I'm afraid not.* Her archangel's voice was the cool mountain wind against her senses. "There is no more time."

They headed up the steps of the plane on the heels of his words.

Aodhan was the last one to board, and he kept his eyes turned toward the window as the plane began to roll down the runway. He didn't look away even after they were in the clouds . . . not until they'd gone too far for even Illium to catch up to them.

9

This part of Morocco was an arid brown and gold landscape broken up only by hardy mountain wildflowers, waving grasses, and occasional groves of deep-rooted trees that provided an unexpected kiss of green to the landscape, but it was spectacular in its starkness.

Elena had been looking forward to the feast to the senses that was Marrakech, noisy and crowded and her kind of place, but they landed even deeper inland, at a private airstrip a considerable distance from the city with which she was most familiar. From there, they flew on the wing over and into the Atlas Mountains and to a sloping peak on which sat a stronghold that was all graceful curves and arches.

Lumia was formed of thousands of small sand-colored bricks that blended into the landscape, and rather than being one big block, it was a sprawling stronghold with myriad pathways and sections that flowed into one another, giving the place a delicate and almost ethereal air. She also glimpsed two domes far apart, one of which looked like glass, the other opaque.

"It's like the Taj Mahal," she said to Raphael when he flew close enough. "This huge thing that somehow has an air of beautiful fragility." The Taj, too, appeared to float against the sky.

"Lumia was designed on the principles of perfect serenity, as understood by the Luminata. Each brick, each pathway in the garden, all of it."

While the courtyard gardens she could see from the air appeared to be manicured and green with precise placement of foliage, mountain flowers covered the hillsides that swept down to gorgeous golden meadows on which it appeared no development had ever taken place.

But for the Luminata complex, there were no other buildings or roads within sight. No vehicles. Not even people on less modern means of transport. She couldn't even glimpse the walled border that Raphael had told her protected Lumia on three sides. There had been no wall on the side over which they'd flown, the mountains providing a natural bulwark. "When you said the Luminata like their privacy, you meant it. Are the borders patrolled?"

Raphael maintained his position at her side with a minute change in his wing balance. "The sect has a small complement of guards who ensure no one breaches Lumia's peace, but for the most part, the people here—mortal and immortal—know that these lands are forbidden to all except by invitation."

"They have a lot of land if we can't see the walls."

"Not so much in the scheme of things. Perhaps an hour's flight from the mountains to the far border at most." Eyes of unfathomable blue met her own. "Is it all you imagined?"

Elena took another look at the compound getting closer with every wingbeat. "I'm not sure. I think I was expecting something more like the Refuge Library." Stately and with a heavy sense of age about it. "Or maybe an austere monastery. This is more grand in a way. Peaceful and quietly lovely, but with an awareness of its own beauty."

She deliberately "nudged" at him with a wing, their primaries barely brushing. "What about you? Is it as you remember?"

Raphael hadn't flown wingtip to wingtip with anyone for a long time before Elena. Smiling deep within at the playful contact, the youth he'd once been rising to the fore, he nudged her carefully back. He was far stronger than Elena, and while she had incredible grace in the air, she'd only been in flight for a mere flicker of time.

Laughing as his nudge spun her to the left, she said, "Whoop!" and flipped over onto her back for a moment that had his heart crashing against his ribs as he prepared to catch her fragile not-yet-fully-immortal body.

If she hit the earth from this altitude, she'd break. She'd die.

But she angled her head down in a gentle curve, her body following, and was right-side-up again in a matter of seconds.

"I am going to kill your Bluebell," he said, dropping two feet so they were wingtip to wingtip again.

A grin. "How did you know he taught me that?"

Raphael just raised an eyebrow.

Laughing again, his unrepentant consort blew him a kiss. "Don't kill Bluebell. He's teaching me to do a downward spiral roll right now."

"Clearly, Aodhan is not the only one suffering pangs of boredom." Raphael felt his lips kick up, the stab of fear retreating under a wave of memory featuring an intrepid little boy with wings of extraordinary blue. "Did he tell you who taught him the spiral roll?"

Elena's mouth fell open. "It was you!" she guessed.

"The Hummingbird wouldn't speak to me for a month afterward," Raphael admitted with a grin of his own. "As for Lumia, the stronghold doesn't appear to have changed in the time since I overflew it—and the splendor of the landscape, yes, that fits what I know of the Luminata way." He'd never truly thought much about the sect, but when he had, it had been to see them as removed from life but not ascetic in the way of the monks Elena had referenced.

"As a very young man," he told Elena, one long-ago memory sparking another, "I once met a mortal mystic, as you did the holy man. He was thin—only tendon and muscle over bone, no fat. Just enough flesh to sustain his mortal body." Raphael remembered wondering how anyone could survive in such a state. "He had a long gray beard, and his skin was cured by the sun from all the hours he'd walked the landscape, but his soul, it emanated perfect contentment."

Raphael been a young and arrogant angel at the time—akin to a mortal youth who'd left home for the first time—but in that instant, he'd felt humbled. "I felt he knew far more than I could ever imagine, though his lifespan could not have been more than six decades to my two hundred at the time."

He'd ended up walking with that mystic for miles, curious and respectful and aware for the first time in his existence that immortals weren't necessarily the pinnacle of existence. "Unfortunately, the lessons I learned in my days of walking by his side didn't hold in the millennium that followed. I had forgotten him until this instant."

"Don't knock yourself, Archangel." His consort's voice held both her warrior spirit and her fierce love for him. "I learned things as a teenager and young hunter that I forgot in the years that followed. Life isn't static, and sometimes, we don't realize the value of knowledge or even of people, until farther down the track, when we're mature enough to truly understand."

At times, Raphael's hunter consort surprised him with her perceptiveness about mortals and immortals both. "The Luminata," he replied, "they're not and have never been like my mystic or your holy man. Their members join after at least one thousand years of existence—no one younger is permitted to become an initiate. And by that stage, they are used to a certain way of life."

"I get it." Elena swept down on a wind current, her joy in flight an incandescent light he could nearly touch. The deep blue of her sleeveless gown glittered in the sun, almost as bright as the blade that glinted with jewels high on her arm.

Her hair was a shining banner of silken near-white.

Montgomery had done well, having chosen a gown with a sleek and tight silhouette that caught no air and created very little drag, but the skirts of which Elena could unzip at the sides once on the ground, freeing up her stride. There was also a cunning opening high up on her thigh on the right. It was only three inches and could be closed with tiny buttons that looked decorative.

But when open, it allowed Elena to wear her crossbow strapped to her thigh—as she was doing now. Not to mention the forearm gauntlets that held her throwing blades as well as a limited number of crossbow bolts, the long knife she wore against her spine under her dress, and the gun hidden in an ankle holster she wore over her boots.

Guild Hunter Elena Deveraux, Consort to the Archangel Raphael, would be landing at Lumia not as a pretty accessory as some older angels were apt to expect, but as a woman deadly in her own right.

Raphael smiled in grim satisfaction.

The Luminata have given up the world, his warrior consort said in his mind, *but their version of giving up temptation is the comfortable immortal version rather than the austere mortal one.*

Just so. Raphael moved to join Elena in her meandering flight over the landscape around Lumia. It was dead certain they were being watched—by the Luminata's guard, by the Luminata themselves, by any archangels who'd arrived before them—but what did he have to hide? The world knew that the Archangel of New York loved his consort.

That he'd fly with her for no reason but to fly with her gave no one any extra ammunition. That didn't mean he'd lower his guard. Not here. Not with the Luminata an unknown and the Cadre a danger he knew too well. *Aodhan, stay high. Alert me of any approach.*

I see other wings in the sky in the distance. A pause. *Silver wings. Solid silver.*

Alexander. No one else in angelkind had wings like those of the Ancient who was once again the Archangel of Persia. *Is he alone?*

No. I see two other pairs of wings. I will need to get closer to identify them.

Stay with us. He wanted any watchers to be aware that his consort would never be alone, because while he knew Elena could defend herself, he also knew immortals had a tendency to see her mortal heart first, her weapons second. *We'll find out soon enough.* Then he rose high, only to drop down beside Elena in a hard, fast dive that required precision timing.

"Show-off." Admiration glinted in her eyes.

And he felt young again, as he felt only with Elena. Not the archangel responsible for millions of lives, mortal and immortal, but a man with his lover. Raphael with Elena. "I must not disappoint our audience."

"Good point." Elena pulled her crossbow free, retrieved a bolt from the forearm gauntlets Deacon had modified for her so she could carry five bolts on her even when it was impossible for her to wear a full quiver. "How about a game, since we're early anyway?" She shot a bolt toward the earth without warning.

Raphael collapsed his wings, dropped like a bullet . . . and caught the bolt. Then he raced up to catch a second she shot across the sky, went sideways to catch a third.

The voice that came into his mind as he caught the final one, which she'd shot so close it nearly grazed his wing, was a familiar one. Ancient and commanding and with more than a touch of arrogance. *My grandson has just fallen in love with your consort, Raphael. He tells me he wants a lover who shoots at him, too.*

Lips curving, Raphael winged his way to Elena to return her bolts to her. As she slotted them away, having already strapped on her crossbow with the ease of long practice, he told her what Alexander had said. She grinned, the wind sweeping her hair back from her face. "Boy has good taste."

Alexander and his grandson—named Xander, in honor of his grandfather—were now visible in the distance. Alexander's golden hair and silver wings marked him out well before the Ancient came close enough for his face to be clear. As for Xander, he was an amalgam of his parents but he was also very clearly Alexander's grandson.

His hair was a rich, dark brown, his skin a brown so light it was dark gold, and his wings a deep black that faded into darkest brown with touches of gold—but spread out, those wings bore an underside of purest silver.

Your grandson flies well, he said to Alexander. *I'm surprised you brought him with you.* At two hundred, Xander was young, green, and Alexander had already lost his son.

Sire, Aodhan said at the same instant. *Alexander's third. I recognize him. Valerius.*

The name was familiar to Raphael: Valerius was one of Alexander's most loyal angelic generals, a man who'd been loyal to that family line for so long that to think of Valerius was to think of Alexander. *You break the Luminata's laws?*

Alexander was close enough that Raphael could see the shake of his head. *The children of the Cadre are always permitted to any such meeting, so long as they are less than two and a half centuries of age.* Anger and sorrow hardened his features. *My son is dead, so my grandson is permitted to attend.*

Raphael hadn't known that rule—but then, he'd never needed to know it. *Are you certain he'll be safe?*

Not answering, Alexander came to flank Elena, maintaining a respectable three feet of distance between their primaries. The Ancient was nothing if not traditional. "Consort," he said in greeting.

"Archangel Alexander," Elena replied, since she and Alexander didn't have a relationship of informality, as she now did with Titus. "No offense, but why did you bring that gorgeous kid?" She nodded at the young male, who'd dropped to fly low over the landscape.

Alexander could've pointed out that Xander was two hundred years old, give or take a year or two, while Elena had barely passed the three decade mark, but they all knew immortals didn't age as mortals did. Xander wasn't actually the kid Elena had named him, but neither was he considered full grown. He was a stripling—around twenty, maybe twenty-one years of age in human terms.

For angels, their third century of life tended to be the defining moment between childhood and adulthood. Some angels were considered true adults after two centuries and a quarter, others required a little more seasoning. From what he knew of Alexander's bloodline, Raphael wagered the stripling would transition to adulthood in a quicksilver heartbeat. Mere decades at most.

But today, in this moment, he remained a youth.

"It heartens me that you and your consort both ask after the safety of my grandson," Alexander said. "Perhaps there is hope for the Cadre."

You know I will not betray you unless you do the same first,

Raphael said, connecting Elena into the conversation through his own mind. *You are the reason one of my Seven is currently able to live freely with his mate.*

Ah, the wild creature. Alexander's lips curved. *As for Xander, I can see to the safety of my grandson better than anyone else—and when I'm not there, Valerius will be. Xander will be better protected than if he was at home.*

Raphael wasn't so certain. *The world has changed since you were last awake, Alexander. Laws have been broken, lines crossed. You know this better than anyone.*

Eyes of pure silver met Raphael's, the lines of Alexander's face brutal in their hardness. *Anyone who touches him will die by my hand, Raphael. I will then annihilate their lands and lines until no trace remains of their blood. This is a promise of which everyone will soon become aware.*

Elena glanced at Raphael but didn't speak, not until he said, *We are private now, Guild Hunter.*

He won't change his mind, she said. *And I don't think it's arrogance—he lost his son, wants his grandson in his sight so he can protect him.*

Raphael understood, but he also understood that Alexander couldn't always be with Xander. *Are you available for babysitting?*

Elena smiled. *Ah, what the heck. It'll keep me from missing Izzy.*

The youngest member of his consort's Guard was closer to one hundred than two hundred, but it wasn't that big of a gap when it came to angelic growth. The difference between a young mortal of eighteen or nineteen and one of twenty, twenty-one.

"Your grandson is welcome to keep company with my consort and Aodhan," Raphael said aloud. "He will, of course, fall further in love with Elena, but the boy will have to risk a broken heart if he wishes to learn to dance with a warrior consort. She may even shoot bolts at him to keep herself amused."

Alexander's laughter was unexpected, a warm, full-blooded sound that had his grandson sweeping around and up toward his grandfather. "Raphael, I envy you." With that, he dropped to meet his grandson, and the two of them angled toward Lumia.

He did not take offense at the offer, Raphael said to Elena. *So you may well find yourself with a young pup at your side. Valerius is an ancient general, a little rigid personally, but brilliant with strategy. Where Xander goes, he's apt to be close.*

Elena frowned. *Is Aodhan okay with Valerius?*

I will ask.

When Aodhan came down to join them, in their slow sweep toward a landing, he said, "I have only had minor contact with Valerius through the centuries, but he has always struck me as honorable. I don't foresee any problems."

Then they were landing in what appeared to be a central courtyard, the pavings of a lighter stone than the walls of Lumia, the plantings around the courtyard simple grasses kept ruthlessly in control.

Alexander and Xander were already down; Valerius landed beside Aodhan. When the general held out his forearm in the way of warriors, Raphael felt Elena tense, touched her gently on the back. *It is no attempt at one-upmanship or insult, but rather the opposite,* he said to her. *Given the gap in their ages, Valerius likely isn't aware of Aodhan's abhorrence for touch.*

Aodhan didn't hesitate. He responded by clasping his hand over the gauntlet that covered the general's forearm, while the general did the same, his hand closing over Aodhan's leather gauntlet. Only someone who knew Aodhan really well would've caught the stiffness of his wings, the relief that colored his eyes when the contact ended.

"Consort." Alexander came over just as Elena finished unzipping the sides of the bottom half of her dress enough to permit her free movement. "Allow me to officially introduce my grandson. Xander, this is Elena."

The young male's smile was shy and it did put Raphael in mind of Izak, or Izzy as Elena called him.

"Consort." Xander bowed his head low as befit a youth of his age in the presence of an archangelic consort; the fact he was an Ancient's grandson made no difference. Warriors earned their own standing and Raphael knew Alexander well enough to understand that the Ancient would expect nothing less from his blood.

Even Rohan, his beloved son, had gone through the same

training as any young soldier. When he made general, it had been through his own skill and efforts.

"Xander." Elena held out her forearm.

The young male seemed stunned for a second before he responded to clasp her forearm. "You honor me."

Elena grinned. "Finally, someone who sees my greatness." The laughing dryness of her tone made even Alexander's lips curve up.

Elena had just released Xander's forearm, the youth even more in her thrall if his expression was anything to go by, when Luminata whispered out of the walls around them.

10

"A well-executed illusion," Raphael said to his consort, his voice low enough that it would reach only her.

Her eyes narrowed. "They're good at it," she replied at the same volume. "I didn't hear or glimpse them until they wanted to be noticed." She brushed her wing over his, the barest contact to slide under the radar of those who might be watching. *I don't know what these Luminata have convinced angelkind is their purpose and aim, but they move like they have combat training.* "I'm starting to think they're more warrior monks than philosophers on the road to enlightenment."

Raphael had to agree with her now that he'd seen the way the Luminata moved, the grace in their bodies, the contained strength beneath the pale, golden brown robes that covered them neck to toe. Including over their wings. That was extraordinary—no angel liked his wings confined.

However, when a light wind lifted the hem of one of the robes, he saw that the robe was in three sections at the back. The fabric was heavy enough not to part over the wings in ordinary movement, but should one of the Luminata wish to fly, they could snap out their wings without problem. Despite that, the effect was subtly disturbing to an angel. Not only did their silhouettes appear misshapen, but they were covering so much of what defined their identity.

Their heads were currently uncovered, but Raphael could see the hoods that lay on their backs, between the covered arches of their wings. Once pulled up, those hoods would shadow their faces, turning individuals into the anonymous many.

That, he realized, was the aim.

And while such anonymity might've made sense in a mortal monastery, it didn't here, with immortals all over a millennia old. Each of them was very much an individual, and nothing Raphael knew of the Luminata suggested they advocated conformity of thought. The path to luminescence, as explained to him, had always been a journey done by one alone, though other Luminata might provide guidance or support.

"Welcome." The word was spoken by a strikingly handsome man of medium height with eyes of a pale green almost as arresting as Aodhan's shattered gaze, and hair of a thick, shining brown that was echoed in his primary feathers, the male's wings otherwise pure white—because of all the Luminata in the courtyard, he alone did not wear a robe designed to hide his wings.

Elsewise, he was dressed identically to the others.

"I am Gian." His skin shone a flawless cool white in the sunshine. "My brothers do me the honor of calling me Luminata."

You didn't say this was a male-only deal.

I did not know, Raphael responded, taking note when Gian's eyes lingered on Elena for a beat too long—it could be simple curiosity about a new consort, but Raphael took nothing for granted. *Angelkind rarely breaks along gender lines. Any demarcation is usually tied to age and power.*

"I am glad to have you here," Gian said. "Please, let us show you to your rooms so that you may refresh yourself." His smile appeared to hold the purest serenity, as if he was no longer quite on the same plane of existence. "Favashi and Neha arrived an hour earlier, and I'm told that Caliane's wings have been spotted on the horizon. The others cannot be far behind."

He swept his hand gently to the left, the movement as graceful as a perfectly balanced sword curving through the air. "My brothers will guide you. Please take no offense that I do not do so myself—I must remain here to welcome the re-mainder of the Cadre."

There is a strange peace in listening to him. Aodhan's voice in Raphael's mind, the sensation of color and light accompanying the words a mental echo of his physical form.

Yes. A strange peace is a good description, Raphael replied, just as Elena said, *That guy is spooky. Not creepy. Spooky.*

Raphael waited to respond until they were following their silent escort down an open outdoor corridor, light pouring in through the curved openings on either side that showcased the astonishing beauty of the landscape around Lumia. *What is the difference between spooky and creepy?*

Creepy is Lijuan. No further explanation was forthcoming—or needed. *Spooky can go either way. You know that holy man I met? He was so much at peace that he was spooky. Like he'd become something different from all the rest of us on this planet. But on the flip side, spooky can mean a seriously dangerous mind—just because a person's not part of this world doesn't mean the world he is part of isn't a whackjob nutso place.*

Do you believe the latter of Gian?

A small shrug. *Got no reason to—honestly, I'd have been a little disappointed if immortal monks turned out to be normal. Have to expect a little spookiness of people who consciously isolate themselves for centuries or millennia, their goal so elusive it must be like trying to find a dream.*

Raphael considered her words as Alexander, his grandson, and Valerius's stocky form were led off through a closed hallway to the right, one that appeared to have no end from this perspective. *They are positioning us far from one another.*

That's good, right? Lines formed between Elena's eye-brows as they passed the entrance to that hallway and the three disappeared from view. *Since it's dangerous if you're too close together?*

It makes no difference when we are all within the same region. The Cadre could remain in close proximity for a short number of weeks before things began to go catastrophically wrong.

The world wasn't designed to allow the close coexistence

of that much power. It began to build and build inside the archangels until the only way to get it out was to attack one another—regardless of whether the sane part of their nature might argue against such an action.

Even Raphael's parents, no matter their piercing love for one another, had been unable to always be together. Nadiel, through no choice of his own, had been missing from Raphael's childhood for long periods. At least until Raphael got old enough to travel occasionally to his father's territory during the times when his parents had to be apart. Caliane's joy at their return had always been a dazzling song that made Raphael's heart ache with happiness that his parents were together again.

But you are right, he added when Elena turned a worried face to him, *the separation is likely a simple courtesy. The Luminata may be taking the safest option, given that they do not know which of the Cadre are enemies with one another and which are allies.* Raphael made a note of their route nonetheless, along with any other corridors and doors they passed along the way.

He knew his hunter and Aodhan were doing the same.

"Archangel. Consort. I am Gervais." Their escort's voice was rougher than Gian's, his face long and saturnine under skin of a dark mahogany. "Your suite." Using one hand, he opened a door of smooth honey-colored wood polished to such a high shine that it appeared like stone.

It was identical to every other door they'd passed.

"Dinner will be announced by use of the central bell," the tall, thin male said, his presence along the same continuum as Gian's—not as oddly peaceful, but with an internal confidence that said the outer world did not matter to him as much as his personal journey. There was certainly no indication that he was intimidated by being in the presence of an archangel.

"We have placed refreshments within your suite. Please rest and explore as you will. The Luminata do not have secrets." Moving back with an unexpectedly shallow bow, he indicated that the room across the hall was Aodhan's, then disappeared down the corridor in a whisper of faded golden brown robes that blended into the stone of Lumia, his wings hidden beneath the heavy garment.

Elena frowned after the Luminata brother but didn't say anything until they were behind the closed door to their suite. "There's something off about this place," she muttered. "Gian's spookiness aside, the sense of peace I expected is missing." She rubbed her hands over her upper arms. "You know, like when you walk into a place of worship? It might not be a religion to which you ascribe, but there's always this hushed reverence about the place."

"I am not mortal, Elena. Mortal religions are not mine."

"Right. Well, think of your mystic, how being near him made you feel."

It had been a long time ago, but the memory was at the surface of his mind after their earlier conversation. "I see your meaning," he said, walking across the thickly carpeted front room and past a seating area of white painted furniture with velvet gray cushions; his goal was the back wall set with a small stained glass window.

When he opened it, it was to find it looked out not onto the outside slopes but an internal hallway identical to those through which they'd walked. "It's not simply a lack of psychic peace. From within, Lumia feels more like the Refuge stronghold of another archangel."

The shallow bow from an escort who had not earned that right, the fact Gian had taken the names of the Cadre without adding "Archangel" to the front, the Luminata who'd watched them from the shadows, their faces hidden under the hoods of their robes, none of it was as it should be.

Elena came to stand beside him as he pulled the window shut. "Maybe it's just because they're immortals who've been by themselves for way too long." Nodding at the window, she said, "They've buried us."

"Yes." Raphael considered their route to the suite. "Did you notice anything about the architecture?"

"Yes, it's not exactly convenient for a people with wings. Ceilings are relatively low for angelic dwellings, and once past the courtyard, there aren't any openings from which to take off." She glanced around, saw a notepad of thick cream paper on a small white writing desk. Beside it was a pen.

Taking both, she began to draw. "These are all the courtyards we saw from above."

"You've memorized them?" He could blast through stone if need be, but his consort wasn't powerful enough to smash her way out.

"Yes, but I'll need to do some exploring, get an idea of distances involved." Putting down the map, Elena stared at the door through which they'd entered. "The corridors are so circular and winding that it's hard to figure out how much time it'll take to go anywhere."

Raphael closed his hand around the side of her neck. "Stay with Aodhan as much as you can. This place . . . it has a darkness to it that may simply be a result of secrecy and long isolation, but we will take no chances."

Elena rose on her toes to brush her lips over his, her hands on his shoulders. "I won't drop my guard. I mean seriously, even if the Luminata are just odd because they spend so much time alone out here, there's still Michaela, Charisemnon, and the others to worry about." She twisted her lips . . . but her jaundiced expression turned suddenly into a smile. "Do you think Astaad will bring Mele?"

"He knows you are friends, so perhaps." Astaad also favored Mele above all his other concubines. "But Mele is a beautiful, fragile bloom—he may not bring her into such a perilous situation." Astaad had his faults but his care of his concubines wasn't one of them. "You will still have Hannah." Elijah's consort was as fragile a bloom as Mele, an artist happier with a paintbrush than with a blade, but custom dictated that she be at Elijah's side for this gathering.

"We've already made plans to meet up." Where Elena wanted to explore the nooks and crannies of Lumia and get into their historical archives, Hannah was itching to look through the repository of angelic art held in trust by the Luminata.

"I figure if we get bored, Hannah'll teach me about art so I can pull off snooty if need be"—she raised her nose into the air and pursed her lips like a stuck-up antique dealer she'd met once during a hunt—"and I can teach her how to throw knives more accurately. Paint knives, of course, since that's her weapon of choice."

Raphael's laughter wrapped around her like the crashing sea. "I'm sure Elijah will be most grateful. Hannah's aim leaves much to be desired, and with the pumas who follow her around like pets, she's beginning to rely on them for her personal safety during the times she's otherwise on her own."

Elena shook her head, conscious Elijah had been attempting to teach Hannah defensive skills for years. "She's stubborn in her own way."

"All consorts worth their salt know how to stand their ground."

"Sweet talker." Her words were light, but Elena's skin prickled; she didn't like how little she knew about this place, saw the same disquiet in the hard lines of Raphael's expression. "Want to look around?"

Raphael's nod was curt. "But first, eat something. Energy is finite and your body is still burning an incredible amount of it as you grow further into your immortality."

Having begun to feel the sharp pangs of a hunger that seemed endless these days, her body so hungry for fuel that she was going through a box of energy bars a day in between meals, Elena didn't argue, just picked up a large handful of nuts and dried fruits. If it was fuel her body needed to become stronger, tougher, then she'd drink every energy shake Montgomery made her, chew down endless bars, eat like a freaking linebacker.

The stronger she was, the less people would look on her as vulnerable prey—and the less chance that an enemy would get to her archangel through hurting her. When she put one of the dried fruits to Raphael's lips, he took the offering with a brush of his lips on her fingers. A sweet kiss. It made her feel like a silly teenage girl—but then, she'd never been that. So maybe she was due.

"Try this." Raphael fed her a hunk of cheese that had a rich, creamy taste to it. "It's a delicacy, meant to be partnered with these peppers."

Elena made a face. "No thanks. I'll stick to naked cheese."

When she leaned forward, he gave her another bite, ate the second half himself. "Make sure Aodhan is eating, too." She knew older angels could survive for long periods without food, but it had an impact eventually. "He didn't eat anything on the plane." She knew she didn't have to tell Raphael why she was worried about the other angel.

The thought reminded her of something else.

Sliding out her phone, she went to message Beth of her safe arrival, saw she had no reception. Raphael took the phone when she muttered under her breath, shook his head. "Too many of the Cadre in close proximity," he told her. "The energy can cause major interference."

"Damn it. I didn't think about that." Putting away her phone, she pressed a clenched hand against her abdomen. "You know how Beth is. She'll have a panic attack if—"

"It is all right, Elena-mine." Her archangel cupped her cheek, brushing his thumb over her cheekbone. "I know your sister is a jewel easily broken—I left instructions with Dmitri to ensure she receives a note from the Tower confirming our safe arrival, regardless of whether Dmitri has heard from us."

Eyes hot, she touched her fingers to the jaw of this deadly being who understood her soul. "Thank you."

"There is no need. Beth is like the Hummingbird, requires a little extra gentleness," he said, just as there was a knock on their door. "Aodhan. I invited him."

No knot in her gut now that she knew Beth wouldn't be plunged into a horrible nightmare until her return, Elena moved to open the door. "Good plan." Waving in Aodhan, she said, "We're snacking before exploring this place. Come grab something."

"I ate the cheeses and nuts in my chambers," Aodhan replied, then, as if catching her skepticism, said, "My task is to be another sword at your back. I can't do that if I'm weak."

There was no way Elena could disbelieve him. To do so would be to question his strength all over again. "Come in anyway. Tell us what you think of this place."

Aodhan entered, shutting the door behind him. "It's not what I expected," he said, as Elena continued to refuel with single-minded focus.

Raphael kept her company by eating the occasional tidbit she fed him.

"Lumia itself is a construct of beauty and grace," Aodhan continued. "But there is an odd resonance beneath."

Elena noticed he was keeping his voice low, only realized then that she and Raphael had done the same since they entered this suite. As if they all believed the walls might have ears.

"The rooms are what you might expect in the home of any

angel past six or seven hundred years of age." Aodhan waved at the fancy furniture, the luxurious carpet. "But the art is missing."

Elena swallowed the cheese in her mouth, chased it down with water. "Isn't that held in some kind of gallery?" It's what she'd assumed when Hannah had spoken about the art she intended to view at Lumia.

Raphael was the one who answered. "Some of it may be, yes. But the walls of Lumia itself are meant to be lined with art, a new wonder around every corner." He resettled his wings and she couldn't help but run her fingers over his primaries in a petting gesture that was openly possessive.

It still struck her mute at times that he was hers.

The funny thing was, he had the same response to her.

Eternity would mean nothing without you. For no power on this earth would I trade my Elena.

The memory of his raw words was a crossbow bolt right to the heart every single time.

"The Luminata," Raphael added, "have collected that art for untold eons. Artists offer them their greatest works, because to be displayed on Lumia's walls is a great accolade."

So where, Elena thought, was all that art? Why would the Luminata prefer anonymous hallways that all appeared the same? Why did they scurry about so secretively and watch their visitors from hidden alcoves? Elena might've missed the first lot of Luminata until they apparently emerged from the walls, but she'd learned from her mistake. So she knew this place had eyes.

And those eyes raised every hair on her body.

11

The hairs on the back of her neck stayed stiff as they exited their suite.

As they'd already noted, the walls had a seamless sameness that sought to deceive the eye and confuse the mind, their color that of the sand-colored stone mined from the nearby mountains, the doors set into those walls identical. Technically, it was soothing and lovely, but . . .

"It's like being in a horror movie," Elena muttered. "Like those scenes where a victim runs frantically down hallways in a hotel where everything's the same and there's no way out."

"What's a horror movie?"

Elena grinned at Aodhan's question. "I'll show you once we get home." Only after the words were out did she realize she didn't know which horror might be Aodhan's own. *Raphael, you're going to have to vet the movies.*

First you throw bread at my head and now you expect me to be a movie critic, was the outwardly haughty response, but he brushed his fingers against her own. *It is to your honor that you care for his heart. I will tell you what he can and cannot bear.*

The eerie sameness underwent a dramatic change once they hit a set of external corridors, the breathtaking scenery beyond Lumia framed by delicate stone archways. From this vantage point, it was possible to see all the way to the mountains over which they'd flown, nothing in between but wildflowers, and, closer to the peaks, the dark shapes of trees designed to survive in this arid landscape.

"The patterns are astonishing."

Elena and Raphael both turned to face Aodhan.

Clearly reading their total lack of comprehension, he smiled that quiet smile that had been known to cause both men and women near enough to glimpse it, to faint. "Look." He went close to a wall, traced lines on it.

It still took Elena well over a minute to see what he was pointing out, the impressions on the stone were so fine. And then she saw them everywhere. Intricate, delicate patterns covered the walls, the arched ceiling, the floor. "Wow." She literally pressed her nose to a wall in an effort to see exactly how the patterns had been created. "Are they all different?"

"No, not on the walls at least," Aodhan said. "They repeat within each hallway, changing only after a turn or once we pass the entrance to another hallway."

Raphael ran his own finger over the stone. "A meditation aid possibly?"

"I'm obviously not mentally enlightened enough for this place." Elena followed one intricate line with her eye, wondering at the patience it had taken to carve it out with such fine delicacy. "I would've never seen the designs on my own."

"Then I, too, am not enlightened enough, Guild Hunter."

"Of course not. Why else would you have had the bad form to fall in love with a mortal? Philistine."

Raphael's laugh had Aodhan's lips curving into a deep smile that was so rare, it made Elena's heart miss a beat. "It is less enlightenment and more a matter of artistic training," he said. "Once you see it, you can't miss it."

Hunkering down, his wings a graceful sweep on his back and the hilts of his dual blades drawing her eye, he traced near-invisible designs on the floor. "I think it's a map, a way to navigate Lumia." He touched his fingers to the nearest wall. "I haven't decoded the map as yet, but what I do understand leads me to believe the walls may open in places."

Elena whistled, crouching down opposite him to examine the lines. "No wonder the Luminata can swan about like ghosts." As if they could walk through walls. "Good way to put people on the back foot."

"I'm beginning to believe the Luminata enjoy holding knowledge above others," Raphael said as they rose to explore further, the three of them walking side by side with Elena in the middle. "They have always been secretive to the extreme."

"Things rot in darkness," Elena muttered, but even as she spoke, she knew she was probably being unfair—her life colored her view. Just because the Luminata were a little weird didn't mean they were in any way dangerous. "Aodhan, you think you can fully decipher the map?"

He nodded, the crushed diamonds that appeared to coat the strands of his hair catching the sunlight coming in from the outside to throw flickering light on the walls. "It appears to have been designed for ordinary angelic senses, rather than for those with extensive artistic training and an inborn spatial sense."

"I see."

Aodhan looked so discomfited at Raphael's toneless response that Elena elbowed her consort. "He's messing with you, Aodhan," she said, having glimpsed the laughter very well hidden in the blue.

The angel created of light glanced from one to the other before his expression warmed, his own smile open and unexpected and—*Wow. Sparkle is freaking gorgeous.* She'd always seen his beauty, but today, she truly understood why people coveted him.

When he is not broken, Raphael said, *he is a shooting star caught midfall.*

The sadness in Raphael's tone had her weaving her fingers through his. *He's coming back*, she reminded her archangel. *And he's powerful enough to kick serious ass. No one will break him again.*

Raphael's fingers locked around hers. *After he was released from the Medica, Aodhan made it clear he wanted to be alone. We honored his wishes at first, but when we realized he was turning recluse, we tried everything in our power to pull him out of the abyss. All of us. Including Galen.*

He'd turn up at Aodhan's isolated home and refuse to leave until Aodhan sparred with him. In the end, Aodhan gave in and turned up to sessions at the weapons salle just so Galen would leave him alone otherwise—in the worst period, it was often the only time he stepped outside his home. They sparred nearly every day during Aodhan's residence at the Refuge. It was always without any physical contact, but the social contact forced Aodhan to stay in the world at least partially.

Yes, there was a hell of a lot more to Galen than Elena had ever realized during her time under his instruction. *If Aodhan was forced to hold his own against Galen for two hundred years, then he's probably far more well trained than pretty much everyone else in the Tower.* Raphael and the others, they had to set him free.

"Aodhan," she said aloud. "Raphael just told me that Galen stalked you for two hundred years."

"Galen is like a storm that you either battle, or surrender to," Aodhan said. "And if you surrender because you do not care, the storm just gets stronger and stronger until the howling threatens to drive you insane and you must pick up the sword just to get a little peace."

Elena's shoulders shook at the bone-dry recitation. "Get flattened a few times?"

"Until I resembled the food your little hunter sister likes. Pancakes."

A snort threatening to escape as she gave in to her laughter, Elena wiped her tears away. "But here you stand."

"Galen would accept nothing less." With that simple statement that held deepest respect, Aodhan paused, stared at the floor for three long seconds before nodding and carrying on.

Right when she thought he was done talking, he touched a hand to the dual blades he wore. "Galen gave me these when he deemed me fit for battle. My originals were . . . lost."

Elena had no need to ask when or how, not with the shadows in Aodhan's eyes and the sudden tension in Raphael. "Damn it," she muttered sulkily, kicking at the floor. "Galen never gave me any weapons."

Shadows fading, Aodhan's eyes filled with a rare light. "It took me a hundred years of daily sparring to earn these. You have time yet."

"Perhaps we should go to the Refuge if you are so eager to see Galen," Raphael murmured.

"I warned you about that sense of humor, Archangel," Elena said darkly while Aodhan struggled to hide a smile.

They walked for an hour but didn't get anywhere near the library, where Jessamy had told Elena she'd find the historical archives; neither did they discover what had happened to the art. Back at their suite, Aodhan sat down and began to draw out the designs so they could all learn the map.

His hand moved strong and sure, the lines that flowed from his pen without flaw.

"This should give us a good start," he said after he was done. "To get back to the suite if you get disoriented, follow this symbol in this grouping." His eyes met Elena's, shattered pieces of green and blue glass spiking out from a jet-black pupil. "There are further symbols I don't yet understand. We will explore Lumia together, unearth their secrets."

Elena nodded, hoping once again that hidden within Lumia would be some small piece of knowledge that might solve the mystery of her ancestry. And if it felt as if she was searching for a way to find her mother through time . . . was that such a terrible thing?

"I want to shower," Elena said after Aodhan left to return to his own room until dinner. "I feel dusty from the flight over the mountains." Despite his consort's words and though she'd already removed her weapons and boots, she hesitated to undress.

Raphael held out a hand.

When she took it, he led her to the bathing chamber and shut the door. There was no shower, but someone had already partially filled the large stone bath with cold water, minerals swirled into the clear liquid. It was a normal angelic courtesy to ensure guests didn't have to wait too long for their bath to fill.

Finding the handle—old but functional—that made the hot water start to gush out from a spout in the wall, Raphael turned it on.

By the time it filled to the top, it would be the correct temperature.

Then he threw his glamour around them both; they were now effectively invisible from any eyes that might seek to watch. His instincts didn't prickle in this particular space in the suite, but regardless, no one was going to see what was his and his alone to view.

"Did we go poof?"

Cheeks creasing because she did that to him, made the capacity for fun come alive inside him, he nodded. "But you must stay close to me for the glamour to encapsulate you."

"What a terrible, terrible hardship." Turning, she lifted her hair off her neck, exposing the soft skin of her nape. "Can you unbutton me?"

There were only two buttons, one each at the top of her wings, the dress designed to be pulled on from the bottom, with wings sliding into the slits created for them, then the dress buttoned into place at the top. Raphael knew that because he'd watched his consort dress, seen her pull the fabric over the black lace panties she wore underneath.

There was no bra, the support built into the dress, so when he undid the buttons and she began to slither the dress past her hips, he, of course, had to curve his arms around her body and cup her breasts. "Just helping keep them in place," he said, kissing her neck.

Husky laughter. "You really are a very helpful lover." Another push and the dress pooled at her feet.

He kept on kissing her neck, his hands bluntly possessive on her breasts.

Shivering, she leaned back into him, raising her arms to loop them around the back of his neck. "You make my bones melt."

He smiled against her skin, moving one of his hands from her breast, down the sleek, strong curve of her abdomen, past her navel, and into her panties. She gasped at the sudden intrusion, her breath coming in rapid pants as he used his fingers to bring her to the edge, her delicate flesh slick under his touch.

Holding her there, he said, "Turn your head." His voice was gritty.

She angled her head to him, met his kiss with primal hunger—and he pushed her over. Body arching as the shudders of her release rocked her, Elena never broke their kiss. And when her eyes opened, they danced with wildfire.

"Raphael." A lazy, sated smile. "You're better than a shower. *Way* better."

And he smiled again.

Scooping her up into his arms, he placed her in the bath, which was nearly full, then stayed right next to her as he undressed. His arousal was heavy and thick, and when he stepped into the bath after shutting off the water, she flowed onto his lap, her arms around his neck and her wings half floating in the water.

This kiss was sweetly tender, two lovers who had total trust in one another taking a moment out of time. Sliding his hands down the sides of her body, he lifted her, brought her down. Had Elena not wanted him to do either, she'd have made it clear. But she smiled against his lips, and when his cock nudged at her heat, she put her hands on his shoulders and bore down.

His back was the one that arched this time, his throat the one that was kissed, his body the one that was petted and caressed. She moved on him slow and sinuous, the sleek muscle of her flexing under his touch. But there was only so much an archangel could take. Holding her hip tight with one hand, his other hand gripping her hair, he took over their intimate dance.

And his consort with the wildfire eyes, she smiled a wicked smile and leaned in to kiss him deep and hot and without restraint as her body clenched around him in a tease that could have only one end. As his spine locked under a slamming kiss of desire sated, he felt the Legion mark go active, felt his wings turn to white fire.

They wrapped around his hunter until the two of them burned up in the heart of flame.

12

An hour after their shared bath, a towel-clad Elena had dried her hair using the dryer Montgomery had packed. As shown by the electric lights in the suite and in the hallways, Lumia had undergone a certain level of modernization at some point, so there had been an electrical outlet his hunter could use for the dryer.

That done, and still protected by his glamour, Raphael seated on the edge of the bath only inches from where she stood in front of the bathroom mirror, he watched her slip into one of the more formal gowns Montgomery had packed for her. She'd made him go out and fetch the gown, saying she felt "creeped out" dressing or undressing in any other room in the suite.

He'd gathered his own clothing at the same time, changed into it before settling down to watch his consort.

It hadn't been a difficult task to find any of the items, since Montgomery packed in a pattern with which Raphael was long familiar after having the butler so long in his employ. Their baggage had arrived while he, Elena, and Aodhan had been exploring Lumia, having been flown in from the airport by a small unit of the Luminata's angelic guard carrying a net for that purpose.

No one had touched it since then, as per protocol.

Archangels might be used to staff, but they were also used to privacy.

The gown Montgomery had packed for tonight's formal dinner was in a shade of midnight blue and it had two wide pieces of fabric that came over Elena's breasts before gathering at her waist and flaring out into a skirt that frothed around her feet.

The back was open but for the fine straps that held the top together—and the long line of the spine knife Elena had slipped into a decorative black and gold metal sheath. Because of course, he'd had to go retrieve her weapons before anything else. She wore the harness below the dress, not because it equaled a more aesthetically pleasing appearance, but so no one could tear it off her without first tearing off her dress.

"Priorities," she'd said to him when he questioned the dangers of having the leather and metal rubbing against her skin. "And Deacon lined the leather of the harness, so I can wear it against my skin without issue."

That lethal blade wasn't her only weapon.

She wore a gun in one thigh sheath, a hunting knife in the other. Both of which she could reach for through invisible slits built into the froth of her gown's skirt. All of Elena's gowns had such adjustments.

Raphael was pleased.

He didn't want the spine knife to be her only choice: guns might not kill strong angels, but a bullet shredding flesh would hurt even the most powerful angel at least a little. It'd give her a second or two to get into a better defensive position should all hell break loose. "You can reach your gun?"

Elena had it in her hand almost before he saw her move.

A sharp grin, then she lifted her bare foot and placed it on his thigh. Circling her ankle with one hand, he watched her hike up her dress to put the gun back into place in the sheath she wore on her upper thigh. "Montgomery makes the tailor do mock-ups of my gowns and I move in the mock-ups to make sure the adaptations work."

Sliding his hand up the smooth skin of her thigh, Raphael made himself a promise that he'd be the one taking off the sheath tonight. "I have your blade."

He allowed her to slip away her foot, then rose to close and buckle up the soft leather straps of the sheath on her upper arm. That sheath glittered with jewels, the buckles brilliant gold. The hilt of the blade itself was as encrusted with jewels, a suitable "show" weapon for an ordinary consort.

Elena wasn't ordinary.

And the blade he'd given her could separate a wrist from an arm without the least problem. "Will you wear your hair sticks?" Jason's princess had given the weaponized sticks to Elena, and Raphael had brought them in with the gown.

In return for Mahiya's gift, Elena had gifted the other woman a crossbow commissioned for the princess that was designed to support her personal style. According to Jason, Mahiya used it every day, not wanting her skills to become rusty.

"Yes," Elena said. "I want to have my hair up so the long knife on my back is visible. The sticks give me another hidden weapon." She twisted up her hair with quick, practiced hands, slid in the sticks to hold the twist in place.

Willing to step out of the bathroom and the shield of glamour at last, she padded to their bedroom and found a case of cosmetics before returning to the bathroom. "This should only take a couple of minutes."

Raphael loved watching Elena ready herself to head out into the world—even more, he loved that while she could spend ten minutes getting the position of a weapon just right, it really did only take her a minute or two to "paint her face" as she put it.

"It's a weapon, too, you know," she said as she focused on dusting her eyelids with finely shimmering color. "The face, I mean. Distraction and obfuscation. Took me a while to understand that."

Raphael admired his hunter-consort's wings of midnight and deepest blue and dawn and so many shades from black to white gold. "Michaela is an expert at it." The other archangel had long ago learned to use her extraordinary beauty to blind others to her power and ambition.

"Yeah, she's good." Elena picked up a small flat disk that she opened to reveal some kind of hard-pressed powder. "Sara's been helping me learn 'next level' stuff—beyond my usual routine."

"I would not think the head of the Hunters Guild would care much for such niceties."

"You kidding? Sara has to deal with powerful immortals every day."

And those immortals, Raphael realized, often put too much emphasis on beauty and aesthetics, forgetting a hunter's skill was her greatest weapon. "What has your friend taught you?"

"I'll show you in a minute. Mahiya taught me something, too, the last time she and Jason came over to stay." A pause. "Don't look at me in the mirror. I want to surprise you."

"I will admire the curves of your body instead." And he did, particularly the long, nearly bare sweep of her back.

Not long afterward, she put down a tiny pot and turned toward him: a warrior princess who looked at him with eyes of wild silver that appeared huge in the dark gold skin of her face, her cheekbones razors and her throat a long line.

"You like it?"

"I like you in all your faces, Guild Hunter." And he knew no matter which face she wore, she remained a warrior first and foremost.

Looking disgruntled, Elena put her hands on her hips. "Come on, I made a special effort with the goop."

Rising to his feet, he cupped her jaw, took in her eyes. "The kohl is from Mahiya."

"Yep." She held up a fingertip smudged black. "Let me wash this off. Mahiya said there are pencils I could use, but she's always used a tiny pot of kohl and her little finger and that works for me, too."

"I thought you a warrior princess when you turned to me." He kissed her on lips she'd left unpainted.

Gripping the black leather of his gauntleted forearm, she opened her mouth to his even as he claimed hers. When they broke apart, her eyes glittered, her skin flushed under a fine shield of cosmetics.

Elena washed off the faint remnants of the kohl on the pad of the smallest finger on her right hand, then checked her face in the mirror before slicking on a lipstick that made her lips appear a little bit plumper. Finished with the primping—*weapon*, she reminded herself, *it's another weapon*—she went into the living area to see that Raphael was putting on his boots.

Since her own boots would only take seconds to pull on, she leaned in the doorway and just watched him. He'd gone for "formal warrior" in his clothing choice and she approved. Black gauntlets covered each of his forearms, the same color as his pants and shirt. That shirt had no sleeves and was patterned on fighting leathers; two thin black strips of leather ran across his shoulders, and in place of the collarless neckline of fighting leathers, this one had a raised mandarin collar closed on the right with a steel black pin that echoed the Legion mark.

Closing down one side of his chest rather than in the middle, the shirt had no visible buttons, but it not only fit flawlessly across his chest, it did the same around his wings.

Aside from the pin, which only became visible at close quarters, there was only a single point of ornamentation on his body—the ring of platinum and amber that he wore as a symbol of Elena's claim. Elena wore her own amber in her ears—and in the blade strapped to her upper arm. It had taken her months of owning the gift to realize there were pieces of highly polished amber embedded in among the gemstones.

Her archangel was just slightly possessive.

Smiling, she walked over to join him when he rose to his feet. The stark black of his clothing threw the brilliant blue of his eyes and the Cascade mark into brutal focus. "You look like a primal warrior barely contained." The sophistication remained, but it had a harsh edge that would remind everyone of his origins as a man honed in combat.

"Good." Raphael watched in silence as she slipped on her soft calf-length "gown boots"—because Elena did not do heels. "Ready?"

"Let's go show them how New Yorkers do things."

The first person Elena saw when she walked into the glass-ceilinged Atrium—as the huge room with the high ceiling had been described by the guide who'd left them at the door—was Michaela. The archangel who'd once been known as the Queen of Constantinople and now controlled the vast majority of Europe as well as part of what had once been Uram's territory was wearing a gown of darkest green that hugged her every curve and had a neckline that plunged almost to her belly button.

In a fairer world, that would've made her look trashy.

This wasn't a fair world: the Archangel of Budapest, Michaela taking her current title from the city in which she kept her court, looked like the embodiment of beauty. Her skin had no blemishes, her curves the catalyst for a million wet dreams, her face all clean lines put together with haunting perfection and her eyes an intense green—jewels without flaw but for the ring of a lighter acidic green that, at times, appeared without warning around her irises.

Uram's taint.

The acid wasn't present today. Michaela had also put up her hair, into a complicated pattern it must've taken someone an hour to create. It revealed the swanlike elegance of her neck.

Then there were the stunning wings of delicate bronze that she held off the floor with effortless muscle control.

There was a reason Michaela was known as the most beautiful woman in existence.

Beyond her, past the cream-colored settees arranged into seating areas, and the meticulously set dinner table, right against the wall on the very far side of the Atrium, stood her psychotic pet vampire, Riker—Elena had caught his jarringly evocative scent when she entered the room: cedar painted with ice. Of course, he was handsome, too, all blond hair and eyes of darkest brown, his wide-shouldered, slim-hipped body that of a fashion model. Psycho didn't mean ugly, not among mortals or immortals.

And Elena didn't think Michaela tolerated physical imperfection.

Catching her glance, Riker smiled . . . and licked his tongue over his lips.

Creep.

She didn't give him the benefit of a response, focusing her attention on his mistress.

Michaela was looking up at Titus and laughing at something the warrior archangel was saying. Big and heavily muscled, his skin gleaming jet and his smile a dazzling thing, his wings powerful, Titus was no slouch in the looks department, but it was his sex appeal that most impacted women. Obviously, even Michaela wasn't immune.

"I don't think I've ever before seen Michaela *actually* laughing," she said to Raphael, the two of them far enough away and the room cavernous enough that no one could hear them. "Not when she's not putting on an act." It made the other woman even more extraordinarily beautiful.

And Elena could see how men would fall for her.

"At least Titus has the brains not to bite down on any lures she may throw out," was Raphael's response. "He has seen through her for an eon."

"Good. I really like Titus." The big angel said what he meant and meant what he said. "I don't see Dahariel."

"Astaad likely left his second in charge at home, as we did Dmitri."

"Right, I keep forgetting that while Dahariel might have slept with Michaela, his loyalty is to Astaad." That messed with her mind. "I don't know if I could ever sleep with a man who wasn't loyal to me."

The crashing wind, the salt-laced sea of Raphael's voice in her mind. *That will never be an issue, Consort. Since you will only ever be sleeping with me.*

Laughing at that icy response, she turned to lock her gaze with his. "Just don't forget—that goes both ways. I'll use the pretty blade you gave me to hack off the head of any woman who touches you."

His lips curved. "Of course." Not shifting his eyes from her own, he said, "It seems Gian is intrigued by you."

"I could feel the back of my neck prickling. Figured it was Michaela shooting poison at me with her eyes." Elena turned back toward the others, keeping her motions natural, as if she was simply taking in the room once again. "I'd quite like to talk to the guy, get his measure."

"This is a good opportunity. It may be nothing but curiosity, but if he's interested in testing the strength of a mortal hunter turned consort, you'll be safer here than if he catches you alone."

Elena tried not to frown. "You think he's dangerous?"

"I've just remembered where I know the name from."

13

Raphael leaned in to speak against her ear, an archangel and his consort sharing a private joke. "Gian was the second of an archangel who has Slept since before Neha's ascension. He is at least five thousand years old and dangerously strong."

Smiling to keep up the illusion of a private conversation between lovers, Elena said, "Got it. I'll watch myself."

"He also had a reputation for being a man who enjoyed the pleasures of life and who had many lovers, all of them women." Raphael's tone was thoughtful. "From that to this bastion of maleness, it's an unusual progression."

"I dunno—sometimes people take stock of their life and don't like what they see. Could be what happened to Gian." She glanced over her shoulder to check on Aodhan.

The angel had taken up a position against the wall of the Atrium nearest the door, alongside several of his fellow escorts. One of those escorts, Elena saw, was a well-armed and gorgeous woman with a blunt fringe of black hair against skin of muted brown—and she was looking straight at Aodhan, invitation in her smile.

Aodhan's attention, however, was on Elena.

Turning back around after their eyes met in a silent

communication that all was well—so far—she asked Raphael about the woman, then held up a hand. "Wait, let me guess. Hmm . . . Neha's escort?"

"Titus's," Raphael told her with a smile. "He adores soft, feminine women, but he also has a powerful contingent of female warriors. I'm fairly certain the woman is the fourth in his command structure."

Reminding herself that all the archangels were multidimensional, she saw that Michaela and Titus were still talking, while Gian remained in another area, in conversation with Astaad. Mele was nowhere to be seen, but Elena glimpsed Hannah and Elijah in the far opposite corner of the Atrium. Alexander and Xander stood with the couple, Alexander dressed in black pants, boots, and a silver breastplate stamped with an image Elena couldn't make out from this distance.

Missing were Neha, Favashi, Charisemnon, and Caliane. "You had contact with your mom?"

"She is about to arrive." Raphael began to move, Elena moving with him.

"Let's wait, greet her," Elena said after a thought. "No harm in everyone here knowing you two are a unit." Caliane might've once been an insane mass murderer, but she appeared sane now—and full of remorse for the atrocity she'd committed in her madness. And she'd stood by Raphael since the instant she awoke from her long Sleep.

Raphael shook his head. "I am not Caliane's son at this moment—I am the Archangel of New York. I wait for no one."

Damn subtle archangelic politics, Elena thought to herself. She'd learned so much but countless things could still trip her up. Because Raphael was right—he couldn't be seen to be waiting for his mother to arrive. And what the hell was he doing now?

"Are you heading toward Michaela?" she asked *sotto voce*. "Good God, why? If you want someone to stab you in the back, I have plenty of knives."

His laughter caught Michaela's attention, her head angling toward them. "Titus and Michaela are the closest to us," he murmured. "It is simple courtesy—and I thought you might appreciate the opportunity to examine her more closely."

"Unfortunately, I don't think you can tell just by looking at someone if they gave birth a year ago." The idea of Michaela birthing a child was still a hard one for her to accept. "She was probably just playing a game, or maybe she was Sleeping off Uram's poison." That was a possibility Elena hadn't previously considered and it made just as much sense as the secret birth of a baby that might or might not have been impacted by the same poison. "Her figure certainly hasn't changed."

Then they were too close to risk further discussion. Mere seconds later, Titus greeted Raphael with a back-slapping hug that made it clear to the room at large that he considered Raphael an ally. Then, as Elena gritted her teeth, Raphael touched his hand to Michaela's in a polite greeting between Cadre.

Titus, meanwhile, was gripping Elena's forearm in the way of warriors—though he'd tempered his strength, likely as a result of a mental reminder from Raphael. The warrior archangel had accepted Elena as a fellow warrior to the extent that he sometimes forgot she wasn't as physically strong as an archangel. "Ellie," he said, using the nickname she'd asked him to use. "When is your next block party?"

His booming true voice filled the room, the enthusiasm in it making her grin. "Maybe after we sort out this whole possible mass bloodlust situation," she said and, forearm shake complete, forced herself to turn to Michaela. "Archangel Michaela," she said politely. "It has been many moons." The words were a stock phrase Jessamy had taught her. She felt like adding: *I hope it's way more moons to our next meeting.*

"Guild Hunter," Michaela responded.

The other woman probably thought she was delivering a subtle put-down by referring to Elena's occupation rather than her status as Raphael's consort, but Elena would never be insulted by being referred to as a hunter.

And Raphael would never be insulted on her behalf.

"Your markings are astonishing, Raphael," Michaela said in a much warmer tone, her sultry voice pitched just right. "I confess I had no idea of their impact from seeing the images broadcast by the media."

Leaving Raphael to handle Michaela, well aware her archangel would never have the extreme bad taste to be seduced by that viper, Elena focused on Titus. "I was looking forward to seeing your own markings, Titus."

The Archangel of Southern Africa had developed gold markings across his massive chest, but tonight, those marks were covered by a gold breastplate, the designs etched into the breastplate almost as intricate as the carvings that decorated the hallways and walls of this complex. As with Alexander, the back of the piece was made of thick but pliable leather.

"Ellie, for you, anything." Titus was back to using the softer tone he consciously adopted in social situations. "I hope we will not always be in meetings." His scowl made his opinion of meetings clear. "If so, I will spar with Raphael. You may watch."

Before, Elena might've taken that permission as condescension. Now she understood that Titus would spar with her, too—if he wasn't so sure he'd rip off her arms when fired up by battle fever. "I'll take you up on that," she said. "Galen still speaks of all that he learned in your armies."

Even as Titus beamed at the mention of Raphael's weapons-master, there was movement near the entrance. Caliane walked in, a woman with haunting blue eyes and raven hair, the template from which Raphael had been cast. Her hair flowing down her back and adorned by the thinnest of diamond tiaras, the gems glittering like ice on fire, she wore a gown in glacial white that turned her into a queen of frost and flame.

However, it wasn't her mother-in-law who caught and held Elena's attention.

Tasha had walked in behind Caliane, now took position among the escorts.

Scarlet haired and with slanted eyes of a vivid green, her wings a rich copper, the scholar and warrior looked out over the crowd. Her lips curved when they landed on Raphael, the archangel who'd once been her playmate, then her lover.

Regardless of the fact that Raphael and Tasha's relationship hadn't lasted, Elena wasn't immune to a twinge of irritation. Why the hell did Raphael have such great taste in exes?

"Ellie."

Turning at the sound of that lyrical female voice, Elena smiled. "Hannah." She hugged the other woman with open warmth.

She and Hannah had first made contact because they were the only two consorts in the Cadre, but their bond had transformed into a true friendship over time: two very different women who'd found common ground.

Drawing back from the embrace after a long moment, Hannah said, "You look lovely and fierce."

"Montgomery," Elena said, admiring how Hannah had woven a fine string of iridescent black pearls through the elegant bun in which she wore her hair. "He's my fashion consultant."

Hannah's laugh was throaty. "I would steal your butler, Elena, except that he is so passionately devoted to you and to his sire."

"You don't need Montgomery's help—you always look gorgeous." That was no exaggeration. Hannah had an artist's eye and knew the colors that looked good against the ebony of her skin. Which, honestly, was pretty much every shade under the sun.

Today, she'd gone for a shimmering copper that made her glow and set off the peach accents in her wings. The dress had a high neck and no sleeves, swept down her body in a column with a slit down one side. Stylish yet simple—but for the touch at the top of the slit: the palm-sized image of a crouching puma picked out in gemstones that ranged from the hard clarity of diamonds to the smoky browns of topaz.

Elena approved of the subtle reminder of Elijah's Cascade-given gift—the ability to command both birds of prey and large jungle cats. "How are the pumas?"

"They know not to invade my studio unless I invite them in," Hannah said in a very stern tone. "In all honesty, I have come to care for the creatures—how could I not when my favorites wait outside the studio for me, then curl up in the sun and watch as I go about my work." She shook her head. "Elijah keeps telling me I'm spoiling them, that they need to be ferocious beasts, not pets, but I know they would protect me to the death should it come down to it."

Elena had to agree—she'd seen recordings of the pumas and they were definitely wild animals. That they adored Hannah was a reflection of Elijah's love for her. "So you're not interested in learning to throw paint knives now that you have a guard of pumas? I told Raphael we'd get up to mayhem."

Hannah's smile turned into a grin, an expression Elena had

never thought she'd see on the elegant consort's face when they'd first met. That was before she'd realized that while Hannah's private face included her elegant side, the other woman also had a wicked playfulness to her.

It made Elena wonder what she didn't know about Elijah.

Because the man who'd won Hannah's heart would have to have a touch of playfulness in him, too. And *that* was a fact that simply didn't mesh with her view of Elijah—he was more like a stable older brother, if that older brother was a brutally powerful archangel.

"Oh, I like the idea of causing mayhem." Leaning closer, Hannah whispered, "Shall we kidnap Tasha and pluck off her feathers?"

"Don't put ideas in my head."

"Consort." The voice was purest beauty, the woman who spoke equally so.

Turning to greet her mother-in-law without cutting Hannah off from the conversation, she inclined her head *exactly* the right amount to acknowledge their relationship without diminishing Elena's standing as Raphael's consort. The funny thing was that it wasn't Jessamy but Caliane who'd taught her that precision bow—a little mother-in-law–daughter-in-law bonding exercise when Caliane realized no one knew how to deal with the protocol between an Ancient mother-in-law and her archangelic son's consort.

Funnily enough, that particular situation had never before come up.

"It is good to see you," Elena said now, going off-script from the ceremonial greeting because she and Caliane had progressed beyond that in the short, stealthy visits Caliane had made to New York, and Raphael and Elena to Amanat, during the past two years. "You know Hannah, of course."

"Hannah, my dear." Caliane closed her hands over one of Hannah's, leaned in to kiss the other woman on the cheek.

The difference in greetings was no insult. Elijah had been one of Caliane's loyal generals before his ascension to archangel, and even afterward, he'd never betrayed her. Rather, he'd looked out for her son.

"Lady Caliane." Hannah's smile held an infectious warmth as she used the same title Elijah continued to use for Caliane, an equal who chose to acknowledge the history he shared with Caliane.

Elijah could do that without repercussions, was old enough to get away with it. Raphael had to tread a far more careful path. His relationship with Caliane had never been of equals when he was younger—he couldn't hark back to it without also reminding the rest of the Cadre of the boy he'd been. More, he'd only been an archangel for approximately five hundred years, a drop in the ocean in angelic time.

"I've almost finished the piece I sketched in Amanat," Hannah said, the words a whisper so others wouldn't overhear of Hannah and Eli's visit to Caliane's city, learn they'd left their territory at times. "I have great hopes of showing it to you within the next six months."

"I will await the unveiling with anticipation," Caliane responded warmly before returning her attention to Elena . . . only for her gaze to skate past Elena, the look in them changing to a piercing love that only appeared when she looked at one person.

"Raphael, my son." She took Raphael's kiss on the cheek in greeting, touched her own fingers to his cheek in return.

It was still a shock to Elena's system to see them side by side. They appeared near to the same age, though Caliane was older by many, *many* millennia. Unexpectedly, Caliane then spoke to Elena. "Consort, I would be pleased if you would walk with me tomorrow eve prior to dinner. I would hear of my son's home, learn how his people are doing."

Why isn't she asking you? Elena said to Raphael, even as she accepted Caliane's invitation.

Her archangel placed his hand on the bare skin of her lower back as his mother moved on to speak to Alexander. Hannah, too, had been drawn away—by Elijah, who'd smiled a hello at Elena, Raphael and the other archangel having already spoken.

She is preempting those who might believe they can drive a wedge between us by using the fact you are not the consort my mother would've chosen for me.

Raphael moved his fingers on her back. *And she has missed speaking to you, I think. She has said to me that you make her remember what it was to be young and fearless.*

Fighting pleasurable shivers, Elena said, *You sure that's not code for young and stupid?*

Raphael's lips kicked up on one corner. *Are they not the same?*

Elena couldn't exactly argue, given some of the stunts she'd pulled as a green hunter. "Have you spoken to Astaad?" She could see the archangel's distinctive wings, the feathers night black where they grew out of his back but fading slowly to pale gray at the tips, like a watercolor done with an expert hand.

"No, let's go do so now."

When they did, Astaad confirmed he'd left Mele at home. "She wanted to accompany me, but she is too gentle, with no weapons of her own." His eyes, a dark shade close to onyx, striking against the cool white of his skin, scanned the room. "Neha has arrived."

The Archangel of India entered the Atrium with regal grace, her silk sari an unusual deep yellow embroidered with threads of blue-gold and her black hair swept back in its usual neat knot. She held her wings off the floor with unforced strength, the feathers icy white with filaments of cobalt in the primaries. Her brown eyes were of the queen she was: intelligent and used to power.

Close on her heels came Charisemnon.

The Archangel of Disease—Elena far preferred that name over his official title—was back to full health and he was physically quite handsome, all rich brown hair and skin of deep gold, his body fluidly muscled and his eyes a darker gold with flecks of brown in their depths.

He still made her stomach turn.

Neha might hate Elena, but Elena liked the Archangel of India for giving Charisemnon a distinctly icy reception when the two exchanged greetings. *I keep forgetting Neha's a warrior, too,* she said to Raphael, *and then she does something like that and I remember she has zero sympathy for people she considers cowards.*

Raphael didn't reply; it wasn't necessary. He was the one who'd told her about Neha's skill with the curved blade of the kukri, told her stories of sparring with the Archangel of India. She knew he missed the relationship he'd had with Neha before he had to execute her murderous daughter.

Favashi entered seconds later, a soft-featured angel with wings of rich ivory and hair of shining mahogany against skin of sun-kissed cream, her beauty lushly feminine and her power the epitome of the steel hand in a velvet glove from all Elena had heard. She wore an intricately beaded dress of rich cream with shimmering cerise accents, the full-length sleeves cuffed at her wrists and the lush skirt coming to just above her calves. Below that were tight cotton leggings of the same cerise and simple gold sandals.

"So, we are all here," Astaad murmured. "Who do you think will attempt to kill who first?"

14

Elena was more interested in the Luminata in the room than she was the Cadre—at least right now. The tiny hairs on her nape kept prickling as people circulated and she was near certain it was Gian watching her.

Deliberately separating from Raphael after warning her archangel she wanted to make it easier for the Luminata to approach her, she spoke to Titus again for a bit, then a scholarly Luminata who turned out to be the head librarian. She was just about to ask him how she could access the archives when he excused himself with a mumble . . . and suddenly she was face to face with the leader of this strange flock.

Razor-sharp cheekbones, dark brown hair that shone with health, those incredible pale eyes that made her think of a creature that hunted in the dark, sleek and intelligent, Gian was not a man who would ever blend into the crowd despite the fact his height put him at least two inches shorter than Elena in her boots. The dun-colored robes of the Luminata served to highlight rather than downplay Gian's physical attractiveness.

But Elena wasn't affected by beauty. She lived with Raphael and he blew every other man on the planet out of the water.

Because her archangel wasn't only physically magnificent, he had a heart. It had started to go cold over centuries and centuries of immortality, but it had woken with a vengeance and it was as magnificent as his body and his face.

She wasn't so certain the deathly handsome immortal in front of her had a heart, but she'd give him the benefit of the doubt. Arrogance didn't equal evil or ugliness of the heart, especially among immortals who had lived for millennia. Often it was an almost inevitable by-product of age and power.

"Consort," Gian murmured, the two of them alone on one side of the Atrium, both with glasses of wine in hand. "I must admit I am intrigued by you. So much so that I've been rude and watched you for most of the night thus far."

Surprised he'd admitted so frankly to staring at her and liking him better for it, she said, "Oh? I'm only a hunter."

His smile was a dazzling flash of light, a sudden, stunning brilliance.

Elena saw in that instant how Gian could win lovers aplenty. She wasn't attracted to him in the least, but she could understand it. This man had the ability to put on the charm, to make people forget the kind of power he held in his grasp. No one stayed leader of a group of angels as generally old and strong as the Luminata without being a ruthless politician.

Again, however, that didn't make him bad in any sense: it just meant he was clever and he liked power. Lot of people like that in the world who also happened to donate to charity and fund scholarships for needy kids.

"The first angel-Made in an eternity," Gian said in a voice that was crystalline without being soft. "A true consort beloved by her archangel. And with such rare beauty."

Elena mentally rolled her eyes at that last. Yes, she cleaned up okay, but not only was she more trained hunter than beauty, she stood in a room with Michaela, Neha, Hannah, Tasha, and more. "Flattery won't get you anywhere with me, Gian."

His laughter was the freaking tinkling of bells. *Is this guy for real or is he messing with my head?*

It's real, Raphael responded from where he stood conversing with Favashi. *My mother tells me that Gian has always had an astonishingly clear voice, that he used to fill colosseums on the rare occasions when he performed poetry in public.*

Poetry? Yes, Elena could see the leader of the Luminata standing up in front of a crowd and holding them in thrall with his presence. He had that charisma thing going on. Raphael did, too, as did the rest of the Cadre—it seemed to come hardwired with becoming an archangel, but with Gian, it was a glow he wore at the forefront of his skin.

"I do not flatter," Gian said with sincerity in every syllable. "I speak only the truth. Beauty is in the eye of the beholder, they say—and my eyes find the placement of your features, the contrast of your hair to your skin, the way you move, quite extraordinary."

"You forgot the weapons," she pointed out, thinking that he was either a very good liar or he actually meant it—weirdly, it appeared to be the latter. His eyes held almost a little too much admiration.

A small shrug in response to her statement, his smile rueful. "Ah, but I am a traditional man. I prefer my beauties without blades."

"I think Neha, for one, would scoff at the idea of that being traditional." As far as Elena knew, angelkind had always boasted female warriors as well as male.

"True. Perhaps I need another word for it. Would Neanderthal be appropriate?"

Surprised into laughter by the self-deprecating statement, Elena found herself reevaluating her impressions of Gian. Yes, he was a little too perfect with that voice and that face, and he no doubt had a bit of a God complex, but he wasn't insufferable and they had a good conversation in the minutes that followed. She also discovered what had happened to the art.

"Many of the pieces were becoming badly damaged by time and dust and the changes in temperature," Gian told her. "In line with our mandate to preserve the art of our people, the Gallery was created to house the art in an environment best suited to preservation."

Elena could see the logic in that. "So you don't have any outside?" It seemed to her that stone sculptures wouldn't molder away, but what did she know? She'd have to ask Aodhan his opinion of Gian's explanation.

"The odd piece that is at least somewhat resistant to time damage." He nodded at a large mosaic on a hanging wall that separated that part of the Atrium into two semi-independent sections. "But once we had the Gallery, it seemed wasteful to leave other pieces out in the ordinary atmosphere, where they would begin to degrade." A deep smile. "I or any of my brethren would be happy to show you the way to the Gallery."

"Thank you," Elena said. "Can I also ask you about your library?"

His eyes never moved off her—and she realized they never had. Her skin pebbled. Okay, that was more than a little creepy, but he hadn't crossed any lines and she had to remember that he'd been isolated out here with a bunch of other Luminata for hundreds of years. Good way to get rusty on social skills.

"We call it the Repository of Knowledge," he said, still watching her with unnerving focus. "And of course. You may ask me anything."

"I was told you collect information." At his nod, she said, "Do you keep any records on human-vampire children?"

A flicker in his eyes, gone so quickly she might've imagined it.

Only she hadn't.

"No," he said with a shake of his head, his eyes shifting to his wineglass as he took a sip. "Why do you ask?"

"I'm pretty sure one of my friends was sired by a vamp who then ran off. You know, the usual deadbeat father story only he was a vampire." She lied because instinct told her to lie. "I promised her I'd look into it so she'd have closure about her history."

"A worthy goal." Gian's eyes lifted to hers again, the cool white of his skin holding no betraying flush of color. "I hope you can help her."

"Me, too. I have a question about myself, too," she said, adding a half laugh to it, as if she wasn't too serious about her inquiry. "My hair and skin, it's really unusual. I don't suppose you've ever heard of anyone else who looks like me?"

No flicker. Nothing but a steady gaze as Gian laughed. "You are unique, Consort. I have never seen a woman such as you."

Damn it. That had sounded genuine.

"Ah well," she said. "I'll see if I have better luck in your Repository of Knowledge."

"You will be most welcomed by the Luminata in charge."

Again, nothing but warmth, but as they separated a minute or two later, Elena thought again of that flicker and wondered. Why had her instincts reacted with a plausible lie? Why didn't she want Gian to know she was aware she might have a vampire ancestor?

She was still chewing on those questions fifteen minutes later when she heard two Luminata say something to each other that made her ears prick. She only overheard the comment because she'd been staring at the mosaic Gian had pointed out—deep in thought, she'd been standing motionless for at least five minutes when she realized there were people on the other side of the hanging wall.

Like the other hanging walls on either side of the large central space of the Atrium, it wasn't closed off on either end. Rather it functioned as a partition that allowed people to gather in different sections of the Atrium, so that they could form small, intimate groupings while remaining part of the bigger whole.

Given her position and motionlessness, and the layout of the room, it seemed the two men on the other side didn't realize she was there. Because Elena definitely wasn't meant to hear this conversation.

"The resemblance is extraordinary, is it not?" A male voice, not particularly distinctive.

"'Eerie' is the word I'd use." Another male, this one with a deeper tone to his voice. "It feels like a ghost is haunting Lumia."

Elena heard that part of their conversation with a peripheral corner of her mind, didn't really pay attention to it.

Then the first speaker said, "The shape of her face and that near-white hair against skin of dark gold . . . *her* skin was darker, but other than that, they could be mirror images of each other."

Elena's entire attention snapped to the conversation. Because there was only one person in the room who had hair of near-white.

"Not quite," the second speaker replied. "The eyes are not the same. Hers weren't silver. I always thought they gave her a feline appearance."

"Yes, you're right."

A pause, while Elena's heart thundered.

"Gian has not said anything."

"Neither will he and you are *not* to mention it." The words were hard, an order. "Or have you forgotten what he was like after her betrayal?"

"A madman . . . or so close to it as not to matter." A whisper of wings, as if the Luminata was settling his feathers. "I will spread the word that it is a matter not to be discussed."

There was more rustling, wings and robes shifting. Elena made a quick decision and turned to go in the opposite direction to the movements on the other side. By the time the two Luminata emerged from behind the partition, she was standing next to Raphael, far enough away that there was no way they could suspect her of having overheard their conversation.

The damn robes that hid their wings made them all so anonymous, but at least their hoods were down tonight. She took note of the two speakers: one was the tall male with mahogany skin who'd first shown her and Raphael to their suite, the other shorter, more square-appearing with silky blond hair. His skin looked to be not-enough-sunlight white with a flush of red underneath.

Guild Hunter, while Astaad appears to believe you are merely being a supportive consort by standing next to me without saying a word, I know different. Raphael's wing spread slightly over hers. *What is it?*

I'll tell you later, she said, trying her damndest to look interested in the conversation Raphael was having with Astaad on the audible level. *I just overheard something so interesting my pulse is doing somersaults. I need a minute to get it together.*

Raphael's thumb brushed over her spine as he replied to Astaad with zero indication he'd missed any of the conversation. She didn't know how he did that—have a physical and mental conversation at the same time. She didn't realize she'd asked him on the mental level until the crisp bite of the wind swept through her mind.

I have had a thousand five hundred years of practice, hbeebti. He turned to smile down at her.

And her overworked heart, it kicked. Because his gaze held affection and love and so many other things she could've never imagined the first time she looked into those eyes of searing blue.

"Ah, you make me miss my Mele."

Astaad's words had Elena turning to the other archangel, even as she leaned a little closer to Raphael, needing to feel his warmth, the strong beat of his life. The more time she spent in Lumia, the more it felt as if this place was cold down to the bone, not in temperature but in its soul.

For a while, speaking with Gian, she'd almost begun to question her initial views on the place, but now that she knew he was a liar, it was easy to see the entire web of charm he'd constructed in front of her. It had been done so skillfully that she'd been partially caught in it even as she believed herself standing separate, critical-eyed.

Elena would not be making that mistake a second time.

"I miss her, too," she said to Astaad. "I wish we didn't live so far apart."

Astaad inclined his head. "And these times of war make travel difficult. Mele did enjoy her time in New York earlier this year. Thank you for hosting her."

"It was my pleasure." The other woman was a scholar rather than a hunter, but she and Elena had clicked from the first. "Mahiya also loved spending time with her. I hope she'll visit again."

"She would be delighted to do so," Astaad said, "but I find it difficult to have her far from me." His features altered, tension humming beneath his skin as shadows darkened his eyes. "I have faith in your honor, Raphael, but I do not have such faith in all our brethren—I can see them harming Mele to get to me. Many know that of all my concubines, she is the most favored."

"I wish I could disagree," Raphael said in a tone as grim. "But honor is no longer what it once was."

Astaad stroked his neat black goatee, nodding slowly in silence.

Elena's blood chilled without warning, her spine stiffening. She caught a sensual, smoky perfume the next second. Not too thick, not cloying. Just right.

Curling her fingers into her palm to still the itch to go for a weapon, she kept her expression neutral with sheer strength of will as Michaela came to stand beside Astaad. "How is Dahariel?" she asked the other archangel. "I have not seen him these many months."

This is interesting.

Archangel, you have a talent for understatement.

15

Astaad raised a thin black eyebrow. "My second is as strong and hale as he ever was. He hasn't succumbed to a mystery illness, gone mad from the toxin, or had an accident befall him."

Michaela threw back her head and laughed and it was an exquisite sound. Her eyes were sparkling when she looked at Astaad again, her amusement apparently genuine. "Ah, you know how to wound me, old friend." She sent Raphael a fond glance. "Not all of my lovers have come to such terrible ends."

The implication was clear but Elena was no new consort easily manipulated by venomous barbs. "If you'll excuse me," she said to Astaad before shooting Raphael a smile, "I see Hannah calling me over."

Raphael held her in place with the gentle pressure of his fingertips on her lower back. "In fact, if you could excuse us both," he said to Astaad and Michaela. "I must speak to Elijah before dinner begins, on a matter to do with our shared border."

"Of course. We will talk again." Astaad lifted Elena's hand to his lips for a good-bye that fit him. She'd come to realize that the Archangel of the Pacific Isles had a decidedly romantic side. She could see why Mele and his other women adored him.

"Careful, Raphael," Michaela murmured with a touch of malice in her tone, "or I'll start to think you do not like me."

"Has there been a man born who does not like you?"

Raphael's question seemed to delight the female archangel. She was beaming when they left—and didn't seem to realize that Raphael had simply posed the question, not answered it. "So," Elena said once they were out of earshot, "the Bitch Queen is still intent on hitting on you."

"Sadly, she will remain forever unfulfilled. I do not sleep with spiders who eat their mates after sex."

Elena bit back a laugh, couldn't quite manage it when Raphael leaned in to say, "I prefer women with knives."

Laughter rippling out of her, she kissed him quick and fast, and as she drew back, she saw Favashi take in the interaction from where the Archangel of Sumeria stood with Neha. There was something sad about Favashi's lovely face at that instant, a terrible, deep-down sadness. It was gone a heartbeat later, wiped away to be replaced by archangelic impassiveness.

"You said Favashi and Rohan were close once."

"Very," Raphael responded. "He would've stood by her side had she accepted it, but Favashi has never been satisfied. She wants the strongest, the most powerful. Alexander's son was a powerful general but he wasn't enough for her."

"I think she's regretting that choice." Her heart hurt for the other woman. "He had a good life before Lijuan murdered him, didn't he?"

"He had a life many a man would covet," Raphael reassured her. "The evidence of that stands beside Alexander."

"Yes." Xander was young and green, but it was obvious even on short acquaintance that he'd been deeply loved and had known stability all his life. The murder of his parents hadn't broken him. It had dented him a little, but he'd recover, especially since he had his grandfather by his side.

"Hannah," she said, the two of them having reached the other woman and her consort. "I'm so sorry but I used you as an excuse to escape a certain conversation. Please talk to me."

Tucking her arm through Elena's, Hannah smiled. "You may use me as an escape from Michaela any time you wish."

Her lips twisted into a very un-Hannahlike expression. "Do you know she tried to seduce Elijah once? After we'd been together for a century!"

Elena's jaw dropped. "*No.*"

"She apparently thought he'd have tired of his 'little artist' by then." An arch look. "Unfortunately for her, Elijah has an astonishing appreciation for art."

Elijah smiled a slow smile at his consort's teasing, his golden hair shining under the lights that poured down from the chandeliers above and his wings a sweep of pure white. "It has always been about the art," he said in a solemn tone that made his lover's eyes dance. "I am Hannah's most devoted patron."

"Talking of art," Hannah said after wrinkling her nose at Elijah in a way that was far too adorable, "come see this." The other woman led her to a section of the Atrium hidden behind a hanging wall.

"Wow." Breath rushing out of her, Elena just stared.

The artwork was another mosaic but it was far more intricate than the one she'd been staring at earlier. Each tiny square had been perfectly fitted to create the stunning image of an angel midfall, a spear through his heart that came out on the other side of his body. His wings were pure white splattered with the red of his blood, his hair a deep brown, his closed eyes making his eye color impossible to see.

Still . . . "Looks like Gian except for the wings."

"I had not seen that, but yes, you are right. Perhaps he was the model for the artist?"

"Maybe," she said, thinking of the conversation she'd overhead, of the "betrayal" the two other Luminata had referenced. Arrow through the heart wasn't exactly a subtle image—and what did it say that Gian had allowed this to stay up here for who knows how long? "It's a strange thing to have here. Aren't the Luminata all about inner peace?"

"Immortals are never so simple, Ellie. The potential for violence lives in the most powerful of us always. We have too much power for it to be otherwise."

Elena thought of all the deaths she'd seen since becoming an angel, compared it to the violence she'd experienced in her previous life, found herself nodding. Immortals took violence to the next level. "There's a signature in that corner."

"Where?" Hannah frowned. "Oh, how did you see that? It's minuscule."

"I don't know. My eye just went to it." She tried to bring the signature into focus but it was too high up in the mosaic to make out. "A shy artist."

"Like Aodhan. He often hides his signature."

They stayed in front of the mosaic for some time, taking in the intricate details as Elena tried to find a clue in the art. She saw nothing she hadn't already seen, but then Gian came to stand beside her and she realized he must've been watching her again. It wasn't as if she and Hannah were easily visible from the main section of the Atrium.

"This piece speaks to you?"

Elena said the expected thing. "Yes." She turned to look at Gian, steeling herself to be the focus of his disturbingly intent gaze . . . and still had to clench her stomach to keep from betraying her surprise at how close he stood.

His wings were almost touching hers, a breach of etiquette that could be deadly for him. Because while Gian was powerful, Raphael was an archangel. And Gian wasn't one of his Seven, whom he trusted to be so familiar with his consort. Elena wasn't as sensitive about her wings as normal angels, but this was inappropriate enough that she wanted to reach for her knife, put it at his throat, and tell him to back off.

Taking a small step away from him instead, using the excuse of including Hannah in their conversation, she said, "Do you know the artist?"

"A mortal collective. Dead many centuries now."

"Oh, I didn't want to hear that," Hannah murmured. "Such talent is rare."

Gian shrugged and Elena expected him to say something along the usual lines about how mortals were born and they died, only for more to be born. Instead, he said, "Great beauty and great talent lie within mortals. I believe they burn hotter with it for their shorter lifetimes."

The silvery sound of a bell broke the strange tension in the air.

"It is time for dinner," Gian said, waving his hand forward. "Please. I will follow."

Elena went ahead with Hannah, and the entire time she had Gian at her back, she was dead certain he was staring at her. She hoped he saw not her bare back but the knife she wore along her spine.

Raphael's hunter said nothing until their escort left them at the door to their suite after the dinner. Then, she said, "I want to fly."

"I was about to say the same." Raphael needed clean, fresh air untainted by politics or secrets. "Aodhan, do you wish to join us?"

"Yes."

The simple answer said all too much about Aodhan's need for freedom.

"Give me two minutes to change." Elena pushed into the suite. "I've got zero desire to flash my underwear at the Luminata."

Raphael's lips curved. No other consort or archangelic lover would ever say those words. Only his Elena. *Would you like a shield of glamour?*

No, I think the bathroom is safe—it doesn't set off any of my instincts. What do you think?

I think even if the Luminata are watching us in some fashion, to spy on the bathing chamber would go against rules of behavior so ingrained that it simply could not be justified by angels this old.

Good.

Deciding to wait for her where he was, in the hallway outside the open door to their suite, he locked eyes with Aodhan, the angel just over a foot away, and spoke in a voice that would carry only between the two of them. "Are the walls impacting you?" He'd learned to be blunt with Aodhan—the angel was too good at deflecting otherwise.

Aodhan spread, then resettled, his wings. The filaments glittered even in the relatively dim light of the hallway. "Yes," he answered after a long pause, his voice almost inaudible. "But I remain able to carry out my task."

"If I thought you incapable, you wouldn't be here." Even before the issue with Remus had come up, Raphael had taken a calculated risk in assigning Aodhan as Elena's backup—the angel had problems being shut inside for too long, but of all the Seven aside from Jason, he was the best at detecting the undercurrents in any given situation. Because even prior to arriving at Lumia, Raphael had worked out that any danger here would be a thing of stealth.

When Aodhan glanced away to the left, his shoulders stiff, Raphael realized he needed to be even blunter. "I wouldn't have made you Elena's backup if I didn't trust you to hold the line to the death if need be. You know what she is to me." *Everything.*

The other angel faced him once more, his spine no longer so stiff. "Sire," he said, a world of unspoken things in that single word.

After glancing down the hallway, as if to ensure they remained alone, Aodhan stayed with vocal speech. Raphael knew he'd already checked the hallway and the suites for any false walls or hidden passageways where someone might hide. The suites on either side of theirs were empty.

Elena had looked for technological devices before her bath earlier today, made the call that the Luminata had only accepted so much modernization, then halted. Electric lights and hot water, yes. Any kind of satellite or antenna, no. Neither did they appear to have phones of any variety. So any spying they did would be of the low-tech variety using their superior knowledge of Lumia.

"I am disturbed by how interested the Luminata are in Ellie."

"Explain." Though he'd been aware of Elena's position in the room every second, Raphael had been forced to keep the majority of his attention on the other archangels rather than the Luminata, the politics of the Cadre currently a perilous sea.

"The brothers watch her when they think there is little or no chance that their interest will be detected. Not all of them, but all those who were at the event tonight—and they are all senior members of the sect, *at least* five hundred years in the fold."

Raphael's blood iced over, not in fear but in a determination as ruthless as it was dangerous. "Is there a threat in their gaze?"

"No, but it's not simple curiosity in an angel-Made. There is something more."

Raphael considered all the options. "It's possible the Luminata are no longer as neutral as they have always previously been. She may be a target."

"I will continue to watch and to listen," Aodhan said. "If there is a threat, given the way the Luminata move and the secrecy that clings to them, it will be an assassin's blade in the dark rather than open battle."

Such an attack couldn't hurt Raphael, but Elena was vulnerable. In many ways, she was weaker than even a comparatively young vampire. "I'll warn her." He couldn't stop his hunter from being who she was, wouldn't clip her wings, but he could give her the weapons she needed to survive.

She appeared in the doorway on that thought, striding out dressed in black jeans and a simple T-shirt in dark gray, the wing slits closed with small buttons at the bottom. She'd pulled her hair back in a ponytail, and though her makeup remained, she was once more the hunter for whom he'd first fallen, her "dress" blade replaced by forearm gauntlets that held her throwing knives, and her crossbow and gun worn openly on either thigh. On her back was the closed sheath that held a full quiver of bolts.

Yes, he loved her in all her faces, but this face, it was her truest one.

They moved in silence down the hallways. And as they did, Raphael told her of Aodhan's observations, warned her of the possible risk to her.

"I think it's something else," she replied. "That's what I wanted to talk to you ab—" She cut herself off as they spotted a Luminata flowing down the hallway. *We'll talk in the air*, she added mind to mind.

Keeping his silence until they reached the courtyard in which they'd originally landed, Raphael then wrapped his arms around Elena's waist. "Let them assume you do not have the ability for a vertical takeoff," he murmured against her ear. "It gives you one more weapon in your arsenal."

A small nod from his consort as she wrapped her arm around his neck and they rose into the air, her weight nothing to Raphael's archangel strength. Aodhan rose after them, having stayed below to watch their backs. Unlike his usual preference, today he remained low while they went high.

Releasing Elena once they were at a high enough altitude that she could sweep out into a stable position without difficulty, he flew beside her as she headed toward the mountains in the distance. They were farther away than they appeared and the three of them only reached the nearest peak after about twenty-five minutes of flight.

Landing, Elena blew out a breath. "Man, that felt good!"

She waved up at Aodhan, who continued to glide across the sky.

The angel dipped his wings to show he'd seen her.

Smiling, Elena walked to the very edge of a cliff and took a seat, her legs hanging over the edge and her wings spread on the stony surface behind her. Raphael sat beside her. Except for the change from day to night, the view was similar to when they'd arrived at Lumia. The stronghold stood in their direct line of sight, all graceful curves atop a gentle hill, its windows glowing with light.

"Beauty and peace in luminescence," he murmured. "That is their motto according to the few Luminata I spoke to in the time prior to dinner."

"Total BS," Elena scowled. "That place seethes. That's the right word. *Seethes*. There's all this stuff below the surface and it's something ugly."

It was a deeply felt reaction to a stronghold and a sect she'd earlier described as merely "spooky." "Tell me."

So she did, laying out the conversation she'd overheard about a woman with hair of near-white and skin of dark gold. She was right—the two Luminata could've been talking only about her. No one else in the entire immortal world had the same looks as Elena. *No one.* "It appears you may have accidentally stumbled upon an ancestor."

Elena blew out a breath. "Sounds like it, doesn't it?" Eyes narrowed, she said, "Funny coincidence, don't you think?"

"Or not a coincidence at all," Raphael murmured. "The entire world saw images of you after the battle in New York." The most iconic images had been taken by people on the ground as he fell with her broken body in his arms, her hair a pale banner and his wings eaten away by angelfire.

His chest squeezed still when he thought of how close he'd come to losing her, losing the chance to build this life that made immortality a gift. "The Luminata had to know I'd bring you with me if they called a meeting."

Snorting, Elena said, "I don't have delusions of grandeur—I don't think they called a meeting of the Cadre just to see me close up, but I do think it might be a nice side benefit." Her throat moved. "But it's clear Gian was involved with someone who looked like me. What are the chances it could've been my grandmother?"

16

Raphael thought of what he'd glimpsed in the eyes of the Luminata leader when he first greeted Elena. Gian hadn't stepped over any lines, which was why he was still alive. But there had been distinct male admiration in his gaze. "We can't know until we track down your family line and discover if the unusual coloring is strong in the line, or if your grandmother was the first."

Lips twisting, Elena stared out at Lumia. "Whoever Gian's lover was, these guys could put me on the path to finding the truth about that side of my history, but I have the feeling no one's going to just answer my questions if I ask."

"The angels you overheard, you should find out how long they've been Luminata."

"Why?"

"Because unless they knew Gian in the outside world, it's possible Gian was already Luminata when he was involved with the unknown woman. And not just a brother—he's been *the* Luminata for centuries."

Elena sucked in a breath. "He'd have broken his vows. Shit, if that's true, no wonder it's verboten to discuss it."

Gripping his protective instincts in a fierce hold, Raphael

spread his wings so that his left wing was lying across her back. "If the Cadre meeting drags on as I expect it to, you'll have several days to explore Lumia and try to unearth the truth. But never forget—angelic secrets can be deadly."

Elena wove her fingers through his. "I can feel you gritting your teeth, Archangel."

Raphael turned to look at her, raising a single eyebrow. It was a look Elena had more than once labeled "pure archangelic arrogance."

Instead of responding with a wicked grin as she so often did, his consort leaned over and kissed him on the cheek with unexpected sweetness, the shadow of his wing shading them both. "Doesn't mean I don't appreciate the effort." The grin peeked out.

No woman had ever treated him with such irreverent affection. Only his warrior. "Teasing an archangel can be a dangerous game."

"Not for me," Elena said smugly, leaning her head against his shoulder. "Not when that archangel is the ridiculously beautiful Archangel of New York."

"Ridiculously beautiful?"

"Those eyes, that hair, those bones." She shook her head. "I mean, it's so not fair to every other man on the planet."

"And why are you thinking about other men?"

Laughing, she lifted their linked hands to her mouth, pressing a kiss to his knuckles. "I just realized how tough it must be to be a man dating in New York when all the women are crazy about you."

"Most women are terrified of me." Only Elena saw the man before the pitiless Archangel of New York.

"Hmm. Good point." Her wing moved under his. "Remember when I was terrified of you?"

"You were never terrified of me."

"Hah! Are you kidding? I was scared out of my skin—but I still thought you were hot. I'm obviously a little deranged."

Raphael didn't laugh. "I'm glad you got over the terror," he said quietly. "The idea of eternity without you is my personal vision of hell."

"*Raphael.*" Eyes silver in the night, Elena touched her fingers to his jaw. "This is my heaven. *You* are my heaven."

And she was his. "Hunt, Elena," he said. "Unearth secrets. But stay safe."

"I'm not the one who's going to be stuck in a room with the most dangerous beings on the planet," she said with a scowl before adding, "I promise to be careful." She gripped his hair in a fist. "Now you promise me the same."

"Done."

Their kiss was a merciless, passionate seal on the promise.

The next morning, Raphael separated from Elena at dawn—it was customary for the Luminata to begin their day with the rising sun, and the Cadre had decided to adhere to that routine to get this over with as quickly as possible.

"The faster we get it done, the faster we can all get back to our territories," Raphael said to his hunter as he dressed at first light, his leathers worn from use and a symbol to his fellow archangels that he wasn't here to play games. "But fast for immortals is still slow, Elena." *You will have time enough to search for the truth.*

She responded mind-to-mind, the two of them in the living area, where they'd shifted their bed the previous night. Unlike the bedroom, which backed onto a wall shared by the suite on the other side, this room had hallways on two sides, the wall to the bathing chamber on the left, and the bedroom wall on the right. It left no way for anyone to spy on them without standing openly in a hallway.

Don't let the Cadre drive you nuts.

I will attempt to hold on to my sanity, though it may be a close thing.

They headed out together.

Elena and Aodhan walked with him to the Atrium, their pace a stroll, as if they were accompanying him to breakfast because they were at loose ends. In truth, the two were continuing to take note of as many corridors and doorways as they could. Aodhan was also attempting to spot any hidden passages.

Is it weird that I'm excited even though I'm frustrated, too?

Raphael smiled. *You are a hunter, Elena. And you have a scent.*

God, but you "get" me, Archangel. Rising on tiptoe as they reached the Atrium, from where Raphael would be going into an inner debating chamber barred to all but the Cadre, his consort kissed him on the mouth, one of her hands curved around the side of his neck.

Branding me, Guild Hunter? Raphael said even as he closed his wings around them.

She bit his lower lip before she broke contact, her eyes shining silver. *I just wanted a taste of you.*

He claimed a taste of his own to take him through the day. Afterward, as he folded back his wings, he glimpsed something over her shoulder. *Tasha is about to enter the Atrium. Perhaps you two will end up friends after being shut up in Lumia for the duration of the meeting.*

Elena bared her teeth at him. *I think you're going too far with this sense of humor thing.*

Raphael laughed and it was at that moment that his mother stepped into the Atrium, having swept down the hallway with Tasha at her side.

A hauntingly clear voice invaded Elena's mind, the howl of age so heavy that she would've staggered had Raphael still not had his hands on her. *You make my son laugh, Consort.* Purest love in that haunting, ancient voice, a shimmer of tears that spoke of incandescent joy. *Never stop doing this.*

Elena?

Swallowing to wet a dry throat as her body threatened to begin shaking uncontrollably, Elena looked into eyes of a blue of such undiluted clarity, their beauty was almost too painful to bear. *Your mother was speaking to me.*

She has done so before. Raphael tightened his grip on her. *You weren't this affected.*

I think she was shielding her voice or something. Her heart raced so hard she felt it in her mouth. *This is so pure it's like heaven and hell at once.*

Sparks of wildfire arced through Raphael's Legion mark, his jaw a hard line. *Go sit down somewhere for a few minutes after you leave me. Trust me on this, Elena. My mother's true voice is potent even for fellow archangels. The impact builds, like a song building to a crescendo. Do not be on your feet when it hits.*

Got it. I can stand now. Her legs were a little jellylike, but they'd hold.

Raphael took his time releasing her, making it look like they were simply indulging in a little PDA. "Mother," he said aloud afterward, turning to greet Caliane. "May I escort you inside?"

Caliane's smile was joyous. "I would love nothing better, my son." Despite her words, her look was careful . . . even a little hesitant. "Are you certain?"

Elena didn't understand the question until Raphael said, "With the Cadre, I must always be an archangel first, your son second." His words were hard and political, his tone gentle for the mother who wore her love for her son so openly. "But that doesn't mean we cannot occasionally remind the others that we are the only bloodline with two places in the circle."

Slipping her hand around Raphael's forearm with a dawning smile, Caliane inclined her head to Elena. Then the two archangels moved on into the meeting chamber located off the Atrium, their wings overlapping—and though Caliane was the Ancient, it was Raphael's wing that was protectively on top.

They didn't stop at the breakfast table. Raphael had already told Elena the Cadre would breakfast later, angels of their strength not needing to eat as often.

Even as his wings disappeared from view behind the heavy metal doors of the inner chamber, the sea crashed into her mind. *Off your feet, Elena. As soon as possible.* A pause. *It is considered an honor to hear Caliane's true voice.*

I don't think I'm strong enough for it.

You will be. Absolute confidence in her archangel's tone. *Now go. I've warned Aodhan of the necessity for speed.*

Elena turned to leave the Atrium, Aodhan by her side—and found Tasha in her path. "Elena," the other woman said with a big smile. "It is good to see you again. Shall we breakfast together?"

Elena thought of how Tasha had fought for New York and held out her arm in the greeting of warriors. Tasha gripped it as Elena's hand closed over her own forearm. And since Elena had a building sense of urgency in her brain, her knees warning her they were about to buckle, she decided to be upfront. "We're never going to be friends, Tasha, but I respect you. I hope you're well."

Tasha's smile turned into laughter, the green of her eyes sparkling. "Ah, Elena. You make it difficult to dislike you. Perhaps we will spar while we are here?"

"Let's not get carried away. I'm not sure I'd trust either one of us in a ring." Shifting a foot to the side as Tasha laughed again, she said, "Sorry to shake and run but I've got a prior engagement."

"Of course."

"You know," Elena said to Aodhan as they walked down the hallway, "it'd be much easier to dislike her if she wasn't strong and courageous and honorable." Elena knew Tasha would die to protect Caliane.

Aodhan's response was unexpected. "She still watches Raphael with the eyes of a lover. Does that make it easier?"

"Yes." Elena bared her teeth. "It definitely does. Thanks."

"You are welcome." He unexpectedly touched her shoulder. "Go right, then left."

Clenching her jaw to keep herself upright, Elena followed his instructions almost on autopilot as the crescendo howled in the back of her head. Natural light hit her eyes after the second turn, made her blink rapidly to adapt, the two of them in an external corridor that looked out onto a courtyard.

"There." Aodhan nodded at a "window" that offered a view into the courtyard; there was no glass in it, the curved arch carved out of the stone. Beyond the archway, a couple of Luminata practiced some type of slow martial art on the stone pavings of the courtyard, their movements compelling.

Realizing that not only had Aodhan found her a safe place to sit but that she actually had an excuse to do it, Elena took a seat in the window with her legs out in the courtyard and crossed at the ankles, the ice blue fabric of her gown sliding over her boots. This gown had a flowy skirt but was a little edgy, from the straight neck, to the way it hugged her torso to the hips, to the silver zipper anchored at her right hip and split out on the diagonal over the fabric.

Elena hadn't been able to figure out a way to wear her crossbow with it, but she had access to other weapons, including the throwing knives in her wrist sheaths, the gun strapped to her ankle, and the long knife down her spine. Hair twisted up with Mahiya's blade sticks, she also wore a bracelet that could snap open to become a garrote.

Still . . . "I hate gowns." Especially in a place that made her instincts bristle.

"You wear them with dangerous grace," Aodhan said as he came to stand beside her on the outside. Together, they watched the two Luminata practice the slow, graceful movements. They wore their robes even for this, hoods pulled over their heads to obscure their faces, but their wings out.

One set of wings was a familiar searing white with dark brown primaries.

!!!!!

It hit her. The impact of Caliane's voice. A roar of sound smashing into her, threatening to explode her eardrums and making her pulse roar, her blood thunder. She kept herself from reacting only by gripping the edge of the stone on which she sat and keeping her gaze blindly focused on the two Luminata in the courtyard.

And she knew she was going to fail.

Caliane was an Ancient, Elena an angel barely-Made. She simply didn't have the capacity to process that much power. *Raphael.*

I am here. An intense wave of a different power, one that tasted of the sea and the wind and the fury of a storm of light and darkness, it shoved back the echo of his mother's voice. *My apologies,* hbeebti. *I'm afraid I grew up with Caliane's voice. I have forgotten how very potent she is.*

Able to breathe now, Elena inhaled shakily, exhaled. Once. Twice. Three times. Her chest still hurt, but her heart was no longer in danger of bursting in a bloody mess. *You heard her as a baby?* The idea was staggering.

I was apparently born with a kind of immunity.

Elena made herself release the stone, two dark red lines on her palms the only sign of how hard she'd held on. *I've got things under control. I know you need to focus on the meeting.*

It hasn't yet begun—we're waiting for Michaela.

Of course. She likes to make an entrance.

Attention returning to the Luminata in the courtyard when

Raphael slipped away a few minutes later, Elena realized her pulse was still erratic. "Aodhan, can I ask you a question?"

"Yes, Ellie?"

"What do you think would happen if Caliane decided to sing again?"

A long pause. "It would either be a sign of great joy on her part—or the return of her insanity."

"Yes." Elena nodded quietly, her skin suddenly chilled. "That's what I think, too." She hoped for the former but was terrified it might end up the latter. Because if it did, then Raphael would have to attempt to kill his mother a second time around. No child should ever have to go through that.

In front of her, the slow dance of the Luminata began to speed up . . . and up.

17

Elena sat up in interest as she realized the two Luminata had pulled out weapons—long sticks with which they danced an intricate martial dance. Replace those sticks with swords, she thought, and they'd be killers. No surprise, not given what she'd already picked up from the way the older Luminata moved through the hallways.

And notwithstanding the other creepy things about this place, the fact the Luminata were warriors didn't immediately negate their stated goal of luminescence. There was contemplation in the physical, too. On a more pragmatic note, these guys had given up sex, money, other vices and sins. They had to get rid of all that testosterone in some way.

Why not in combat?

. . . it's possible Gian was already Luminata when he was involved with the unknown woman. And not just a brother—he's been the *Luminata for centuries.*

Raphael's words reverberated in her mind at the thought of vows and vices.

Right then, Gian made a particularly smooth move that had her releasing a quiet whistle. His hood fell back at the end of the move, hair of dark brown exposed to the morning sunlight.

The two men drew apart a few seconds later and bowed to one another, sticks held out to the side. The still-hooded male left via the external corridor to the left, but Gian turned directly toward Elena, telling her he'd been aware of her presence the entire time. "Consort," he said formally.

Going with instinct, Elena smiled. "Just Elena." If she wanted to learn Gian's secrets, she had to earn his trust.

A responding smile that turned the leader of the Luminata from handsome to devastatingly so. "When we are alone, Elena then."

Something in that statement raised the tiny hairs on her arms, made her fingers itch for her long knife, but she kept a smile on her face and got to her feet. "What's it called? The martial art you were practicing."

"Contemplation." His eyes, pale and striking, held her own. "That is its purpose, to put us in a mental space where we have absolute purity of thought."

Forcing herself to shake off her negative reaction to being watched with such unnerving concentration, Elena grinned. "Yeah, and you don't sometimes fight just for the hell of it."

Gian's laughter was deep, that of a man who was delighted with his partner in conversation. "Ah, but that is our secret." He held out the stick, suddenly just a handsome angel who happened to enjoy her company. "Would you like to learn? It takes hundreds of years to master, but I can show you the basics."

Closing her hand over the smooth wood, Elena found it unexpectedly heavy. "I'm always up for learning new weapons."

Gian kept scrupulous distance between them as he fetched another stick and showed her what he called "the first path." Given the weight of the stick, the movements were difficult, even at slow speed. But Elena wasn't an ordinary consort or a mortal—she was hunter-born and Guild-trained. She picked up the motions with a quick fluidity that had Gian giving her a look that said he couldn't decide whether to be pleased or discomfited.

Ah, but I am a traditional man. I prefer my beauties without blades.

Given his views on women, Elena half expected him to call a halt to the exercise, but he upped the ante and the speed. Her breath began to come harder, but she didn't falter. She'd seen Gian move, knew he could push it to a speed where she simply couldn't keep up—she wasn't that immortal yet—but he brought things to a smooth stop well before she reached the edge of her endurance.

"You are skilled," he said, his face flushed from the exercise. "Even a Neanderthal can accept the beauty of such warrior grace."

As a compliment, it was a good one. Even better was the self-deprecating smile that accompanied it. Only it no longer rang true to Elena. It was the eyes. Gian's eyes never changed, no matter what the rest of his face did. And those eyes watched her as if he was trying to peel her down to the bone.

Not so much male admiration as a scientist with a bug.

"Thank you," she said, wondering if she was just seeing such negative things in him because she knew he'd lied, if only by omission. "But you're a master at this."

"I will be happy to give you lessons during your time here," the Luminata responded with apparent sincerity. "I'm sure a hunter will begin to chafe at being trapped in such a quiet place. No rogue vampires here for you to hunt."

"Activity's always welcome," she replied, handing him the stick she'd borrowed. "I'll see you tomorrow morning then?"

A nod of Gian's head. "It will be my pleasure." He glanced at Aodhan, a gentle disappointment in his gaze when he looked back at her. "You do not need a guard with me, Elena."

"Aodhan's not a guard," Elena said. "He's a friend—and if I had to guess, I'd say he's composing a painting in his mind." She had no such belief, but she knew Aodhan would back her.

Gian's expression was suddenly suffused with light. "Ah, of course. This is a new environment for him. All artists absorb the new." He looked in interest at where Aodhan remained by the wall, out of range of their conversation. "Will he begin to create it here? We have supplies—some of my brothers prefer to search for luminescence through art rather than martial contemplation."

"I'll ask him," Elena said. "But I know he spends a lot of time thinking before beginning to create." Aodhan had told her that once as she was sitting in his Tower studio reading a backlog of Guild bulletins while he just looked out at the stormy skies beyond.

First I must see, Ellie. Only then can I create.

"I will ask my brother Natal to come here tomorrow morning during our practice," Gian said, and again, he was suddenly standing much closer than he should've been, the movement so quiet she hadn't caught it. "He and Aodhan will have much in common."

Regardless of the crawling feeling across her skin, Elena stayed in place. She knew Aodhan would be with her in a heartbeat if she gave the slightest indication of trouble, but she wanted to get a handle on Gian. Secrets and lies aside, was he just weird because he was old? Or was he something far more dangerous?

"You've led your brothers for a long time," she said. "Aren't you tired of it?"

A slight cocking of his head. "You've asked about me?" His eyes filling with light, his wings flaring out before closing back in.

"You are *the* Luminata. I was curious."

"Yes, of course you would be curious. It is in your blood," Gian said almost absently.

The words were stones thrown into a still pond.

Elena wanted to clutch at them, claw out the answers she needed. But she couldn't show her hand. Not yet. Not when she was stumbling in the dark. "Yep. Hazard of being hunter-born, I guess."

Gian blinked, stared at her for a second as if she wasn't who he expected, then smiled. "Yes." A glance up at the sun. "Alas, I must go. It is time for my first meditation—but I look forward to meeting again."

Saying her good-byes, Elena walked up to Aodhan while Gian left the same way as his previous partner. "Just so you know," she said, "you're contemplating creating a new artwork."

"You did not lie, Ellie. This place does interest me on an artistic level." Eyes of shattered light met hers. "Gian stands too close to you."

"Do you think it's because he's been here for hundreds of

years?" She nudged her head and they walked down the corridor. "His social skills might just be rusty."

"No." Aodhan's response was firm. "He only does it with you, no one else."

Elena thought of how Gian had stared at her so strangely there at the end. "I remind him of the woman he was involved with." She'd updated Aodhan on that piece of information after their flight the previous night. "I'd probably stare, too, if I met a man who looked like Raphael. And if the breakup was bad, if Gian's lover did betray him, it explains why he hasn't mentioned her."

Aodhan nodded, but she saw he wasn't convinced. Neither was Elena: she was just forcing herself to look at every possible angle. She couldn't allow herself to be unduly influenced by the fact that those tiny hairs on the back of her neck? They'd quivered upright the entire time she was with Gian.

A sudden wind whistled through the courtyard.

Elena shivered, hearing within it a woman's desolate moan.

Raphael sat next to his mother in the internal chamber. There was nothing in this room beyond ten armchairs arranged in a circle. On his right was Titus, next to Titus sat Elijah. Alexander had taken the seat directly opposite Caliane. Next to him sat Michaela on one side, Favashi on the other. Charisemnon had the seat between Michaela and Elijah, while Neha sat next to Caliane on her other side, Astaad next to Neha.

The Cadre of Ten was in session though there were eleven archangels in the world for the first time in known history.

"We shouldn't be here," Charisemnon said into the quiet broken only by the rustling of Neha's silver-shot maroon sari as the Archangel of India crossed her legs.

Neha's hair was in its usual elegant knot and she wore a teardrop-shaped bindi in jewel blue between her eyebrows.

Raphael knew that while Neha may have stopped wearing mourning white, she would never forget—or forgive—the death of her daughter. Regardless of how much he respected her, or how much he missed the relationship they'd once had, he could never forget that simple fact.

Vengeance defined Neha.

And it was she who responded to Charisemnon. "So sure, Charisemnon—have you had contact with Zhou Lijuan?" Her voice was poisonous grace, but that poison wasn't malicious—Neha was the Queen of Snakes and Poisons after all. Then again, given the way she was looking at Charisemnon, maybe it was very much on purpose.

As Elena had pointed out, Neha did not suffer cowards.

And as far as Raphael was concerned, Charisemnon was a coward who brought shame to angelkind and who needed to be erased from existence. The Archangel of Northern Africa had gained the ability to create immortal-harming diseases in the Cascade, had used it in attacks on Titus's and Raphael's territories. In Raphael's case, it had led to the Falling, when angels fell from the sky to be shattered and broken.

Hundreds had been horrifically injured.

Five had died.

Been murdered.

Including young Stavre, a promising youth on his first placement.

The fallen had been carried home from New York by an honor guard of angels, their funeral biers covered with flowers as they traveled the sky road they'd so loved in life. When the honor guard passed by Neha's lands on the way to the Refuge, they'd been joined by another squadron. The new squadron had carried lanterns to light the way, those lanterns refreshed all the way to the fallen's final home in the mountains where each had been born.

The Archangel of India was a complicated woman.

"If I had met Lijuan," Charisemnon said with a smile that dripped charm, "I would've spoken up when this ridiculous summons was first sent." He remained boneless as a cat in his seat, a handsome man with flawless skin. No sign remained of the disease that had ravaged him when his abilities turned on him; he was once again an archangel who attracted lovers in droves and who had a liking for young flesh in his bed. Too young.

That one was always full of himself even as a boy.

His mother's voice, that stunning symphony of sound,

broke into Raphael's thoughts. *Sometimes*, he said, *I forget that you knew everyone here as a child. What was Alexander like as a boy?*

Her eyes met his for a fleeting instant, the incandescent blue flame burning with memory. *As ambitious and as honorable as he is today.* She turned to face the others once more. *Though now he carries a violent rage deep within.* Sadness in her tone. *I hope he will not allow it to poison him.*

Xander is helping. Lijuan had murdered Alexander's only son as well as Rohan's wife, but that son had left behind a son of his own. *Alexander can't drown in grief when he has a boy to raise.* Like Elena's adored Izak, Xander needed seasoning, needed a firm guiding hand as he grew into his wings and learned his own strength.

Yes. Caliane's agreement was soft. *But it is a harsh thing to outlive your child. Some never recover. I have seen this in my eternity of life.*

Raphael could say nothing to that; his mother had lived so many years that he might never know quite when she'd been born, when she'd taken her first steps. Across from her, Alexander raised his eyebrows very slightly and he had the feeling the two Ancients were talking to one another.

Charisemnon, meanwhile, was still attempting to convince the rest of them to dissolve this meeting and give Lijuan more time to surface.

Raphael decided it was time to get things back on track; he had no intention of being stuck in Lumia for weeks. Especially not when the Luminata watched Elena from the shadows, their intent unknown. "We can't cancel this meeting," he said when Charisemnon paused for breath. "Bloodlust has already hit."

"Isolated incidents." Astaad stroked his goatee as he had a habit of doing when deep in thought. "While you all know I believe vampires must have a strict hand on them regardless of age, it is a big thing to depose an archangel. We *must* be certain."

Neha inclined her head, her tone far less poisonous in response to Astaad. "I share a significant border with Lijuan. Any outbreaks of bloodlust could well spill over onto my lands and yet I would not declare her derelict in her duties or gone to Sleep without irrefutable proof."

Neither statement surprised Raphael. Astaad was an ally, Neha an unknown at this point in time, but both were archangels who believed in tradition over change. "The incidents are no longer so isolated," he said in the pause that followed their exchange.

18

A piercing silence.

"Jason got word to me before dawn this morning."

"How?" Charisemnon sat up in his seat. "Mortal technology cannot presently penetrate Lumia and the borders of the stronghold are heavily patrolled."

He may as well have called Raphael a liar.

Strangling the ice cold anger that would disrupt the meeting and give Charisemnon a victory, he shrugged and spoke to the room at large rather than deign to respond to an archangel he planned to kill as soon as it became feasible. As far as he was concerned, Charisemnon was a cockroach, a scourge on the earth.

"Jason isn't known as the best spymaster in the world for nothing." It was a deliberate dig—Charisemnon had once tried to lure Jason away by promising him lands of his own to rule.

The other archangel had never understood that, to Jason, such an offer wasn't freedom: it was a cage.

"I don't care how that black-winged shadow of yours got word to you, Raphael," Titus said. "I want to know what he said."

A number of the others nodded, though Charisemnon's

face was rigid, the color of an overripe tomato and as attractive.

"A moment." Reaching into his boot, Raphael retrieved the thinly rolled map that had been slipped under the door to his and Elena's suite during the early hours of this morning. Raphael would've questioned its veracity except that Jason had reached out with his mind to confirm his presence, before the spymaster disappeared back the way he'd come, a shadow among shadows.

He was no longer anywhere near Lumia, having flown back in the direction of China the instant after passing on the map and the information. His parting words, however, hadn't been what Raphael expected from his long-silent spymaster. *I hope you settle this fast, sire. I wish to return home to Mahiya.*

Jason's princess understood who and what he was, accepted that he needed to travel to distant lands, but she missed him desperately. So much so that when Jason was away, Elena, Honor, and those of the Seven located in New York City, as well as all the other friends she'd made, worked together to keep her company as often as possible.

The last time Mahiya visited the Enclave, she'd told Elena and Raphael that she was training so she could accompany Jason on missions that didn't require stealth Jason alone could pull off. *Your princess is thinking about joining you*, he'd said to the other man. *Not on this journey. Others.*

Jason's response had been so aggravated that Raphael had laughed—his spymaster had not sounded so very "real" in an eon. *Yes, we are in discussions about her plans. She refuses to listen to reason so it appears I must teach her how to be a spy.*

The memory of that unexpected interaction faded as he unrolled the map, then rose and used a mere dusting of his power to meld the edges into the stone of the wall behind his armchair. It showed Lijuan's territory in detail. The fine tide of red that licked at China's northeastern border needed no explanation—the line was nearly unbroken.

A gasp of sound, erupting from more than one throat.

"Surely that isn't true." Michaela's tone was, for once, pure archangel, no undertone of seduction or nastiness. "Your spymaster has noted cases of bloodlust all along that region? We would've heard had it been so."

"The outbreaks have only ratcheted up in the past forty-eight hours," Raphael told them, tapping at a red dot on the map. "A dot of this size denotes one or two fatalities." The vast majority of the dots were of that size.

"Sporadic breaks," Elijah murmured, two deep grooves between his eyebrows. "Those happen everywhere in the world. The worrying thing is how close the outbreaks are to one another."

Getting to her feet in a rustle of silk, Neha came over to examine the map more closely, the pleats in front of her sari opening and closing with quiet grace as she walked. "Raphael, are you certain?"

He ignored the biting, jagged edge of her. "You know Jason, Neha."

A sigh, a nod. "Yes, I know Jason. He wouldn't report this unless he'd confirmed it twice over."

Alexander's silver wings caught the light as he leaned forward, his expression grim. "We have time yet, but not as long as we'd hoped."

"I refuse to believe this until I see it with my own eyes," Charisemnon countered, jumping to his feet. "Lijuan deserves that from us. She was the oldest among us until Caliane's rise."

"I agree," Titus said, as Astaad nodded. "It is a titanic decision and we can't rely only on the word of even the best spymaster in the world." His dark eyes met Raphael's. "You understand."

"Yes." Not simply for reasons of honor and tradition. "If we make a mistake and place two active archangels in the same territory, we risk igniting a catastrophic war." The Cadre had to be dead certain that Lijuan had gone into Sleep.

Favashi spoke for the first time. "The tide of blood is concerning, but it *is* sporadic yet. I say we come to a decision as to what would be the best course of action should Lijuan indeed be in Sleep, *then* make our inspection. That way, should Lijuan prove to have disappeared, the archangel or archangels in charge of her former territory can take over at once."

Michaela tapped a finger on the arm of her chair. "Why waste time discussing a 'what if' scenario? I say we go to China now, scare the vampires into good behavior, investigate, then make our decision."

Raphael wasn't in the habit of agreeing with Michaela, but she was right: why waste time and energy if there was no reason for it?

"There is no *decision*," Favashi said, her steel showing. "We are all dancing around the very large elephant in the room." Her eyes went to Alexander. "You and I are attempting to share a territory that should belong to only one. If Lijuan is dead, I take over her lands and you keep Persia. That is the only viable option."

Having retaken his seat after Neha took hers, Raphael waited for one of the more land-hungry of the archangels to dispute Favashi's point. But no one did. *I didn't expect such quick agreement*, he said mind to mind to Elijah.

I think the possibility of war is in everyone's thoughts, and right now, Favashi and Alexander are ripe for it—you cannot put two such aggressive powers next to each other and expect peace.

Still, Raphael responded, *Charisemnon seems the kind who would encourage a war that would decimate his enemies.*

I see your point. Elijah's eyes lingered on the Archangel of Northern Africa. *We must not forget, Raphael, that for all his faults, Charisemnon has ruled for two thousand some years. He may have more sense in him than we realize.*

Michaela waved a languid hand. "Your solution is simple, Favashi," she said with a smile that was a wonder of physical beauty. "However, there is a reason Lijuan is the Archangel of China—and it's not because it was the land of her birth. Her territory also includes a significant portion of what was once Uram's."

Astaad nodded. "Michaela is right. Lijuan's is one of the physically largest territories."

"Michaela's territory is as large now," Favashi countered. "She, too, controls a sizable percentage of what Uram once did."

"But those lands contain areas that are largely uninhabited, and the overall population in Michaela's lands is in the same vicinity as Astaad's," Neha said with crisp pragmatism. "China, in comparison, has *the* largest number of vampires in the population, and Lijuan was the most powerful among us for a long time."

That was a very, very good point.

"Are you implying that I can't control the vampires under my command?" Favashi's whip of a question was directed not at Astaad but at Michaela.

Titus boomed an answer, his voice echoing off the stone before he tempered it—*after* he had everyone's attention. "We are all archangels," he said. "But I am quite prepared to accept that some of us have more power than others—and Lijuan has proven that multiple times. You are the newest member of the Cadre, Favashi. It would be irresponsible to hand you China and Lijuan's associated lands."

Favashi's face tensed, her bones pushing out against the cream of her skin, but it was Michaela who next spoke—and very strangely for her, she didn't ask for a piece of the pie for herself, or suggest they redraw the borders of all the Cadre territories. "Lady Caliane," she said, her tone respectful. "The easiest answer is for you to take over a larger section of Lijuan's territory, while Favashi oversees the rest."

Favashi's angry expression faded into thoughtfulness. "A workable solution," she said at last. "And your lands, Lady Caliane, are currently the smallest in the Cadre. Such is not respectful to your status as an Ancient."

The truth was that Caliane didn't want anything more. The only reason she'd taken over Japan was that she and her people needed a home.

"I have done my ruling, child," Caliane said, and from her, the world "child" was no insult. In this circle, only Alexander was her compatriot. "Unlike some of my friends"—a glance at Alexander that held dry amusement—"I have no desire to step back into that arena. I wish to live in peace with my people. Japan is enough for me."

"I think you do not have a choice, old friend." Alexander leaned forward again, muscled forearms braced on his thighs. "There is a reason that we two are both awake—and I think it's partly because of this. The world does not need eleven archangels. It needs ten for optimum balance."

Caliane's wings glowed with power. So did Alexander's.

Had any other archangel in the circle done that during a meeting, it would've been a sign of aggression. With Ancients, it had become clear that such things were often accidental.

They had so much power running through their veins that it poured out of them without their conscious knowledge.

"Alex," Caliane said softly, "do you not think we should leave the world to the young?"

"Callie, you know we cannot. They have made a mess of it."

Everyone else in the circle sat in stunned silence. Even Raphael was startled. As he forgot his mother's age at times, he also never thought of her as young. But once, she must've been. Once, she'd been simply Callie, not Lady Caliane.

Now, she laughed, the sound haunting music that made several archangels close their eyes and just listen. "Such arrogance," she said to Alexander. "We made our own messes and we cleaned them up. We should leave them to clean up theirs."

Alexander's smile was open, containing none of the distance so often in it when he spoke to younger archangels. "It is the time of the Cascade," he replied. "The normal rules do not apply."

Sighing, Caliane gave a reluctant nod. "Perhaps you are right." Her expression was quiet for a long moment, the quiet of ages long gone. "I will assist young Favashi to maintain order—and when she is old enough, I will release the lands to her. Will this satisfy the Cadre?"

Favashi's expression was openly surprised—archangels weren't known to give up territories they'd claimed. Recovering quickly, she said, "I thank you, Lady Caliane."

Will you truly be able to work with her, Favashi? Raphael asked. *You are used to total control.* Like him. Like every other archangel in the Cadre.

Favashi didn't look at him as she replied. *Yes. She is not one of us—she is an Ancient. And unlike Alexander, she truly seems to want to be left in peace. Do you believe she will suddenly wish to rule again?*

Raphael thought of the sorrow that sat heavy on Caliane's heart, the losses that still marked her, the tiredness he glimpsed in her eyes too often, and said, *No. So long as you do not encroach on the small territory she has claimed as her own, my mother will assist you as she has stated and leave you alone the rest of the time.*

"Well," Elijah said, "that settles it. Together, Favashi and

Caliane are more than strong enough to control Lijuan's territory." As he spoke, Raphael realized the other man was one of the archangels who didn't see Caliane as Ancient first; to him, she would always be the warrior he'd once served. "The only question is whether or not we have the right to dispose of that territory."

"There is another matter," Astaad said, looking a little uncomfortable. "If Lijuan *is* still awake and alive, then we have a serious problem in Persia."

Tension gripped everyone in a tight fist, because his words were an understatement of the highest order.

"Eleven archangels," Caliane murmured. "It is not natural. There is no possible way to maintain the necessary distances long term with eleven."

Alexander glanced at Favashi. "I have no quarrel with you, but I *am* awake and I want my territory, a territory I ruled for eons before you were born. I will not give it up."

Favashi's response was curt. "You've made that clear, but I, too, am an archangel." A reminder that she wouldn't go down easy. "It does not matter yet. We must resolve the Lijuan question first. At that point, there may no longer be an issue—but if there is, then we will hash out a solution, since the Cadre will already be in one place with no need for a separate meeting."

"Favashi's logic is sound," Astaad said.

Neha nodded, so did Titus, then slowly, everyone else.

"That leaves only one question," Neha murmured. "How are we to determine whether or not Lijuan is simply recovering from an injury, or if she has gone into Sleep, or perhaps . . . into death?"

19

Elena and Aodhan wandered deliberately aimlessly through Lumia that morning, giving anyone watching the impression that they were just killing time while Raphael was in the Cadre meeting. When they spotted Xander doing flight drills with Valerius in another courtyard, they waited until he was done, then asked both males to join them.

"We're going to meet Hannah," Elena told them. "She said she'd be in the Gallery." They'd met the other consort an hour earlier by chance.

Valerius inclined his head, his blond-streaked brown hair tightly curled, and the white wings arching over his back holding filaments of the same blond. "We will join you after we clean up." A pause. "A young warrior should learn art as well as weapons if he is to be a man of strength in all its facets."

"That sounds like something the Hummingbird would say."

At Aodhan's words, Valerius's stern face cracked in a small smile that brought warmth to his eyes. "She was stuck in Alexander's territory once for two years—she spent that time trying to bring culture to those of us far more at home with the sword and the crossbow."

So many connections over the eons lived by an immortal,

Elena thought, so many strands of lives entwining. Never would she have linked this usually dour general with the fragile Hummingbird, but from the smile that lingered yet in the greenish hazel of his eyes, that connection had been one he'd enjoyed.

Xander, his dark brown hair damp with sweat, gave Elena a small smile as Aodhan and Valerius fell into a quiet conversation. "I have a younger friend in your tower, Consort," he said. "Izak. Is he well?"

"Izzy?" Elena couldn't help her affectionate grin. "Last I saw him, he was determinedly learning to shoot the crossbow to pinpoint accuracy under the tutelage of a number of my hunter friends."

Xander blinked, while Valerius's eyebrows came down heavily over his eyes, the general clearly having kept one ear on his charge's discussion with Elena. "An angel being taught by mortals?"

Not all the hunters in the Guild were mortal now, but since Izak's tutors all were, that was a nonissue. "Angels can survive a crossbow hit," she pointed out. "Mortals mostly can't—so hunters learn to be very, very, *very* good at hitting the other party first." Survival instincts gave mortals an edge immortals simply didn't possess, especially when young.

Valerius nodded slowly, and though his expression remained reluctant, it wasn't intransigent in the way of some of the older angels. "Galen is in agreement with this?"

"He's the one who suggested it." Galen was always aware of the best resources in Raphael's territory, whether mortal or immortal, and he utilized them well. "We'll see you in the Gallery?"

Xander and Valerius nodded before they headed off down a hallway to the right, Xander taller and more slender in comparison to Valerius's more solidly muscled form. She saw the boy ask the general something, heard the deep rumble of Valerius's reply. They disappeared from sight after making a turn off the hallway.

"Do you know the way?" Elena asked Aodhan. "I forgot to ask Hannah."

Shaking his head, Aodhan said, "I haven't worked out all the symbols. But there are Luminata everywhere. We can ask one."

Elena had noticed that, too—the Luminata *were* every-where. "Guess they don't all have the same meditation times," she said, thinking back to what Gian had said.

"Or it's used as a convenient excuse when needed."

Elena sighed. "Damn it, Sparkle. Don't go cynical on me."

Shooting her as close as Aodhan ever came to a glare, he said, "Illium is a bad influence on you."

"Way I hear it, he's been a bad influence on you since you were tiny tots."

A deep smile that creased his cheeks, his beauty once more stealing her breath. "We took turns."

Around them, Elena was aware of the Luminata going motionless—yeah, Sparkle's smile had a certain effect. "Let's stop one of the brothers who *isn't* trying to be stealthy." No reason to tip their hand, showing these men that Elena and Aodhan were highly conscious of being shadowed.

The one they approached was heading down the corridor toward them. About Elena's height, his face was in darkness because of his hood, his wings covered. However, when they asked about the Gallery, he immediately pushed back the hood. And his smile, it was a bright thing, his teeth white against skin of darkest mahogany and his black hair cut close to his skull, his cheekbones like razors, his eyes a startling sky blue.

She was surrounded by pretty men today.

"If you would not mind the company," he said in a mellif-luous voice, "I would be happy to guide you." His expression turned apologetic. "I'm afraid the Gallery is deep in Lumia, the route to it complicated. We would protect our treasures from all possible natural threats."

"We'd love it if you came along," Elena said. "This place is a maze. Fun to explore, but I can see how we could end up going around in circles."

"Yes, it took me a year to learn how to navigate it," their guide admitted. "I used to constantly end up doing my brother-hood meditations in the hallways because I couldn't make it back to my room in time."

A silvered chime sounded in the air.

"The breakfast bell for us," their chatty guide said, begin-ning to walk. "I will go there after taking you to the Gallery.

We breakfast long here, brothers coming and going as they finish their personally chosen meditations."

Elena had her guard up so high she could barely see over it, and still she found herself wanting to like this angel who seemed an open book. "I don't suppose you have a historical map of Lumia we could see?" she asked because, hell, why not? "It'd be interesting to see how the place has changed over the years."

"I do not know of one," the Luminata said slowly, "but I will search the Repository of Knowledge for you." A smile so honest and innocent that Elena was suddenly afraid for him. "I am Ibrahim, Consort."

"Elena." She glanced to her left. "You know Aodhan?"

"We have not met but yes." He and Aodhan acknowledged each other. "We carry pieces of your art in the Gallery."

Aodhan tilted his head to the side. "I would've thought my age would disqualify me?"

"No, my brothers who are in charge of the art archive judge only on the merits of the work—and you are a student of the Hummingbird." A smile that held shy admiration. "I am but an initiate yet learning of art, but in my opinion, you are the best student she has ever had. You have taken her teachings to heart but you haven't tried to emulate her. You are Aodhan as she is the Hummingbird."

Maybe it was empty flattery meant to put Aodhan at ease, but though Elena was no art expert, she agreed with Ibrahim. Aodhan and the Hummingbird were both astonishingly talented—and each was unique in what they created. "Do you have many of her pieces here?" she asked Ibrahim.

"As many as we have been able to acquire." His expression became mournful. "Her work is beloved by those lucky enough to have obtained a piece. Not many will pass them on even though the Luminata wish only to hold her art safe for future generations."

And keep them out of view of the world, Elena thought privately. It wasn't as if this Gallery were a museum anyone could come by to visit. In fact, it struck her as being more like Lijuan's creepy "Collection Room," where she apparently pinned up dead angels with beautiful wings: a secret hoard.

As Aodhan and Ibrahim exchanged further comments, it

became clear that Ibrahim wasn't only a student of art but a practitioner, too. "I am an unknown, nowhere near your level of skill," he said modestly when Aodhan asked him about his work. "But it gives me joy." A soft smile. "It is my contemplation."

"The greatest art," Aodhan replied, "comes from great joy and great despair."

Ibrahim's smile faded. "I think for the Hummingbird, one turned into the other centuries ago."

The comment resonated within Elena. There was such terrible sadness in the Hummingbird now, but she'd seen a work in Raphael's Refuge stronghold that Illium's mother had created two millennia ago—it burned with such radiant joy that to look at it was to smile.

However, even as she thought about art, even as Ibrahim told them about his favorite works in the Gallery, she was noting every step they took, creating a mental map of this sprawling maze. The stone of Lumia itself began to change as they got closer to the secret heart of the stronghold. Carvings done with time and care became apparent on the walls, while the floor beneath their feet turned into a delicacy of mosaics.

Those mosaics were earth-toned and gentle at the start, but the pale turquoise blues and faded reds slowly flowed into jewel tones so brilliant Elena wondered how the colors had been captured with such depth. And on the walls, the carvings turned into paintings of great events in angelic history.

"Who painted this?" Aodhan asked, stopping in front of a breathtaking piece that appeared to show an angel bursting into flame. His tone was dangerously quiet.

A heartbeat later, Elena noticed that while the angel's hair was gold, his face was one with deeply familiar lines. She'd always thought Raphael strongly favored his mother, but the face that stared out at her from that painting was his. Change the golden hair to midnight, the equally golden eyes to a blue too pure to be mortal, and she'd be looking at a portrait of her archangel.

Wait. "His eyes aren't golden." And the hair whipping across his face was created of flame.

"No," Ibrahim replied. "His eyes show angelfire burning him up from within." Ibrahim's entire body seemed to sag. "The artist is one of the brotherhood. He was once a healer, but now he chooses seclusion and art. But this is the only scene he ever paints. Over and over."

"Was he a friend of Nadiel's?" Because Elena was certain beyond any doubt that she was looking at an image of Raphael's father in the moments before his death.

"He has never said." Ibrahim tucked his hands into the sleeves of his robe. "The older Luminata tell me that he came to us in silence and in silence he has remained forevermore." Pausing, the blue-eyed male seemed to be about to say something further, but then simply shook his head.

Lifting her fingers, Elena traced the lines of Nadiel's face. It was eerie, the resemblance . . . but even if the hair and eyes were changed, she would never mistake one for the other. There was something in Raphael that was missing in this man, and there was something in Nadiel that she'd never seen in Raphael.

A brokenness. A subtle madness that was visible even in the final throes of his life.

Magnificent but broken, that was Raphael's father. And this painting captured his death, when his beloved consort had been forced to execute him lest he drench the world blood red in his insanity. "He *never* speaks?" she said to Ibrahim. "The brother who painted this?"

"Never with his voice. I was more curious than I should've been," Ibrahim added, "and I looked up his record in the Repository. He once bore the name 'Laric,' but my brothers have come to call him Stillness."

Poetic and sad.

And an erasure.

Elena knew one other person who'd given up her name— Sorrow had chosen that name in despair over the changes ravaging her body, so it hadn't exactly been a free choice, but it had been *her* choice. It didn't appear as if this healer artist had made any choice at all. "Where does Laric live in his seclusion?"

"The north tower." Ibrahim nodded in that direction. "I do not mean to say he never emerges. He does. It is simply that he rarely interacts with us, and so he carries his seclusion with him."

Aodhan's wings flickered, a surprising movement from an angel who knew how to be still, until you could almost forget him despite his shattering otherness. "I would meet him."

Ibrahim looked at Aodhan for a long moment. "You, too, were silent for a long time," he said unexpectedly before inclining his head. "He seems to exit for sunset most often." A pause. "I walk with him at times. I do not know if I intrude on his seclusion, but he has never given any indication that he wished for me to leave." A hesitant but very real concern in his tone for this brother who lived in aloneness.

"Thank you." Aodhan's voice.

Forcing herself to walk away from the disturbing but compelling painting of Nadiel, she said, "Do you know when Laric first came here?"

"It was not in the records that I saw." Ibrahim shrugged, then winced. It was followed by a sigh. "I am new to the brotherhood. Only on the first step to my path for luminescence." A lopsided smile that was infectious. "You will not report my behavior?"

The more time she spent with this man, the more she liked him. And the more she worried that he was a hapless lamb among wolves. "Your secret's safe with us. Right, Aodhan?"

"We are vaults."

An actual grin before Ibrahim seemed to remember himself and suddenly was all contemplative quiet again.

"Who did the work on the Gallery?" Elena asked out of curiosity. "I mean, the Luminata are meant to be a closed sect and, no offense, but I can't see your brothers learning construction skills."

Ibrahim winced again. "I think I am not meant to talk of such."

"Let me guess—the rules get bent now and then?"

A subtle nod. "As you say, there are certain things we need that we cannot provide for ourselves. And those of the angelic squadron that patrols our borders also have need of supplies, so Lumia has certain ties with the closest town."

"What about shelter for the squadron and their lovers or families?" She hadn't seen any soldiers in Lumia.

"None who have families are asked to serve here," Ibrahim replied. "Those who do live in barracks located by the eastern wall, and during their rotation in Lumia, they maintain their chastity." Flushing almost immediately on the heels of those surprising words, Ibrahim said, "I talk too much. Gian is in despair that I will ever achieve anything close to luminescence."

"According to the angels I know," Elena said, "even a hundred years of doing something barely makes you competent at it, so you've got a few thousand years at least to figure out luminescence."

Ibrahim's face creased into a smile at her dry tone. "Yes, this is so. But here, surrounded by so much peace, I wish to hasten my journey."

"Have you ever considered that you might not want to be Luminata?" As far as Elena was concerned, he was too good for this place.

"Of course," Ibrahim said at once. "That is part of the path—all of us who wish to become Luminata are given a century to make our decision. It is the rarest initiate who ever chooses to leave." A tranquility to him that, all at once, made Elena believe this man would achieve the luminescence he sought. "A thousand two hundred years of adventure, excess, wealth . . . nothing in that life spoke to me as do the ancient teachings on which Lumia is built."

Aware of Aodhan listening with concentrated focus even as he kept his eyes on their surroundings, Elena had the worrying thought that he might be considering this place . . . then mentally shook herself out of it. Aodhan had made it clear that he wanted to live, wanted to experience life in vibrant color after disengaging from the world for two hundred years.

Still, she'd ask him, make damn sure. She wasn't convinced he wasn't still shaken up after the fight with Illium.

"What about love?" Elena asked this initiate who appeared to have no hidden agendas, too new to have been inducted into the Luminata's secret society.

20

"Love?"

"Ellie means to ask if there was not a person or people you loved?" Aodhan said into the quiet. "To be Luminata is to leave behind such ties, is it not?"

Instead of answering the question, Ibrahim gasped. "You call your archangel's consort by a diminutive?"

"He's my friend," Elena said, proud of the fact she'd earned Aodhan's trust. "And I'm never going to be like other consorts—I'll always have a mortal heart."

It is your greatest strength.

Words Keir had spoken to her the last time he'd visited New York. The healer had placed his hand over that heart as he spoke. Coming from another man, it might've been a come-on, an invasion of her personal space, but Keir was . . . Keir. She knew he was a sexual being, had seen clear evidence of it, but he never interacted with her in that way. To her, he was a healer, wise and gifted. And his hands held only a healer's gentleness.

Never lose your heart, Elena. No matter if the world tells you it makes you weak. Immortals have so much power. It is good to have a weakness.

Elena wasn't certain she agreed with that last—especially when it came to Raphael. She never forgot that *she* was Raphael's greatest weakness, and it both infuriated and scared her. She didn't want her archangel to have any weaknesses, not when he swam with the vipers of the Cadre on a regular basis.

But in one thing, Keir was right: her mortal heart made her Elena. Give that up and she might as well lie down and die.

"A mortal heart." Ibrahim paused in a corridor awash in color, the tiles having become ever more vivid step by step, the mosaics intricate bursts, and the paintings on the walls expressionist splashes of pigment. "You say that with pride and yet mortality is a fleeting thing without any hope of luminescence." Rather than arrogance, his words held confusion and a question.

"Let me tell you a story, Ibrahim," Elena said as they began to walk again. "About a holy man I met three years after I first became a hunter."

The story was one of peace, of transcendence, of an awareness that mortality was but a shell and that the soul soared free in an immortality even the angels could not understand.

"You teach me," Ibrahim said sometime later, the three of them at a stop in front of stone doors carved in complex patterns. His expression held equal amounts of awe, bewilderment, and thoughtfulness. "And I am humbled."

Those sky blue eyes met hers. "I understand now: A thousand years or ten thousand years of life does not automatically proffer more wisdom. It is only fitting that I learn this from— forgive me for my boldness—a consort who is an infant in angelic terms."

Elena shook her head. "I'm not wise, Ibrahim." She was reckless more often than she should be, hadn't made peace with the memories that haunted her, had so many other faults. "But someone who *is* wise once told me to treasure my weaknesses. They are what make us."

Beside her, Aodhan reached forward to haul open one of the stone doors. The air that whispered out was noticeably cooler than the external air, though by no means chilly. "Thank you for showing us here."

"It has been my pleasure." Ibrahim bowed low. "If I may be so forward, Consort," he said upon rising, "I would speak to you again."

"Only if you call me Elena," she said.

Ibrahim's smile was that open and oddly innocent one. "Then I will see you again soon, Elena." He pulled up his hood as he turned away, but paused to add, "I have not forgotten my promise to look for a map."

"Thanks, Ibrahim." Elena didn't say anything further until she and Aodhan were inside what appeared to be some type of an antechamber, a relatively small room richly carpeted in deepest blue and hung with small artworks. At the other end of it was another door. "An airlock?"

"I do not know this word," Aodhan responded.

When she explained, he nodded. "Yes, I believe so. To ensure the air within and without do not mix to destabilize the constant temperature needed for the more delicate works of art." He indicated the pieces on the walls. "These are relatively new, created only two hundred years ago at most. They do not need the extra care."

Jerking her thumb over her shoulder, she said, "What about the stuff outside?"

"The mosaics were created in situ, likely purpose-done, and the paintings are brilliant but did not strike me as rare."

Elena thought back to what Ibrahim had said of Laric's compulsive painting of that one scene. Which reminded her, "You're not being seduced by the idea of luminescence?"

"The idea, yes," Aodhan replied. "This place, no."

"Phew. Because I'd come drag you out if you lost your mind and joined this cult. Though Illium would probably beat me to it."

Aodhan stared at the floor. "Do you think he's all right?"

"Jason would've got word to us if anything was wrong." She went to touch a hand to his forearm, stopped herself in time. "You want to look at these paintings or shall we go in?" She figured Xander and Valerius would find them easily enough when they arrived.

"No, I am eager to see the older works." A small smile that nonetheless lit up his face. "Illium is always teasing me about my liking for 'moldy old relics.'" The smile faded as quickly as it had appeared.

"You two have been friends for centuries," she reminded him. "Fights happen."

"Not like this. Not so he wouldn't come to see me off on a long journey."

Elena shook her head. "You're wrong. Sara and I didn't talk once for three whole weeks." It still hurt to think back to that time, to how much she'd missed her best friend, a woman who was her family by choice. "It was a stupid disagreement that dragged on, both of us too young and too proud to say sorry first—but through it all, I *always* knew she had my back, as she knew I had hers. Do you doubt that about Illium and you?"

"No, never." He looked away from her, to the door in front of them. "Illium has never been so angry before. He doesn't stay angry. Not with me."

"But you're angry, too," she pointed out. "No point ignoring that or you two will just fight again. When we go back, have it out with him." She played a blade through her fingers. "I recommend getting swords and going at it."

Aodhan's eyes were so difficult to read, but when he faced her again, she thought he might be laughing. "Perhaps you are right. I was . . . closed within for a long time. I think Illium has forgotten who I was before I was broken."

Pulling at the final door with one hand, Elena found she couldn't budge it. She waved toward Aodhan. "So remind him," she said as he hauled it open. "But don't forget that all the time you turned recluse, he was also growing and living his life. He's not the same person, either."

Aodhan didn't reply, but she knew he'd absorb and think about her words. Aodhan always listened and considered—

"Holy shit." Her mouth fell open.

In her mind, she'd thought the Gallery would be like a museum—the walls hung with works of art, sculptures artfully arranged or lit up in little cubbyholes. She'd pretty much expected the high ceiling because of the second, opaque, dome she'd seen when they overflew Lumia—but she could've never expected this.

The dome was part of the Gallery all right. It was an astonishing display high above her head, the underside painted with exquisite attention to detail and softly lit to showcase the artwork. But the dome was just the start. She and Aodhan stood on a gangway about ten feet wide that went around the entire room. In the center of the room was a plunging hole that

appeared bottomless. In the center of that hole hung a staircase that spiraled down with pathways splitting off on various
sides to lead viewers into other sections.

The Gallery was a misnomer. This was a tower of
galleries.

The designers had left enough room that you could fly
down if you didn't want to take the stairs—though if you took
the stairs, you'd see far more of the art even if you didn't step
off on every level. On the other hand, it would take forever to
walk down—because though she hung out as far as she could
without unbalancing and falling into the hole, Elena couldn't
see the end of the Gallery.

It kept going and going and going until it disappeared into
what looked like shimmers of gold. As if she was looking into
the heart of a distant sun. "How deep is this?" she whispered,
not really expecting an answer.

Having leaned over the edge with her, Aodhan said, "Shall
we find out?" The exhilaration in his tone reminded her of
what Raphael had said: there was a reason Illium and Aodhan
had become lifelong friends.

She grinned at him in answer but didn't immediately jump.
"We can't go straight down—the staircase and pathways off
to the different levels create obstacles. We'll have to go floor
by floor." In preparation, she closed the split diagonal zipper
over the top of her dress that appeared to be nothing but a decorative detail. It closed by pleating the extra fabric inward,
making her gown snug enough that it wouldn't fly up—she
really had to give Montgomery and the tailor props for thinking outside the box.

Aodhan pointed to their first landing spot, then they both
grinned—she'd *never* seen that look on Aodhan's face—and
stepped off the edge. A rush of cool air turned slightly colder by
their momentum and they were on the second lower level. It was
all freestanding marble sculptures here, the pieces no doubt
priceless. Elena, however, was far more interested in exploring
just how far the Luminata had dug the Gallery into the earth.

"That spot next." She pointed to one two levels down. "No
obstructions."

Aodhan dropped.

Laughing, she followed, the shattered light of his wings a

glorious sight below her as he came to a halt in a spot that gave her plenty of room to land herself. Her heart thumped as she glanced around. Two Luminata stood on this level, their hoods down. They appeared to be talking very quietly about a leather-bound book one was holding.

Seeing Elena and Aodhan, they both frowned. It was a very "hush in the library" look.

Elena tried to look suitably chastened before nodding at the next spot to Aodhan and they were falling. This time, they landed by a portrait gallery, an endless number of stunning images on display. So much sheer *beauty.* "Angelkind really won the genetic lottery," she said to Aodhan. "No wonder they're so jaded." When this was their normal, it became difficult to admire anyone or anything.

"They are not all angels." Aodhan motioned to a portrait in their line of sight. "She is a vampire. Nine thousand years of age and considered a beauty to rival Michaela."

That got her attention.

The woman in the picture had skin of an astonishing pure cream. No blemishes, nothing but a luminous flawlessness. Her nose was aquiline, her eyes a huge, soft aquamarine, and her hair cascades of lustrous red. *True* red. Not orange-red. Not rust-red. Not auburn. *Red.* "Talk about winning the genetic lottery." The vampire's beauty was the kind that caught the eye and held it, the brain trying to figure out how this person was put together that she was so perfect in every way.

Elena had been caught in that same loop with Michaela once, before she saw through to the female archangel's toxic heart. "But . . . there's something missing. Something Michaela has that this vampire doesn't." She couldn't put her finger on it, but Michaela just shone brighter. "It's not power, or not only that."

Aodhan gave her an approving look. "You see it. And though you don't like Michaela, you don't immediately favor Renate."

Renate. It seemed the right kind of name for this beauty. "Fact is fact," she said with a shrug. "And obviously, Michaela knows Renate doesn't hold a candle to her at second glance, or Renate would've met with an unfortunate accident long before reaching nine thousand years of age."

"I think you are correct." Aodhan took in the image again,

his eye clinical. "The fault is not the work's—the artist has captured her perfectly. What is missing is the spark of intelligence. Renate has air in her head."

Elena blinked. "Bit harsh, Aodhan."

"I'm not being cruel," he said. "Fact, as you say, is fact. In nine thousand years, Renate has not sought to improve her mind in any way—it has even been suggested that perhaps she was impaired during her Making, but I once overheard a healer speaking." He lowered his tone, his head leaning toward her own. "Renate's original master had tests done on her and it was found that she isn't impaired. She simply does not have that inner fire that pushes one to seek knowledge. Neither does she possess any ambition."

Pushing back his hair where it had fallen over his forehead, light sparking off the tumbled strands, he added, "If she was not so beautiful, she would've had a hard life as a vampire. As it is, she is a beloved pet—and I say that in the truest sense of the word. Her lover of the past five hundred years adores her, but he does not look upon her as a partner."

Elena whistled. "Nine thousand years and she isn't bored of just existing?"

"My sister tells me she combs her hair a lot."

Elena's mouth fell open. Swiveling on her heel, she glared at him. "Since when do you have a sister?" she hissed under her breath. "Nice of you to share with me."

He actually looked a little abashed. "I don't often think of her," he admitted. "Imalia was seven hundred years old when I was born. We only ever see one another when our parents summon us both home." A shrug. "She is a near-stranger, though she is not unkind. If I were to ask for her help, she would give it without hesitation. But we were born too distant in time to be true siblings."

Elena felt her mad begin to fade. Seven hundred years was an insane age gap. "I get it," she said. "I'm only nineteen and sixteen years apart from my two half sisters, but if Eve wasn't training to be a hunter, I wouldn't have much in common with them, either."

As it was, she never got to speak with Amy. The teen had refused any contact with Elena out of loyalty to her own mom. Elena understood. As the eldest of Elena's half sisters, Amy had a far deeper understanding of her parents' relationship than Eve—she'd figured out that Jeffrey Deveraux would never love her mom as he'd loved Elena's. "You and Imalia have the same parents?"

Aodhan nodded. "Such long gaps are not unusual among angelic families. Though children are rare gifts, there is no known end to fertility."

"Huh, guess that makes sense." She pointed to the next drop as, from above them, came a pointed, "*Shh.*"

They dropped . . . to find Hannah gazing in fascination at something in a glass display case, her vampiric escort, Cristiano, leaning lazily against the wall not far away. The handsome male with skin the color of darkest caramel and eyes of a chocolate brown gave an impression of liquid grace that was oddly feline. It intrigued Elena that one of Elijah's most trusted people would echo the prowl of the pumas that came to the archangel's call.

"Ellie," Hannah said softly, waving her over. "Come see this."

Crossing the short distance to her after smiling at Cristiano, Elena saw the other woman was fascinated by what appeared to be a map drawn on what looked to be animal hide. It was so fragile that it was in pieces an archivist had carefully placed next to one another, like a complex jigsaw. "It's the Refuge," she said in realization, "but the gorge is missing." That gorge bisected the angelic stronghold, was unmissable.

"This is from a time before the land shakes that created the gorge." Hannah's eyes glowed. "But it's not simply the age of the map—look at the artistry of the work itself. Aodhan, do you see?"

Having come to stand beside Elena, his wing just brushing hers, Aodhan nodded. "It is one of Tarquin's. The hand is unmistakable."

Elena frowned; she'd heard that name before.

"He was an archangel in the time of Caliane and Alexander," Hannah told her before she could ask. "An Ancient who went to Sleep some fifty thousand years past." Her slender, elegant artist's fingers touched the glass. "This was discovered long after his descent into Sleep, the damage already great, but the Luminata have done astonishingly well in managing to keep it as whole as it is."

Elena tried really hard to be interested, decided it was a lost cause. "Have you been to the bottom of the Gallery?"

"No, it would take me many months to get there," Hannah whispered, tucking back a curl that had escaped the intricate knot at the back of her head. "I skipped all the levels above to get to this one—it was so *hard* to make a choice as to what treasures to view first." Her dark eyes met Elena's, sudden laughter suffusing the awe in her expression. "Shoo. Go explore and then come back and tell me if I should go to a particular level."

Grinning, Elena nudged her head at Aodhan—who'd gone to talk with Cristiano—and they continued to dive down. Each part of the Gallery held endless treasures. One of Elena's favorites was the glass level. Full of finely blown glass created by mortals and immortals both, the fragile items were safely encased behind far more rigid glass shields, their dazzling colors glowing under strategically placed lights. This exhibit she *could* imagine spending hours in, lost in the iridescent wash of color.

Aodhan had a different favorite—a strange level filled with "artworks" that made little sense to Elena. "What do you see?" she asked him.

"This is the exhibit of possibility," he told her. "The pieces that were never finished, or those that were found half done after the artist's death. The stories are not yet complete, and so, there are endless futures to explore."

Elena tried to think through that lens, caught the barest glimpse of what he meant. But what struck her most was that he'd taken the positive interpretation over the negative. Because it could as easily be said that this was the exhibit of lost dreams. None of these pieces would ever be finished, no hope in them.

Elena was no healer, but she didn't have to be one to know that Aodhan's interpretation was a sign of soul-deep healing on his part. "You want to hang here?"

"Later perhaps. First, we must get to the bottom—Illium would never forgive us otherwise." A determined look. "I will make him listen to me after I return and then I will tell him of our adventure."

Nodding in approval of his plan, Elena flew down to a landing spot, Aodhan's wing brushing hers again as he landed a little too close. His primaries were impossibly soft when contrasted with the way they glittered as if coated with broken glass. He didn't apologize for the contact and she didn't want an apology.

The glancing brush was unremarkable among friends . . . but it was one Aodhan would've gone to great lengths to avoid when they first met.

21

Elena swallowed the knot in her throat, glanced around. The works on this level were of the earth—clay and stone and other natural materials. Again, she thought it was an exhibit she'd enjoy, but they had places to be. Next came an exhibit of precious metals and gemstones, tiaras placed beside necklaces and next to rings so dazzling they threatened to outshine Aodhan.

Attracted to the dazzle, she and Aodhan both stopped to peer more closely at a number of the pieces. Beside most were cards that had a lettering she didn't understand. "Can you read that?"

Aodhan stared at the letters, lines forming between his eyebrows. "I should be able to—we learned it in school. But it has been an age since I have used it." He scanned the text again. "I'm fairly confident it says this ring is a borrowed item, not a permanent part of the Gallery. The owner has lent it to Lumia."

Elena made a face. "I could understand that if this was a public museum," she said. "But why give it to people who'll just hide it away?"

"I believe there is a certain cachet in being able to say that a piece of art you own was deemed acceptable for Lumia's archives."

"Ah. Bragging rights. Got it." She looked at a necklace that was ropes of lustrous white pearls placed on a blue velvet background, thought that Sara would've liked to see it. Her best friend liked pearls—and even though she now owned the real thing, she still wore the imitation pearl bracelet Elena had given her for her twenty-first birthday.

"Ready for the next level?"

She nodded at Aodhan's question.

Metal sculptures, paintings of every kind, pencil and charcoal sketches, a collection of feathers that spanned every shade from pure white to gleaming obsidian—and included a feather of deepest magenta that she was certain came from the inner curve of Jessamy's wings, the exhibits kept surprising them, delighting them.

"Do they have one of your feathers?" she asked Aodhan, having not spotted it in their quick walk-through.

"I don't know. Perhaps—if someone picked one up and handed it in."

And then, finally, they were at the bottom of the Gallery.

Not quite believing they'd made it, Elena looked around, but there was definitely no more staircase. Only a floor that was a sunburst of golden filigree over white marble, the design so spectacular that Elena released the zip on her dress so she could move more freely and went down on one knee to run her fingers over the artistry of it.

When she looked up, it was to see that Aodhan's wings had turned golden, his feathers reflecting the room. Tapestries shimmering with golden threads, sculptures created of gold, paintings done in shades of gold, old-fashioned lamps with golden casings, a graceful carved settee upholstered in golden velvet and with a frame of golden wood, and ornately framed mirrors that reflected the gold to turn the entire space into a burst of sunshine.

"It's happy," Elena whispered. "Does that sound strange? This exhibit, the way it's set up, it feels happy. Alive."

"Art is meant to evoke emotion—but the emotion is not necessarily the same from person to person. Where you see joy, I see a delighted pride." His wings brushing the floor as he deliberately lowered them, as if to experience every aspect of this room, Aodhan stared at a painting that was all thick, textured paint, the shades of gold within it endless.

Though the painting had no structure, it reminded Elena of the sea, a crashing wave of color under a sky glowing with the hopeful tones of sunrise.

"Come look at this, Ellie."

Rising to join him, she lifted her fingers to touch the paint, found it as thick as it appeared. "You think there's actual gold in this paint?"

"Yes." Aodhan's eyes, the shattered light of them, glowed with endless reflections as he turned from the painting to look up. "But that's not what I wanted you to see."

She followed his gaze, gasped. She'd noticed the chandeliers attached to the bottoms of each part of the staircase as well as the pathways that led to each exhibit, but the overall effect was only now apparent. All those chandeliers created a shower of shimmering light, scattering a dazzling rain over them and turning this room into even more of a dream.

"Okay," she whispered, "the Luminata might hoard art, but they sure know how to show it off, too."

Leaving Aodhan to his contemplation of an intricate tapestry that had caught his eye, she wandered around trying to take in as much as possible. It was unlikely she'd have a chance to return—because, open as it was to all Luminata, she couldn't see the older members of the sect hiding any secrets here. And even this beauty couldn't compare to Elena's need to unearth the truth about the woman with hair of near-white who had looked so much like her that the Luminata found the resemblance eerie.

It feels like a ghost is haunting Lumia.

Skin pebbling, she decided she and Aodhan should head to the library next. Though what had Gian and Ibrahim called it? The Repository of Knowledge, that was it. That, too, was a public space, but with so many millennia of knowledge there, it was possible there were secrets that had fallen through the cracks, small clues she might be able to string together to form a coherent picture.

Not just yet, however. Leaving the Gallery too quickly would betray her impatience, arouse suspicions. And Aodhan was enjoying this. Happy to wait for him, she eventually found herself looking into a glass cabinet in which lay a tumble of golden artworks in miniature. Tiny sculptures, paintings, jewels, all of it sized for dolls.

Delighted, she took out her phone—which she carried around out of habit—to grab a few shots for Eve. She knew her youngest sister would enjoy zooming in to see all the different objects. It was only after she slipped away her phone that she realized this place was probably "No photography allowed," but oh well, at least she hadn't used the flash.

Leaning in closer, she smiled at the cheerful way this space had been organized. Someone in the Luminata had a sense of joy, understood that art didn't always have to be in perfect lines. She was about to move to the other side of the case when her eye fell on something half hidden beneath a tiny bust of a hawk-nosed man. It was the edge of what looked like a small painting.

The surround was aged gold, but there was a miniature canvas within, and from what she could see, that painting was of someone with long hair of near-white. It could be nothing, a truly ancient archangel or vampire, or just a blond woman whose image had faded over time, but Elena's heart thundered. She couldn't walk away without seeing it. But no matter how carefully she looked, she couldn't see a way to open the case.

She didn't realize Aodhan had noticed her preoccupation until he came up right next to her, their wings overlapping and the bare skin of his biceps almost touching her own arm. "Ellie, what is it?"

Elena glanced around before whispering, "You think this place has security cameras?" There'd been none in their suites, or in the hallways, but this Gallery held treasure after treasure.

"I would bet my wings it doesn't," Aodhan said. "Many angels believe such technological intrusions disrespectful to the contemplative space required for art. The Luminata are highly likely to fall into that category."

Breath coming a little too fast and shallow, she touched her fingers to the case. "There's a miniature painting right at the bottom with a portrait inside that I want to see."

"Which one?"

She tapped her finger on the glass to point it out. "Under the bust."

Aodhan's expression sharpened as he realized what had

caught her interest. "I can break the seal." His tone was as quiet as hers had been. "But the damage would be obvious."

Shaking her head, Elena looked up, the lights of the chandeliers now frustrating because they blinded her to anyone who might be watching them, or who might be heading to this level. "No," she said after looking back down, spots of black light dancing behind her eyes. "We can't risk the Luminata becoming suspicious—if they figure out I'm searching for information about the unknown woman, I think they'd bury any other clues that might've been inadvertently left lying around." She was pretty certain the miniature, if it *was* a clue, had been overlooked because it was so small and part of a jumble of other objects.

Aodhan's eyes remained golden, reflecting all the metallic surfaces here. Like glittering fire. And again, she remembered Illium's words about people wanting to own Aodhan. "Give me a minute," he murmured. "Any case such as this will have an official way to open it so the archivist can rearrange the objects within."

Though it almost physically hurt her to do so, Elena wandered away from the case to look at a collection of gold-handled hand mirrors that Aodhan pointed out to her. If anyone was watching them, it'd appear as if she'd gone from one fascinating object to another. Nothing unusual. And lingering on this level could hardly be unexpected—it was a room designed to captivate.

The tiny hairs on her nape prickled the entire time, her skin tight, so when Aodhan spoke her name softly, she nearly burst apart. Turning with deliberate laziness, she strolled over to him. "Success?"

"I need a very thin blade, the thinnest you have, with the narrowest tip."

Mahiya, Elena thought, *I owe you one.*

Reaching up to the hair she'd twisted into a roll at the back of her head, she removed one of the blade sticks. She was careful to keep the movements ordinary, everyday, nothing but a woman fixing her hair. Palming the blade stick while appearing to slide it back in, she passed it over to Aodhan by placing it on the very edge of the case, near the thick metal rim. Then she turned and, blocking the case and Aodhan's hands with her wings, pointed out the carvings on the bottom of the staircase to this level.

"Look at that." She didn't have to pretend wonder. "They've utilized every surface." Because the carvings weren't on the area, they were attached to it.

A slight movement against her wings, as if the case was being lifted up . . . just as a pair of large wings was silhouetted against the lights of the chandeliers above. A gust of wind hit her face as one of the Luminata came to a hard, firm landing on the floor.

Folding back wings of dark gray scattered with feathers of white dotted with gray, the heavyset male with pale skin tanned to light gold looked more than a little abashed. "My apologies." He bowed from the chest, his thickly silver hair falling over a face that appeared no older than her own. "I would not have landed so enthusiastically had I known others were present."

Elena forced a smile through her thundering heart. "This place does encourage enthusiastic landings," she said, stepping forward a little. "Aodhan and I landed there." She pointed to the far end of the starburst on the floor and the man's head swiveled in that direction as she'd hoped.

Elena couldn't glance back at Aodhan, check it was done. Instead, she went to the Luminata's side. "And," she said, "I'm pretty sure the tips of my right wing almost brushed one of the paintings. *Shh.*" A finger lifted to her lips.

The Luminata's dark gray eyes were warm when he met her gaze, his face not traditionally handsome in the angelic way, but compelling all the same. "You are truly unlike any consort I have ever met."

She tilted her head to one side. "Have you met many?" Currently, there were only two: Hannah and Elena.

A small nod. "I am as old as Lumia, I sometimes think. My hair is a family trait, but these days, it also tells the truth of my years on this earth." Tucking his hands into the wide sleeves of his robe as Ibrahim had done, he smiled. "But for once I am not the oldest in this place. Not with Caliane and Alexander in attendance."

A slight rustle announced Aodhan moving about, but he didn't speak and the Luminata didn't interrupt him. Likely out of respect for quiet contemplation of art. Lowering her voice, as if she, too was being respectful of Aodhan's apparent absorption in a piece, she made herself continue the conversation in spite of the clawing impatience in her gut. "*Were* you alive when Lumia was built?"

A gentle laugh, a shake of his head. "No, I am not that old. An exaggeration on my part earlier." He paused, lines fanning out from the corners of his eyes. "I was born in the same year as the Archangel Lijuan." He released a breath. "We were playmates once upon a time, though that time is shrouded in the hazy mists of memory."

Elena felt her eyes widen.

Intellectually, she knew Lijuan must've once been a child. Emotionally, however, it was difficult to accept that fact. "What was she like then?" she murmured and, when the Luminata's face gained a subtle tension, added, "It's just . . . I have difficulty imagining her as anything but the archangel she is now." Insane and power-hungry and terrifying in her delusions of godhood.

Her companion's expression softened, turning a little distant at the same time. "It was so long ago, Consort." His voice was lyrical, that of a storyteller. "I remember, she was a small girl. One of the smallest in our class. And so clever. A nimble mind."

Strangely, Elena could see that. No one could ever say that Lijuan was anything but fiercely intelligent. "Did you guess who she would one day become? I've heard people say Raphael burned with power from the instant he was born."

"Those people are right," the silver-haired Luminata confirmed, "but perhaps it is also true that he was watched far more closely for signs of power than other angelic babes for he was the child of two archangels." Dark gray eyes locked with Elena's, and unlike Ibrahim's innocent peace, they held a darker, older wisdom. "You must know, Consort, such a pairing is beyond rare—usually lasting only for a short period. Even rarer is a child born of that pairing."

"Jessamy told me." No one knew of any other child born to parents who were both archangels. Elena had even asked the Legion, received—for the Legion—an unusually straightforward answer: *He is the only one. His birth resonated through the world until we heard of it in our long sleep.*

"Ah, the Historian." Affection and respect in the Luminata's tone. "She does her vocation justice."

Together, the two of them walked to take in a small painting that was all white golds and intricate curves.

"I am Donael," he murmured. "My apologies for the tardy introduction. It is not often we meet new people in Lumia."

"I can imagine," Elena said, even as impatience screamed in her.

"In the outside world," Donael said, his eyes once more on the painting, "I knew the artist who created this. He was old even then, may have gone into Sleep now." A long pause before he spoke again. "Lijuan was like me, like all our other friends. Nothing in her indicated she would one day become an archangel. She wasn't precocious in any particular way—ah, I had forgotten that." He smiled. "I taught her to fly better. She was as wobbly as a baby bird."

"*That*," Elena said dryly, "I can't imagine no matter how hard I try."

A soft laugh. "But think of this, Consort—in ten thousand years, you will be tempered and strong and there will be young angels who cannot imagine you as a fledgling angel, and mortals who cannot comprehend that you were once one of them."

Elena just stared at him. "Damn, that's a scary thought." *Ten thousand years.* Hell. Who would she become in ten thousand years?

"I do not think you need to fear the future," was Donael's response. "You will never walk the path alone."

"No, you're right." Her archangel would always be by her side; he'd pull her back if she faltered and she'd do the same for him. "Who walks with the Luminata?"

"We are brothers but each path is unique." Donael's smile was beatific, no hint that he found his choice lonely. "Will you contemplate this part of the Gallery today?"

Unclenching her gut with conscious effort, Elena could no longer fight her urgency. "No, I'm afraid I have to run—I promised to spend time with Xander and Hannah and I've been down here all this time. Will I see you again?"

The Luminata seemed pleased to be asked. "I will make myself known. I hope you do not think me presumptuous, Consort, but it gives me pleasure to speak to someone so very young. You are not scarred with life."

Elena felt her face set itself into harsh lines, the response one she couldn't control. "A false impression," she said, her mind filled with the drip, drip sound of blood falling to the floor from Belle's mutilated body. "We are all scarred by life. And mortals die where angels recover."

A moment of heavy silence before Donael released a long breath. "I am foolish. A mortal lives an immortal lifetime in a mere century or less. That their scars are quicker to form makes those scars no less painful."

No, Elena thought. It didn't. Angry at this man for stirring up the nightmare that lived always inside her, she nonetheless knew his opinion was hardly an isolated one. Most older immortals simply didn't "see" mortals.

She dug up a more pleasant expression because at least Donael was willing to accept that he might be wrong. "I look forward to speaking with you again." Joining Aodhan on those words, she said, "I'm going up to see if Xander's arrived. Do you want to come?"

His nod was immediate. "I think I have drunk up too much of this room. I must clear my senses to fully appreciate it once more."

As he spread his wings, Elena thought about doing a vertical takeoff, realized she'd be weakening herself for no reason. "We could take the stairs for a few flights," she suggested. "It'll let us look a little at the galleries we winged past on our way down."

Aodhan closed his wings in silent agreement, then the two of them walked to the stairs, while Donael appeared lost in artistic reflection. But when she looked down two flights of stairs later, she saw him looking up, as if attempting to track her passage.

Chills rippled over her skin, goose bumps appearing on her arms.

22

"Do you know anything about Donael?" she asked Aodhan after another flight. "He said he's the same age as Lijuan."

"Yes," Aodhan murmured. "I know only because . . . I was told once." He added nothing to that for almost a minute and she didn't have to guess hard to realize it was Remus who must've whispered the knowledge to him while trying to break him.

"I was told of an angel many millennia old who held enough power to be *the* Luminata," he said at last. "And not only that, an angel who was far enough along on the path to luminescence that he was held in awe by the others."

Elena wasn't so sure about the latter. Donael had seemed confident and serene in his choice to be Luminata, but she'd felt nothing otherworldly around him. "So how come Gian's the head guy?"

"Because Gian is better at playing politics." Aodhan's tone held an unfamiliar bite of cynicism. "Even in this place meant for finding the deepest truths of existence, such manipulation can turn men's minds."

"Yep, I can see that." She peered over the edge of the hanging staircase, no railing to stop her, but Donael was too far away to

glimpse now. "A man who's lived that long," she said after drawing back, "is probably very good at controlling his expressions."

"Yes. I wouldn't trust your senses with him or any of the
Luminata."

Elena nodded. She might only be a "baby" angel, but she'd
learned lessons in her mortal life that stood her in good stead
in the immortal world. One of those lessons was that, sometimes, the worst dangers wore a pretty or "trustworthy" face.
Slater Patalis had been as handsome as sin.

Chest tight as they went up another flight, she said, "So?"

Aodhan's only response was a slight nod.

Exhaling in a rush, Elena spread her wings. "Okay, I've
had enough stair climbing." From this height and configur-
ation of exhibit levels and staircases, she could drop down
then wing her way back up, making it appear as if she was
simply taking in a lower level before flying up.

Aodhan waited for her to spread her wings and fall before
he followed. He'd clearly figured out what she planned to do,
mimicked her exactly—as if, as her escort, he'd been warned
of her intent. They winged up beat by beat, no air currents
here to ride. Reaching the exhibit where they'd originally
found Hannah, they saw she was still there, only on the other
side of the staircase.

Xander stood next to her, Valerius having taken a seat on a
beautifully carved wooden bench not far away. It was clearly
meant to offer a place from where to contemplate a particular
piece of art, but the general was currently polishing his sword,
which he usually wore across his back.

Cristiano was seated on the ground, playing a knife through
his hands as he chatted to Valerius.

Elena felt her lips tug up at the corners. Yeah, she could
only take so much of museums and galleries, too. "Xander,"
she said as she walked closer. "You enjoying the Gallery?"

The young male flushed a little, reminding her once again
of Izak. "I'm afraid I am more fond of the physical arts." He
turned red almost as soon as the words were out.

It took her a moment to figure out why.

Laughing, she patted him on the arm. "Don't worry, kid, in
this company, we understand you were talking about knives
and swords and fists." Michaela, on the other hand, would've

probably eaten him alive for that slip. "Even Hannah has her specialty weapon."

"My paint knives," Hannah said proudly. "I can sever a jugular with one now."

Xander stared at the elegantly gowned woman as if she'd grown another head. "But you're a consort."

Scowling, Hannah waved a slender hand at Elena. "So is she."

"Yes. But she was a hunter first. You were an artist."

Elena just pointed at Aodhan, renowned for his artistry and the fact he was a warrior both.

Swallowing, Xander nodded. "I meant no offense."

So young, Elena thought, struck once again by how a being could live a hundred years and still be a youth. Angelkind, she'd come to learn, developed at a different pace, children remaining children for decades, their brains and bodies maturing in line with the eternity they were intended to survive.

Sweet Sameon, whom she'd met soon after waking and with whom she talked at least once a week, was still much the same little boy though several years had passed. It would take up to ten years for him to show distinct development. It made Elena an anomaly that she'd lived less than any angelic youth, and yet was very much an adult.

Human lives burned hotter, faster.

"None taken," Aodhan said, as Hannah added, "In truth, a few years ago, you would've been right—I didn't believe I needed weapons. But"—sadness a heavy note in her voice—"the world is changing." She reached out to touch her fingers to one of Xander's hands, her nails painted a translucent shade that caught the light. "You know that better than anyone."

Xander glanced away, blinking rapidly.

Elena felt for him. He'd lost his mom and dad in a single strike. That he'd discovered his grandfather was awake might cushion that loss, but not enough, never enough. Some hurts were forever.

Leaving him to get himself under control because pride was pride and grief didn't always need an audience, she moved to stand next to Hannah. "What are you looking at now?"

"An illustrated manuscript." She traced the beauty of the graceful script through the glass. "Stunning, is it not?"

"Hmm. I've seen better."

Hannah glared at her. "When will I get to see the Grimoire?"

"When you go to the Refuge." The only reason Elena had seen the ancient book Naasir had found for Andromeda was because the couple had come to New York a year earlier. Normally, the Grimoire lay in Jessamy's keeping at the Refuge Library, but as the one who'd unearthed it, Naasir had exerted his right to travel with it.

According to him, he'd had to "fight" Jessamy for it, in the end resorting to stealing it out from under her nose and leaving a note in its place promising its return.

Jessamy had threatened to strangle Naasir.

He'd just looked smug and pointed out it was Andromeda's Grimoire, on loan to the Library. Andi, in turn, had told him to behave, though she'd been laughing at the time. The memory of Naasir's unrepentant smugness—and of the possessive, wild kiss he'd taken from Andi, leaving his mate breathless—had Elena grinning despite the tension in her gut.

"Hey"—she nudged Hannah's shoulder with her own when her friend pretended to ignore her—"at least it's not entombed in Lumia, accessible to only the rarest of the rare." With the corner of her eye, she noticed Aodhan speaking to Xander, saw that the young male was paying attention.

Valerius stayed in his seat, his attention apparently on his sword, but Elena had no doubt he was aware of every possible threat in the room. Those eyes missed nothing.

Cristiano appeared more lax, but Elena had come to know the vampire during her friendship with Hannah, knew he was as dangerous as Aodhan. The man might give off a lazy vibe, might've once told her he liked nothing more than sunning himself like a cat, but he could move lightning fast when necessary.

"Yes." Hannah glanced around, grooves forming around her mouth. "I appreciate the idea behind the Gallery. So many of our people's treasures would've been lost or damaged without the stewardship of the Luminata, but I cannot agree with the limited nature of access to it."

The jeweled pins in the elaborate bun in which she wore her hair caught the light, sparkling in beautiful shatters. "When I create works of art, I do it because it is part of me and I *must* create. But afterward, when the work is done, I hope that it'll speak to people, that it'll open up their hearts or their minds. That cannot happen if the art is buried for safekeeping."

"It's a kind of hoarding, don't you think?" Elena murmured. "The Luminata renounce sex, worldly possessions, all that, but they have this archive of treasures that belongs to them."

"It belongs to all angelkind."

"Lip service, Hannah." Elena glanced down at the exhibits all but empty of life below them. "If a random, nonpowerful angel rocked up and asked to enter the Gallery, do you think he or she would be admitted?"

Hannah bit down on the lush curve of her lower lip, but despite the hesitant act, she was very much a consort in that instant. Contained and graceful, and with a spine that held a pure, unbreakable strength. "I want to think so, Ellie," she said softly, "but being here, feeling the pulse of this place. It is . . . not right."

"Secrets have a way of rotting foundations when those foundations are meant to be built on truth and honor." Her gaze wanted to go to Aodhan, her soul itching to look at the miniature he'd retrieved.

Forcing patience, she kept her attention on Hannah. "You ready to leave, get some air?"

The other woman looked torn. "An oddness to the air or not, there is so much here for me to see. I do not know when Elijah and I will be able to return, not with the upheaval in the world." She put her fingers to the glass again. "Will you be very angry if I stay?"

"Of course not. This is your jam."

Hannah sighed. "I will be a very bad friend this trip, I'm afraid."

"I'd be the same if you threw me into a room full of weapons across the ages." She frowned. "Speaking of which, where are the weapons? I know for a fact that at least one of Deacon's pieces was never used, but was commissioned to be displayed for its artistry." Her best friend's husband might be mortal, but his skill was revered by vampires and angels as well as humans. If he hadn't been so loyal to the Guild, he could've worked only for the immortals and wallpapered his home with money.

As it was, the Guild's hunters always came first for Deacon—hunters, he said when queried about his choice, needed their weapons to stay alive. He'd repair those weapons, create new ones when needed, then work on pieces for immortals. First the weapons meant to be used in combat. Last came the commissioned "art" pieces, or ones he guessed were meant to be displayed.

"I build my weapons to be used, not to be kept shiny and clean and under glass," he'd said to her the last time she'd been over at their place for dinner. "I only do the odd show-piece because it means the immortal involved owes me a favor— which means he or she owes Sara a favor."

And the head of the Hunters Guild did occasionally need to call in those markers.

Raphael had gone with her to that dinner, had nodded at Deacon's reasoning. The two men had become friends of a kind over the past two years. Not the type of friendship Raphael shared with his Seven—it was too soon for that—but one that wasn't simply a surface acquaintance. They'd been forced into contact because of Elena and Sara's relationship— after Elena declared that the Archangel of New York would henceforth be attending all social events to which she was invited.

That had caused a certain ripple.

The funniest had been the day she landed at Guild Academy for a party and Raphael landed beside her. Everyone's jaws had dropped. The sole person who'd bet that Raphael would turn up that night—Ransom—had made a killing. Of course, her archangel hadn't stayed long, aware that his sheer power altered the balance of the situation, put everyone on edge.

It was different with Deacon and Sara: though they, too, felt the impact of his power, they weren't in awe of him, saw him first as Elena's man. Everything else, even the fact he ruled North America, came second.

"It is as when I met Dmitri," Raphael had said to her after

their third dinner with the other couple. "I knew I had met a friend and it made sorrow fill my veins to know that he would be gone in a mere heartbeat."

Except Dmitri had been Made a vampire against his will, while Deacon was content to live a mortal life. Elena knew because she'd asked both her best friend and Sara's husband if they wanted to be tested to see if they could become vampires. Not everyone had the right biology for it. Beth didn't.

Sara had hugged her, smiled, then shaken her head. "We're happy to be mortal, Ellie."

Her hug had held a fierce love; Sara understood that Elena was terrified of the day when Sara would no longer be there. The other woman had made Elena see that her own life was as dangerous, that it was possible Sara would outlive her, but what nothing could change was that Elena was becoming ever more immortal and her best friend, her sister of the heart, wasn't.

As for Sara and Deacon's daughter, Zoe, she adored Raphael, had no fear of him.

Elena had noticed that about her archangel. He terrified adults, but children gravitated toward him, tiny hands patting at his wings, small faces smiling up at him. He'd been known to take Zoe into his arms and fly so high that Sara complained of heart palpitations. But Raphael always returned Zoe safe and sound and so excited she couldn't stop dancing.

"Perhaps the weapons are displayed in a different area?" Hannah's voice broke into her thoughts, had her lost for a second until she remembered that she'd asked about a weapons exhibit.

"Maybe," she replied. "I'll ask Gian the next time I see him." It would give her an excuse to talk further to the Luminata. He was the key to the secrets of Lumia.

23

Ten minutes later, she, Aodhan, Xander, and Valerius were in the skies above Lumia, the miniature still with Aodhan. Elena wanted to scream with impatience but she kept it together. This was a normal thing for warriors to do when trapped in a place where they had few other outlets—fly, stay strong, get some exercise. And she had to be normal right now, because people were watching.

Could be it was paranoia on her part, but she didn't think so: people *were* watching.

Always.

Beside her, Xander did an acrobatic flip that had her clapping. "Almost as good as Bluebell," she called out.

He grinned, handsome and cocky. "Illium is famous for his skills."

Together, the four of them flew for about an hour, and at one point, she was aware of Aodhan and Valerius flying wing to wing, discussing something. It wasn't until they'd landed in a large courtyard that Aodhan came to her. Bending to speak with his lips close to her ear, his breath warm against her skin, he said, "Valerius believes Xander is being monitored."

"Why?" Yes, he was Alexander's grandson, but surely no

one was idiotic enough to think to go after him? Alexander had kept his sanity after losing his son, but he'd raze the world in a rage if he lost his grandson.

"Likely the same reason we are being monitored," Aodhan replied, his jaw a grim line. "I want to examine your and Raphael's quarters again."

Elena nodded. "I still get the creeps if I step into the bedroom to retrieve stuff from the wardrobe."

"Consort." Xander bowed in front of her, the movement unexpectedly elegant. "Would you and Aodhan do me and General Valerius the honor of accompanying us for lunch?"

"Only if you promise to call me Elena."

His pupils dilated to fill his irises, even as a shy delight warmed his skin from within. "Thank you, but my grandfather would be displeased."

Elena sighed. "Guild Hunter, then."

"Guild Hunter," he said with a smile.

"Let's go grab lunch." She was starving after missing breakfast.

That lunch was laid out for them on the large dining table in the Atrium. The only other person in the cavernous room right now was Riker, Michaela's pet vampire propping up the wall beside the inner chamber. Waiting for his mistress.

Elena had a feeling he'd been here since Michaela went in.

Ignoring him when he blew her a kiss, she took in the room in daylight. She'd noticed the glass dome of the ceiling last night, now saw the glass was carved with complex patterns that scattered sunshine on the walls of the room, turning the stone into a living artwork that would change throughout the day.

"Wow," she said. "I might not have artistry in my veins, but even I know that's incredible work."

Aodhan was also staring rapt at the walls. "This is one of Ophelia's pieces. She was renowned for her light work."

"She Asleep?"

"I don't know," Aodhan said. "She was long gone from the world by the time of my birth, only her art left behind to tell us of her gift."

A groan of sound, the large doors of the inner chamber opening.

188 Nalini Singh

The first to exit was Michaela, a cruel kind of amusement writ large on her features. She was wearing a bodysuit in deepest red, with a skirt of the same color that had a large split along one thigh that revealed her boot-clad leg with every step. Giving the table straining with food a disdainful glance and not even bothering to sharpen her verbal knives on Elena, she walked straight to the other door and out.

Riker followed at her heels.

Astaad exited next, followed Michaela out. His expression was more pained than anything, his fingers rubbing his temples as if to ease a headache.

Other archangels left the inner chamber one by one and they all, each and every one, headed out of the Atrium. Elena didn't blame them—she'd have searched for clear air, too, if she'd been trapped inside half the day.

Raphael emerged after Titus, Elijah at his side.

Archangel, she said. *You want to fly?* Then she noticed that his wings weren't solid anymore. *Did that happen in the meeting?*

No, just now. He spread them, to gasps from those who'd never before seen those wings of white fire.

Even Elijah looked impressed.

Caliane and Alexander exited as Raphael closed his wings. Caliane's face went white for an instant. Whatever she said to Raphael, it wasn't audible, and then Raphael was turning to say something to her in return, his head leaning toward her own.

Mother and son, Elena thought, that's who they are at this instant, not archangel and Ancient.

Walking around them, Alexander went straight to Valerius and Xander. "Come," he said. "I need fresh air."

Elijah was the next to pass. "I assume my consort is in the Gallery?" he said, the power of him shoving against Elena's senses.

Sometimes, she wondered how Hannah could possibly be with someone so *other*, then she'd realize Raphael was exactly the same. "You guess right."

"No, you do not, Eli." Hannah's gentle voice from behind them, a smile in her tone. "I was hoping the Cadre would set itself free for a break at midday." Placing her hands on her consort's chest, she rose on tiptoe and brushed her lips over his.

They were astonishingly beautiful together, Elijah's golden hair glinting in the sunlight that came in through the dome and the sharply handsome lines of his face looking down into Hannah's, her skin glowing with life and her elegance innate, her eyes a luminous dark. What made it even more beautiful were the small smiles on their faces, the smiles of two people who had loved one another so long that they needed to make no big declarations.

"I will paint them," Aodhan whispered to Elena. "Just like this, with the light from Ophelia's work scattering a filigree over their bodies and Eli's wings unfolding unconsciously as if to curve around Hannah."

"Ah, you must love me then, Hannahbelle." Elijah's smile grew deeper, the golden brown of his eyes as luminous as his consort's. "To have torn yourself away from the art of which you've been speaking since the instant we heard of this meeting."

Hannah's response was silent, but whatever she said, it made Elijah laugh and slide one hand to her lower back as they walked out, Cristiano joining them at the door.

"Hannahbelle?" she asked her archangel when he came to stand in front of her, Caliane moving past him to meet Tasha, who'd just arrived.

"I have never heard anyone call her that," Raphael said. *But I have never heard anyone else call you Elena-mine either,* hbeebti.

You have a point. It delighted her that even after all these centuries, Hannah and Elijah could play with one another. *Is your mom okay?* She hadn't looked okay.

Raphael's expression was difficult to read. *Seeing my wings ignited a memory of pain. My father—he died in a blaze of fire.*

Yeah, about that. She shot a glance at Tasha. *Can you reach Tasha with your mind?*

Raphael raised an eyebrow. *I am an archangel.*

Elena didn't tease him like she usually did—there was an edginess in his tone that said he was at the end of his patience. Not with her, with whatever had been going on in the meeting chamber. *Tell Tasha to make sure she doesn't take your mother down a particular path if they go to visit the Gallery. Aodhan can give you the exact mental map—there's a painting of Nadiel's death there.*

Raphael's features grew hard and cold. *If there is, the Luminata should've covered it as a mark of respect.* His eyes locked with Aodhan's, then seconds later, he looked toward Tasha.

It was only because Elena was watching her that she noticed the very slight jerk of Tasha's shoulders. Caliane was facing away from them, her attention on something Tasha was saying, and didn't seem to notice. Looking back at Elena, Raphael cupped her cheek. *Thank you for caring for my mother's heart, Elena. Even to the extent of asking me to speak with Tasha.*

"Come on, Archangel, I think you need some air."

"Sire, she has only eaten two energy bars today."

Elena's jaw fell open. Swiveling to face Aodhan, she said, "Did you just nark on me?"

A small smile, hidden laughter. "It won't take you long to refuel if you choose high-energy items."

"*Elena.*" Hauling her to the table on that growl of sound, Raphael picked up a tray of meat and handed it to her. "Eat."

"Ugh." She put the tray down, grabbed a plate, and began to fill it up with her own choices. "If you two are going to stand there and loom, it'll give me indigestion. Eat something."

They did, though most of their attention was on making sure her plate was never empty. Feeling as if she'd put on ten pounds by the time she couldn't take anymore, she groaned and leaned against Raphael as they headed out. "I will definitely need a boost to get into the air."

"That, *hbeebti*, is never a hardship."

They were in the sky soon afterward, Aodhan beside them and Elena's gown zipped up once again. After releasing Elena, Raphael flew high—and in a direction where there were no other wings. Most of the archangels had to have taken off, but the majority were no longer anywhere in sight, though she could see glints of Alexander's silver, and Michaela's bronze.

She, Raphael, and Aodhan aimed for the mountain where

she and Raphael had landed the previous night. When she began to tire, she and Aodhan landed on the mountaintop to wait for Raphael to burn off his energy. She couldn't even see him now, he'd gone so high, but she could feel him. About to ask Aodhan for the miniature—*finally!*—something made her glance up.

Just in time to go flat on the ground with a yell as Raphael skimmed over her and Aodhan's heads, having dropped silently at a speed she couldn't even imagine. "Raphael!" she yelled when she scrambled up, a shocked-appearing Aodhan still seated on the ground in front of her. *Come down here right now, Archangel!*

Raphael landed in a glory of wings of white fire. "I was testing my speed."

"No, you weren't." Folding her arms, she tapped her foot. "You were dive-bombing us. Admit it."

Smile heartbreaking, he pushed back his hair and walked over to hold out a hand to Aodhan. The angel took it without hesitation, allowed Raphael to pull him up. "Have you been possessed by Illium, sire?" he asked in a disbelieving tone.

"He did seem to be having a lot of fun, so I decided to try it." Dropping Aodhan's hand, Raphael thrust his own hand into Elena's hair, sending her remaining blade sticks to the earth, and brought his mouth down on top of hers.

Her body sighed, her blood heated, and she had the tip of a blade to his throat even as his tongue licked over hers. Ignoring it, his lips still curved over hers, he just kissed her deeper. And since she had zero defenses against him when he got like this, she slid away the blade and took the kiss. She'd seen him at dawn but it felt as if she'd been missing him forever.

Breathless when he finally released her, she tried to muster up a scowl. "You got my gown all dusty."

"I'll brush off the dust." He ran a hand over her breast, down to the curve of her hip, the action protected from view by the way he'd curved his wings around them.

Her toes curled. "You were faster than fast," she said as he folded back his wings. "I didn't even feel the whistle of wind passing over your wings." Glancing at where Aodhan stood some distance away, giving them privacy and watching out for threats, she called out, "Aodhan! Did you have any idea Raphael was heading for us?"

Shaking his head, Aodhan made his way back to them through the golden grass. "Your wings are of pure silence."

"One hell of an advantage." Elena reached out to play her fingers through the white fire of them—they did feel solid in a sense, but there were no feathers. It didn't burn, was cool to the touch, and . . . "It tastes of you." Like the crashing sea and the wild wind and power that tasted of *life*.

Fingers still in her hair, Raphael shook his head. "It tastes of us."

Her eyes widened before she nodded. "Yes." The wildfire that lived in him, it was formed of both of them, a strange alchemy no one who knew could understand. "I don't think Lijuan could hurt your wings if these were your wings during a battle."

"An intriguing idea, but unfortunately, I can't control when they come and go." His jaw tensed. "Lijuan is far ahead of me in that sense, appears to be able to take her noncorporeal form at will."

Elena clenched her stomach, Aodhan going motionless beside them.

"The Cadre has decided that Zhou Lijuan is alive?" he asked.

Raphael shook his head. "We have decided nothing." It was a gritted-out statement. "The answers are all there, hashed out in the first ten minutes. Favashi to take over Lijuan's territory with Caliane offering assistance. But we must have consensus for this decision and Charisemnon is refusing to budge. He insists we leave Lijuan to run her territory as she sees fit."

Elena bared her teeth; she wanted to stab the Archangel of Northern Africa in the eyes.

"Unfortunately," Raphael said, moving his hand to curve it around the side of her neck, "we cannot cut off his head and just vote on his behalf until it grows back, or one of us may have tried it by now."

"Is Charisemnon the only holdout?" She began to run her hand on the underside of his fiery wings.

A long exhale before Raphael said, "He is the most recalcitrant. Astaad continues to struggle with interfering in another archangel's territory but is unwilling to let things go on as they are, especially given Jason's information."

His Legion mark sparked with white fire, glowing bright for a second, and when the mark settled, Elena felt feathers under her touch. His wings were once more white gold, but the left wing bore an astonishing scar of darker gold created when she shot him back during what might've been the scariest moment of her life.

He'd bled so much, this man who wasn't supposed to be able to be hurt.

"Enough about that." Tugging her close, he pressed a kiss to her temple. "Did you two discover anything?"

Elena forgot all about Lijuan and bloodlust and stabbing out Charisemnon's eyes. "Aodhan."

Reaching under the straps that crisscrossed his chest over his leathers, providing a brace for the double sword sheaths he wore on his back, Aodhan pulled out first the blade stick he'd borrowed, then the miniature. He held on to the former, putting the latter on the open hand she held out.

24

How could anyone have painted Elena so quickly?

An instant after the question passed through Raphael's mind, he realized the woman in the miniature wasn't Elena. Her eyes were a shimmering turquoise, her skin a darker gold than Elena's. Her face, too, was narrower, more hawk than hunter. None of it took away from her startling beauty—or her startling resemblance to Raphael's warrior.

"I think we can safely say that you are on the right track, Elena-mine."

Hand trembling, Elena stared at the tiny canvas.

"If I may, Ellie." Reaching for the miniature, Aodhan took it, turned it over, then lifted the blade stick with his other hand.

"Don't damage it," Elena cried out.

"I promise, I won't. But sometimes, the artists will write of the subjects on the backs of these miniature pieces."

A very careful insertion of the tip of the blade stick, an expert lift . . . and Aodhan had separated the miniature from the frame. Frowning, he looked down at the tiny writing on the back. "Majda," he said. "I think that's what it says."

Raphael took the miniature, looked at the writing; it was in the same text Elena had seen in the Gallery. "Yes."

Elena blew out a breath. "That doesn't sound anything like Elena." Folding her arms, she watched as Aodhan put frame and image back together. "My mother told me that my grandmother's nickname was Elena."

"There is apt to be more to her name," Raphael said as she nodded at Aodhan to hold on to the miniature, her dress not having many hiding places. "With this name and the initial *E* that your mother remembered being on her baby blanket, you have avenues of investigation beyond Lumia—starting with the closest township."

Looking out at the distant stronghold, she threw her gaze even farther forward, but the town that existed beyond the border wasn't visible. "I'm not sure I want Aodhan and I to be that far from you while the Cadre is in session." No matter her hunger to dig up the truth of her ancestry, leaving him without backup wasn't an option.

"If there is to be a battle among the Cadre, Guild Hunter, I would rather you not be anywhere in the vicinity. Remember Beijing."

The city no longer existed. The smoke was long gone but the crater remained a brutal scar on the landscape—and some said there were parts of it that were hot to the touch to this day. Elena wasn't sure whether to believe those reports or not, because most people stayed far, *far* away from the evidence of what could happen when archangels fought one another.

"Being in the town won't protect me from that kind of battle," she said bluntly. *And my only fear is losing you.*

Raphael closed his hand over hers while Aodhan once more stepped away to offer them privacy. "If you keep your movements erratic, it protects you."

She couldn't argue with that. Wandering Lumia's endless hallways was a good way to get trapped—and to distract Raphael with worry. He didn't need any distractions, not when he was crossing swords with the Cadre of Ten.

"Maybe this afternoon," she said, "Aodhan and I can go do a reconnaissance of the town, see if we can get a feel for it. Caliane and I aren't supposed to meet for our walk until the evening." She leaned into Raphael on the heels of her words, the heat of him a burn she craved. "Stay safe, Archangel."

"Do not fear, *hbeebti*." The Legion mark glittered in the sunlight as he pressed his forehead to her own. "I don't think anyone on the Cadre is keen for a repeat of Beijing." A pause. "Of course, if Lijuan decides to pay us a visit, then the end-game may be upon us."

Watching Raphael return to the inner chamber had her gut in knots, but Elena kept it together, a casual expression on her face as she forced herself to nibble a little further from the lunch spread. Might as well keep up with the fuel since her huge meal appeared to have digested at the speed of light.

"You were in an energy deficit," Raphael had said when she mentioned that. "Remember, each and every cell of your body is transforming from mortal to immortal. You are fast-forwarding through a process that takes an angelic babe at least a hundred years."

Put that way, was it any wonder she was eating like a bodybuilder?

Eyes on wings of white gold, she consumed nuts and dried fruit with mindless efficiency. Dried meat would probably be better, but Elena had her limits. A little jerky on the road? That she could deal with. Eating it piece by piece by piece? No thanks.

Then the doors to the inner chamber slammed shut with a portentous bang, sealing Raphael in with the rest of the Cadre once more.

He wasn't alone, she reminded herself. Along with the enemies, he had allies in there. And he was a freaking *archangel*.

"He is also the only one who has displayed an ability to keep Lijuan in check," Aodhan murmured to her, having clearly followed the path of her thoughts. "Self-interest alone should keep him from being attacked by the others. No one wants Lijuan free to cause mayhem."

"Except Charisemnon," she pointed out, once again ignoring Riker when the vampire tried to catch her eye.

"I'm no expert in Cadre politics," Aodhan said, "but I

believe the Archangel of Northern Africa has few friends in the Cadre. He went too far with the Falling."

"Coward." She crunched down on a bunch of nuts on that single word, reminding herself that every mouthful she ate was another step closer to true immortality. Her bones were getting stronger day by day, her tendons less difficult to snap, her skin harder to bruise.

Of course, it was all relative.

The vampire walking toward her was far stronger than her. "Elena," Riker said with a smile that was full of psychotic charm, the cedar and ice scent of him as incongruously beautiful as always. "Want to play?" He stepped close enough that their boots touched.

The swish of steel leaving a sheath. "Consort, would you like me to cut off his head?"

Aodhan's toneless question had Riker looking up with narrowed eyes, but whatever he saw in Aodhan's eyes had him paling before he gave her space. "I'm only being friendly."

She felt as if she were being covered with slick black oil with every word he spoke. It would've been easy to let Aodhan handle it, but she was a hunter and she was Raphael's consort. She hid from no one. "How's your heart these days?" she asked with a razor-sharp smile. "I haven't had a close look at it lately."

Hissing out a breath, his eyes hot red, Riker fisted his hands. She almost wished he'd say something that crossed the line so they *could* legitimately cut off his head and rid the world of his nastiness, but he just bared his fangs and said, "It's inside my ribcage, where it belongs."

"You should try to keep it there."

An unblinking stare before he turned on his heel and walked back to where he spent his time waiting for Michaela.

"I didn't know you could be scary enough to terrify genuine psychopaths," she said to Aodhan.

"Galen made me practice."

Shoulders shaking at the cool statement, she ate more of the damn nuts.

"Hungry, Elena?" Tasha's voice, the warrior angel strolling into the room to pick up a grape from the table and pop it into her mouth.

Elena was glad she hadn't taken a seat at the table. Being seated while Tasha stood would've irritated the hell out of her. "All this lounging around looking at art gets tiring."

Tasha watched her eat a piece of high-fat cheese. "Yes, Lumia is a little too peaceful for me, too." Shrugging her shoulders, she drew a sword from a thigh sheath and, moving away from the table, swung it through the air.

"Aodhan, will you spar with me later today? I need a little activity to relieve my boredom and Titus's Mau'lea has already made plans to train with Astaad's escort." A glance at Elena. "I know the sword is not your weapon of choice."

It wasn't, but Elena was learning. "That's a heavier blade than I would've expected you to favor." Yes, Tasha was stronger than her, but why go for a heavier blade when a lighter one would use up less strength and get the job done as well?

"It's what my trainer used," Tasha replied, sliding the sword back into its sheath. That sheath wasn't a decorative one—like Aodhan, Tasha was dressed as a warrior, dressed as Elena wished she could dress. "I suppose I became used to it and it is what feels right in my hand."

"If you two want to spar, I don't mind," she said to Aodhan and Tasha both. "Maybe I'll learn a few new tricks by watching."

Tasha's eyes narrowed. "I can't tell if you're being gracious, or if there's a little venom there."

Swallowing the last bite of a little quiche she'd picked up, Elena said, "Venom sinks into the blood and I don't want to end up like Michaela one day." No matter how much Tasha annoyed her, Elena wasn't going to waste her energy on unnecessary jealousy.

Raphael's heart was hers. If she ever lost it, it wouldn't be because of Tasha, but because something had gone catastrophically wrong between her and her archangel. She couldn't even imagine what that might be.

"I hate it when you make sense, Elena." Walking to the table, Tasha ate a few more grapes. "Aodhan?"

"Not today," he replied. "Perhaps tomorrow. Today, Ellie and I were planning to fly to the closest township, stretch our wings."

Elena frowned inwardly—why would Aodhan give away their plans?

Face brightening, Tasha said, "Do you mind if I join you? I swear I'll lose my mind if I have to wander one more hallway or speak to one more of these hooded men." A sneer. "All of them afraid of women and hiding it under the veneer of a 'brotherhood.'"

Damn it. There she went again, saying something that made Elena want to grin. "Sure, you can come," she said, since any other response would've been odd. "Maybe we should ask Xander and Valerius as well. I know Xander's definitely bored."

"I saw the boy in the nearest courtyard," Tasha said. "I'll go speak to him. When shall we meet?"

"I need to change," Elena said, having zero intention of exploring the town while in her Lumia getup. "Say, twenty minutes?"

"Done."

Elena waited to speak to Aodhan until they were away from the Atrium and headed to her and Raphael's suite. "Why did you tell her?"

He bent, spoke close to her ear, his breath whispering over her skin once more, the touch of his wing over hers almost familiar. "We may need to go to the town multiple times. It would be highly suspect if it is only the two of us who keep turning up. A group of bored escorts, on the other hand . . ."

Oh. "You're good at the sneaky stuff," she said approvingly.

"Jason made me practice that," he said in the same cool voice as earlier. "It took seventy-five years before he declared I'd be passable as a spy if I didn't glow in the dark."

Laughing so hard that her stomach hurt, Elena tried to see if he was joking. "Did they ever leave you alone?" she asked when she could speak again.

"No, no matter how hard I tried." A smile that held an ineffable joy. "They were always there, Ellie. Constantly hauling me back from the edge of the howling abyss." He swallowed. "Illium . . . he used to sneak into my house and leave art supplies everywhere, until what could I do but start using them or be buried in them."

Elena dared link her fingers to his for a second, felt her heart squeeze when he curled his own around hers. "We lucked out with the people who love us, didn't we, Aodhan?"

His answer was a smile that lit up even the secret-shadowed hallways of Lumia.

*   *   *

Tasha, Xander, and Valerius weren't the only ones waiting for them in the courtyard. Titus's escort, Mau'lea, was also there, as was Neha's general, Hiran.

It appeared everyone was ready for a field trip.

Seeing her and Aodhan, Tasha said, "Magnus has already left. He'll go overland, meet us in the town."

Magnus, she remembered, was the vampire Astaad had brought as his escort. The other man had arrived on a glossy black stallion he left to run wild, calling it back with a whistle when he needed a ride. Elena had no idea how they'd got the horse to Morocco—maybe the gorgeous creature was used to planes. "Cristiano?" she asked Tasha.

"He's going to stay with Hannah—she's still drinking up the Gallery."

Seconds later, they all spread their wings in preparation to rise, and then the sky was filled with wings as they took off one by one, careful to give one another space to get lift without the risk of tangling wings.

Elena waited right to the end, until only Aodhan was left. It would make it more difficult for the others in the sky to judge how much effort it took her to achieve a vertical takeoff. As for the Luminata, hopefully, since she stood in the center of the courtyard, they were far enough away not to catch any betraying nuances.

"Ellie, I can give you a boost."

She shook her head. "No, I've decided I want the Luminata to know I won't be easy prey." There was a time to play games of stealth, and there was a time to showcase your weapons so your enemies would think thrice over before considering any hostile action.

That the Luminata had done nothing threatening to this point didn't change the fact that her skin crawled with an awareness of danger every instant she was in this place. Keeping her face expressionless despite her emotions, she spread her wings, gathered her strength, and launched. The familiar strain pulled across her shoulders, made itself felt in her chest, sent sparks of sensation shooting down her back.

But then she was airborne and able to glide on an air

current while Aodhan came up to join her. "Go high, Aod-han," she said to him, her fitted black T-shirt sleek against the wind. "You'll be better able to keep an eye on things."

"I can't protect you if I'm too high."

"I can hold off anyone in this crew until you're here to back me up," she pointed out, patting the crossbow she'd strapped on over her jeans. "I'd rather have eyes above so you can monitor any strange movements."

So brilliant in the sunshine that it was hard to look at him, Aodhan nodded and then he was winging his way to the clouds, where he turned into a distant shatter of light, an inde-pendent piece of the sun.

The others had all scattered across a wide area, each one flying independently while staying with the wider group. When Neha's general fell back until he was next to Elena, she had to stop herself from checking that her gun remained within easy reach.

25

"Consort," said the black-haired angel with wings of dark sienna, the color one she'd seen on no other angel.

"General Hiran."

"I have instructions from General Rhys to ask after Mahiya," the male said, his expression impassive. "Is she content?"

Thinking back, Elena remembered that Mahiya had spoken warmly of Rhys and his wife. They'd never treated her badly. "Yes," she answered. "She's finding her wings." For the first time in her life, Mahiya was free to be exactly who she wanted to be and she was extraordinary.

"The spymaster treats her well?" Hiran gave a thin smile. "The question is General Rhys's—he says he knows it is not his right to ask such questions, but Mahiya has no father to watch over her."

No, her father had been Neha's consort and a useless waste of space from what Elena knew. "She has a very scary mother."

"Nivriti loves her, this I do not doubt," Hiran murmured thoughtfully, "but I think for Neha and Nivriti, they have ever been one another's most important relationship. Even in hate, they are forever bound."

It was an unexpected and insightful comment. Mahiya's mother and Neha were twins, but it wasn't that bond alone that bound them. It was centuries of emotion, of memory, of betrayal. Elena understood. The same mess of emotions bound her to her father. "Jason and Mahiya are very happy," she said, knowing she gave away no secrets.

What she didn't say was that the man known for his impenetrable darkness would do anything for his princess. *Anything.* It would've made the spymaster painfully vulnerable had Mahiya not possessed the exact same vulnerability. If Jason asked, Mahiya would carve out her own heart.

"I'm certain General Rhys will be pleased to hear that," Hiran said with enough warmth that she knew he respected the other man a great deal. "His heartmate, Brigitte, has sent a gift for Mahiya." A pause. "With the cool relationship between your consort and my lady, they have felt disloyal in reaching out to Mahiya, but they could not let this opportunity pass. It would be a great favor if you could take their gift to her."

"I can do that," Elena said, knowing she'd also go through the gift with a fine-tooth comb. No way in hell would she take anything back to Mahiya that had the potential to hurt her.

"I will get it to you before it is time to leave Lumia." Hiran inclined his head in a polite good-bye and then he was sweeping away, his wings beating powerfully as he caught up to Valerius.

Xander, meanwhile, was flying far below, skimming close over the golden landscape of this sunlit land, the gold filaments in his wings and the silver on the underside afire as he dipped this way and that with youthful exuberance.

Reminded of Izzy and Illium both, Elena dropped to his altitude. "What's so interesting?" she called out when she was close enough.

"There are animals below!" he yelled back. "Goats perched on such narrow ledges that I can't believe they aren't falling off!"

Elena joined him in goat-spotting. Not an activity she'd ever before considered. This was definitely not New York. But it kept them both amused—and Xander was right: some of those goats had to have glue on the bottoms of their hooves or something. The landscape below wasn't particularly hilly, but the hills that did exist were steep and devoid of heavy foliage.

"Magnus!"

The lion-maned rider below them looked up at Xander's cry and waved a hand before going down low over the neck of his black stallion again, a man clearly at home with that means of transport though he lived in an area where it wasn't exactly common. But angels and vampires, as she'd learned, had long histories.

Magnus could well have been born in a landscape filled with horses.

When she, Xander, and the others eventually passed over Lumia's walled border, the aerial guard dipped its wings but didn't get in their way.

The first thing she noticed was the lack of any guards without wings—vampires need not apply to Lumia in any capacity apparently, not even as guards. The second thing was the sheer size of the defensive squadron—and what she was seeing was only the part of the force assigned to this section of the border.

Raphael, do you know Lumia has an army of its own? She didn't have the strength to "send" that far, but Raphael could hear her from great distances.

The crisp bite of the wind sliced through her mind an instant later. *How big?*

This is only an estimate, Elena said, then gave him the numbers.

Interesting. Raphael's tone was cool—not Archangel cool but thoughtful cool. *Lumia has always had a guard complement fed by volunteers from all of the archangelic territories. Unless one of the others in the Cadre has seconded large numbers of people here, the Luminata must have recruited beyond the volunteers.*

Elena twisted her lips. *I can't see any of the archangels weakening their defenses to supply a heavy guard to men who are meant to be a bunch of monks.*

It could be that these monks are no longer neutral and are providing a service to an archangel, Raphael pointed out. *I've asked Aodhan to keep a sharp lookout on your return, see if he can identify any of the angels in the squadron.*

See what you can discover in the town, he added. *If the angels and vampires who live there are aggressive, it may be an overreaction or posturing on Lumia's part. I, meanwhile, will attempt to keep from killing Charisemnon.*

That last didn't sound like a joke. *What's happened?*

Nothing. But I look at him and I see Stavre.

The youngest angel to have died in the Falling, his funeral bier covered with flowers placed there by his warrior brethren. *We'll kill the evil bastard one day*, she said. *Better yet, I like to imagine his disease-causing power turning back on him again, but this time in a slow, tortuous, but eventually fatal fashion. Don't give him your energy.*

Wise advice from my consort. I shall attempt to follow it.

Blowing him a mental kiss, Elena winged to a slightly higher altitude as the first buildings came into view on the horizon, a hive of life in the midst of an otherwise arid landscape. Interestingly, nothing appeared much over two stories high—angels tended to go up when they built, though low dwellings weren't unheard of depending on the weather and topology of an area. Lumia itself was gracefully low to the earth—though it did sit on a rise—so maybe that had influenced the architecture of the town.

Elena wanted to get an overview of the place before she landed, see how big an area it covered, guesstimate how many people she'd be dealing with in her hunt to unearth the identity of the woman in the miniature. For all she knew, that miniature had been painted centuries ago and no one would have the faintest clue, but she had to try.

The homes on the edge of town were very small and colored in earth tones, blending into the landscape. Then came the fruit trees—fig and orange maybe—followed by the shocking green of fields planted with vegetables and irrigated against the harsh sun and dry environment. Cows looked up placidly at the shadow of wings passing overhead and children pelted to their homes.

Elena frowned.

Kids ran under angelic shadows in New York, too, especially in Central Park, but they always tried to *follow* the wings, not divert away from them. Could be Raphael was right and the angels who lived in the town were aggressive and

violent. Not that she could see any of them; the only wings in
the sky were of her group.

Trees and houses broke up the patches of lush green. The
farms were small, each field easily traversable on foot. The
deeper they flew into the town, the more the houses began to
cluster together, the greenery coming in smaller patches that
were probably private gardens. Earth tones permeated
throughout.

No mansions. No railingless balconies that she could spot.
Nothing beyond the two stories she'd already noted. A few flat
roofs that could be used as landing spots, but the people she
spotted on them had no wings.

More and more of the town's denizens began to come into
view, some seated under the shadows of trees, others going
about their business with their faces covered by colorful
scarves. Those scarves were necessary under the merciless
heat of the sun. Elena had thrust one into a side pocket when
she and Aodhan swung by the suite earlier; it was a bright
purple thing with silvery threads in it that she'd picked up on
her last trip to Morocco.

In flight, the wind cooled the sun's kiss and any damage
was quickly repaired by the immortal ability to heal such
small surface wounds, but on the ground, the heat could be
punishing. Those of the Lumia group who hadn't thought to
bring scarves would probably make a few of the local traders
very happy very soon.

The town's central marketplace appeared below them not
long afterward.

Elena had traveled the world as a hunter. Bustling market-
places were one of her favorite parts of any city or village,
whether that marketplace was an open air one on a small trop-
ical island, only a tin roof keeping off the afternoon rains
while people haggled, or one situated in the narrow maze of
streets that was often the center of an old city.

Strip malls didn't have the same impact, though Times
Square did.

It was the unpredictability she enjoyed, the not knowing
what stall or store she'd find around the corner or what random
sights she'd see. Like the time she'd seen silk threads being
colored and stretched along a wall, or when she'd walked into

a small café in an old city and found herself in a Michelin-starred establishment. Then there was that G-string-wearing woman in Times Square.

Nothing too unusual about that except the human woman had been dressed like Illium, complete with a wig of black hair dipped in blue, gold contact lenses, and faux wings she wore with a harness that showcased breasts she'd painted a glittering silver. Elena wouldn't have known whether or not to be horrified for her friend's sake if he hadn't been the one to point out the performer to her—Illium thought it was hilarious.

He'd posed with the ecstatic performer, made Elena take a photo.

From what she could see, this marketplace, like Times Square, was a permanent installation, little shops set snugly against one another with sloping roofs that extended several feet out to provide shade for the goods displayed in front of the shops. Sunshine rained down on the entire area, but some clever town planner had left room for a number of large trees that provided shoppers with shade, meaning they'd linger.

Circling the largest tree was a wooden bench on which she glimpsed men and women sitting and chatting as they drank something. Fresh mint tea, she hoped, her mouth watering at the memory of the taste that was an integral aspect of her impression of Morocco.

The marketplace wasn't only a single street but set out in a ragged wheel, the spokes uneven in length. At the end of the longest spoke, the one that went to the very western edge of the town and had no homes around it, she glimpsed—and caught a whiff of—a tannery. Other stores or industries that created noxious fumes or smells were probably also located near that edge, similarly to how larger cities separated out their industrial districts from retail or residential areas.

The people below all looked up as Elena and the others passed, but no one waved. In fact, they seemed to go oddly immobile. Angelstruck? *No*, Elena thought. Those humans who were so in awe of angels as to become enthralled into a frozen state by their presence were rare.

The reaction could just be surprise: the Luminata wouldn't often—if ever—fly out here, since their whole deal was to find their way to luminescence by contemplation while encased in their pristinely controlled environment. Haggling with mortals and being faced with the harsh realities of life didn't exactly fit into that, no matter how you cut it.

It had to be the guard squadron that got supplies and anything else Lumia might need. But the guards were angels, too. So why this disturbing reaction? And where were the town's own resident angels?

Continuing on past the marketplace, their entire group flew to the very edge of the town, where once again, the homes became farther apart and green fields became a mainstay. Tasha was at the leading edge, and when she turned, the rest of them followed suit. Elena wasn't sure if everyone wanted to land, but she had no intention of leaving here without speaking to the townspeople.

With that in mind, she angled her way toward the marketplace once they got closer to the center of the town. The flyers in front of her kept going before someone glanced back and started a chain reaction. By the time she came down on her feet in the center of the marketplace—by the tree circled by the wooden bench—it looked as if everyone had decided to join her.

Elena glanced up at the dusty blue of the sky and hoped Aodhan wouldn't feel compelled to land. He might be okay with small touches from those he most trusted, but he'd hate the marketplace, be hurt by it. Better for him to stay aloft and alert her if there was a problem.

A rush of sound as the angels landed . . . and then shimmering quiet.

That ghost that was haunting her, it walked over Elena's grave again. Because it wasn't surprise she glimpsed on the faces around them. No, it was a far darker emotion, one that pushed bone white against skin that shaded from deepest browns to sunny golds, and that made people's breath come in ragged beats.

Fear?

Wings folded back tight to take up as little space as possible, she watched the other angels begin to explore. Nearest to the landing area were fruit and spice stalls, with other goods spreading out behind them. Instead of walking on, Elena shifted to under the canopy of the sitting tree as if she just wanted to be out of the sun, and tried to tune into the whispers around her.

She didn't know why she was wasting her time—she didn't speak or understand Moroccan Arabic beyond a few words that her mother had passed on to her, those words ones Marguerite's own mother had spoken often to her. That Marguerite remembered anything at all was a miracle, given how young she'd been orphaned.

But the words Elena's mother had remembered were almost all ones of love, ones a doting mother would say to a cherished child. Marguerite had been loved, deeply so, that truth a distant but potent memory that had allowed Elena's mother to survive foster care with her soul undamaged.

". . . Raphael . . ."

The single word sliced right through her preoccupation.

Looking to her left, she caught the eyes of the slender teenage boy who'd been speaking. Maybe fifteen or sixteen at the most, he paled under the light brown of his skin, his hazel-brown eyes going huge. "What about Raphael?" she said with a smile.

If anything, the boy paled even further, while his friends looked at her as if just waiting for her to pull out a crossbow and punch a bolt through the boy's heart, leaving him broken and bleeding on the dry earth.

The chill inside her grew harder, colder.

26

"I'm Elena," she tried again, keeping her tone friendly and hoping he spoke English. "What's your name?"

His Adam's apple bobbing desperately, the boy found the courage to say, "Riad."

Waving him over, Elena didn't make any sudden movements.

Sweat broke out over his face, but he came. Then he blurted out, "You want me?"

It could've simply been his grasp of English, but the blunt question struck her as subtly wrong. "Just to talk," she said once he was close enough that she could speak to him without raising her voice—though the friends who'd come along with him in a silent statement of solidarity could no doubt hear her. Good. "I don't harm kids. If you know who I am, you know that to be true."

Swallowing again, Riad whispered, his eyes wide, "Hunter angel."

Elena groaned at the moniker that haunted her. "Yeah, yeah." Putting her hands on her hips, she glared. "Guild Hunter, if you don't mind."

For some reason, that seemed to make the teenager relax.

A faint smile emerging out of the fear, he said, "I heard stories. You fought ten vampires all together." He lifted one hand, punched the air. "Pow!" Another air punch. "Pow!"

Grinning while his friends nodded as if synchronized, she said, "I might have." She glanced around the area before turning her attention back on Riad. "Why so scared?"

"No reason." Scuffing at the dirt, he stared down, his face pale once more and his pulse so rapid, she could see it jumping in his neck.

Elena decided to let it go for now. "How about being my tour guide?" she said instead. "Show me the best stores."

Taking out the scarf, she wrapped it around her head like a Moroccan hunter friend had shown her. This pattern of wrapping would provide shade, protecting her face. It also had the side effect of hiding her hair, which might be a benefit if she didn't want to freak people out with her resemblance to Majda—that is, if there was anyone still alive who'd known her. And if she'd had any connection to this town at all.

Mouth falling open, Riad said something in the local tongue that had all his friends daring to step closer. All five boys stared at her. When she raised an eyebrow, four blushed and pulled back. Riad was the one who spoke. "You look like . . ." A scowl, a quick discussion before they seemed to decide on the right word. "Like a cousin," he finished. "Like us but different."

"My grandmother was Moroccan."

The excitement that lit up their faces was a bright, innocent thing. "Really?" another of the teens asked, seeming to forget his fear in the face of this unexpected piece of knowledge.

"Really," she confirmed. "Who knows, maybe I have ancestors here."

They all laughed, taking it as a joke, but she had an escort of five teenagers when she walked into the market proper, the others of her group having spread out until she couldn't spot anyone in the immediate vicinity. Her impromptu escort seemed to confuse the wary storekeepers and citizens until the boys chattered at the adults and a few smiles began to cut through the heavy miasma of fear that shadowed every face.

She figured out soon enough that the boys were sharing her Moroccan heritage. To her disappointment, however, no one looked at her in a way that hinted that they saw her as anything other than a foreign angel. Interesting maybe, but that was it. Definitely no sense of being recognized.

It had been a long shot anyway. Morocco was a big place and the woman who might be her ancestor could've come from any part of it. Just because Majda had been at Lumia and known Gian didn't mean she'd been a local.

Then came the carpet maker.

The elderly man stared at her with faded brown eyes, his frown so deep that it dug dark furrows into the wrinkled skin of his forehead. "You wish to buy a carpet?"

"Not today." Elena ran her fingers over the handwoven threads. "I come only to admire."

The carpet maker made a noise at the boys that was clearly an order that they stay out of the store, the interaction so familiar she guessed the boys belonged to market families and had grown up running wild through its streets.

Scuttling out, the teens yelled that they'd wait for her outside.

She laughed, went to make a comment about teenage exuberance, and as she turned, her scarf slipped down to reveal her hair. The carpet maker sucked in a breath, staring at her as if he'd seen a ghost.

"Did you know her?" Elena asked softly, not wasting time. "Majda. Did you know her?"

Terror stole all the color from beneath his skin, his bones seeming to shake. "Lady, I think my store is too poor for you."

Glancing around to make sure no one was lurking inside with them, Elena said, "I will do you no harm."

The whites of his eyes showing, the man—who had to be seventy-five at least—went to a corner that held a little table set with tea things. "I will make you mint tea," he said, but his hands were shaking so badly that he couldn't handle the stainless steel pot that held the hot water, clattering it to a stand on the similarly brightly polished tray.

Sounds outside, two women bustling into the store and freezing when they saw Elena. The terror on their faces was a visceral stab, a dagger of ice. But the younger one, she found the courage to run past Elena. Dropping the package in her hands to the floor, she placed those hands on the carpet maker's upper arms as he stood facing the tea service. "Abba?"

Father.

Elena had learned that word on her own during her travels. Jeffrey had always been Papa to her as a child, Marguerite *Maman*, her mother far more at home in her adopted language.

Whatever the man said, his voice trembling, the daughter turned to Elena with a fear-pinched face that held a courageous determination. "My father is old and tired. He wants only to live in peace."

So take the trouble you bring to our door and go.

The girl had no need to speak those last words—Elena heard them loud and clear. Disappointed but not willing to terrorize an old man for her answers, she pulled up her scarf, once more covering the hair that had triggered his response.

"I'm sorry I distressed him," she said. "If he ever wants to speak to me, he can find me through New York's Archangel Tower. My name," she said, not assuming that the doings of a faraway city were of any interest here, "is Elena." Moving past the older woman, who still stood frozen near the doorway, she found her escort of teens lounging around sharing a packet of candy.

"Elena! Elena!" They swarmed around her the instant her foot hit the street.

She let them show her their market, and she listened, and she watched.

And she learned that though *no* angels lived in the town, *everyone* here was terrified of them—but beneath the fear burned a cold hatred. She was insulated from most of it because of the boys' enthusiastic adoption of her, but she caught dangerous hints in the eyes that turned her way when they didn't think she was looking, saw it in the twists of countless pairs of lips, felt it in the subtle way they avoided her, their shoulders stiff and their hands clenched.

It wasn't hard to do the math.

Archangel, can you hear me?

His response was delayed by about two seconds. *Of course,* hbeebti. *I am arguing with Astaad—he is beginning to be swayed by Charisemnon's arguments.*

Elena made a swift decision. *This isn't urgent. Do what you have to do—we'll discuss things tonight.*

A kiss of the tumultuous sea in her mind as Raphael retreated, rippling waves of sensation left in his wake as the minute amount of wildfire that lived in her blood reacted to his voice.

"Wow." Riad's whisper and wide eyes had her angling her head in a silent question.

"Your eyes just"—a frustrated pause, a debate with his friends—"grew fire," he finally said. "White fire around the black center." He opened his fingers out in a burst then closed them. "White fire then no white fire."

Great, her eyes were acting even weirder.

She spotted Xander around the same time that the thought passed through her mind; he was walking toward her with Valerius at his side. While Valerius's face gave nothing away, Xander's distress was obvious. He tried to hide it, but he was young, and she suspected that what had set him off was totally outside the realm of his experience.

Heading over to him, she told her five teenage guides to come along with her. They did, but stayed safely behind her, their faces wary once more. "Xander," she said. "I'd like you to meet my escorts." Then she introduced each boy by name.

Xander's face glowed with an inner light, the anguish retreating. "I am Xander," he said with a small incline of his head. "My grandfather is Alexander."

Gasps went from boy to boy, making it clear they all knew the legend of the silver-winged archangel who had risen from a long Sleep. However, in contrast to their nonstop chatter with her, and though it was obvious they had a thousand questions for Xander, the boys didn't voice any of them.

"Xander is only a little older than you," she said in an effort to "humanize" the young angelic male. "In human terms, he's—"

"About twenty, perhaps twenty-one on a *very* mature day," Valerius unexpectedly supplied.

"Yes," Xander said. "I am in training." He winked out of sight of Valerius. "And because my father was a great general"—a fast swallow, a hitch in his breath—"and my grandfather is Alexander, I can't miss a single session without being called on the carpet."

A tentative set of grins from the human teenagers before one dared to ask what kind of training Xander was doing. He immediately began to tell them about crossbow drills and aerial maneuvers. Ten minutes later, Elena left him happily surrounded by fascinated teenagers and being bombarded by questions on every side, and came to join Valerius where he stood a short distance away.

"He is a young man growing into his strength and will soon be considered a true adult, but he found himself lost today—he is not used to being looked upon with hatred and fear," Valerius said under his breath, a humming anger to him that she sensed only now that she was standing right next to him. "Not after growing up in his father's territory, training in Titus's, only to return to the wave of love and respect commanded by his grandfather."

Elena wasn't familiar with how Xander's father had treated the people in his region, but she knew Titus was beloved. Not just by the women he took to his bed, but by all his people— mortal and immortal alike. Elena could well understand why. The big warrior archangel was one of her favorite people in the Cadre. He believed in honor on the deepest level. "Titus never harms the weak, doesn't consider it honorable."

"Yes—and this lesson, Xander has learned from all three of the defining men in his life. I, too, seek to show him the same." Valerius's tone held a deep pride, but the anger remained. "As such, he has never been faced with fear in a child's eyes or had a woman lose all color when he smiles at her. Like most pups, he is more used to smiles and flirtation in return." A harsh exhale. "This town . . ."

"Yes," Elena said though he hadn't finished his sentence.

Together, the two of them stood watch over Xander. Valerius missed nothing. Neither did Elena. So she noticed that, around them, the hatred was morphing into confusion as the boys chatted with Xander, while she and Valerius stood nearby but didn't interfere.

When Xander pulled out the short sword he wore at his waist, horror crept back into those faces with the suddenness of a bloody strike . . . only to fade into open bewilderment when he gave the sword to the awed teens to handle, even going so far as to show them the correct way to hold it.

Then a little girl maybe three years of age, dressed in an orange-red dress trimmed with thin gold rope, her black hair in two neat braids and her feet in pretty golden slippers, escaped her mother to run straight for Elena and grab at the edge of her wing.

Elena caught the look of primal terror on the mother's face as she bent down to pick up the little girl. "What are you doing, *azeeztee*?" she said in a chiding tone that she totally spoiled with her smile. "Your mama is worried."

Having gone to that pale-faced woman to ease her concern, Elena blinked in shock when the woman, who was maybe in her late twenties, dropped to her knees and, head bowed, began to speak very fast. Elena couldn't understand her, reacted on instinct, dropping to one knee herself, her wings spread on the earth behind her. "Here," she said, holding out the child. "She's safe."

The woman snatched at her daughter, kissing her face over and over again as tears streaked down her own cheeks. The child whimpered, scared by her mother's fear. Again, Elena didn't think—she reacted. Reaching for a feather she could feel was about to come loose anyway, she tugged it off and held it out.

It happened to be one of the shimmering pale feathers near the edge of her wings, the color most often described as dawn. "Here, *azeeztee*."

The mother froze again, but the child gave a wobbly smile and closed tiny fingers gently around the feather. "*Shokran*." It was a shy whisper.

Elena smiled. "You are welcome." Rising to her feet, she held out a hand to the mother.

The woman remained distraught, but she took Elena's hand with a shaky one of her own and allowed Elena to help her up. Then, swallowing, she met Elena's gaze and said something in her native tongue.

Gesturing for her to wait, Elena looked over her shoulder to see Xander and the teens frozen in place, their attention on the small drama. "Riad!" she called out. "I need a translator."

The teenager ran over at once, a redness in his cheeks that spoke of a fearful rush of blood only moments earlier. "What do you want to ask her for?"

Ask her for.

Again, a very telling construction.

"Nothing," Elena said. "She spoke something to me. I didn't understand it."

Riad spoke. The woman replied.

"First, she says thank you for not hurting her baby." A pause. "Then she says why you use this word, *azeeztee*?"

Respect bloomed inside Elena for the woman in front of her; she'd been terrified, was still scared, but she was asking a question. "My mother used it with me and my sisters," she said, her voice growing thick as memory hit out of nowhere of her mother's soft hands and sparkly eyes, the way Marguerite spoke in an accent all her own.

Looking away, she breathed deep while Riad translated.

When she glanced back at the woman, her dark eyes were soft with understanding, the words she spoke as soft. Riad sucked in a breath, but he translated. "She says when you first became Raphael's and she saw pictures, her grandmother told her that you—" A deep frown, a sudden snap of his fingers. "That you put her in memory of a woman who lived here once. You understand? This is right word?"

Throat dry, she nodded. "What was her name?" she asked not Riad but the woman who still held her child in her arms, the little girl stroking her finger over Elena's feather.

Dark eyes met her own. "Majda," she said, and Elena's heart turned to thunder.

27

"Almost white hair and this skin but more dark." Riad pointed to his own arm, his voice penetrating the cacophony inside her skull. "The family had light hair many times in daughters, but she says Majda was first daughter with so light hair." Pointing at Elena this time. "But her father knew Majda was his daughter. She had mark here." Pressing his hand to the left of his abdomen. "Like father."

Elena could barely breathe, her mind filled with a day long, long ago when she'd watched her mother dress for a night out with her father.

"*Maman*, why do you have a map on your skin?"

Laughter. "It is a treasure map, of course, *chérie*."

A birthmark in the exact same place as that indicated by this woman. "How long ago?" she asked the woman in front of her, a woman who wasn't that far apart from her in years. "Was Majda your grandmother's age?"

A nod after Riad translated . . . and Elena knew Majda must've been her grandmother. She'd be cautious, investigate everything, but there were too many pieces that fit for it to be otherwise. Majda's age. Her Moroccan origins. Her unusual coloring.

"What happened to her?"

The response had Riad scowling. The other woman spoke other words, her tone sharp. Rolling his eyes, the teenager said, "She says this is not for my ears." His tone made it clear what he thought of that. "She will tell it to you and you must ask the English from a grown-up you like."

"I understand. Go talk to Xander again. I think he's bored with all the adults at Lumia." She'd deliberately used the name of the Luminata stronghold and she was watching for his response—so she saw the ugly fear that choked Riad before he turned and ran back to the others.

Shifting her attention to the woman who'd confirmed Majda's residence here, Elena nodded.

And the woman began to speak.

Thank you, Jessamy, Elena thought, as she memorized the words without understanding them. Elena's memory had always been good, but it was the angelic Historian who'd taught her memory tricks designed to help her absorb and recall the vast amounts of political and etiquette data she was expected to know as Raphael's consort. As if she'd gotten a damn download into the brain the instant she fell so hard for her archangel.

"*Shokran*," she said afterward.

Smiling openly now, the woman turned to press a kiss to her daughter's cheek, her tone chiding when she spoke. The little girl laughed and waved her feather with delight. It made Elena think of Zoe; affection in her heart, she hunted out a few more loose feathers.

Unexpectedly, Valerius came to join her, handed her a number of his feathers before leaving in silence. "Here," Elena said, giving all the feathers to the woman. "For those children." She indicated the big-eyed kids hiding behind their parents' legs a few feet away.

Her smile impossibly deeper, the other woman moved to pass out the treasures. The adults stayed silent—at least until Elena's back was to them. Then they began to whisper so furiously she knew they were grilling the woman who'd spoken to her.

Light shattered high in the sky the next second, so bright that Elena caught it with her peripheral vision.

Guessing what was about to happen, she quick-stepped her

way to a relatively clear section near the tree. Aodhan landed
two seconds later, with enough room around him that he wasn't
forced into unwanted physical contact. "A large squadron is
headed this way. Uniforms are dark gray with red markings."

Lijuan's colors.

"Valerius! Xander!" She pointed up.

To their credit, they didn't question her, just stepped back,
opened their wings, and took off. Elena gritted her teeth and
made a vertical takeoff, Aodhan right behind her. The others
of their party must've spotted the four of them, because they
rose into the air not long afterward, Magnus heading out on
his stallion beneath them.

It didn't take long for everyone to figure out why they were
airborne.

Lijuan's squadron was a growing smudge on the horizon.

Elena, I am on my way. Raphael's voice, the sea dark and
stormy.

I'm very glad to hear that, Archangel. Because if that
squadron was hiding Lijuan in its midst, they were all going
to be in bad, bad trouble.

Raphael had broken up the meeting the instant he got
Aodhan's message. For once, no one argued, the entire Cadre
lifting off in a rush of violent power that had the Luminata
staring up at them.

Raphael didn't bother to tell those of the sect what was going
on—if Lijuan was coming this way, everyone would know soon
enough. He flew at archangelic speed, spotted Elena within
minutes. She and Aodhan were in the middle of the group heading toward Lumia, Xander and Valerius leading. *Get behind us.*

Raphael—

I know. That she'd never let him go into war against Lijuan
alone. *I need you safe until I know if it's Lijuan we're facing.
And the Archangel of Death isn't the only threat in the air.* It'd
be easy for one of the other archangels to "accidentally" send
Elena tumbling from the sky.

Shit, yeah, I get it. She and Aodhan dropped in preparation
for passing under the Cadre.

Xander and Valerius dropped a second later, with the

others following like dominoes. The two parties passed each other a minute later, going in opposite directions. But Raphael knew Elena and Aodhan would be turning to stay on the Cadre's tail. Not only because they were stubborn and loyal, but because of a truth no one else in the Cadre could ever know: that Raphael's power to hurt Lijuan was rooted in how Elena had made him "a little bit mortal."

He carried a piece of his hunter in his blood. And while the wildfire was too powerful to truly live in Elena, touches of it burned through her blood nonetheless, for it was a creation of life and his hunter burned so very bright. *Elena, Aodhan, tell me if the members of the Cadre behind me make any unexpected movements.*

Got it.

Sire.

The Luminata's protective squadron had risen into the air ahead of them, dropped so suddenly Raphael knew one of the other archangels had ordered them down. The leader of that squadron had a brain that he'd obeyed so quickly and efficiently; he'd taken his squadron down but kept it in battle-ready formation on a low flight path to the left of the Cadre.

Ahead of them, Lijuan's squadron made an unanticipated move: they began to drop slowly, in a fashion that telegraphed their intention to make a landing. The Luminata squadron flew forward and landed behind them, close enough to be a threat, far enough away not to step on the Cadre's toes.

Raphael and the other archangels waited until Lijuan's entire squadron was down before they landed. It wasn't planned, but they ended up in a neat, straight line all the way across. Somehow, Raphael wound up at the center of the line, face to face with the squadron leader. "Do you escort Lijuan?" he asked the square-jawed blond male with eyes of blue.

"No. I have a message from my lady." He held out a sealed envelope with both hands, formal and practiced.

Michaela, standing next to Raphael, was the one who took the envelope. "It took an entire squadron to deliver this?"

The squadron leader didn't react to the acid in Michaela's voice. "We had to be certain the Luminata guard would permit us access to the Cadre. Our instructions were to hand the letter to only the archangels as a group."

That made a certain amount of sense.

Of course, it also made sense that Lijuan was in her non-corporeal form and the squadron's task was to distract them while the Archangel of China readied herself to strike. Then the squadron leader bowed from the waist. "My instructions are to return as soon as I have completed my task."

"I assume none of us wish to delay him?" Neha said coolly before nodding to the squadron leader, who'd risen back to his full height. "You have performed your task as asked. Good journey."

The blond male seemed to unbend a fraction. "I thank you, Lady Neha."

He spoke a command in Mandarin Chinese and the squadron lifted off as one. The Luminata squadron followed them out, but Raphael knew they'd stop at the border to Lumia. *Aodhan.*

I have it, sire.

Alexander, Mother, can you spare your escorts to join Aodhan?

Both answered yes and Tasha and Valerius fell in with Aodhan, ready to track Lijuan's people far enough out that they couldn't double back in a surprise attack.

Alone on the field of golden grass but for the others of the Cadre around him, Raphael touched his consort's mind. *Any thoughts, Guild Hunter?*

Lijuan is playing games, was the grim response. *Or Xi is covering for her, hoping to give her enough time to finish whatever it is she's up to.*

Yes. He saw Michaela hand the letter to Caliane.

"I think of all of us," the green-eyed archangel said, "you are the one least likely to be accused of tampering with this on the trip back to the meeting chamber."

Caliane took the letter but didn't spread her wings. "There's no need for any accusations. We read it here." With that, she broke the seal and the Cadre came together in a circle, close enough to hear but not close enough that their wings would overlap.

Raphael found himself on the opposite side of the circle from his mother.

"'To my fellow archangels,'" she read out in her crystal-clear voice, "'I write this knowing you meet at Lumia. There is no need. I am fully capable and in charge of my territory. As a goddess, I do not accept the authority of the Luminata to call me to order—no one holds that power over me.'"

Favashi spoke into the pause, her voice toneless but her words blade-sharp. "Well, it sounds like Zhou Lijuan in any case."

"Xi has known her a long time," Astaad pointed out, because for all his traditionalist views on respecting a fellow archangel's territory even with bloodlust licking at the edges, he'd been Cadre for over two thousand years. He understood politics.

"Shall I continue?" Caliane asked. "I think we can all guess the rest."

"She may surprise us yet." Michaela's acerbic tone.

"Indeed." With that single word that said nothing while communicating a great deal, Caliane continued to read the missive. "'I have no need to prove my existence. It lives in the strong and ordered beauty of my territory. I will emerge when I wish. Until then, you should return to your own territories. They are vulnerable without you.'"

The threat couldn't be much clearer.

"Despite her delusions of godhood, she has signed it 'Zhou Lijuan, Archangel of China,'" Caliane said. "I assume the Historian will be able to verify the veracity of that signature?"

"It does not matter, does it?" Elijah said with the calm for which he was known. "Nothing in that letter says it was written yesterday or a month ago or even a year ago."

"She knows we are at Lumia," Charisemnon pointed out, his arms folded across his chest.

It was Neha who responded. "An easy guess if she was preparing for this in advance."

"And," Favashi added, "we don't know how many different letters she wrote and left with Xi. She could well have written one to be sent should the Cadre have decided to meet with no interference from the Luminata."

"Or," Charisemnon said, his jaw jutting forward, "the letter could be legitimate and we are wasting our time here."

"Do you never cease repeating yourself?" Alexander

sounded as pompously Ancient as anyone might expect—except those who knew him. It had been many centuries since Alexander went to Sleep, but Raphael had known the Archangel of Persia for all of his life before then. As a result, where others might hear pompous, Raphael heard aggravation and a temper close to the edge.

Charisemnon squared his shoulders, locked gazes with the Ancient. "Careful who you mock, old man."

Alexander laughed, his amusement appearing genuine. "Ah, the arrogance of youth." He shook his head, a handsome man with golden hair and wings of silver who would not appear in any way old for countless millennia, if ever.

In truth, Raphael had never seen any adult angel who showed signs of visible age once they'd reached their prime in terms of physical appearance. It was theorized that they *did*, in fact, age after a certain point, but at so very slow a rate that it was all but invisible. The other theory was that they reached their prime and stayed in that state. Raphael tended to believe more in the former than the latter—because he'd seen changes in himself. Nothing anyone else would notice . . . except an eagle-eyed consort.

Elena was dead certain he hadn't yet hit his prime. "Alexander calls you a pup and I think he's right, at least in terms of your immortality. You're still maturing and becoming impossibly more beautiful with every day that passes."

Holding back a smile at the memory of her glare as she'd said that, Raphael glanced at Titus, who'd been unusually quiet. The warrior archangel's forehead held two deep vertical grooves, his attention on the far horizon where the squadron had vanished. But then he gave a nod as if he'd come to a decision and said, "Enough of the debating. We could be here all year." His voice boomed. "There is only one way to decide this and that is to go to China."

Several heads nodded, but it was Elijah who spoke. "If Lijuan is still awake and in control, she'll be furious at our intrusion and will rise to confront us."

"Then we can all go home." Michaela's curt words bristled with impatience, her wings held a little too tight to her body and her arms folded as aggressively as Charisemnon's.

She'd been pushing for an end to this meeting from the

start. Nothing unusual in that except the other archangel usually enjoyed politics and could be counted on to draw things out for her own amusement. Yet now, she wanted to get back to her territory as fast as possible.

To a child?

Or was there something more dangerous going on?

Because it was equally possible that the toxic contamination she'd suffered at Uram's hands had gone active. Perhaps she knew she'd betray her unstable state if she stayed too close to the rest of the Cadre.

"We need to come to a unanimous decision," Charisemnon insisted, a hard light to his eyes. "That is the law."

"There is no written law," Neha countered. "It is simply that we usually decide by consensus. In this case, however, with bloodlust threatening to consume China, we must act and act fast, even if that means a majority vote."

"I'm not certain we have that right," Astaad began.

"I have no quarrel with you, Astaad," Neha said, "but your lands are an ocean away, while mine border Lijuan's. I cannot and will not wait for the rest of you when my territory is at risk of a spillover of bloodlust." Her tone was of the Queen she was, one who had held power for a millennium. "It is a question of protecting my territory."

"Neha is right." Alexander's tone said he'd made up his mind and that was it. "The Cadre has no right to stay her hand. And as the outcome of any investigation will affect all of us, we must take her lead."

"So you would leave me in my territory, close to my armies?" Charisemnon's smile was sly. "I think not."

"If you stay," Titus said with a grim smile of his own, "I stay. That, I believe will even things out and allow the rest of the Cadre to head to China."

His smile wiped out, Charisemnon looked at Titus with unhidden ill will. The two had been at odds for a long time, their morals and ethics sharply opposed. Raphael had always been on Titus's side, seeing in him what an immortal should be, while in Charisemnon, he saw what an immortal could become if he gave in to the worst excesses of their kind.

"A vote." Neha's sari rustled in a rasp of silk as she spoke, the Archangel of India skilled at flying in the garment and landing as elegant as when she'd taken off. "Who does *not* wish to travel to China to confirm whether or not Lijuan is present in her territory?"

Everyone stared at Charisemnon.

Face going a hot red and fists bunching at his sides, he said nothing.

"So," Neha said after a full minute, "we are decided. We will head to China."

28

"We go on the wing," Alexander stated. "Only the Cadre, no one else."

Raphael frowned inwardly. *Surely you cannot expect Elijah and I to leave our consorts*, he said mind to mind with Alexander. *I know you do not want to leave Xander.*

As others began to speak around them, Alexander replied on the mental level. *It has been pointed out to me*—a quick glance at Caliane—*that I may be doing my grandson a disservice by having him always at my side.* Eyes of undiluted silver looking into Raphael's own. *I did not become a warrior that way. Rohan did not. You did not.*

It was an inarguable point. Yet so was Raphael's. *There are those who would hurt the pieces of our heart to get to us.*

If we bring them with us, this will take much longer. They cannot match our speed and endurance.

Having kept an ear on the audible discussion, Raphael spoke to back up Elijah. "The Luminata may have a reputation as being worthy of trust," he said, "but they are not my people, and now that I have walked the hallways of Lumia, I'm not so certain of the clarity of their quest. To ask me to leave my consort here is an exercise in futility."

"I can understand that." Favashi's words were quiet, heavy with emotion. "Had I a consort, I would not leave him in unknown lands with an unknown sect, either."

The other archangel gave an excellent impression of still mourning Rohan, but Raphael remained chary about the truth of her emotions. Favashi appeared one of the gentlest members of the Cadre, but she hadn't survived this long by being anything but a clear-eyed operator.

"I suggest a compromise." Astaad's tone was of a peacemaker. "It is already deep into the afternoon. We leave tomorrow midday for China, while consorts and other escorts leave for our home territories at dawn, giving us time to fly with them a good distance before we return to Lumia for the trip to China."

It appeared the most feasible solution. Raphael could get Elena to the plane in that time and Elijah could fly Hannah out of Morocco, Elijah's consort old enough to make the trip home on the wing. Though she'd have no escort, since Cristiano was a vampire. *Eli, if you prefer Hannah not return home alone, she's welcome to join Elena on the jet.*

Thank you, my friend, but there is a plane waiting for her, too—Cristiano flew in on it, while we came on the wing. If she is to return without me, I will ask that she go with Cris to save my heart the worry. A small smile. *Hannah prefers the open sky whenever possible.*

Raphael knew that in two or three hundred years, he'd be making the same response when it came to Elena; his hunter loved to fly, was held back only by her limited endurance and strength. "I have no argument with Astaad's suggestion," he said when it was his turn to speak to the Cadre on the proposal.

No one else demurred, either.

"I'm sorry, *hbeebti*," Raphael said to Elena after the Cadre rose into the air and he swept out to fly wingtip to wingtip with her. "It appears you will not have as long in Lumia as we'd hoped." He told her of the Cadre's decision.

Her face fell, the two of them close enough that he could see every nuance of her features. "Damn. But I get it—a possible surge of bloodlust-ridden vamps trumps my curiosity about my family history any day." She tucked back a strand of near-white that had escaped the twist in which she wore her hair. "Shall we wait for Aodhan?"

Raphael considered it, nodded. "Yes. I don't want you alone in case one of the Cadre calls another meeting after we reach Lumia."

Landing in among the wildflowers after riding down on a gentle wind, Elena folded back her wings as he did the same with his own. "I discovered something disturbing today."

He listened as she told him of the lack of angels in the nearest township, of the fear and hatred she'd glimpsed in the eyes of the populace—and of the fact that Majda had indeed come from the town.

Intrigued by the latter but deeply troubled by her report on the townspeople, Raphael said, "Did you see many vampires?" As hunter-born, she could scent them even if they didn't reveal their fangs.

Elena blinked. "No," she said after a while. "In fact, the entire time I was there, I didn't scent a single vampire."

She stared at him. "Raphael, that's more than odd. In a township that size, there should've been at least a few in the marketplace."

Folding her arms, she scowled down at the inoffensive wildflowers around them, the colors soft pink, lacy white, and a bright, spiky yellow. "Mortal-only towns are pretty much a myth except when people put up their own gated compounds— and even those only last a generation at best. Someone in the family *always* ends up wanting to reach for the almost-immortality of vampirism."

"An irrefutable fact proven through eternity." Which meant there was a reason both angels and vampires were giving the township a wide berth. "Let me see if Aodhan has heard anything." He reached out easily to the member of his Seven who was still heading away from Lumia.

Aodhan's answer had him raising an eyebrow. "He knows nothing of why there are no vampires in the town, but according to what he learned from Remus, it's possible angels don't settle there out of respect for the Luminata."

Elena's lips pressed into a thin line. "I guess I can understand that given the reputation these guys have in angelic circles. But doesn't it strike you as giving them their own little fiefdom?"

Yes it did. "I think I need to visit the town myself." He wanted to see firsthand exactly what the Luminata had been doing cut free from all Cadre oversight. "It must be today. We won't get a second chance until after the threat of war no longer looms on the horizon."

Wincing, Elena reached back with one hand to squeeze the opposite shoulder. "I'm not sure I can go back with you right away. I've already spent significant time in the air today and I did two vertical takeoffs."

Not that long ago, his consort wouldn't have admitted the stress on her wings, considering it a weakness. And not that long ago, he'd have challenged her decision instead of asking what he did next. "The takeoffs were necessary?"

"Yes." A grim reply. "I want the Luminata and everyone else to think twice before believing they can trap me."

Now that they'd been in Lumia long enough to have picked up the disturbing undercurrents, Raphael saw nothing but ruthless practicality in her decision. "How bad is the strain?" He reached out not to the injured section but a little bit to the left, massaging the area gently with his fingers.

Eyes closing, his consort released a sigh of pleasure. "Nothing torn, but I'm fairly sure if I make the return trip to the township again, I might snap something." A pause. "But you have to go even if I can't. My gut says what's happening there ties in with the Luminata as a sect and exactly how far the Cadre can trust them."

"I need your contacts, Elena. The vast majority of mortals are terrified by archangels to the extent of muteness." He knew exactly what would happen if he landed in the town without his mortal consort—their fear would overwhelm every other response and he'd get nothing.

"I should be able to ease the strain on your wings." His healing abilities remained erratic, but he'd learned to access a certain low level of power at will—it should be enough to settle a minor strain.

Elena gripped his wrist, her fingers strong and warm. "After we're back at Lumia. I don't want you distracted out here."

Since Lijuan's squadron was by no means the only possible threat with so many of the Cadre in the vicinity, Raphael nodded. "You'll also need to refuel and rest your body a little." Meanwhile, he'd keep an eye on her flight patterns to make sure she didn't need an earlier landing.

Hand dropping off his wrist, she said, "Raphael, I've been thinking . . . the way that painting of Nadiel was left where Caliane might've seen it, it can't have been a simple oversight."

"It reads as a power play to me, too." And it made him wonder what other small aggressions the Luminata had taken against the Cadre. "If the Luminata have become so arrogant as to challenge archangels, then they have become a danger that needs to be swiftly eliminated."

The survival of the world depended on the archangels being the ultimate authority. The Cadre had to be the fear beyond fear. The instant anyone began to question that, they empowered vampires and mortals to do the same. The end result of any such insurgency was always the same: a tide of horror and death.

"When I was a boy," he told Elena, "a small group of powerful angels in a distant part of Caliane's lands mounted a rebellion. Not because she was a bad leader." His mother had been sane then, and beloved by her people for the most part. "They just believed they were too old and too experienced to be under an archangel's yoke."

Elena frowned. "Most archangels seem to leave the older angels pretty much alone to keep an eye over their areas of influence. I mean, you don't interfere with Nimra or Nazarach when it comes to the day-to-day running of their regions."

"It was no different then." The wildflowers swayed in the wind as he spoke, brushing against his wings. "But the angels objected to even the fine thread that linked them back to Caliane and made her their official liege."

"What did she do?" Wariness in Elena's expression.

He didn't blame her; his mother had earned her reputation for mercilessness. "She was tired of their behavior so she told them they were free to rule their section of the territory with no oversight from her."

"I have a feeling this story doesn't have a happy ending."

"The angels bragged to anyone who would listen that they

reported to no archangel." Raphael could remember the whispers in the Refuge, had been aware even as a boy of the tension that whitened the lips of more than one adult. "Word soon got out to the vampires that they were under the angels' control, with no archangel in the mix."

"We're talking angels as strong as Nimra and Nazarach?" Elena shifted their positions so she could take his hand, tug him on a walk through the wildflowers. "Those two are plenty strong enough to keep vampires in line."

"These angels were even older and stronger." Arrogant men and women who were used to people cowering before them. "But we live in a world of predators and prey, Elena. And while archangels can only be killed by other archangels, even powerful angels *can* be killed by anyone."

Elena snorted. "If anyone has a tank or five and a hail of burning hellfire, and oh, maybe eight layers of armor."

"Truth—but vampires chafing at the bit don't think with such logic." He wasn't talking about people like Dmitri or Cristiano, who owned their vampirism, but creatures weak of character and selfish of need. "Such minds are blinded by hunger until they see only the possibility of total freedom to glut themselves on fresh prey."

Eyes stark with the knowledge of a woman who'd survived just such a monster, Elena stared at him. "How many died?"

"Five thousand mortals, four hundred and seventy-three vampires, one angel."

Her fingers clenched on his. "An angel?"

"A predator attacking the herd goes for the weakest link." Vampires in a twisted kiss were akin to a pack of feral dogs, hunted in that same instinctual way.

"In this case, a number of violent and *old* vampires decided to attack a scholar who was maybe six hundred years old. He stood no chance, was cut into pieces in front of his household." As Jessamy would stand no chance against Dmitri—angels weren't automatically stronger than vampires, a fact most mortals never understood.

"Jesus." Elena's face was white. "And once that first boundary is crossed, there's no going back."

She'd seen it, the point he was making, his consort's mind

as sharp as the blades she wore with such lethal grace. "Do you want me to finish the story?"

A jerky nod.

"The vampires then slaughtered the angel's small household of mortals and other vampires." Raphael had been too young to be allowed anywhere near the scene, but he'd heard adults talking about gobbets of flesh flung at the walls and bloody feathers ground into the carpet, steaming piles of innards left on the welcome mat.

"The vampires moved on to their next target soon afterward, but only after crowing of the kill so the news ran like wildfire through the region."

Elena just shook her head, her features set in harsh lines.

"Their next target proved stronger than expected, killed the vampires, but the genie was out of the bottle. Other vampires began to strike at angels while feeding on mortals like they were disposable cattle—entire villages were left full of only the dead." He'd looked up and read the historical records once he was older, discovered the maddened vampires had ravaged anyone in their path.

Elders with fragile bones had been thrown against the walls, children's soft throats torn out, young men and women abused vilely while those who would protect them were murdered in brutal ways. "The mortals paid the highest price, but the angels who survived the assaults didn't do so unscathed: a number had their wings hacked off, the vampires having learned to do that first to keep their targets earthbound."

He thrust a hand through his hair. "There were rational vampires, almost-immortals of iron control and will who tried to halt the tide and who fought heroically to protect the mortals in their areas." Good men and women who'd fallen in defense of the vulnerable. "But bloodlust is infectious among the young and those already predisposed to violence. And just knowing that they *could* kill an angel, it was enough to snap the leash."

"Where were the ruling angels in all this?" His consort's voice reverberated with anger.

"Flying from scene to scene, helping injured angels, executing vampires. But not even their most brutal punishments could slow the vicious rampage, much less bring it to a halt. Nothing did—not until Caliane said enough and swept in. It took her a single day to bring the entire region into order."

Elena's response was hard with the ruthless understanding of a hunter. "Because no vampire can *ever* kill an archangel."

"And we live in a world of predators and prey," Raphael repeated. "Remove the top predator from the chain and the entire chain collapses."

"It's not chance the Luminata cleared out the vampires from this region."

"No, it appears to have been a strategy to maintain their fiefdom—but that strategy hinges on a single fragile fact: that no murderous kiss of vampires will catch wind of an entire town full of defenseless prey."

29

Landing at Lumia approximately forty-five minutes after the others would've returned, he and Elena made to go to their suite, while Aodhan requested leave to seek out a healer and artist named Laric, whom the Luminata called Stillness because of his unwillingness to speak.

"According to our source, he isn't usually out at this time of the afternoon," Aodhan told him. "But I still wish to attempt to make contact."

"Go. Talk to him," Raphael said, holding the splintered blue-green of Aodhan's eyes as the three of them stood alone in the courtyard. "But remember, you have found your voice. And that voice is beloved by more than one person."

A slight nod. "I will not lose my way, sire." Pausing for a heartbeat, he added, "I want to live in a way I did not live for two hundred years. I kept *myself* in a cage and that is a truth I must accept and get over."

And Raphael realized Aodhan wanted to help Laric rather than become like him. "We will be in our quarters for an hour, then we'll head back to the township. It's apt to be dark by the time we return."

"I'll ensure I'm present to provide escort."

Raphael made a snap decision. "There's no need. Stay here," he ordered this member of his Seven who was so very luminous that sometimes, he blinded people to his brutal intelligence. "Listen. Learn."

"Sire."

Wings brushing Elena's as they split with Aodhan and began to head in the direction of their suite, Raphael was surprised to see a Luminata walking toward them who pushed back his hood and beamed at Elena in a most un-Luminata way, something in the openness of his face putting Raphael in mind of the pure innocence of a child.

"I have found it, Consort!" He lifted a rolled-up piece of paper before seeming to collect himself and incline his head respectfully toward Raphael, the pale hue of his eyes bright and the dark brown of his skin flushed. "Archangel."

"Raphael," Elena said with a smile, "this is Ibrahim. He promised he'd look for a historical map of Lumia for me." She touched her hand to the slender male's forearm in a silent thanks that made Ibrahim's smile even more incandescent.

"Ibrahim," Raphael said in greeting. *Why a historical map?*

Taking the map from Ibrahim, Elena replied to his mental comment the same way. *If the Luminata are hiding things, I didn't think we'd get access to a current map, but we can extrapolate from an older one.*

Or, Raphael pointed out, *depending on the age of the map, we may see what's missing or what's been added.*

Elena's eyes gleamed in appreciation of his point, before she returned her attention to the Luminata who continued to glow with that inner purity so rare among the sect. "Did you find this in the Gallery?"

Ibrahim shook his head. "There is a dusty old room where—" Glancing around, he ducked his head and lowered his voice. "It's where the archivists in charge of the Gallery stack damaged items or things that are not seen as fit for display." A wince. "They never tell the artists and I don't know if that is a kindness, or if it's because they don't want to expend time and energy on restoring items they deem inferior."

How did you win this Luminata's trust so quickly? It was obvious Ibrahim was struggling with having shared what he had, his expression heavy with guilt, yet he *had* shared it nonetheless.

Ibrahim's new, Elena responded, *and I get the sense he's questioning his vocation now that he's been here a while—he's sniffed out the corruption but he's having trouble coming to terms with the fact his heroes have feet of clay. I just gave him an outlet.*

"Thank you for searching," she said to the Luminata, placing her hand on his forearm again for a second—her demeanor appeared almost protective to Raphael. "This map will make it much easier to explore the stronghold. Not that we'll have long."

"No?" Ibrahim's face fell. "You are leaving?"

"Tomorrow, I'm afraid." She held out her arm, offering it in the grip of warriors.

Ibrahim took her hand between the two of his instead, like a scholar or another of a gentler vocation. "It has been an honor, Consort. I hope you will return to Lumia one day."

"I hope so, too." Smile gentle, Elena held the rolled-up map to her side as they left the Luminata to continue the walk to their room.

Placing it on a small decorative table set with a mosaic of semiprecious stones once they were inside, she turned to slide her arms around his waist. He wrapped his wings around her in turn, cocooning them in privacy both because he didn't trust these walls, and because he liked having his Elena so close.

Sliding his hands up from her waist to her wings, he said, *Where does it hurt the worst?*

Elena listed the areas with the pragmatic knowledge of a hunter who saw her body as a tool she had to keep in fighting condition. Absorbing the information, he spread his hands over two parts of her wings and reached for the energy inside him that was life. His hands glowed with a slight blue fire that was concealed by his wings.

Sighing as the energy sank into her, Elena rested her head against his chest, shifting until she was right over his heartbeat, as if listening to it. "Even though it frustrates me that we have to leave tomorrow, I'm glad, too. I really don't like this place," she murmured in a tone that was soft, private. "I can't point to any one thing as the reason why, but—"

"I feel it, too." While the warmth of her against him settled his protective urges, his skin continued to prickle with an awareness of subtle wrongness. "I spoke to my mother as we were flying back. She says in the past, the Luminata had vampiric border guards as well. The complement was never only angelic."

"The change fits with what we were talking about earlier, doesn't it." Elena kept her head against his chest as he moved his hands to different parts of her wings, easing the strain and healing muscles that might've sustained microtears. "Only . . . vampires given that position would be pretty solid, not the type to go nuts even if they figured out the Luminata were ruling their own little mortal colony."

It was an excellent point.

Then she made another one. "Maybe it's because while angels seem to revere the Luminata enough that even the Cadre's left them alone for a long time, vampires would be more clear-eyed."

"Especially," Raphael murmured, "vampires of the age to be stationed here. It's far too sleepy a region to send experienced warriors—they'd consider it a punishment. I know Galen tended to send no one over two hundred and fifty."

"It's a place to get a little seasoning, then move on." Elena nodded. "Vamps like that probably wouldn't see the Luminata as anything but a bunch of angelic monks. No reverence, no looking the other way." She began to play her fingers up the inner surfaces of his wings, the caress an intimate one between consorts. "I feel back to normal wing-wise."

"Good." Giving her one last pulse of healing energy, he bent his head.

She lifted hers as if he'd spoken, the kiss they shared a soft brush that was about connection, about being one in this place filled with outsiders, not all of whom wished them well. Raphael wanted to do so much more with his consort, but time was their enemy today. "I do not like abstinence," he said against her lips.

Laughter in her eyes. "Great minds." She ran her hands down his chest, his leathers soft under her touch. "We'll make up for it when we're back home."

The dark gold of her skin pulled taut over her cheekbones, her laughter erased between one pulse and the next. "I don't want you to go to China."

"I must."

"I know. Doesn't make me any happier. The entire thing could be a giant trap."

"It's possible—but I don't think even Lijuan is delusional enough to take on two Ancients at once, forget about the rest of the Cadre."

"Since Her Creepiness thinks she's a goddess, that fact lowers my worry levels by point one percent at most." She touched her fingers to the Legion mark on his temple, and where her fingers brushed, wildfire sparked, as if drawn to her. "Shall we look at the map when we're away from here? I can carry it easily in the same sheath as my crossbow bolts."

Raphael nodded, aware the sheath had a cover she could zip up to protect her bolts from falling out during flight. It'd do as well to protect the map. "You need fuel first."

"I'll have a couple of energy bars." She went to her travel case and opened an inner pocket to retrieve the bars. "I'd rather buy food from the marketplace. It'll give us an excuse to talk to people, too. And then I don't have to change to go to the Atrium."

Catching the bar she threw over, Raphael bit into it.

It was as they were about to leave five minutes later that Elena said, "It would've been useful if I could've had a translation of what the woman in the marketplace told me." It had clearly been important enough—and dangerous enough—that the woman hadn't wanted Riad to hear it.

"I don't suppose you have a local contact who can translate Moroccan Arabic," she said jokingly. "And oh, someone who you trust to give us the correct translation." It was the latter that was key, because the Luminata no doubt spoke the local language.

Raphael's lips tugged up a little. "You will not like the answer, *hbeebti.*"

Surprised by his comment, she parted her lips to ask him to explain, then groaned. "Don't say it."

"I'm afraid I must—Tasha spent many years in Morocco once upon a time. She speaks the language flawlessly."

Gritting her teeth, Elena said, "Can you contact her mind to mind, get a translation? And oh, damn, I'll need to reschedule my walk with Caliane, too, since we won't be back in time."

"Of course I can contact Tasha. But I will not."

"It's fine." Elena waved a hand. "I won't do the jealous lover thing. She just annoys me because she's so damn impressive."

Raphael cupped her jaw. "She is not my warrior."

Spreading her wings, Elena pressed her hand over his heart. "I really can handle it, Archangel."

"I know. But I would not play with Tasha's heart, either. Warning her about the painting was a courtesy that could not be misconstrued as anything more personal. This may cross a fine line."

Elena remembered what Aodhan had said about Tasha watching Raphael with the eyes of a lover, nodded. If the other woman did still have feelings for Raphael, it wouldn't be fair to give her hope that it might ever be reciprocated.

"But," Raphael said, "we can go see my mother, speak to Tasha there."

Raphael contacted Caliane as he and Elena left the suite. *Mother, Elena needs to consult Tasha on something. We would like to meet you outside in an open space.*

His mother's response was immediate, the purity of her voice the song of his childhood. *So you feel the eyes in this place, too, my son*, she said. *There is a garden that Tasha discovered, if you would meet us there.*

Raphael got the instructions, told his mother they were on their way.

He and Elena ran into Gian not far from the garden. "Archangel, Guild Hunter." A deep smile, not even the faintest incline of his handsome head. "May I offer any assistance? I know Lumia can be a maze."

"My mother says there is a garden nearby," he replied, noting Gian's subtle insolence and disguised condescension while deliberately downplaying his ability to navigate Lumia. He had incredible power, but strategy and intelligence still counted in a battle.

Especially against a foe on home ground.

The other man's smile appeared genuine, but Gian had been alive a long time, had headed a secretive sect for hundreds of years. A sect that was meant to change leaders every five decades. Nothing in Gian's face could be trusted.

"Yes," Gian said, smile holding, "it's just down this way." The Luminata began to lead them there, all helpfulness. "Did you enjoy your flight to the town?" he asked Elena.

"Pretty place."

Gian nodded, expression serene. "Yes, I hear that is so."

As if he's never been there. Total BS if he was involved with Majda. Elena's blade of a voice in his mind. *He lies while breathing. I can't believe I almost fell for it.*

Touching his hand to her lower back, Raphael stroked gently. *He has had a long time to perfect his public persona,* hbeebti.

I wonder if he fooled my grandmother, too. No doubt in her now, that the woman in the miniature was her blood.

Having seen the similarity, Raphael had to agree with her conclusion.

Maybe, Elena continued, *Majda ended up in Paris because she realized what he was too late. But who fathered my mom? Where's the vampire in the family tree? It could be several generations back.*

She was a hunter who'd caught the scent. And she was magnificent.

Even as his consort thought of the hunt, the hallway opened out into a courtyard that held a manicured garden, the hedges so neatly cut it was mathematical. *It's unlikely,* Raphael said in response to her supposition about her vampiric ancestor. *He'd have had to be under two hundred to have sired a child, but while he was clearly strong, I know of no vampire of that age who would have power enough for the kiss of his blood to last beyond a second generation.*

"Many of the brothers find it calming to work in this garden," Gian told them at the same time. "It's a little too sedate for me"—a smile that was grace embodied—"but we all find different paths to luminescence."

Spotting Caliane's snow-white wings on the other side of the garden, Tasha's copper ones beside her, Raphael said, "It seems my mother has beaten us here."

"Thanks for being our guide."

Gian's eyes glowed at Elena's words. "I hope you both enjoy your walk," he said, but he was looking only at Elena. "The garden is beautiful at sunset."

Raphael ran his hand down his consort's stiff spine after Gian disappeared down the hallway, ice coating his words when he spoke. "He looks at you with covetous eyes in front of me." The only reason Gian wasn't dead right now was because he had answers to Elena's questions.

She closed her own hand over the edge of his wing, stroked down in a firm caress. "Don't let him get to you. Even if we have to come back after the world settles down, we'll expose all his secrets."

It was a promise.

"Mother." Having reached Caliane, Raphael greeted her with a kiss to the cheek.

His mother, her hair a fall of midnight down her back and her body clad in a flowing gown of white with the barest tinge of green on the edges, smiled and slipped her arm through his, but not before she turned to Elena and said, "May I steal my son for a few minutes, Consort? I have missed him."

"Of course." Elena's tone was gentle in a way Raphael knew his mother didn't realize—and neither, he was certain, did his hunter. Elena had a soft spot for his mother now that it had become clear how much Caliane regretted what she'd done to Raphael.

It wasn't only that, of course.

His consort would do anything to see her own mother again, couldn't find it in her heart to hold on to anger against Caliane.

Knhebek, hbeebti.

Elena's response was a kiss against his mind before she fell back with Tasha.

30

"Did you ever visit Lumia before this?" he asked Caliane.

Nodding, she said, "Yes, several times. I had a friend who was Luminata long ago, before you were so much as a speck in the universe's eye." A remote smile, her gaze filled with eons of memory. "He was as thin as a reed and the funny thing was that his name was Reed. We teased him so, but he always had such a smile about it. Such inner peace."

"After he became Luminata?"

A shake of Caliane's head. "He was born that way, I think. Like some children are born with a placid, happy nature." Glancing up at Raphael, she laughed, no longer a distant Ancient but the mother who'd once kissed his hurts. "You were not like that. You had *very* firm and loud opinions for a babe."

"I had two archangels for parents."

Laughing again, she said, "Reed was born of two scholars and he was scholarly himself. I wasn't surprised when he told me he was drawn to Lumia." She went silent for a while, as the older angels were apt to do, their memories tangled skeins they had to unravel. "He was the kind of person who *should* be here. It seemed as if he had an ability to see beyond the veil."

"I've met people like that in my life." Ibrahim was one—young but with a purity to him that sang. "It doesn't seem as if most of the current Luminata are as your friend."

"I should've known you'd sense it, too. So intelligent and perceptive even as a babe." Memories in her voice again, her smile a haunting echo of the woman she'd been before unspeakable tragedy and madness. "Talking of Reed, I find I miss him. He had such a quiet, warm sense of humor."

"Does he Sleep?"

"I do not know." Sorrow colored her features. "He disappeared two millennia before your birth, and no one knows where he went. At the time, most hoped that he'd chosen to slip quietly into Sleep, but I hoped he'd found luminescence, was inhabiting a plane of existence unknown to the rest of us."

A soft smile, so many memories shadowing her expression when she lifted her head to meet his eyes that his soul ached. "Now I'm more selfish—I wish him to be Sleeping, so that he might wake one day and I will see my friend again."

Raphael thought of what it would be like if he lived a hundred thousand years, two hundred thousand, and began to lose friends to Sleep, or to retreats from society. Even vampires did the latter. They didn't have the ability to Sleep, but the old ones had been known to shut themselves away for eons.

Immortals called them the Withdrawn.

The Withdrawn relied on trusted retainers for their blood intake, with some families remaining with the same vampire for generation after generation, the only ones who ever had contact with the recluse or recluses. Raphael had known one such retainer a hundred years earlier; the man had told him that his master was tired but "his god does not permit self-annihilation." So he had chosen a life of total seclusion, blood supplied to him through a hole in the door to his suite.

"It must be a hard thing," he said to his mother, "to be awake in a world where so many of your friends Sleep." He knew he would never be alone that way—he and Elena would always wake and Sleep together. Not only could he not imagine life without his hunter, he'd seen the terrible harm it could do when one half of a pair went into Sleep unilaterally; he'd never hurt Elena that way.

"At least Alex is awake now." Caliane's sigh was heartfelt. "A troublemaker still. He always wants to take control—even as a boy, he was determined to lead."

"Have you tracked down any others of your compatriots?" He knew she'd asked Jessamy to do a search for her.

"Not from so long ago, but others I met through the ages, yes." Midnight strands of her unbound hair brushed over his arm as they walked. Many who only saw her outside Amanat thought she always dressed this way—in flowing gowns with her hair down, but Raphael knew that was only one of his mother's skins. She was as comfortable in weathered leathers, with her hair in a braid.

"Tell me," she said. "What is it that brings your consort to talk to Tasha?"

Elena and Tasha walked in silence for several minutes, and oddly, that silence wasn't awkward. It felt like walking with another hunter, both of them keeping an eye out for threats without making it appear they were doing so.

"Raphael told me you speak Moroccan Arabic," Elena said as, up ahead, Caliane and Raphael walked side by side, their wings overlapping.

Elena and Tasha, on the other hand, had made every effort to ensure their wings didn't so much as brush against each other.

"Yes," Tasha replied. "I learned it when I lived here for a time during my youth." A smile in her voice, she added, "Raphael traveled through here as well, you know."

"Knock it off, Tasha. You won't rattle me with stuff like that."

A shrug. "I'm simply speaking of an old friend."

Deciding to let that battle go when it was obvious Tasha was in a mood where she wanted to dig at Elena, Elena said, "Raphael also told me I can trust you to do a translation."

A frown from the other woman, her hackles so far up Elena could almost see them. "Of course you can trust me in this. We may both be the lovers of the same man, but I have honor."

The prickly response seemed honest. "I apologize," Elena said. "I wasn't questioning that . . . hell, yes, I was. This fucking *place*."

Tasha's stiff tension turned into a caution directed outward, her eyes going dark before she scanned the area once more. "Yes, I feel it, too. There are ghosts here."

Fighting off a shiver at the memory of the ghost that had twice chilled her skin, Elena said, "If you can, please translate this for me." Reaching into her mind, she spoke the words exactly as the woman in the marketplace had spoken them.

"Wait." Tasha frowned. "Repeat that more slowly."

She asked the same two more times before saying, "I have it. The repetition was because it appears the original speaker used a particular dialect. I had to match up the words I know with the words you spoke—you realize this means I must guess some meanings from context?"

"Got it."

After taking another minute to order her thoughts, Tasha began to speak. "'My grandmother told me the story of Majda, a woman with moonlight hair, born to a small merchant family. The family is no more, for she was the only daughter and the parents are now dead and she disappeared long ago.'"

Tasha gave a hard shake of her head. "Wait, that's not right. It wasn't the word for 'disappeared.' It was 'taken.'"

A woman who was taken.

Elena's heart thudded. "Was that all?"

"No. There was also this: 'All traces of this family and of the woman with the moonlight hair have been erased from the town, and those who know are elderly, their memories fading and their bodies too fragile to rebel against the silence that hangs over the story. If others know, they stay silent, for to speak of her is to draw the attention of the angels.'"

A quick breath before Tasha continued, "'My grandmother told me Majda's story in secret. I think you will not betray me and you, too, have skin like her and moonlight hair'"—Tasha's gaze grew sharp—"'so I tell you this.'"

Blood roaring through her veins, Elena reached for Raphael's mind, shared what Tasha had told her. Aloud, she said, "Thank you," to Tasha.

"You seek your ancestors?"

"My mother was orphaned as a small child," she told the other woman, since that was no secret if anyone cared to look into Marguerite Deveraux's history. "Her mother came from Morocco, that's all I know."

"A woman with moonlight hair," Tasha murmured, her gaze flicking to Elena's hair once more. "Personally, I think you look as if you were fried in a lightning storm, but to each their own."

Elena found herself laughing. "That's pretty good for an on-the-spot comment."

"It's possible I've been working on it for a while." Tasha's lips tugged up in a clearly reluctant smile. "Will you not insult me in turn?"

"I called you Tasha McHotpants once," Elena said, and as Tasha burst out laughing despite herself, Elena thought once again that she and the other woman could've been friends if not for Tasha's unhidden desire to turn back the clock.

The angel simply didn't understand that some things were set in stone, were forever.

Elena-mine, are you ready to fly?

Her lips curved at the sweet, wild caress of the sea over her senses. *Yes.*

My mother has expressed a desire to accompany us. I think she wishes to escape this place, too.

I've got no problem with that, but warn her of the reception she'll be getting. Turning to Tasha on the heels of her discussion with Raphael, Elena found the other woman's jaw clenched tight, her eyes grim. "Caliane let you know the plan?"

Tasha nodded. "I don't want her to be hurt. She's used to living in Amanat, where her people adore her."

"If you need backup getting her out of there, let us know."

"She's stubborn," was Tasha's response. "Not often, but when it matters to her, she will do exactly as she will do."

Ahead of them, Caliane spread her wings.

Tasha took off after Caliane, but Elena walked into Raphael's arms and let him lift off for both of them. She'd already proven her skill at vertical takeoffs; there was no need to be stupid and waste energy when she had a much better option. And while she was at it, she decided to take advantage of her position and kiss her archangel's gorgeous, sexy mouth.

Life was for living.

You are distracting me, hbeebti. Despite the stern words, Raphael kissed her back with a passion that curled her toes, all power and heat and love. So much love. It nearly hurt, to know she was that deeply loved.

"I could kiss you forever," she said against his lips . . . and he dropped her.

Sweeping around with a laughing "Whoop!" of sound, she flew to line up wingtip to wingtip with him. "You know how to court a girl!"

A dangerous smile. "I aspire never to bore my consort."

They kept to a steady pace, arriving at the township as the sky glowed a dark orange streaked with pink, sunset a long process in this land. More people were out in the cooler weather—though "cooler" was a relative term.

Their landing had a predictable effect: people froze, then they began to pull away as unobtrusively as possible, ducking inside shops or hunching their shoulders to make themselves smaller targets. The four of them had come down near the edge of the canopy of the sitting tree, and within seconds, everyone on the bench that circled the trunk had somewhere else to be.

Glancing at Caliane, Elena saw Raphael's mother take in the fearful—and deeply if quietly angry—response with no visible reaction. As she watched, Caliane went to sit on the bench that circled the tree trunk, her wings draped gracefully on either side; her ebony hair, jeweled eyes, and gown of white brushed with green turned her into a goddess at rest.

"I will stay here," she said to them with an enigmatic smile. "I miss my people when I am far from them. Listening to this town's heartbeat settles the ache." Her eyes met Tasha's. "Explore, my dear."

Shaking her head, Tasha remained standing by her side. "I am with you, my lady."

"There's not much anyone can do to me, child."

"I'm sure Father will be very understanding when I explain why I left you alone in an unfamiliar marketplace."

Caliane's laughter was pure music, her voice holding a piercing beauty even when she was doing nothing to amplify it. "Ah, Avi, he taught his daughter well." A nod. "Then stay, listen, and perhaps we will come to understand why this town is haunted by a malignant fear."

Extending a hand to Raphael, she said, "You and your hunter will do much the same?"

Raphael closed his fingers gently around Caliane's. "Yes. Tell me if you sense anything we should know."

The two were focused on each other so they missed what Elena saw: the way people's eyes lingered on their handclasp, and on how Caliane smiled at Raphael. Though she was an age-less beauty, that smile was a mother's. No one could mistake that. As no one could mistake that they were mother and son.

Leaving Caliane and Tasha seconds later, Elena and Raphael stepped out into the amber and red of day transition-ing to night. Had the streets been full, they might've had trouble navigating through them with their wings, but with people so wary, there were no obstructions.

At first, all they did was walk through the market, looking at various things.

When Elena spotted a short, skinny man cooking some type of filled bun, she wandered over to the cart he'd parked in front of a closed shopfront. Hot and with a touch of spice, the scent had her stomach rumbling, her mouth watering. "Two," she said to the cook, who'd gone as motionless as a deer who'd spotted a wolf.

Nodding jerkily, he prepared two buns with expert hands, then half wrapped them in greaseproof paper, providing an easy way to hold the hot items as they ate. Elena dug into her pocket and placed enough local currency on the counter to cover the cost—the night before her and Raphael's dawn de-parture from New York, she'd rung Sara and asked if the Guild could convert some dollars for her; she knew it held a small amount of all types of currencies.

Izzy had picked up the money for her and dropped it off at the Enclave. Because while plastic might be fantastic, a hunter always carried actual cash for moments like this.

The cook's eyes went huge at seeing the money.

Shaking his head, he began to push it back with a trembling hand. Elena just took the food and gave one bun to Raphael. "Try it," she said after taking a long sniff of the aroma. "If you don't think it's delicious, I'll swallow my favorite blade."

The cook made a small, choked sound.

Ignoring the overwrought man, Raphael took a bite and

gave a decisive nod. "There is no need to swallow your blade, *hbeebti*."

Smiling, Elena took a bite of her own bun before they walked on, leaving the stunned cook to collapse into a chair behind his setup, a tea towel held up to his sweat-drenched brow. From the corner of her eye, Elena saw a nearby shop-keeper run over and pat his shoulder before collecting the money and putting it in the little tin in which it should go. Her eyes, too, were wide as she handled the money.

These people don't expect us to pay for what we take. Raphael's mental tone was frigid, though his expression remained unchanged.

31

Yeah, looks like the Luminata don't believe in a fair transaction. Elena's own anger was a cold pulse inside her—immortals had so much, had centuries upon centuries to gather wealth. These people weren't dirt poor, but they weren't rich, either. Not by any calculation. They were just ordinary citizens trying to eke out a life.

With Lumia so close, they should've had a thriving economy supported by custom from the stronghold. Instead, it appeared Lumia preferred to bleed them dry. Though . . . *They have to pay enough for the goods they take that the town doesn't go under*—because Lumia needed the town—*but I bet you it's nothing close to market value.*

Having finished their first snack, Raphael bought them juices made fresh by another roadside seller working from what looked like a semipermanent cart. He paid with a coin that had the juice man's throat moving convulsively as he swallowed. "What was that coin?" she asked after taking a drink of the cold, refreshing liquid.

"Angelic currency, accepted worldwide. He can exchange it for his local currency at any exchange house or bank—and the coin I used will equal triple the cost of the drinks." A brush of his wing over her own. "I'm afraid, Guild Hunter, that I assumed you knew about it and just preferred to use local coin."

Frowning, Elena said, "You know, I have noticed those coins over the years but I guess I had no reason to pay attention." A pause, before she lowered her voice and leaned closer to him. "You think it's a good idea to pay with that here? I'm not sure he's going to get fair value from whoever it is that does the exchange."

"Angels do not handle the exchange," Raphael told her. "Mortal financial institutions are kept apprised of the exact value of the coins—and they understand what will happen if they short anyone. Each coin is linked to a particular archangelic territory, and all transactions are monitored via a computer network that, in my case, connects back to the Tower."

"I should've known." Raphael had always been one of the archangels most in step with the world. A lot of that was because of Illium—the blue-winged angel was fascinated by technology.

Having finished their juices, they put the disposable cups in a nearby trash receptacle, then walked deeper into the market, taking in the reactions all around them while maintaining their impassive fronts. It was about ten minutes later that they discovered a hole-in-the-wall operation that was selling what looked like fresh-made tagine, each creation in its own tiny clay pot with the characteristic conical lid.

The kitchen, busy with two fast-moving bodies, was behind the large square window from which a smiling, dark-eyed woman passed out the food, prettily painted chairs and tables set out on either side of the restaurant window.

"Do you think your mom and Tasha would like some?" Elena asked, standing in line behind the stooped shoulders of an elderly couple who'd clearly not noticed the angelic pair behind them.

The counter clerk, meanwhile, was trying frantically to mouth at the couple to move away—at least until Raphael shook his head at the hyperventilating woman. "I will ask." A pause before he said, "Mother tells me she convinced Tasha to go a short distance and bring them back mint tea and a plate of sweetmeats. They don't need anything else for the moment."

In front of them, the elderly man's age-spotted hand held a

tremor as he tried to pay for the food he'd purchased. It was the tremor of a life long lived, not fear, and when the money slipped from his grasp to flutter to the ground, Elena thought nothing of bending down and picking it up.

Turning, the man went to smile . . . and caught sight of her wings, of Raphael. His face turned sheet white under the sun-dark brown of his skin. Scared he'd have a heart attack, Elena smiled as gently as she could, touched him on the upper arm in silent reassurance, then placed the money on the counter.

By this time, the man's wife was staring at them, too.

Eyes a little bleary, the elderly woman suddenly smiled a smile so dazzling it was breathtaking and stepped toward Elena. Tears rolled down her cheek, her water-logged but joyous outpouring incomprehensible to Elena but for a single word: "Majda."

I'm asking Tasha to translate, Raphael said, while the woman went as if to throw her arms around Elena.

Jerking to life, her husband started to pull her back, but Elena was having none of that. She closed her arms and her wings around the woman's fragile body with care, the elder's bones like a bird's under her touch. The woman cried and continued to talk, and her hands, they patted at Elena as if she was a daughter long lost come home.

When Elena drew back after a long moment, folding her wings once more to her back, the woman's face was incandescent with joy and wet with tears. Elena wiped those tears away with gentle fingers.

Tasha says this woman is calling you Majda's blood. Madja was her friend's child, and when she was lost, it broke her parents' hearts. They died far too young. Raphael paused as the woman spoke again. *She is so happy the child survived.*

She has to be talking about my mother. Elena knew she'd been reaching from the start when it came to Majda, but it simply didn't make sense to her that the two of them would share such similarities without being related. And now, another piece that fit. A child. "I want to tell her the child was my mother, that her name was Marguerite."

Tasha came through, giving Raphael the words Elena needed to say. When she spoke them, the elderly woman sobbed again and hugged her, while repeating Marguerite's name over and over. It was at least a minute later when she drew back and began to speak to her husband.

Patting Elena's hand afterward, she beamed and stepped back.

Elena wanted so much to ask her more questions, but the fear in the husband's eyes stopped her. She wouldn't hurt this sweet couple, wouldn't repay the woman's affectionate welcome by terrorizing her husband.

Letting the white-haired pair take a seat at a nearby table with their food in front of them, Elena and Raphael placed an order of their own. When the food came, she glanced at the couple and felt relief kiss her skin like a cool rain. The man no longer appeared full of terror. Instead, he was looking at her with thoughtful eyes, as if seeing what his wife already had.

Lighting up as she caught Elena's gaze, the man's wife waved her and Raphael to the two spare chairs at the table.

"Elena!"

She'd just taken a seat, glanced over her shoulder at the call to see Riad . . . whose eyes bugged out of his head at seeing Raphael in the chair beside her. But when she angled her head in welcome, he came over nonetheless.

The elderly woman chattered at him, making hand motions.

"My great-grandmother says I am to sit and speak English to you." It came out a squeak.

Elena noticed every hair on his arm was standing up. "Grab something to eat first." She put some money into his hand. "Get what you want, then come join us. I want to talk to your great-grandmother and I need a translator."

The teenager nodded jerkily before running back toward the bun seller.

"This family has courage," Raphael murmured, his eyes on Riad's great-grandmother. "And I think it comes from this woman."

"Yes," Elena said, "I think so, too." She wasn't really interested in the food but she ate a few bites to make everything appear normal while waiting for Riad to return.

The teenager returned within minutes, his chest heaving.

Dragging over another chair, those hairs on his arms still up and his hair starting to crackle, too, he gulped from a bottle of water. His great-grandmother seemed to chide him for his manners.

Raphael, all their hair is beginning to crackle.

*I'm afraid my power is surging. A Cascade effect, I be-
lieve. It has an impact on mortals in close proximity, but it
should do them no harm.*

Having been speaking to his great-grandmother between
bites of his first bun, Riad now told them what Tasha had already translated about Majda having been the daughter of a
cherished friend. "She says Majda's baby had the same hair
but lighter skin. Like the other lady said to you, my great-
grandmother also says light hair was very strong in the girls
in the family, but still it was . . . I don't know the word." He bit
down on his lower lip.

"Unpredictable?" Elena suggested. "Sometimes the coloring appeared and sometimes it didn't?"

"Yes! Unpredictable. But Great-grandmother says Majda's
husband—who she loved like he was the stars and the moon—
had golden hair and pale skin like milk with just a little honey,
so the baby had a good chance of moonlight hair like yours."

Elena's blood ran hot. "Was Majda's husband mortal?"

A rapid-fire transfer of information before a white-faced Riad
whispered, "We're not supposed to talk about this. I told—"

It was his great-grandfather who spoke now, his voice
unexpectedly strong.

Riad's lower lip shook, the second bun he'd bought forgotten. "He says that they are old anyway, about to head out
on the final journey. What can the angels do to them now?
They take only the young—the prettiest women and the most
beautiful men." Eyes wet, his distress unhidden.

Touching his shoulder even as fury tore through her, Elena
said, "You love them both very much, don't you?"

A quick nod. "I don't want the angels to hurt them."

The angels. The Luminata.

"No one will." Raphael's voice silenced everyone at the
table. "Tell them this: they are under my protection. I will
make certain no one dares lay a finger on them."

Won't Charisemnon be an obstacle? Elena asked as a
breathless Riad translated.

*Charisemnon doesn't care about a small town. This is
Luminata business and that's who we have to deal with.* His
jaw set. *If need be, I'll leave Aodhan here to watch over these*

*people until we can return and dig out the rot at the heart of
the Luminata.*

Elena hadn't thought she could love Raphael more, but at
that instant, her heart overflowed with love and pride both. For
this archangel who had compassion enough to treat such fragile mortals with care. *Thank you for being you.*

Eyes of endless blue met hers. *You made me remember myself, Elena. Without you, I might've turned as cold as those
who would prey on the weak.*

Elena thought of the scar on his wing, of why she'd shot
him, and felt a chill ripple through her. *Never again,
Archangel.*

You live in me now, hbeebti. He touched his hand to her
hair. *I cannot ever return to who I once was, no matter what
eternity brings.*

Quiet words spoken in a feminine voice that quavered drew
her attention back to the table. Riad's great-grandmother was
saying something as more tears rolled down her cheeks.

"She says Majda's husband loved her, too, even though she
was mortal and would die while he'd keep living." Riad listened, then spoke, his eyes huge. "He didn't want to live without her, but he couldn't find any angels to make her a vampire
like him."

Another kick to Elena's heart, another jolt in the bloodstream at the unambiguous statement that Majda's lover had
been a vampire. And he hadn't simply been her lover. He'd
been her *husband.*

"My great-grandmother says Majda's husband was strong,
but he was just a young soldier who didn't know anyone so
powerful like Raphael." The last word came out an awed
whisper, Riad only daring to look at Raphael through the
corner of his eye.

"The angels in *that* place refused to help him." The bitterness of his tone made it clear Riad was referring to Lumia.
"They said he wasn't old enough to ask to have his mortal
turned into a vampire."

"Do you have any idea what happened to Majda or her husband?" Elena asked the elderly woman who'd hugged her with
such love.

Riad's quick translation was followed by an answer for

which Elena didn't need a translator. It was a sad shake of the head, the words spoken melancholy.

"She says Majda's husband went away first, soon after the baby was born." Riad made "poofing" motions with his hands and Elena understood the vampire had vanished without a trace. "Majda searched and searched for her husband, but when she didn't find him, she was afraid, so afraid; she said she had to run before she was made to go away, too."

A deep frown as he listened to his great-grandmother. "They thought the baby was dead when they saw Majda's ghost years later."

"Wait." Elena sat up, a chill running down her spine. "Her ghost?"

"My great-grandmother didn't see her," Riad translated. "But some of the other people in town said they saw her running down the hills from that place one night. Her hair, it was so bright under the moon."

Another biting of his lip. "When the angels heard the whispers, they hurt the people who spoke them, and so no one speaks of it any longer. My great-grandmother didn't see Majda's ghost, but she says why would the angels be so angry if it was just stories?" A very teenage shrug.

"Indeed," Raphael said, looking directly at the older couple. "You define bravery. Thank you for speaking the truth."

Riad's translation had the older couple sitting up a little straighter in open pride. They spoke more, but there was nothing else the couple could tell them except the name of the vampire who had been Majda's husband.

"He came from a faraway land," Riad's great-grandmother said, the teenager translating. "He helped guard that place, but he lived in the town. All the vampires and angels who were guards lived in the town then."

Riad's great-grandfather nodded his agreement with those words. "They were part of our town and it wasn't the first time a vampire fell in love with one of us." Riad pointed to himself as he translated, to indicate he meant mortals. "The vampire's name was Jean-Baptiste Etienne."

A last name beginning with *E*. Another piece of the puzzle slotting into place.

The realization that she'd just heard her grandfather's name reverberated in Elena's soul. "When did the vampires and angels stop living here?"

"Soon after Jean-Baptiste went away." That poof-disappearing motion again. "And *those* angels told the other vampires who lived here that they couldn't stay anymore." The elderly woman's expression made it clear what kind of tactics the Luminata had employed to pass on that message. "Then later, the angels who were guards stopped living here, too. The angels from that place came and made the townspeople tear down the tall homes left behind, the ones that touched the sky."

A fiefdom indeed, Raphael said in a tone gone ever colder.

Elena nodded. *Selfish as it was, tearing down the angelic homes wasn't just about ensuring the townspeople didn't make use of them.*

No, Raphael agreed. *It was a message to the rest of angel-kind that the Luminata prefer they do not settle their wings in this place.*

A haunting sound cut through the air before Elena could reply, a sound so pure that it made her heart hurt. "Raphael, your mother is singing." It came out a whisper touched with wonder and fear both.

The last time Caliane sang to mortals, thousands of them died.

And if Caliane had lost herself to madness again, it was Raphael who would have to stop her . . . who would have to attempt to kill his mother a second time around.

32

There's no need for worry. Raphael's wing arched over her, shadowing her face. *She does not sing any harm to these people.*

Shuddering, her chest no longer so tight, Elena put her hand on Raphael's thigh and just listened, giving in to the clarity and splendor of a voice unlike any she could've imagined. Around them, the entire marketplace had gone silent. Some people sank to their knees after a while, tears streaming down their faces, while others began to walk toward the tree where Caliane sat.

And in all those faces, Elena saw no fear or worry, only sweet serenity. *She's doing something, though, isn't she?*

I believe my mother is singing away the knot of hard, cold fear that lives in all these people. She is giving them a moment of perfect peace and untainted joy. It will hold only so long as she sings.

It was manipulation . . . but Elena couldn't argue with it. Not here. Not when reality would return as soon as the song stopped. Every person she'd seen in this town looked as if they could break at any moment, the strain on their shoulders a painful burden. If Caliane could offer them a small respite without asking for anything in return, if she could put a balm on their pain for a short period, then how could Elena say that was a bad thing?

Yet she knew it was. *She's stealing their choice.*

The Luminata have already done that, Raphael argued. *She's simply balancing the scales.*

Torn as she was herself, Caliane's voice a gift not many mortals would ever be lucky enough to hear, Elena didn't pursue the argument. *It's not affecting us.*

I'm shielding you.

She lay her head against his shoulder, let Caliane's song sweep over and into her. Her eyes stung, her soul wanting to soar but held to this earth by what she'd learned today. All of it, it fit.

The vampire who'd sired a daughter with a mortal.

The woman with hair of moonlight who'd disappeared with a baby.

The birthmark on both Majda and Marguerite.

The baby who'd been orphaned as a toddler.

The way Gian and the older Luminata looked at Elena when they thought she couldn't see.

And the "ghost" seen running from Lumia one quiet night.

Raphael heard the faraway echoes of thunder in the air twenty minutes after his mother began to sing, felt the air turn unseasonably cool at the same time. Something prickled across his skin. An instant later, Elena sat up, frowned. "The air's sparking."

"Stay here, Guild Hunter. Keep watch. I'm going to check the sky." Rising, he moved to the center of the pedestrian road, where the people stood or sat in thrall to Caliane's song, and spreading his wings, rose skyward.

It could be expected that the sky would be darkening as night started to fall in earnest, but the darkness he saw on the horizon was a roiling blackness that reminded him of the unnatural clouds that had crawled across the New York sky before hundreds of birds landed around him and Elena as they stood on a barge on the Hudson.

This storm, however, wasn't created of birds, wasn't a

message from beings who had spent eons in the silent deep. The black clouds had a malevolent purple tinge; he knew the lightning arcing inside it could crash even an archangel to the earth. He'd witnessed its like when Alexander awoke, seen powerful angels go down with shredded wings when they attempted to get above the clouds.

Because this wasn't ordinary lightning. It was Cascade-born. Unpredictable. Dangerous.

Elena, this storm is unnatural. Order the boy to tell people to go inside. I will ask Mother to stop her song. He knew no one would leave while she sang.

Caliane stopped the instant he told her of the Cascade storm building to killing fury. *I will sing them to return to their homes*, she replied a heartbeat later.

Not arguing against the manipulation that could save lives, Raphael landed back in the marketplace. People were bustling this way and that in the wake of Caliane's song of warning. He knew that song would reach every corner of the town, Caliane having amped up the voltage without raising her voice.

The boy was gone, as were his great-grandparents—along with Elena.

Guild Hunter.

I wanted to make sure Riad and his great-grandparents got under shelter. She appeared from around a corner even as her voice filled his mind, her wings held tight to her back. *Their house is literally just behind the market street.*

Reaching him, she said, "Is there anything else we can do?" Her hands were on her hips and her eyes sharp as she took in the activity around them.

"No, but I think the people here should be safe until the storm passes." Raphael watched a young man pick up a little girl and run into a shop that was putting up storm shutters. "These buildings are low to the ground to begin with, and most are likely to have a lower level underground, where it's cool."

Elena nodded. "Riad said he'd take his great-grandparents down to the cool room. That must be what he meant." She looked around. "Let's do a flyby, make sure no one's been caught outside for any reason."

Raphael took her into the sky, then splitting up, the two of them did a quarter-by-quarter flyover. They found no one in distress, children and elders and the infirm being assisted by the able-bodied, as should be in a healthy town. Clearly, this place had no problems of its own. The fear and horror came as a direct result of the Luminata situated on their doorstep.

Elena, start your flight back to Lumia. You need a head start. His consort was dangerously vulnerable in this situation. *I'll do another sweep, follow with Mother and Tasha.* Both of whom were still in the town as Caliane continued to sing people to safety.

His hunter flew down to check on a child who was being pulled inside a house, swept back up to face him. "I think everyone's inside or will be soon. Maybe we can just stay here until it passes?"

Raphael shook his head. "Caliane and I may attract the power of the storm." The Cascade acted in strange ways and its effects were concentrated mainly on those of the Cadre. "We can't take the risk of driving lightning down on this town."

"You promise you'll be following?" Elena asked as rain began to come down in hard stabs that had her wiping a hand across her face.

"I promise." Raphael had no intention of abandoning her alone in the dark. "I'll catch up to you before you've covered a quarter of the distance."

After reaching out to touch her fingertips to his, Elena turned and flew in the direction of Lumia, wings of midnight and dawn disappearing into the murk created by the rain and the rapidly falling night.

Mother, you need to get in the air. The people are safe. He understood her weakness, understood that she was trying to make up for the horror of what she'd once done, singing the adult populations of two thriving cities into the sea. She hadn't touched the children, but they'd died nonetheless. Of sorrow, of heartbreak.

Are you certain? Guilt in her tone, thousands of ghosts in her voice.

Yes. The streets are all but empty and the stragglers will make it to safety in the next two minutes at most. We must fly if we are to make Lumia before the storm hits—or we may draw the lightning to this place.

Caliane's body appeared in the distance, her wings spread, Tasha behind her.

Waiting for them to pass, Raphael swept along behind them. As he'd predicted, they overtook Elena within minutes, his hunter's young immortal body unable to reach anything like the punishing speed Tasha was maintaining. Caliane had slowed to match her escort, now said, *Raphael*—

I will bring her home, Mother. She is mine to protect. Even as he spoke, he dropped down to below Elena. *Guild Hunter, collapse your wings.*

That she didn't even hesitate at what could be a deadly order undid him.

Moving with the wind when it pushed her falling body to the left, he caught her in his arms and swept up in the same motion in an effort to get above the cloud layer, while Elena wrapped her arms around his neck as the rising wind whipped strands of hair that had come loose from the twist in which she wore it, across her face.

"I hate being a damsel in distress!" she yelled in a distinctly disgruntled tone.

He grinned because that description would never fit his warrior. "I can feel your crossbow digging into my arm. Be ready to shoot if anything comes at us."

Laughing with a fierce wildness that spoke to the same in him, she tucked her face against his neck, pulling her body in even further to lower the wind resistance. He took a moment to glance behind them, saw the storm was licking at their heels. When he looked forward, he saw only a single pair of wings in flight. *Mother, where is Tasha?*

Flying low. She's searching for a natural lee where we can shelter should we have need.

Raphael looked down, couldn't spot Tasha through the darkness. *Tasha, it's too exposed for this lightning. Head to Lumia.* They'd pass the barracks on their way, but those barracks weren't as well constructed as Lumia. The angelic guards should be fine—but they wouldn't be if Raphael and Caliane joined them and the lightning followed.

The rain became a torrential downpour an instant later, punching a heavy weight on his wings. Having reached Caliane, he saw Tasha come up on her other side, her wings almost crumpling under the combined pressure of the rain and the wind. "Sire!" she yelled to his mother. "Go! I will be behind you!"

Caliane didn't answer, but neither did she put on archangelic speed. Like Raphael, his mother would never leave one of her people behind. Tasha didn't waste her breath asking again, just flew on, though it was clear she was having trouble maintaining her place in the sky. Elena, meanwhile, shifted up carefully so she could look over his shoulder, leaving him free to keep his attention forward.

"How bad?" he asked, the two of them close enough that they could hear each other over the noise of the storm without having to shout.

"The lightning goes on as far as I can see, but it looks like the town's only being hit by scattered strikes. The heaviest mass is chasing us—or it's being dragged toward Lumia." She continued to look. "You think since there're more archangels there to draw the storm, that you and Caliane could land and have the lightning pass over you?"

"We can't risk it." Neither Elena nor Tasha would survive even a single strike.

Using one hand to wipe the wet strands of hair off her face, then his in turn, she said, "Then we need a plan B. Because we're not going to outrun it." Her tone was practical, not panicked. "Not at this speed."

Mother, you need to fly Tasha. Caliane appeared slender, but she was an archangel, had power humming through her every cell.

She will never agree.

Raphael spoke directly to Tasha, told her what he'd suggested. *This needs archangelic speed, Tasha. Don't be proud and get us all lightning-struck. If Elena can do it, so can you.*

I can't believe you are comparing me to a once-mortal, was Tasha's bitter response, but Caliane dropped below her seconds later and Tasha collapsed her wings so Caliane could capture her. Not in her arms, but in a net of sparkling white power.

Then he and Caliane *flew.*

A lightning strike singed the very tip of his left wing just as he landed at Lumia, Caliane having landed right before him. Ignoring the burn until they were under the shelter of the nearest external hallway, he placed Elena on her feet while his mother released Tasha from the net of power. Tasha's hair was an electric halo around her head, cracking with echoes of that power; her body shook a little, the tremors apparently uncontrollable.

"My lady," she said, sounding as if she was having to form her words with utmost care, "I think I am drunk."

"It will pass," Caliane promised, pushing back her wet hair from her face.

Elena, meanwhile, had turned her attention directly to Raphael's wing, kneeling down so she could look closely at the injury. "Damage is deep."

He glanced down, saw what she meant. The lightning strike had sheared off the very tip of his wing. He needed those feathers to maneuver, couldn't risk being without them—they'd heal, of course, but not at high speed. Wings never did.

The idea of being grounded in Lumia, even for a day or two, was intolerable but his Cascade-born healing strength, at least the amount he could access at will, hadn't yet regenerated after he'd used it to ease Elena's wings.

She looked up right then, her eyes shining silver. *Take it from me.* The words were an order. *The wildfire is all about life, right? Test it, see if it'll fix your wing.*

It was a good point—he was used to seeing it as a weapon against Lijuan, but it did taste violently of the energy of life . . . and of his hunter's mortal heart. *Let me attempt to direct the wildfire that lives in me.*

That attempt failed.

He could call it to his hand, could've attacked Lijuan with it or driven out her poison, but it dissipated into his blood when he tried to direct it to his injured wing. *It doesn't work.*

You don't know my wildfire will act the same, Elena insisted. *It exists because of my love for you. Its only purpose is to protect you.*

When he hesitated, loath to weaken her in any fashion, her eyes narrowed. *I accepted being a damn damsel in distress for you. You can be the hunky archangel in distress for once.*

Lips twitching despite the danger of the moment, he used the contact of her hand against his wing to *pull* at the wildfire that lived in her, as if a rope connected them and he was wrenching on his end. Her teeth clenched, her free hand fisted, but otherwise, she gave no outward indication of what he'd done.

His mother and Tasha, behind her, had no reason to suspect anything.

A heartbeat later, pain burned through him as if he was lightning struck on the inside, even as a white-hot glow pulsed off the injured section of his wing. Her wildfire had arrowed directly to the wounded part of his body, his once-mortal consort loving him with a fierceness that was a storm wilder than the one that raged outside.

Releasing a shuddering breath, Elena rose to hug him tight. He noticed her legs were a little shaky, tightened his own grip so no Luminata watching might guess that she'd literally just given him a piece of herself. And his heart, it pounded like a thousand horses across a wild plain because only now did he allow himself to think how close they'd come to disaster.

A single strike and Elena could've been erased from the world.

He hadn't known fear before loving Elena. He hadn't known life, either. *Hbeebti?*

I'm good, she replied, running one hand down his back. *You?*

My wing is healing. As for the other—love meant learning to live with fear.

As he released her, his mother turned from where she'd been watching Tasha to ensure her escort steadied with no ill-effects. Her eyes reflected the lightning just beyond the covered hallway. "It appears," she said, "that we may not be leaving Lumia at dawn after all."

Elena hissed out a breath.

33

Pissed off at the idea that they might be trapped in this place with its ugly secrets and its dark whispers and its walls that watched them, Elena stalked through the corridors with Raphael by her side. They were taking a shortcut to their suite that she and Aodhan had figured out, one that involved passing through hallways so narrow, she and Raphael couldn't have walked side by side had they minded their wings overlapping.

Water dripped from her hair down her back and onto her face, while their wings tracked water through Lumia despite the fact they'd both shaken off those wings before heading to their suite. Not that it mattered—as wet as they were, it wasn't as if they could avoid leaving a watery trail.

Lumia was eerily quiet around them, though, despite the lightning-seared darkness, it wasn't that late. "Wonder if people are prepping for dinner," she said, one of her throwing knives in her hand without her conscious volition.

"Perhaps."

Yeah, clearly her archangel didn't buy that explanation, either.

Wiping off the water dripping into her eyes, she stifled a sneeze. "Damn it. Shouldn't I be immune to sneezes by now?"

Raphael's smile made her want to kiss him.

Instead, she wove her fingers through his, uncaring of who might see. If people didn't know they adored each other by now, they had rocks in their head, she thought just as she turned the corner and saw a robe-clad body crumpled on the ground. The fallen angel lay on his side, his wings exposed and limp, another distressed-looking angel kneeling beside him, his trembling hands hovering above that crumpled body.

"Ibrahim!" Knife held in readiness against a threat, Elena strode to the downed angel's side . . . and saw Ibrahim's bloodied face, the crushed pulp of his right hand. That wasn't the worst of it. His robe was sunken in on the side she could see, as if his ribcage had been crushed inward.

She knelt down beside him.

Sliding her hand gently under his head after putting away her knife because, trained response aside, Raphael had her back, she looked hard at the angel with eyes of dark gray and hair of silver who knelt on his other side. The one she'd met on the lower floor of the Gallery: Donael. "What happened?"

"I do not know," he said, his features stark. "I've just found him. This is *Lumia*." His voice shook. "There is no violence here."

Jaw tight, Elena took in Donael's spotless robe, the lack of injuries on his knuckles or anywhere else on him, and was forced to believe him. Ibrahim's injuries looked very recent from the lack of any apparent healing, and she didn't think the strong young angel would've gone down without trying to fight back.

Raphael's wing was heavy over hers as he knelt down beside Ibrahim, the warmth of the still-healing tip pulsing through her own feathers. "He is badly hurt," he murmured. "Crushed windpipe. That's what's keeping him under."

And Raphael's healing ability was wiped out for the moment. "What can we do?" The idea of just leaving Ibrahim to hurt was not something she could accept.

"Make him comfortable so he can heal. And keep him safe." Sliding his arms under Ibrahim, Raphael rose with the broken male in his hold. *Can you scent another angel or a vampire on him?*

Elena tried, shook her head. *No vamp but I don't know about an angel.* Her ability to scent normal, non-toxin-maddened angels continued to be hit and miss.

"His quarters are through here," Donael began, but Elena shook her head, her crossbow in hand so she could watch Raphael's back as he carried Ibrahim.

"We're taking him to our suite," she said, having no need to check with Raphael on that—she knew her archangel, had heard the fury in his tone.

Donael didn't argue. "Of course, of course." His breathing was ragged, white lines bracketing his mouth. "I don't understand. We do not have violence at Lumia."

The repetition of the patently untrue words had Elena snapping. "Yeah?" she said, her tone harsh. "What about the violence visited on the townspeople? That's apparently okay?"

Donael looked at her with a complete lack of comprehension as he tried to keep up with her and Raphael's long strides. "I have no reason to go to the town. There is no peace there, as is oft the case with mortal places. Always moving this way and that, always living their lives in fast-forward."

The sea rolled into her mind, touched with floes of ice. *He is old, Elena. Truly old. He may not ever go into the town.*

Maybe. And maybe he's just a really good actor.

"Why would anyone harm Ibrahim?" Donael's voice had settled, but his expression remained shaken. "He is a child, one with a calling, but a child nonetheless." A careful look at Raphael. "We have many non-Luminata here."

"And I've seen Gian and others practicing martial arts," Raphael's consort bit out. "Violence isn't off-limits in Lumia."

"Controlled violence," Donael protested. "A form of movement to aid meditation. It's different from this atrocity."

"True," Raphael responded. "But we can debate who it was that hurt Ibrahim later. For now, do you have a healer in Lumia?"

"There is only the one called Stillness." An angling of his head, a pause that said he was riffling through his memories to find the correct one. "The boy had another name once, and under that name, he was a student of healing."

Aodhan, Raphael said, reaching out with his mind. *We need a healer. Can you find Laric?*

I'm with him at this moment, sire. Where shall I bring him?
To our suite.

When they reached their rooms, Raphael laid Ibrahim down on the bed he and Elena had moved to the living area, and as he did so, Ibrahim's right arm slid down the injured male's side. The movement was so strangely fluid that Raphael gently pushed up the sleeve of the man's robe.

"His arm is in pieces," Elena gritted out, her free hand fisted, the one holding her crossbow pointing it safely down and away from anyone in the vicinity. "Like it's been deliberately smashed."

Elena was right. It was as if whoever had harmed Ibrahim had focused his rage on this one arm after taking the angel down. But the rest of Ibrahim's body hadn't escaped insult by any measure. When Raphael opened Ibrahim's robe and tore open the fine tunic he wore beneath, he saw the man's ribs had been crushed inward, likely perforating his organs and causing bleeding on the inside if the swelling in his abdomen was anything to go by.

His face, too, was battered and fractured.

Bruises bloomed on every part of him that Raphael could see.

Though Donael called Ibrahim young, he had to be over a thousand years old to have been permitted to become a Luminata initiate. "He'll survive," Raphael told Elena, because his hunter knew very well that immortals *could* be killed. "He may, however, go into *anshara*." The healing sleep might be the best thing for him.

Aodhan entered the room without knocking, the hooded Luminata by his side short of stature and small of form with shoulders that were hunched in and a gait that was hesitant. Laric came to Ibrahim's side at once, the hands he placed on Ibrahim's broken body an icy white marked with ridged scars of dark pink.

Stepping back to give the healer room to work, Raphael and his hunter both turned to Donael. It was Elena who spoke first. "Did you see or hear anything before you found him?"

A deep frown before Donael nodded slowly. "Yes. I heard muted thumps." Dark gray eyes lingering on Ibrahim. "Such as could be made by punches being thrown into flesh. I did not like the sound, knew it was wrong in this place, so I called out." His hands trembled as he tucked them into the sleeves of his robe. "I soon heard footsteps moving quickly away and there was no one but poor young Ibrahim in the hallway when I arrived."

If Donael was telling the truth, he'd surprised Ibrahim's attacker. That, however, brought up another question. "How long would that hallway usually be empty at this time of night?" Raphael asked.

"Close as it is to the dinner bell, it is not a time for contemplation for most of us," Donael said slowly. "And the hallway is a crossroads for many. A 'shortcut,' the young ones call it." The angel released a quiet breath. "I wouldn't expect it to be empty for more than five minutes at most."

"I don't think this was a five-minute beating." Elena's voice was gritty. "An angel as old as Ibrahim couldn't be so badly hurt so quickly . . . unless it was more than one person."

"No," Aodhan interrupted. "Laric says it was only one."

Raphael turned to the angel, not asking how he was in communication with the silent healer. "Why?"

"He's no expert, but there doesn't seem to be enough variation in the blows."

"Then someone else, *more* than one someone, must've seen Ibrahim being beaten," Raphael said with grim understanding of exactly how deep the rot was in Lumia. "Given that it is a Luminata shortcut, the likelihood those bystanders were Luminata is near to a hundred percent certain. As is the fact they chose not to stop it."

Or were too scared to, Elena said mind to mind, the steel of her a gleaming blade today. *There are always people who have more power than others in any given situation. Old and respected as he is, Donael has power of his own, enough that the attacker didn't want to take the risk of being seen by him.*

Raphael considered it, realized she was right. *The Luminata clearly give way to Gian, but as you've just pointed out, the old ones like Donael also hold considerable power—and he's not the only one of his generation here.*

Elena's nod was reluctant. *Yes, much as Gian creeps me out, I can't see him just losing it like this. He's always in control, the kind of angel who'd take his time, be subtle.*

And what had been done to Ibrahim was in no way subtle.

"He is in *anshara*," Aodhan said, and this time, Raphael saw how he was speaking to the healer.

Laric was using his scarred hands to sketch fluid, shallow movements into the air. It was an old language that relied on understated motion rather than sound. Rarely spoken these days, it was used mostly by those who wished to withdraw from the world, including vampires who chose seclusion. Aodhan had never used it as far as Raphael was aware, but clearly, if he knew it so well, he'd thought about it.

Rising, the healer continued the purposeful movements.

"Ibrahim needs to be in a safe place," Aodhan translated. "Laric is happy to watch over him in his own quarters, but believes he shouldn't be moved until the dawn. His body will have knitted together a little by then and movement will not cause him further harm."

Do you trust him, Aodhan?

Yes, sire. He isn't like many of the others, is as guileless as Ibrahim.

The healer moved at that instant and a stray beam of light from the overhead lamp caught on his throat and lower face. The scarring was the worst Raphael had ever seen on an immortal. Angels simply did not scar that way.

He felt Elena go motionless beside him, knew she'd caught it, too, but neither one of them said anything, letting the healer move to Ibrahim's other side to further check his injuries and do what he could to ease them.

Looking to Donael, Raphael said, "You should inform Gian what has happened." His words were a command. "Tell him we'll speak with him after my consort and I have had a chance to get out of our wet clothing."

Inclining his head, Donael went to leave—but he paused on the doorstep. "We are not who we once were." Melancholy in his tone. "This would've never happened in the time of Reed."

Waiting until after Donael closed the door behind himself, Raphael left Aodhan on watch while he and Elena retreated to the bedroom to change. "Don't waste energy on glamour," Elena said, her eyes dangerously focused. "I'm going to check the walls, and this time, I'm not stopping until I figure out what the fuck is making my skin crawl in this room."

Raphael did the same, but it was Elena who found it almost thirty minutes later.

Hearing her mutter a harsh word under her breath, he moved to join her. Wisps of her damp hair had begun to curl around her face, her clothing stuck to her, but her concentration was a laser. "Where?" he asked.

She pointed the tip of a knife at a detail in the painting at which she was staring; it was the artist's impression of a knot of wood on a tree. The hole was a pinprick, but it was very much there. Wings glowing in blinding fury, Raphael pulled the painting off the wall and threw it on the floor, exposing the hole beyond.

Elena thrust her knife into it. "No screams. Too bad. I was hoping to stab out someone's eye."

Not satisfied with that, Raphael punched a hand into the wall with archangelic strength. It collapsed in a spiderweb of cracks about four feet in diameter. He tore out the pieces to expose the entire interior.

Elena looked inside the hole after waving away the dust. "It's a goddamn hidey space built *between* two rooms."

"Maybe so the spy or spies can watch both." Raphael stepped inside, saw that the hole apparently connected to nothing on either end. But there was a door in the center. "The entrance is via the other room."

Squeezing past him, Elena opened that door—which proved to be the back of a closet. "Bet you the room's empty."

It was—and there was no clue as to who'd been utilizing the hole.

"At least we frustrated the spy or spies the entire time we've been here," Elena muttered in cool satisfaction. "I hope they enjoyed watching an empty room." She secured the door by thrusting a blade through the locking mechanism so no one could open it from the other side, then the two of them stepped back fully into their room.

Staring at the wall that had concealed the hole, Raphael spoke through the ice-cold anger chilling his veins. "This will not go unpunished."

"Your wings are glowing, Archangel." Elena ran the edge of his wing through her fingers. "Don't explode just yet. Keep it in reserve for when we find out who hurt Ibrahim and which of these assholes have been terrorizing the town."

It took at least a minute for Raphael to get himself under control. Then he and Elena, in silent agreement, checked the other walls again. There were no more peepholes, but despite Elena's admonitions to save his power, he threw his glamour around himself and his consort. He would allow no one to spy on her.

As for their voices, no one would be able to hear them if they kept the volume quiet.

Elena, her own temper still shimmering a silver light in her eyes after she finally stripped off her damp clothing, pressed her naked body to his in a silent statement that they were one. Always. It calmed him enough that he could think. "We'll find the answers hidden in this place, *hbeebti*. Even if we have to come back a hundred times."

Rising up on tiptoe, Elena kissed him soft and tender. It was a delicate touch from his tough hunter, but he was used to such kisses now and then. Because Elena had a well-hidden core of softness that only came out with the vulnerable, and with those she loved. Stroking his hands over the sleek line of her back, down to the toned lower curves of her body, he sank into the kiss, sank into her.

It felt as if she breathed life into him, washing away the darkness that lingered so heavy on the horizon. Closing his wings around them to protect her even further, though his glamour hid them from all eyes, he kissed his lover, his warrior, was kissed in turn.

"I love you, Raphael." A whisper against his lips, eyes full of ghosts holding his. "Don't ever go."

"*Elena.*" He pressed his forehead to hers. "You are thinking of your mother and your sisters again." The loss haunted her, made her afraid of losing the people who mattered to her as she'd once lost Marguerite, Belle, and Ari.

Shields down, her face painfully bare, Elena traced his Legion mark with a single fingertip. "My grandmother's body was never recovered after the bus crash in which she was meant to have died, did you know that?"

34

Elena hadn't ever before spoken of how Marguerite had been orphaned. "You think she—Majda—was never on that bus, that she was taken and brought to Lumia." The "ghost" who'd attempted to make an escape on a moonlit night.

Nodding, Elena continued to trace his mark, the wildfire reacting to her as it always did. "I managed to track down newspaper reports of the accident when I was a teenager." She ran her hand down his jaw to place it flat on his chest. "It wasn't hard since it was such a big accident, doubly so because so many of the bodies were washed away by the snowmelt-fed river at the bottom of the ravine. Easy and convenient accident to arrange if you were powerful enough."

Raphael's eyebrows drew together over his eyes; there was a problem with her theory. But he needed more information before he could be sure. "How did they know your grandmother was even on the bus?"

"She told the nun with whom she left my mom exactly which bus she'd be on—she didn't want to take my mom since the long round trip would be too grueling."

Stroking her hair, her back, Raphael said, "Elena, if a powerful angel wanted to take a human woman, especially one who was alone in a large city but for a child, he—or she—would just take the woman. No need to go to the trouble of staging an accident to cover it up." The victim would just disappear.

Raphael had seen too many twisted immortals to believe such things didn't happen.

Elena stared at him. "You're right," she said in the tone of someone who'd missed the obvious. "So I guess the ghost was just someone's imagination and the Luminata overreacted because of guilt over something else."

"Jean-Baptiste's disappearance," Raphael suggested. "Majda ran because her husband was taken."

"Do you think Gian murdered him out of jealousy?"

"I wish I didn't, but the facts line up too neatly for it to be otherwise . . . and Gian watches you with eyes that are—"

"Stalker-creepy," Elena suggested, a shiver rippling through her but her voice razor-sharp. "He watches me like I'm a pretty bug he wants to put in a glass jar and keep."

Gripping his rage in a fist that anyone would dare look at his consort that way, Raphael nodded. "Just so." Gian would die as soon as they had the answers to Elena's questions.

"Majda ran to protect her child's life," Elena said. "And she never made it back home, never made it out of the river at the bottom of the ravine." She swallowed. "I'm glad. I'm glad she wasn't trapped at Lumia, far from her child."

He kissed away the tears that streaked her face. "*Elena.*"

Hands closing over his wrists, his hunter said, "She dressed my mother up in a pretty dress and coat, left her with a bag full of snacks and toys. She loved her baby."

"Did someone keep the clothing, the shoes?"

Elena shook her head. "The nun took a photograph of my mother the day my grandmother died. She knew that once my mother went into the foster system, her history would be lost and she'd never know how much she'd been loved."

More tears, her eyes haunted. "As a child, I didn't understand how scared my mom must've been when her own mom didn't come back for her. She was so small, so vulnerable."

Kissing away her tears once more, Raphael said, "Your grandmother left her in safe hands, hands that cared for her long after others would've forgotten her."

"It doesn't seem fair, does it, Raphael?" Elena shook her

head, the yet-damp strands of her hair brushing against the wings he'd curved around her. "Marguerite lost her mother, then she lost two of her daughters. No one can be expected to bear that much sorrow." Her shoulders shook, a sob catching in her throat.

Wrapping her tight in his arms, Raphael held her close as Elena cried for a woman who hadn't been able to bear that awful reality, no matter that she had two living daughters who loved her, needed her to kiss away their own shocked horror. Marguerite Deveraux had put a rope around her neck and ended her pain—and it had been Elena who'd found her. For that, Raphael would never forgive Marguerite, no matter how much pity and sadness he felt for what she'd suffered.

Elena's nails dug into his back, her wet cheek pressed to his chest. "It's like our family is cursed."

"If it was," Raphael said, "then you have broken the curse." Cupping the back of her head, he pressed his jaw to her temple. "No one will take my Elena from me. I'll destroy the world before I allow that to happen."

"You're scary, Archangel," his hunter whispered, shifting back to face him with a tear-wet face that nonetheless held a smile. "But I want to dance with you anyway."

The words were an echo of the ones she'd spoken to him as they fell in New York, Elena's broken body in his arms and his wings shredded and useless. *Knhebek, hbeebti.*

He took another kiss, poured power into her until her skin glowed with it, tried to kiss away the pain that lived so deep in her. He wanted to love her in the most primal way, to drive away the dark with raw pleasure, but in the next room lay a broken Luminata, and above them, the skies pounded with lightning.

"We'll dance when we are home," he said, the words a promise.

"Done." A shaky breath. "It's such a rush when you do that thing you do." Her breasts were flushed, her nipples tight.

Raphael smiled. They'd only been able to experience this little eroticism of late, as she became strong enough to bear the merest hint of power he shared with her, bonding them during intimacy. Her body couldn't hold on to that power for longer than a few seconds, but it was more than enough to ignite pleasure through both their bodies.

"Imagine how much better it'll feel as we grow together," he whispered, dropping his head to kiss one pouting nipple.

Elena shuddered. "You're lethal. And I"—a tug on his hair, a hard kiss—"am your willing victim."

Elena dressed in the full set of warrior leathers she'd packed just in case, complete with boots that came up to her thighs and would double her protection against knife strikes. The top was sleeveless but had a high neck, and the blades strapped to her upper arms should give pause to anyone who wanted to strike at her. Over her wrists and forearms, she wore metal reinforced leather gauntlets that had been a gift from Titus.

For Raphael's warrior, he'd written in the note that had accompanied the gift the Archangel of Southern Africa had sent her after the block party in New York.

They fit perfectly and, even better, weren't decorative but meant to be worn as protection. On the underside, there was a built-in knife sheath, which she now utilized. Then she strapped her crossbow onto her right thigh and, pulling aside her ponytail, slipped her long spine knife into its hidden sheath. The crossbow bolt sheath was easy to wear on her back, designed as it was to sit on her spine and not get in the way of her wings. "Can you pass me those knives, Archangel?"

Raphael handed over the small, sleek throwing knife set she always had on her. With the glamour still around both of them, she could be sure no one was watching as she secreted the blades all over her body.

Her lover's eyes glinted. "You're missing something."

"I am?" Elena glanced at herself. "I'm pretty sure I'm bristling with as many weapons as possible." She was pissed off at what had been done to Ibrahim as well as the brutal fate that had probably befallen her grandfather—and that had led to her grandmother's death in a land far from her home.

Raphael lifted a closed fist, opened it. On his palm lay a deadly blade star that could cut a throat if thrown just right. "Ashwini came over to give this to me the morning of our departure, while you were in the shower."

The other hunter was an expert with the stars, could probably decapitate someone with a slightly larger version, and she'd been teaching Elena how to use them effectively. Eyes wide, Elena picked up the star with utmost care, aware it could slice right through her finger if she wasn't cautious. "Why are you giving it to me only now?"

"Your strangely prescient friend told me to give it to you once we'd found the broken man."

As long as Elena had known Ash, her friend's occasionally spooky predictions still made her shiver. "Did she say anything else?"

"Only that you'd need it." Raphael's jaw grew hard. "If you do, use it. Sever the arteries, do whatever you have to do to survive."

"I have no intention of letting anyone hurt me, Raphael." Her words were a vow. "These bastards might have terrorized my grandmother, but I'm no simple town girl. I'm a fucking hunter, and I'm the fucking consort to the Archangel of New York."

Hauling Raphael down to her after slipping the blade star carefully into a spot in her leathers built to hold the weapon, she kissed him with red-hot fury. "Now let's kick these assholes into oblivion."

Raphael bit at her lower lip. "Are you tired? From the wildfire transfer?"

"Not tired, but I feel like I'll need more sleep than usual when I crash." Another kiss. "But I'm not crashing anytime yet."

"I'll be there to catch you if you do, my damsel."

"Ha ha. Funny. *Not*."

Raphael's smile was a kick to the gut.

He, too, had discarded his wet clothing, now wore a set of faded brown leathers that had stood the test of time. He carried no weapons, but if he needed one or three, she had more than enough for both of them. It was good to be a consort.

The room still held only Aodhan, Ibrahim, and the healer with the terrible scarring on his neck and face. But Aodhan stepped aside from the door at Elena and Raphael's return. "Gian wishes to enter. I told him to wait."

Good call, Elena thought, as an angry-faced Gian was allowed in at last.

"What is the meaning of this?" the coldly furious Luminata leader demanded, staring down Aodhan as if he was some underling who'd crumple under pressure. "I am the head of the Luminata. On whose authority do you bar me from seeing to the welfare of one of my own?"

"Mine."

Had Elena's hair been unbound instead of in a tight ponytail, it would've been pushed back from her face at the sheer force of the power pulsing off Raphael. He was glowing again, the glow hard enough to hurt mortal eyes . . . but it didn't hurt Elena's. Not any longer.

Near the door, Gian drew up his shoulders, his hands tucked into the sleeves of his robe and his face devoid of any marks that fingered him as Ibrahim's attacker. That didn't necessarily mean anything—Gian was old enough to have healed superficial wounds by now. And while Ibrahim would've fought, he would've also been taken by surprise. It was possible he hadn't done any easily visible damage.

"Lumia does not fall under the Cadre's authority," Gian said, his eyes hard though he'd schooled his expression into Luminata calm.

"No, Gian." Raphael's tone told the other man to tread with care. "I had the records checked prior to the meeting. Lumia falls under no one archangel's authority. It falls under that of *all* of us. That stipulation is how Lumia achieved independence."

Elena's mouth would've fallen open had she not been clenching her jaw at the sight of poor Ibrahim lying so hurt nearby. Laric had pulled a blanket over his wounded body, continued to work on him with gentle hands, but there was no hiding the extent of the damage.

Gian smiled a small smile that was so astonishingly sincere Elena would've believed it had she not already learned that he lied with flawless ease. If he'd been human, she'd have called him a psychopath.

As if he'd caught her thoughts, his eyes flicked to her for a single heartbeat before he said, "That is untrue." His confidence was a peaceful thing. "Lumia is an island of self-governance, our laws and rules our own."

"On the contrary." Neha's elegant voice as the Archangel of India appeared in the open doorway.

She'd changed out of her sari into something akin to warrior leathers, though her clothing was of a tough-looking dark green material that appeared new. Elena wasn't fooled by the latter. Raphael had told her how good Neha was in combat. Just because she chose to be a lady most of the time didn't mean she wasn't also a deadly fighter.

"Raphael is quite correct," Neha said, the elegant lines of her face exposed by the French braid into which she'd plaited her hair. "The stipulation is on Lumia's founding documents." An icy smile shot in Raphael's direction, but no audible words.

What did she say? Elena asked Raphael mind-to-mind.

35

*That it is a pity she can never forgive me for helping to murder
her daughter, for I am still as intelligent and as dangerous as
I ever was.*

Even though Neha's daughter, Anoushka, had been a monster who'd gone so far as to brutalize a child in her quest for
power, Elena might've still felt sorry for Neha for losing the
child she'd loved so deeply, except that she now knew how
Neha had treated another child in her care.

Mahiya rarely spoke about her time in Neha's court, but
Venom and Dmitri both had contacts there and Elena had
picked up enough through those two to know that Mahiya was
a miracle: a woman who'd held on to her kind spirit and heart
through sheer effort of will, despite a childhood not only
utterly lacking in love, but filled with acts of what Elena considered flat-out torture.

"However," Neha added, "be that as it may, I do not believe
the Cadre needs to be involved in internal Luminata matters."
Her eyes went to Ibrahim's broken body, but from her
position—and taking into account how Laric was hovering
protectively beside his patient, while Gian's stiff form further
blocked her line of sight—she could likely only see part of his

lower half. "Especially given the ferocity of the storm outside. That should be our priority."

"Why are you here, Neha?" Raphael asked.

"As it happens, I was simply walking the hallways." A graceful movement that was as close as Elena had ever seen Neha come to a shrug. "I want to leave this place and find out what is happening in China. However, it appears we are trapped here for the time being, and since we are . . ."

The Archangel of India's eyes went to Ibrahim again. "I cannot see his face, but that appears to be blood on his robe. He is injured?"

"This novice was beaten to a pulp," Raphael said flatly. "Kicked while he was down."

"A distasteful act." Neha pursed her lips. "We may as well discover who was behind it."

It was an ironic thing to say, given what Anoushka had done to one of Raphael's vampires. Then again, the Queen of Poisons steadfastly chose to believe in her daughter's innocence despite evidence to the contrary.

Her eyes lifted to Gian, who was icily furious at being told his little fiefdom wasn't actually a fiefdom at all—but who was doing an excellent job of hiding it. His calm facade never cracked, but Elena saw the truth in the flatness of his gaze, the rigid tension of his body.

"What do you know about this man?" Neha's question was a cold demand.

"He is new here." Gian's voice was as unshaken as always, a leader well on the path to luminescence. "Only with us for five years."

Elena hadn't realized Ibrahim was *that* new. In angelic terms, five years was literally the blink of an eye. The slender male wouldn't have had time to gain the trust of anyone here—but neither would he have been drawn into whatever it was that was going on beneath Lumia's shining surface. He wouldn't have known not to do something.

Mouth drying up, she stared at him in horror. *Raphael, he got us that map.*

Raphael met her gaze, the blue of his eyes a metallic shade that denoted an anger so cold, it came from the primal core. *You think that caused this?*

I think it might be part of it at least. Ibrahim was being helpful probably without realizing that certain things are off-limits.

Then, Raphael said, *there must be something on that map we're not meant to see. Do you have it on your person?*

Yes, it's still in my crossbow bolt sheath. It had survived the rain thanks to the fact she'd closed the sheath out of habit—it had only taken losing a bolt onto the city streets to learn that lesson. She'd been lucky she didn't accidentally hurt anyone.

Raphael turned to respond to something Neha had said, but his attention remained with Elena. *Go with Aodhan, see if you can discover what it is that we weren't meant to find. I'll make sure your friend is safe.*

"Aodhan." Elena looked into the splintered shards of Aodhan's eyes. "Let's go back to the spot where Raphael and I found Ibrahim. There might be a clue there."

To Aodhan's credit, he didn't question why she was leaving the injured man. He just held open the door for her, and as she strode past him, her wing brushed his chest. The contact was nothing momentous, not now, not between friends, not when Aodhan had given her permission in multiple small ways but she felt eyes boring into her back.

Sliding out a blade as if playing with it, she used the polished surface to catch a glimpse of who it was that was staring at her and Aodhan.

Gian.

And he wasn't focused on her but on Aodhan.

It could be nothing, his calmly stifled anger directed outward at whoever happened to be in his line of sight, but that look . . . it made her glad Aodhan was going to be nowhere near Gian's vicinity.

A second later, she and Aodhan were in the hallway and heading in the right direction. "Ibrahim found that historical map I asked for," she explained to him after they were out of hearing distance and alone. "We need to figure out if there's something in there we shouldn't know about."

"We'll need a place to examine it." He thought for a moment. "There's a small library in the tower where Laric makes his home."

"Let's head there." Elena had zero doubts that Gian would know soon enough where they'd gone, but it would take a little while for the message to filter back to the Luminata leader. Long enough for them to get a head start on whatever was happening here.

They passed a number of the sect in the hallways, their faces hooded and their hands tucked into the wide sleeves of their robes. None spoke. "Creeps," Elena muttered after the most recent one had slithered down the corridor. "Why not look people in the eye, show your face?"

"I think your view has been impacted by what was done to Ibrahim," Aodhan said quietly. "Laric does not cover his face because of a lack of courage."

"Shit." Elena blew out a breath, rubbed her forehead. "I'm sorry. I didn't mean it that way. These Luminata, though— they hide things."

Aodhan didn't argue. "I think secretiveness has become embedded into their culture."

"What happened to Laric?" Elena asked. "Did he really come here to find luminescence?"

"He was in the sky when Caliane executed Nadiel." Aodhan's words were like rocks thrown into a still pond. "He wasn't close, was attempting to land when he saw what was about to happen, but he wasn't fast enough. The flames from Nadiel's death crawled across the sky like the 'most violent lightning fire' according to him, and he was caught in the inferno."

"Hell." Elena couldn't begin to imagine the pain Laric had suffered. "Why hasn't he healed?" She'd seen angels heal from all kinds of things, including wings that had been sliced off.

"Even Keir can't give him an answer to that." Aodhan led her down a narrow corridor. "He *is* healing, but at a glacial pace. In the over a thousand years since Nadiel's execution, he says the scars have become less rigid, freeing up the movement of his hands. But there is no outward sign of that softening, no indication the scars will one day disappear."

Elena thought about what Aodhan was telling her. "He was caught in the backwash of an archangel's death at the hands of another archangel. That violence of energy . . ."

"Yes. It would burn even an immortal to the bone—only

the fact he was so distant and descending rapidly saved him, I think."

They walked in silence for several minutes, and a number of times, as they entered covered external walkways, Elena felt the pummeling force of the wind, saw lightning stabbing at Lumia, the clouds above thunderous black. Nothing would be flying in that until it was all over. "Good thing Lumia's built to last."

"This lightning is scoring the stone nonetheless." Aodhan pointed out the signs of charring she'd missed in the erratic flashes of light. "If the storm doesn't abate within a day, it may threaten the integrity of even this place that has stood for millennia."

Because the Cascade made its own rules.

Her eyes took in the purple-hued sky split with lightning. "You know what that would mean." Raphael and the other archangels would have to fly out, drawing the lightning with them—and risk being smashed to the earth by the bolts.

"It won't kill him," Aodhan reminded her softly.

Elena's hand fisted. "But it'll hurt him badly." Forcing herself to flex her hand after they passed back into an internal hallway, she blinked away the after-images of lightning on the backs of her eyes. "Let's not borrow trouble, focus on the now." Thinking of Raphael heading out into the malevolence of that unnatural storm made her stomach churn, a cold hand choking her throat.

"I think Laric is hiding here," Aodhan said after nearly a minute, the words heavy. "As I hid in my home in the Refuge. At least I was protected in a sense by my appearance. It is unusual, but also coveted by many." A long pause before he continued. "Immortals do not have to face physical ugliness in anything but a fleeting manner—many were not kind to him. Especially the girl he was courting at the time of the fire."

Elena thought of her own comments about immortals winning the genetic lottery, her mind awash with the searing beauty of the angels and vampires she knew. And she thought of Jessamy, so gifted and kind, but with a twisted wing that defined her in the minds of many immortals.

Her heart squeezed. "He's been here the whole time?"

"From about a decade after the incident," Aodhan told her.

"He says this place had a kind heart once, that the Luminata in charge had true luminescence in his soul, and he offered Laric sanctuary with no end date attached.

"Not only that, Laric says the Luminata sat with him for many hours, offered him wise counsel, urged him to return to his studies at the Medica, and spoke to him in the silent tongue." Aodhan moved his hands to show what he meant. "But that man has long been Asleep. I think he is afraid, Elena, afraid that the heart of Lumia is gone and he will be shoved out into the world again."

Elena thought of how Laric kept his shoulders hunched in, his face angled in a way that kept light from illuminating his scarred face. "How old is your new friend, Aodhan?" From everything Aodhan had said, she didn't think Laric was very old. "Or I should ask—how old was he when he came here for sanctuary?" Because he'd stayed in stasis since then, no matter the physical passage of time.

"A hundred and twenty."

Elena sucked in her gut. "He was a baby." So close in age to Izzy that the difference didn't matter a damn.

Aodhan nodded. "He was far too young to request entry into Lumia, but the then leader of the sect made an exception for him—the sole exception ever made—because he came not to be a novice but as a terribly wounded being who needed refuge." Aodhan's voice was no less potent in its emotion for being quiet. "The Lumia of today, however . . . I don't want to leave him here, Ellie. It's not a good place."

"We'll figure something out." If Laric wanted to leave with them, no one was going to stand in his way, Elena would make sure of it. "Is that his tower?" It was at one far corner of Lumia, a light burning in the window high above.

The covered but open corridor that led to it howled with wind, lightning slamming into the stone directly above their heads and gusts of rain pelting their faces and bodies as they ran to the tower. Aodhan took the windward side, his wing raised to block out the worst of it.

"Thanks," she said, her heart thumping as they reached the end.

Folding back his wing, he gave her one of those rare smiles that lit him up. "I ran with a girl like this once," he said, a wonder in his tone that said the incident had been long buried under far darker memories. "I wasn't even eighty yet. She let me kiss her afterward, called me her hero."

Even in the storm-lit darkness and with the ugliness of what had happened to Ibrahim fresh in her mind, the story held a stunning sweetness that had Elena's cheeks creasing. "Your first kiss?" He'd have been a young teen in human terms, if she was doing her calculations right.

A slow nod that made the fine droplets of rain on his hair waterfall with translucent light, his smile growing. "I strutted for months afterward." He pulled open a side door to the tower that was old but appeared in good working order.

Elena entered to find they were on a lower floor that was basically just stone with a staircase in the center. Aodhan told her to go on up to the first floor. "I must follow, Ellie," he said, once more her grim-eyed escort. "The danger is more apt to come from the outside rather than the inside."

Moving without delay, Elena went up, her gun in hand. The staircase opened out into a small library that had books on three walls, a fireplace set into the fourth, with two antique armchairs suitable for angelic wings placed in front of the small fire Laric must've left going. The carpet on the floor was as ancient, this place frozen in time but for the books she could see stacked here and there.

"Where does he get his books?" Somehow, Elena didn't think Laric would've caught on to the Internet and mail order.

"There are some Luminata who are still kind to him. Donael is one, Ibrahim another," Aodhan added. "They make sure he has books."

"Glad to hear they're not all bastards." Reaching out with her mind, she touched Raphael's. *Any news?*

Not yet. We have asked Gian to gather all those who might've walked through the nearby areas at the time Ibrahim was attacked.

She told him about Donael getting Laric his books. *Not sure what that tells us except that he's not totally self-absorbed in his quest for luminescence.*

I will keep that in mind.

Elena found a small table in front of the armchairs, and taking a seat in one since the table was too low to use standing up, she put her gun on the table, then retrieved the map and spread it out. She placed a throwing blade on each edge to keep it pinned down. "It's beautiful."

Shock had her staring.

She'd been expecting an old-fashioned blueprint at best, but this was a three-dimensional artwork that showed Lumia as a dollhouse peeled open, with more detailed smaller drawings around the edges for areas where the dollhouse approach didn't permit an inside look.

Candles, books, even tiny pots and pans in the kitchens, they'd all been drawn with stunning attention to detail. And of course, there were Luminata scattered throughout, going about their daily business. "They're not all wearing robes."

Instead, they were dressed in various types of clothing from warrior leathers to flowing garments of color and more prosaic outfits that said "everyday wear" to Elena. The robes *were* present but not many of these Luminata wore them with the hood pulled up. In fact, in the scenes she could see of people passing each other in the corridors, the one with the hood was always shown as pulling it back to greet his fellow resident.

Only one thing remained the same: this was a brotherhood. No women.

Not an inexplicable choice, Elena found herself thinking— hard to keep sex out of the equation otherwise.

No, wait.

I have been alive thousands of years, have learned that love does not always wear a single face.

Keir had said that to her after she saw him flirting with a male warrior—where previously, she knew he'd had a female lover. As with mortals, immortal sexuality was a wide-ranging canvas with many variations. So having a male-only environment wouldn't necessarily take sexual temptation off the table.

"Why just men?" she murmured.

A shrug from Aodhan. "Why did human men create gentlemen's clubs in earlier times? And why does Caliane have a temple in which only her maidens are permitted?"

"Hmm." She twisted her mouth to the side, thought about what he'd said. "I see what you mean. Might be nothing more complicated than the fact the angels who set up Lumia wanted it to be a male club."

"Whatever their reasons for not admitting women, Lumia
has changed in a profound way since this map was created,"
Aodhan said. He'd remained standing beside her, but he'd
pushed aside one of the armchairs so he could look down at
the map without compromising his ability to move quickly
should he need to.

His wing lay half across hers, a warm weight. "Does it have
a date?"

36

Elena searched all over the map at his question, found a scratching of words in the corner. "This looks like that angelic language we saw in the Gallery." She'd have to see if she could learn some of it at least; she hated not knowing things. Then again, every hunter had his or her specialty—ancient languages were more up Honor's alley.

Leaning in, Aodhan looked carefully at the writing before nodding. "There is no exact date, just the millennium. It was done at least a thousand years earlier."

"How many Luminata leaders since then? Did Laric mention it?"

"Remus did." His tone didn't change as he named the angel who'd sought to break him when he'd been hurt and vulnerable. "After the one Laric spoke of, there have been only two."

"So it's not only Gian who's ruled for longer than the fifty-year-term Luminata are meant to serve. He's only been leading for four hundred years."

Aodhan nodded slowly. "Yes, you're right. Before him, it was Hanjel who held the position. He gave up the title to Gian after deciding he wished to find luminescence walking the hidden roads of the world."

Elena jerked up her head. "No shit," she whispered. "I always figured that was an urban legend." At Aodhan's curious look, she said, "Over the years, a number of hunters have reported seeing an angel walking along isolated roads and forest trails on bare feet, his wings coated in dust—as if he'd been walking forever. The reports are rare for how long he must've been around, so he must stick to really remote regions."

Shaking off her surprise, she said, "So which one of them began the change?" From Lumia with a heart to Lumia with cold, hidden secrets and violence. From a place where the brothers cheerfully showed their faces to one where shadows ruled.

"Gian," Aodhan said definitively. "Remus was here during the second century of Gian's rule and he said the more established Luminata spoke of the difference in management styles. Hanjel was focused only on his own inner luminescence, left Lumia to run itself as it would."

"While Gian thinks of Lumia as his personal territory."

"Even if he began it, others had to agree," Aodhan pointed out. "A man does not stay in power without support."

"Yes, this is definitely not a one-man show." She stared at the map. "Okay"—she pointed to a familiar glass dome—"this is the Atrium."

"And this is where our rooms are situated," Aodhan hunkered down to touch his finger to the right location.

"The Gallery is already there." That was a surprise. "Wow, I would've placed it at Gian's feet—it seems a testament to ego that fits him." The disconnect was another reminder that she had to be careful not to get tunnel vision; Gian was creepy and a liar, but that didn't mean he was behind the subjugation of the town, for example.

"Perhaps Gian exists because of a subtle sense of superiority that was present in earlier Luminata," Aodhan murmured. "They've been left to live as they would for millennia."

Elena nodded. "The seeds must've been sown over a long period, just waiting for the right Luminata to take it to the next level." She thought of Donael, of how old he was, how experienced. "It's even possible Gian is an unknowing puppet."

"A stalking horse?" Aodhan lifted a shoulder, dropped it in a liquid shrug. "I don't see Gian as anyone's fool, but arrogance can be blinding."

"Yes." Now that she'd oriented herself within the map, Elena tried to figure out if something was amiss. "Damn," she said after a few minutes. "We don't know Lumia well enough to figure out what to look for."

Aodhan was silent, his attention on the Gallery. Turning the map toward himself, he continued to stare. "We flew through all the levels of the Gallery," he murmured, as if speaking to himself. "There is no discrepancy with the number of levels, but . . ."

He lifted the map, sending her blades sliding off.

Tucking them back into the various sheaths and taking over the watch so Aodhan could concentrate, Elena waited. Aodhan had very good spatial skills. At last, he gave a curt nod and put the map back down. "Look here, Ellie."

"It's a door." On the bottom floor of the Gallery.

"No, Ellie, it's a *trapdoor*."

Elena's eyes widened, realization slamming belatedly into her. "And if we were on the very bottom floor, what the hell lies underneath?"

"More importantly, that trapdoor wasn't covered by a rug or other easily removable object when we were in the Gallery. The entire floor was smooth marble."

"What's the best place to bury something?" Elena whispered. "A place that no one knows even exists." Her heart thundered.

Was she looking at her grandmother's grave? The graves of countless other men and women taken from the town because Luminata wanted them—or as with Majda's vampire husband—because they stood in the way of someone else the Luminata coveted?

"Ellie." Aodhan's voice was gentle, his wings sparking wildly in the firelight. "You must make no assumptions. If it was a burial place for a mortal, no one would care." The harsh words made her flinch then stiffen her spine. "You know what most immortals think of mortals, and you've seen evidence of how the Luminata treat the people of the town."

Elena fought not to strike out at him—she knew he didn't believe the same, was just giving her the perspective she needed to keep in mind. "So what the fuck is down there that has Ibrahim lying in *anshara*?" Because it was the map that had caused the angel to be beaten to a pulp, of that Elena had no doubt. "He gave us this and he paid for it."

"It could be the Sleeping place of an angel, one that is known to the older Luminata," Aodhan pointed out. "If so, we have no right to disturb it."

"But if it was that, all anyone had to do was drop a word in Raphael's ear and none of us would've gone near it," Elena said. "Why beat Ibrahim so badly?"

"Ibrahim could've been beaten for some other, totally unrelated reason. Such as the fact he fell afoul of a Luminata who wished to take an unwilling man or woman from the town."

Elena hadn't even thought about that option, and damn it, she could see innocently hopeful Ibrahim being shocked by such an abuse of power.

Glaring at Aodhan, she said, "Stop being a devil's advocate."

A faint smile. "Your Bluebell is not here, so I must carry the banner."

"Ha ha. How did you know about what the Luminata are doing in the town anyway?" She hadn't had a chance to brief him after their first trip, and he hadn't come along on the second.

"The sire spoke to me soon after you discovered the spyhole in your quarters." He touched his temple to indicate how Raphael had contacted him.

Rolling up the map after biting back a snarl at the memory of that hole, she slipped it into the crossbow bolt sheath once more. "We have to find out if there's another way to get underneath that final level of the Gallery and we only have until the storm passes." Soon as the lightning stopped, the Cadre would have to move. Bloodlust across China was a far more lethal threat than the insanity of a small, power-mad cult.

Aodhan appeared thoughtful. "I can ask Laric what he knows. Before Lumia changed, he didn't always stay in his tower. He used to walk the hallways and talk sometimes with a few others who know the hand language."

"He can't vocalize at all?"

"No, the scarring is too severe." A pause. "He says none of the new ones but Ibrahim bothered to learn the hand language if they didn't know it already. Ibrahim is apparently terrible at languages, but he is dogged."

The more Elena learned about the hurt novice, the more she liked him. As for the others who hadn't bothered with a simple kindness for a living being in pain . . . "That's what happens when the rot comes from the top. People turn into mindless sheep." She got to her feet. "I want to talk to Hannah, too. She spent the most time in the Gallery, could've seen something she doesn't realize the importance of."

"Donael will know if there is a hidden part of Lumia beneath the final level of the Gallery," Aodhan said as they left Laric's library. "He was here when this map was created."

"Last resort." Elena played with a blade to keep her anger under control. "I don't know if we can trust him, even if he doesn't give off the creepy vibe."

"Because if he's been at Lumia so long," Aodhan murmured, "he either knows of the secrets in these walls, or he has stayed deliberately blind."

"Like you said, Gian didn't appear in a vacuum. If Donael had stuck up for what was right when Gian began to take control—or even earlier, when Lumia first began to change, we might not be here today." A focus on personal luminescence didn't, in her book, excuse willful blindness to evil occurring right under your nose.

Archangel, she said, reaching out to Raphael, *can you tag Elijah, find out where Hannah is? I need to talk to her.* She told him what they'd discovered about a possible hidden underground section to the Gallery.

Sea winds kissed her mind moments later. *Eli and Hannah are in their suite. It's almost exactly on the opposite side of Lumia to ours.*

Thanks. She followed Aodhan down the staircase.

There is a deep vein of fear within the brothers who live here, Elena, almost as deep as that in the town. It stinks up the air when I speak to those who might have seen Ibrahim in the moments before the attack.

I'll take care, she said, because while she'd fight him always when he slipped back into seeing her as a vulnerable mortal, she also understood that fear was a new concept to Raphael.

He hadn't tasted it for eons until he fell in love with her, until he tied his heart to that of a woman who could be wounded or killed by his powerful enemies. After all, Elena worried about him even though he was one of the most violently powerful beings in the world.

Telling Aodhan their new destination just before he opened the door on the lower level of the tower, Elena jerked back at the slap of wind that rattled that door, as if trying to rip it from his grasp. The storm wasn't just holding, it had increased in size and violence. The lightning now fell like rain, punching into the earth over and over, and where it hit, it left behind only scorched earth. The stone walls of Lumia bore several new scars that she could see, but that stone was still holding up under the assault.

Heart thumping at the beauty of the primal display despite the danger of it, Elena looked at Aodhan. "Ready?"

To her surprise, he took her hand, gripped it hard. "Wings tight to your back, body low. The wind is strong enough to blow us off the path if we're not careful."

"Wait." Tugging her hand from his grasp, she unstrapped her crossbow and gave it to him to hold, then pulled out the garrote bracelet she'd stuffed into a pocket at the last minute. It actually had a far longer length of thin wire inside it than was necessary for twisting it around someone's neck.

She snapped the bracelet into two parts with the wire in between, tied one part to the front end of a crossbow bolt, was about to twist the other end over her own gauntleted wrist when Aodhan held up his. "I'm stronger."

Because he was, Elena wrapped the metal wire over the top of his gauntlet and gave him this end of the bracelet to hold. They couldn't afford to tie it to something on the tower side without first knowing if they'd have enough length to make that possible. "Grab on to something."

After fixing the door open with what looked like a heavy chunk of rock meant for that purpose, Aodhan used his free hand to grip the staircase railing behind them and stretched out his body so that she had as much wire to play with as possible. And she shot the bolt. It went at too fast a velocity for the wind to impact, slamming home safely on the wall of the hallway at the end of the path.

While Aodhan maintained his position, arm muscles rigid, she quickly unwrapped the wire from his gauntlet, then together, the two of them got it hooked around the stairwell railing. The length proved just enough. The only problem was that the metal was so thin it'd shred their hands if they gripped it with bare palms. "I have an idea." Racing upstairs, she cut out two pieces of Laric's old rug using one of her knives, came back down.

Aodhan took one look at what she held and nodded. "I'll go in front. Use my body as a wind shield and grip the back of my pants."

Two seconds later, they headed out. And Jesus, the winds were brutal. A gust actually lifted Elena off her feet at one point, only her dual grip on the wire and on Aodhan keeping her on the path. Face and body wet on one side from the driving rain, she stumbled into Aodhan on the other end, colliding with the soft smoothness of his wings. "Sorry."

He wrapped an arm around her and pulled her firmly out of the wind.

"The wire," she said, pushing damp strands of hair out of her eyes. "I was going to cut it at this end, but with the ferocity of the wind, it could whip around and accidentally garrote someone."

Putting a bare hand on the wire, Aodhan released a touch of the same energy she'd witnessed him use in battle. It raced along the wire to spark against the stairwell . . . and behind it, the wire disintegrated. "When do I get superpowers?" she muttered, retrieving the bolt she'd shot and sliding it away.

"Perhaps once you're no longer around the same age as Sam."

Surprised into laughter and threatening to brain him with her crossbow, Elena forced herself to look away from the wild fury of the storm. She and Aodhan made good time to Hannah and Elijah's suite, to find Hannah alone but for Cristiano's languid form, the vampire as loose-limbed as always. Those dark brown eyes, however, they were of a cool-eyed predator who'd eliminate any threat to Hannah or die trying.

"Elijah has gone to join Raphael," Hannah said to Elena after Cristiano let them in, the vampire and Aodhan staying by the door to talk in quiet tones. "Gian is insisting the violence must've come from one of the Cadre's escorts. He is pointing the finger most strongly at Riker."

Elena had zero love for Michaela's vampire guard—and

that was a *grand* understatement, but making him the fall guy was a little too convenient. "He sticks as close to Michaela as permitted," she pointed out. "When she's meeting with the Cadre, he lurks outside. So if he beat up Ibrahim, that means Michaela was watching."

Aimlessly rearranging a vase of flowers, her deep green gown simple and elegant and her hair in a neat knot, Hannah raised an eyebrow. "We both know that could happen."

"Normally, yes. But Michaela wants out of here—she wouldn't have countenanced anything that could cause a delay." She folded her arms. "And I know Riker's scent. It wasn't on Ibrahim."

Nodding, Hannah abandoned the flowers. "Why did you want to speak?"

When Elena told her, Hannah frowned. "Another level below the Gallery? I saw nothing that indicated a hidden area."

"Are you sure?" Elena pressed. "You were on the map level for a long time. Maybe they forgot something, left it on display." Visitors, after all, were rare in this place.

Picking up a sketchpad, Hannah began to make strokes with a charcoal pencil that had been lying beside it. Again, it seemed aimless . . . "Oh, damn," Elena murmured, ice in her own veins. "You're worried Elijah is going to fly out of Lumia to draw away the storm."

Hannah swallowed hard, her expression bleak when she looked up from the sketchpad. "He was talking about it before you left, how it was the only option if the storm didn't abate in the next three to four hours—else Lumia will begin to collapse. Has Raphael said anything?"

"No, but I know he has to be considering it." Elena had succeeded in putting the possibility to the back of her mind, but faced with Hannah's fear, her own nipped at her with cold, hungry teeth. "They're archangels, Hannah. Don't forget that." It was as much a reminder to herself as to Hannah.

"I know, but that lightning, it's not natural." Shuddering out a breath, the other consort continued before Elena could reply. "I am sure about what I saw on the map level. Absolutely nothing that indicated a hidden level to the Gallery."

Disappointment sank leaden fingers into Elena's blood, joining the icy knot of fear in her gut. "Damn. It would've been nice to have confirmation."

"I'm sorry," Hannah said.

"I don't suppose you've heard the name Majda or Jean-Baptiste?" Elena threw out without hope.

But Hannah's eyes widened.

37

"Majda?" Hannah said. "Yes, I saw that name very recently."

Elena's pulse rocketed. "What? Where?"

"In a book." Hannah pressed her fingers to her forehead before dropping her hand and locking gazes with Elena. "Elijah and I went to sit in the Repository of Knowledge for a little while earlier tonight, together with Astaad. I got up to wander and discovered a handbound volume of poetry that had fallen behind a tall shelf."

Lines on her normally smooth brow, she said, "I only glanced at it before handing it to the librarian on duty. He appeared shocked at what I held and I couldn't understand it at the time. I thought perhaps he was dismayed that something so obviously handmade had made it into his library."

Elena didn't know how poetry could help but she waited, listened.

"The book had an inscription on the flyleaf: *To my love, Majda.*"

Elena stared at Hannah, who couldn't know the import of what she'd found. "Was it signed?"

"Just with a *G*."

Fighting not to betray her response to that piece of information, Elena said, "Anything else?"

"There was a poem in there that I glanced at, about a woman with hair of moonlight." Her eyes went to Elena's own hair, sudden comprehension in their depths. "It wasn't very good poetry, you see. That's why I only glanced at it before handing the book to the librarian so it could be properly shelved."

"Bad poetry? Like the kind a besotted man might write for a woman?"

Hannah nodded slowly. "Yes, exactly. Bad love poetry, delightful for the recipient but not a literary gem by any measure."

Elena tried not to grab on to that *G.* It could belong to anyone. She certainly didn't know the names of every single Luminata in this place.

"Do you want me to see if I can get the volume back?" Hannah said, her interest unhidden. "The librarian can't lie to me about its existence, since I handed it directly to him."

"I don't want you to put yourself at risk," Elena began.

"Ellie." Closing her hands over Elena's, Hannah squeezed. "I'm good at taking care of myself and I also have Cristiano." A deep smile. "He moves like a lazy cat and behaves like one when at rest, but he is a cagey, dangerous mountain lion at heart.

"Plus," Hannah added, "I don't think even the Luminata are arrogant enough to strike at the consort of an archangel. They know Elijah would annihilate this place, along with every single member of their sect."

Elena wasn't so sure. "These people take arrogance to a new level, Hannah. They're used to operating without boundaries."

"I will ask Titus to go with me, then," Hannah said, clearly at peace with the fact she was no warrior. "He is restless in this place and I think he will find even a small diversion attractive."

"Titus in a library?" It would be like finding Elena in one, to be honest. Titus was far more at home with a weapon, his body in motion.

"It is not his normal habitat, it is true." Hannah laughed.

"But there is a display of ancient knives on one wall that should be of interest to him."

That answered the question of where at least some of the Gallery's weapons collection was displayed. "Promise me you won't go if you can't get Titus to come along."

"I promise," Hannah said, a soft curve to her lips. "You know I am older and stronger than you?"

"Yes, but you don't have a killer instinct." For better or worse, Elena did. Perhaps she'd been born with it, or perhaps it had come to life in the months and years after the brutal murder of Elena's sisters, when Elena learned that, sometimes, to fight a nightmare, you had to become an even more dangerous nightmare.

Leaving her fellow consort, Elena considered their next move. It was Aodhan who said, "Your advice to Hannah was sound."

Her lips kicked up, the ache of memory retreating to the background in the face of the current reality. "And I should follow it?"

"It would be prudent."

"We should get back to Raphael anyway, see if he's dug up anything." And so she could make sure he wasn't planning to head out into the murderous lightning that pounded Lumia.

As it was, things had come to a dead end with the investigation.

None of the Luminata were talking and none of the Cadre who now knew of the incident—Raphael, Elijah, Neha, and Titus—could justify more extreme methods of questioning, as that would violate boundaries so important it might tear a permanent rip into the fabric of angelic society.

Returning with Raphael back to their suite, a suite guarded by Titus's escort—who left on their return—Elena saw that Ibrahim was breathing easier. Laric sat beside him, his shoulders bowed and his hood tugged forward to shadow his face, but his hands gently ministering to the badly wounded angel as he did what he could despite his lack of training.

That was when she remembered. *Archangel, I have to tell you something about Laric.*

Raphael's expression grew progressively darker as she shared the story of the deadly fire that had consumed the sky, catching a young angel in it.

I didn't know there were any collateral victims, he said afterward, *and I don't believe Mother does, either.*

I don't think many people do. Elena wove her fingers through his. *If he wants to leave Lumia, we can offer him a home, right?*

A wild blue inferno met her gaze. *Such a soft heart you have, Guild Hunter. Yes, we can offer this healer a place, but he will still have a hard life. Many immortals are unforgiving of physical imperfections.*

The words echoed Aodhan's earlier ones, and they weren't cruel, simply factual. *I know*, she said. *But I think if we can give Laric a place where he can grow strong inside, he might do much better than he's doing here. He's buried himself alive.*

Jaw held in a grim line as an impossibly desolate shadow passed over his face, Raphael nodded before returning his attention to where Aodhan had gone to stand by Laric. The angel's hands moved quickly. The smaller, slighter healer moved his scarred hands in turn, their conversation apparently intense.

That was when Elena noticed that Laric's wings were much smaller bumps beneath his robe than they should be. Her eyes burned at the realization that the fire had done catastrophic damage to his wings, too—and yet he had the heart to heal others still. That was far more luminescent, in her mind, than anything else she'd seen in this place.

Swallowing the response, she went to sit by Ibrahim, gently touching her fingers to his hair. It was tightly kinked and so soft. "Come on, Ibrahim," she whispered. "Don't let the bastards get you down."

The biting wind kissed her mind, touched with the salt-laced air of the sea. *Aodhan asks us to come close.*

When they joined Aodhan on the other side of Ibrahim's supine body, the angel spoke in a soft voice. "Laric says there was something beneath the Gallery once."

The silent healer nodded from where he stood beside Aodhan.

"He never went there, assumed it was for storage of un-wanted things. He only has a vague memory of the trapdoor in the Gallery itself, but he remembers a door set into a wall near the Gallery entrance, which was sometimes open and from which he could see a flight of stairs."

"The stairs would have to be impossibly steep, given the description Elena has given me of the Gallery," Raphael said.

"Laric only caught a glimpse, so he cannot say."

Blood pumping hot and dark under her skin, Elena looked at the healer. "Can you lead us to that door?"

He seemed to start at being addressed directly, but his hands began to move. Aodhan translated. "Laric wishes to stay with Ibrahim, in case he falls out of *anshara* and is in pain, as sometimes happens, but he can give us instructions."

Raphael looked to Elena as Aodhan got those instructions. "I think we should wait until after the bell for the Luminata's nightly contemplation. That time is sacred enough to them that Gian asked the Cadre itself not to disturb it."

It was difficult to make herself wait when instinct was screaming at her that something monstrous lay beneath Lumia, but Elena nodded. It made sense to wait until the brothers had all scurried back into their rooms, leaving the hallways clear.

Thunder crashed outside seconds later, so loud it vibrated through Elena's bones. Eyes locking with Raphael's, she reached for his mind. *You are not going out there.*

He cradled the side of her face, just shook his head, the midnight strands of his hair framing a face of blinding power. And she knew. If that was the only choice, then Raphael would make it. Because he was an archangel. He stood a chance of survival even in the midst of the aberrant Cascade-born storm. If Lumia collapsed and the lightning hit her or Aodhan, they'd die.

Body rigid, she threw her arms around him and just held on tight.

It was twenty minutes later that Cristiano came by with a note for Elena.

The librarian insists he destroyed the book, that it was a "worthless item that should've never been" in the

*Repository of Knowledge. I don't believe him, but I
can't call him a liar to his face without causing grave
insult that the Luminata may use to stir up trouble, for
we both know the world needs no more chaos right
now. I will, instead, keep scouring the shelves in case
they have forgotten something else.—Hannah*

It wasn't what Elena wanted to hear, but at the same time,
the librarian's caginess lent further weight to the fact that
Hannah had inadvertently stumbled upon something important. Sliding the note into a pocket in an instinctive effort
to keep it safe and away from prying eyes, she forced herself
to leave Raphael—who was chatting to Aodhan—and went to
sit next to Laric.

"Do you want to stay here?"

When the healer froze at her question, she simply waited.
You didn't push a broken, scared bird. That would just make it
attempt to fly away. It was at least two minutes later that he finally lifted his hands, dropped them again to glance over at
Aodhan. But the member of the Seven wasn't looking this way,
his concentration on his low-voiced discussion with Raphael.

Elena looked around, grabbed a notepad off a nearby side
table, and gave it to Laric along with a pen, before retaking her
seat. He held the pen oddly and she realized the scarring on
his hands made it difficult for him to write smoothly.

He could, however, still write.

When he handed the pad back to her, Elena saw he'd written the words in painstakingly formed English: *There is nowhere else where I will be left in peace.*

Frowning, she said, "Do you want that? Isn't it lonely?"

The healer said nothing for a long time. Then he wrote
again: *People are cruel.*

Young, Elena remembered, he'd been so *very* young when
he'd been injured. Regardless of his physical age, he was still
that boy inside who'd been rejected by his lover, then looked
on with pity and maybe even distaste by the immortal world.
Still . . . "Do you know Jessamy?"

An immediate nod, those scarred hands writing carefully
on the page: *She is strong. I am not strong.*

"I don't think you've ever given yourself a chance," Elena

murmured and, acting on instinct, placed her hand on his shoulder.

He went stiff before slowly relaxing. But he didn't pull away. That's what she'd thought: this boy wasn't like Aodhan, who'd shunned touch. People had simply stopped touching him. "Think about it," she said. "There are a lot of unusual things in New York—you won't stand out as much as you think."

Grinning, she said, "The other day, I saw a man dressed as a chicken walking with a briefcase. He kept looking at his watch as if he was late."

His surprise was such that she almost caught a glimpse of his face before he angled it so the shadows of the hood concealed him, clearly practiced at the maneuver. Picking up the notepad, he wrote: *Angelkind does not want its mistakes out in the world.*

Anger burned Elena's blood, but she couldn't tell him that wasn't true. Even Jessamy had said something similar.

"Watching one archangel execute another in the skies of New York," Jessamy had murmured, "is a far different case from seeing an angel with a malformed wing." A soft smile that told Elena the other woman was at peace with who she was. "One is an otherworldly thing beyond mortal ken, the other far too close to their own reality. Angelkind cannot ever afford to be that real, Elena. It would shatter the foundations of the world."

On the heels of that memory came that of Raphael's bloody story about the angels who'd wanted to rule without any archangelic oversight.

We live in a world of predators and prey.

And the consequence of seeing an angel with a "mortal" ailment could be thousands, tens of thousands, of mortals dead after some idiot decided they could take on the angels and win.

Because mortals could *never* win.

Gritting her teeth, Elena narrowed her eyes. "There must be a way," she muttered. "There's always a way. We just have to figure it out."

Laric appeared to be staring at her. What he eventually wrote on the notepad made her grin. "Yeah," she said, "I'm not like other angels. I'm a hunter angel." What the hell—people were already using that term. She'd just co-opt it. Then she'd make Demarco and Ransom and all her other hunter friends who insisted on wearing the ridiculous hunter angel T-shirts, bow down to her in homage.

The idea made her want to laugh, regardless of the brutal storm outside and the subtler malice within Lumia. "Hunters are a different breed."

The healer didn't respond, but she could feel him staring at her again. "Did you ever try to get your scars excised?" she asked. "Adult angels have an incredible healing ability from what I've seen."

Laric's hand moved slowly across the page. *The scars are impossible to cut through.*

Elena tried to process what he was telling her, considered the amount of energy that would've been released at the violent death of an archangel. There'd been no similar blowback when Raphael executed Uram, but those two had extracted a hell of a lot of power from their environment, then expended it during their fight, Manhattan a war zone. Badly damaged high-rises and a burned-out electrical network had only been the start.

And in comparison to Caliane's and Nadiel's battle, Raphael's and Uram's fight had been between young "pups," as Alexander was wont to say.

Nadiel had been younger than Caliane, but not *young*. The amounts of energy involved . . . It must've seared the scars so deep into Laric's body that they went to the bone itself. *Raphael, do you think you could try your ability to heal on Laric once you're back from China?* Not before. Not when they had no idea of what he might face there.

I've been considering how best to utilize it.

Elena met those eyes of endless blue, of an archangel whose heart was no longer in any danger of turning cruel.

He spoke again, the cool winds of him a caress across her senses. *We will not abandon him, Elena. Aodhan says as you did—that Laric is dying slowly here.* A dangerous pause. *The boy is afraid of being shoved out for interrupting the "serenity" of this place with his scars, so he rarely ventures out now.*

That idea didn't just magically appear in his head. It had been planted there by men who searched for luminescence in unkindness. "You've done an amazing job with Ibrahim," she said aloud to Laric and it wasn't just talk—Ibrahim was breathing easier, his color better. "Especially since you've only had a little training."

Laric wrote again on the notepad. *The damage is not so bad. He will heal.* He seemed to accurately read her shock at that description of Ibrahim's injuries, because he added, *No signs of weapons being used. Nothing to cause damage deep on the inside.*

The hairs stood up on Elena's arms.

38

Taking the notepad, she walked over to show it to Aodhan and Raphael. "Fists and kicks, that skews personal to me."

"Someone in a rage." Aodhan's voice was quiet but his shattered eyes were shards of ice. "As the sire said, he had to have been kicked after he was down; fists alone wouldn't have collapsed one side of his body or pulverized his arm."

A rustle, Laric coming to hover awkwardly nearby.

When Elena waved him closer, he came. It was only once he was part of the circle that his hands began to move. Aodhan watched, his face increasingly grim. "He says he's certain it wasn't undirected rage—the injuries are too closely grouped for that. One side of Ibrahim's body was targeted. Particularly his arm."

Elena stared at the ground with a scowl, trying to focus her thoughts. "Why that arm?" She raised her head. "I mean, I could understand targeting both arms if it was about him giving us the map, or if it was punishment because he touched something out of bounds, but one arm?"

"Not something." Firelight flickered on the top arch of Raphael's wings, and then those wings were white flame.

She heard Laric suck in a breath, stagger back a step, but

when the fire stayed confined to Raphael's wings, he came back in a show of unexpected courage.

"You touched Ibrahim on that arm."

She stared at Raphael, his words vibrating inside her skull. "That doesn't make sense. I belong to you. Everyone knows that."

His smile was coolly satisfied, his wings flickering back to normal as quickly as they'd switched to flame.

Making a face at him, she said, "And you belong to me, Archangel." She gave him a smug look of her own.

Laughing, he put a hand over his heart. "I would wear your brand on my skin, Elena-mine. Even if it meant searing it anew each day when I woke."

"Ahem." Elena pointed to the wing that bore the bullet scar. "You already wear my mark, Archangel."

He unfolded his wing, smiled in open satisfaction. "So I do."

Laric had been turning his head back and forth as they spoke.

Elena could all but feel his flabbergasted surprise at the conversation. Apparently, everyone expected archangels and their consorts to walk around being otherworldly and powerful, not act like the lovers they were. Though, at least with Elena, there was an expectation that she was apt to be a little odd, since she'd once been a mortal.

It was Hannah who held the capacity to surprise the heck out of everyone: Elijah's consort was nowhere near as flawlessly ladylike as even Elena had once believed. If she'd really thought about it, she'd have realized the truth long before she and Hannah became friends. No artist ever walked in a straight line. And no warrior as powerful and as intelligent as Elijah would so deeply adore a woman who was a graceful ornament.

"Regardless of the fact you are mine," Raphael said, folding back his wing, "it is too much of a coincidence that Ibrahim was beaten so badly within hours of interacting with you in a way that, to a jealous eye, would've been unacceptable."

"If you're right, then they must hate you." Her knife was in her hand between one breath and the next, the hilt a familiar hardness. "Whoever it is must want to annihilate you." She bared her teeth. "Good thing you're an archangel."

Raphael's responding smile was as lethal. "Yes. As I do not believe this is one of the Cadre, I am in no real danger."

Glad her lover was such a tough and dangerous opponent, Elena put both hands on her hips. "I agree—I don't think anyone in the Cadre is carrying a secret torch for me," she said dryly. "Which leaves one of the guards or escorts or the Luminata. I know who I'd bet on."

A sudden thought had her focusing on Laric. "Did you ever see a woman here who looked like me? It would've been decades ago. She had hair like mine, skin a little darker."

Instead of moving his hands to answer in the silent tongue, he took the notepad and wrote out his answer. *No. But I have heard rumors of a woman with moonlight hair who threatened Gian's luminescence with her seduction.*

Elena hissed out a breath. "Everything I've learned so far says this woman loved her husband, was true to him. She wasn't having an affair with anyone, much less Gian."

Elena.

She met Raphael's eyes, forced herself to breathe. *She loved her husband, Raphael. Like he was her stars and her moon. And she loved her child enough to run to protect her.*

People make mistakes. He held her gaze. *I'm not saying she betrayed her mate, but she was involved with Gian in some way. We must not dismiss the possibility out of hand.* Aloud, he said, "Everything points to Gian."

Elena nodded. "There's a chance it's a loyal flunky, but my money is on Gian." Those eyes that watched her, the lies he'd told, the *G* in the book of bad love poetry Hannah had found. "Can we move on him?"

"I can kill him now," Raphael said flatly, his eyes metallic in their coldness.

"And it'd cause all kinds of political issues." Elena put her hand on his forearm. "No, we get evidence no one can dispute, then we confront Gian." *You don't need more problems with war hanging on the horizon.*

Laric was writing again, held out the notepad a moment later.

"Well fuck," Elena muttered, turning the notepad to Raphael and then Aodhan. On it was written: *Gian's closest*

*ally in Lumia is a tall and thin man named Gervais. Like a
shadow, he does what Gian does.*

"Not the lover but the man who coveted what the lover
had?" Raphael's eyes remained cold. "Possible."

"Whether it is Gian or Gervais," Aodhan said, "a man who
would beat someone so badly for the 'crime' of having Elena
touch him, this to me speaks of obsession."

"Transference?" Elena braced her hands on her hips. "The
Luminata was obsessed with my probable grandmother and
now he's transferred that obsession to me?"

Aodhan nodded.

Laric wrote something on his notepad, held it out with a
hesitant hand. When Raphael rather than Elena took it, his hand
trembled. The kid was clearly intimidated by standing this close
to an archangel. Just like Elena had once been—but she knew
this man now, saw Raphael, not the Archangel of New York.

"This is no surprise after what we learned in the town,"
Raphael said, turning the notepad toward Elena.

*The Luminata vow celibacy when they come to Lumia as
initiates, but I think they do not all hold to that vow. I have
seen mortals flown in late at night.*

Elena wondered if those mortals came here by choice, was
forced to admit the vast majority likely did—angel groupies
were a serious thing. "I guess, technically, I'm your number
one groupie," she said to her archangel.

Raphael raised an eyebrow, in pure Archangel of New York
mode. "I should hope that to be the case."

An unexpected laugh built in her, faded all too soon.
"Groupies or not, I can't forget the fear in the town, the way
Majda was scared of being taken, what Riad's great-
grandfather said about the Luminata's interest in 'the prettiest
women and the most beautiful men,'" she murmured. "Clearly,
they're not just scooping up the groupies. But why would
angels need to coerce mortals when so many throw themselves at angels?"

Married or unmarried, single or in a relationship, it didn't
much matter. Angels apparently didn't count when it came to
infidelity—she'd heard that gem from a married hunter she'd
met, a man who'd lusted after angels. This had been before

Elena herself had become an angel and consort to one, but even then, she'd disagreed on a gut-deep level.

Fidelity was fidelity in her book. The end.

"For some," Aodhan said quietly, "it isn't about sex at all. It's about power."

His words made far too much sense given what they knew of the Luminata. "Taking and abusing and killing people to keep the town in line? Or just because they can? Yes, that fits with how the Luminata seem to operate."

"There is also the fact that a particular mortal who catches an angel's eye may not wish to play the game," Raphael said, a chill in his tone. "We both know a once-mortal who was coveted by an angel who would not take no for an answer."

Dmitri.

Elena sucked in a breath. She didn't know all the details, but she knew that Dmitri had been made a vampire by force by that same angel. "Yes." The word came out gritty, hard. "That means—"

"The woman with moonlight hair may well have been someone who said no," Raphael completed.

Red across her vision, Elena said, "Has enough time passed?" She wanted proof, wanted whoever was involved in terrorizing the town—likely the same people who'd made her mother an orphan—brought down.

"No. A little longer."

It was an hour later that Elena and Raphael exited their suite, the hallways of Lumia lit more softly than usual during this time of contemplation. They left Aodhan watching over Laric and Ibrahim, not trusting the Luminata to keep their distance should Laric be alone with the injured angel. From the careful way Laric had continued to monitor Ibrahim, Elena had the feeling the healer would fight to protect him— but he was small and weak, would only end up brutalized.

Aodhan had protested their going out alone, but he'd clearly been torn—he understood that Laric and Ibrahim were far more vulnerable than Elena and Raphael as a unit. In the end it hadn't been a long disagreement and he'd taken up a guard position outside the room, making it clear the two angels within were under Raphael's protection.

As for anyone—even several anyones—who tried to take on Aodhan, good luck to them. Elena had seen him in battle. Not only was he a beautiful demon with a sword, but he had that violent power in his veins that he could use to decimate parts of Lumia itself if he so wanted.

"You are smiling your lethal hunter angel smile."

Snorting out a laugh in surprise as they headed toward their ultimate destination, she punched Raphael lightly on the arm. "That was a good one." It made her grin when he continued to look icily archangelic on the surface. "I was thinking about how dangerous Aodhan is."

Raphael broke out his own scary smile. "Yes. No one but an archangel will get through him—and the majority of the Cadre is uninterested in this 'domestic drama.'"

"Neha?" They turned into a part of Lumia that faced outward.

A nod. "She returned to her suite when we got nowhere with our questions."

Lightning flashed in searing bursts beyond the windows and thunder reverberated through the air, but the hallways of Lumia were once more eerily empty. "When the Luminata retreat for contemplation, they really retreat."

"This way, Elena." He tugged her right when she would've gone left.

"Sorry, woolgathering."

"Your thoughts are on what lies beyond that hidden door."

Her skin pebbled, chilled. "Bodies," she forced herself to say. "I think we'll find bodies there. Men and women who said no and who were never seen again. Plus their spouses, lovers, fathers, or anyone else who dared get in the way of the angels." Exactly what had happened to Majda's husband.

Raphael's response was arctic. "If that is so, know that the punishment will be a final one."

"Not all immortals think us mortals matter in any way, you said that yourself." Because she was still mortal in her heart, would always be a mortal in her heart.

Raphael's hand closed over her chilled one. "Enough do," he told her. "Elijah, Titus, even Neha, will agree with my judgment should we prove abuse. Astaad has a more old-world view of mortals and may abstain from a vote, but I do not think he will speak against any measure I propose. Michaela is apt to speak for it."

She jerked up her head in disbelief.

"She may be many things, Elena," Raphael murmured, "but she is also a woman. Sexual violence against a woman or child in her territory is punishable by death—that is the only possible punishment. It is said her territory is the safest place to be a woman or child alone even in the very darkest corners of a city."

"Jesus, Raphael, I can't believe you're telling me something that makes me want to *like* Michaela."

"Do not worry, *hbeebti*, the urge will pass."

"I sure hope so." Feeling better now she knew Raphael wouldn't have to take a stand against the rest of the Cadre to bury these bastards, she realized they could no longer see the lightning, the thunder muted to an ominous rumble.

Not a surprise since they were heading deeper into Lumia, toward the Gallery. But as per Laric's information, they would take a hallway that split away from the main one to the Gallery. Before that, however, they passed the wall which had borne the painting of Nadiel. Whatever Tasha had said to the Luminata, the painting hadn't simply been covered over; it was gone, literally cut out of the wall.

In its place sat a hastily constructed mosaic.

"Was it there?"

She nodded at Raphael's flat question. "Don't try to track it down," she said, shooting him a glare as his wings began to glow. "You don't need to see it."

A pause, his jaw tight, before he inclined his head. "Once was enough."

And she knew he wasn't talking about the painting but the real event. Sliding her wing over his, she said, "Hey, don't go all Scary Raphael on me."

"Scary Raphael?" His voice held an immortal power that had awakened the Legion, the mark on his temple pulsing with wildfire and his wings continuing to glow.

"Ice and danger and scariness."

The ice began to thaw. "Your affection overwhelms me, *hbeebti*."

Chest no longer so tight, she winked. "You can call me Scary Elena. I'd like it."

Wings of white gold brushing against hers, the glow subsiding, Raphael nodded left. "There's our turn, my terrifying consort."

Elena grinned, but deep inside, she was cold, scared of what she'd find. "I don't want any more murdered women in my family, Raphael." It came out a painful rasp. "I've had enough."

39

The murders of her sisters and the effective murder of her mother—Marguerite Deveraux had never truly left the room where Slater Patalis had tortured her—was why Elena was so deeply protective of Eve, Amy, Beth, and little Maggie.

It squeezed her heart each time she held her sister's baby. Beth, sweet, sometimes feckless Beth, still carried hurt in her soul. But she'd named her baby not in sorrow, but in love. "So Mama, Ari, and Belle don't get forgotten," she'd whispered. "So they know we remember them. And Maggie, she'll know all about her grandmama and older aunts."

Marguerite Aribelle Deveraux-Ling.

Such a big name for such a tiny little girl. Elena would help her niece grow into that name, had already started teaching the two-year-old how to hold a weapon.

Those faux-weapons came courtesy of Sara and Deacon. Deacon had been building little Zoe baby-appropriate weapons for a while, and as Zoe outgrew them, they kept the painstakingly crafted pieces to pass on to friends.

Maggie was currently learning to bang things with a polystyrene hammer.

"I thought Beth would freak when I brought Maggie the

first weapon, but she was so happy." It had made her realize once again that her baby sister bore more scars beneath her sunny personality than most people would ever know. "She said she wants her baby girl to grow up to be like me. Strong. So no one can hurt her."

"Your sister is a good mother."

"Yes, she is." Maggie was always full of smiles, a gorgeous little girl with a shock of silky black hair and sweet brown eyes who knew she was deeply loved. And who had been rocked to sleep in an archangel's arms more than once.

The first time Beth had asked Elena to babysit, her sister'd almost had a heart attack when she came to the Enclave to pick Maggie up, only to find her baby snuggled up happily in Raphael's arms. Beth was better about handling things now, but she still had trouble with the sheer amount of power that lived in Raphael.

Maggie, meanwhile, like all children, had no trouble at all.

Speaking of power . . . "Can you blast these walls open if we need to?"

"Yes, but if there is someone alive behind a wall, it could kill them."

Elena nodded, muscles tight. "So that's out." Even if there was a slim chance the area wasn't just a graveyard, she wouldn't risk going in with violence—the Luminata could be keeping captives, or just hiding their peccadilloes. "Any groupies who came voluntarily could've still been trapped in Lumia by the storm, been hidden away until they could be snuck back out."

"If the Luminata were indeed arrogant enough to bring these mortals here while the Cadre is in session," Raphael said, "then the entire Cadre will be united in any punishment. There will be no debate."

Elena needed no explanation as to why. It was all about respect and the chain of power. She wished immortals would simply treat mortal lives as important, but immortals had had millennia to build their prejudices; nothing was going to change that overnight, if ever. She was realistic enough to accept that and be satisfied that punishment would be meted out for any abuse.

"Did you hear that?" She froze, her head angled in the direction from which the noise had come. *There it is again.*

It sounded like wind whistling into the hallway from the outside—but they were deep inside Lumia. Communicating with a single glance, she and Raphael moved silently toward the sound . . . until it cut off with a clipped suddenness. As if the wind had been blocked. *A door?*

Possible, Raphael responded, the two of them continuing to move. *The more interesting question is, who is moving about during the Luminata's time of contemplation?*

Yes, they're very serious about that. So serious that all the good Luminata are shut up in their rooms, contemplating their personal luminescence, leaving the hallways clear for the ones who are interested less in luminescence and more in their own power over others.

Because this wasn't about sex or about the sadism that drove so many jaded immortals. These Luminata were drunk on power, on being able to live outside the boundaries set by their society—and at present, being able to flout those rules right under the noses of the Cadre of Ten. That had to be a rush. Far too addictive of a rush to abstain from regardless of the danger.

There is no door where Laric indicated it should be. Raphael crouched down in front of a wall, his hair gleaming blue-black.

As she watched, he tugged a downy inner feather from his wing and held it near the bottom edge of the wall. The delicate filaments didn't move. Rising, he did the same test two feet over. The movement was minuscule, but there should've been *no* movement in this corridor devoid of motion but for the two of them.

Sucking in a breath, Elena took the feather from him, slid it into a pocket. They wouldn't leave anything for those who might be coming or going to find—and she'd give the feather to Maggie, who loved to stroke them with her small, soft fingers. Zoe already had several of Raphael's in her growing collection. *Do we go in?*

From the sounds we heard, someone entered only moments ago. Raphael stared at the wall. *No one exited or we'd have caught sight of them as they turned the corner.*

Elena's pulse raced. She didn't want to wait, didn't want to give any more time to whatever evil was going on behind those doors. Because it was nothing good if it had to be so darkly hidden. *We have to wait*, she forced herself to say. *We don't know how to get in and we can't risk harming someone by using your power.*

Raphael nodded, but his gaze held unrelenting determination. *Storm or bloodlust, we will not leave until we have the answers*, hbeebti.

Swallowing her furious impatience, she satisfied herself—for now—by dropping a blade into her palm. *We'd better hide so we can try to see how to get in.*

Raphael smiled and opened his wings.

Her eyes widened. *I am an idiot.* Walking into his arms after he shifted to put his back against the opposite wall, she let him close his wings around her as she faced forward, her own wings against his chest. She couldn't feel the glamour, but she knew from the outside, they no longer existed. *Good thing the Luminata didn't think to have security cameras.* She'd checked.

Being hidebound is an immortal's greatest weakness. Raphael closed his arms around her shoulders, held her close to the muscled warmth of him, his scent so deeply familiar to her that it settled her on the innermost level.

He was hers. She was his.

And together, they were something far better than either one of them was alone.

Stroking the underside of his wings, Elena stared at the wall on the other side, willing it to open. She jerked when it did only five minutes later. The Luminata who walked out was the tall and thin one who'd been their guide the first night.

Gervais. Gian's best buddy.

His hood was off and he had a smile on his saturnine face that was more a smirk.

Pulling up his hood with spidery fingers, he glanced back over his shoulder and spoke in that rough voice she'd noted the first night. "You'd better hurry. You know he doesn't like anyone else inside when he goes into the special chamber to see his pet."

". . . got here."

"You should've come earlier. Of course, you can delay if you want to stay in there permanently."

A second angel huffed out, this one short and stouter than any angel Elena had ever seen. Angels just generally didn't carry any extra fat on their bodies—partly because of the immortal metabolism and partly because winged flight took serious energy. This one wasn't so much overweight as just really *solid* and round. Hard fat, she realized. A man who'd been fit but who'd let it go.

For that to happen to an angel, it meant he wasn't bothering to fly much.

Right now, his face was hot red and he was in the midst of pulling on his robe over what looked like a pair of pants and a tunic. "That's the quickest coupling I've ever had in all my centuries of existence."

Gervais clapped him on the shoulder. "Never mind. You'll have plenty more time once the Cadre has left us in peace. The sluts and toys will spread their legs on command or pay the price."

Elena didn't realize she'd pulled out the knife she'd slid away until Raphael closed his hand over her wrist. *Later, Elena. We will take care of them later.*

Her body vibrating with rage, she somehow managed to keep her blade from leaving her hand. Then, as Gervais and the other angel walked away, the wall beginning to shut behind them, she and Raphael moved. Not so fast as to create a gust of air that would alert the two Luminata, but not so slow that they'd miss the door. And then they were in and at the top of a flight of stairs that wasn't as steep as it should've been.

The door shut behind them in smoothly oiled silence. However, what was a seamless part of the wall on the hallway side was clearly a door from this side. Having separated from Raphael so that they could move independently, she tucked her wings back tight against her spine. The staircase was easy to navigate side by side, the lights on the walls guiding their way.

And then they reached the bottom.

Raphael's fingers clamped on to her forearm. Since she'd begun to fling out that same arm against his chest in an unconsciously protective move, she figured they were even. Both steady now, they looked over the edge of the doorway into nothingness. The only way to tell that they were looking down a deep shaft dug into the earth were the lights placed a regular distance apart going down.

"We're next to the Gallery," she said, the words a whisper. "Why would the builders dig a hole but not utilize all of it?" This shaft was nowhere near the diameter of the Gallery— maybe a tenth the size—but it was significant. And while it had exposed beams, it was structurally shored up.

"I think it was to provide a back way for the archivists to enter different levels of the Gallery." Raphael pointed out what looked like an old door across the way, the wood a little warped and not appearing as if it had been opened anytime recently. "It may have been specifically created so the archivists could reach the final, hidden section without disturbing any guests in the Gallery."

Elena blinked. "This shaft is an angelic elevator?" Which meant that final level had once had a legitimate use, likely for handy Gallery storage as Laric had assumed when he saw the staircase.

"Aptly put." He turned to take her into his arms. "We arrive together."

"Done."

With that, Raphael jumped off the edge and opened his wings in silence. The lights flashed up one after the other and they landed on square paving stones in a matter of seconds, the pavers set neatly into the dirt, as if they'd just been laid—though it was clear from the discoloration that they were old. The door to the hidden level was propped open with a rock, the corridor stretching out beyond well made but narrow.

Too narrow for Elena and Raphael to walk down it together.

Elena pulled out her gun, aimed it forward as she took the first step. *I am not going second this time, Raphael,* she said when she felt him shift behind her. *Don't even try it.*

A pause. *If there is danger you cannot handle, drop.*

That I can do. It'd give him a clear line of sight.

The passage was clean of dust and well maintained, clearly a place that was used often. Other than professionally installed electric lights every two feet—lights that told her some poor, hardworking electrician probably lay buried nearby, since this was a place no one outside a clandestine group could know—there wasn't anything on the walls or on the floor to give them any clues. Definitely none of the faint carvings that marked the navigation pathways around the rest of Lumia.

Then she caught the first hint of a scent. *Perfume*, she said to Raphael.

Female, he replied. *Heavy enough to linger—or to sink into another's skin during intimate contact.*

Elena thought of the two Luminata who'd recently exited, felt her jaw go tight. *Musk,* she said, breaking down the scent in an effort to think past the anger that lay hot and heavy in her gut, *rich on the oils, expensive.* It was the kind of scent that was overwhelmingly opulent, the kind you simply couldn't ignore. Getting used to it took a little doing for a born hunter, since scent was her business, her nose more sensitive to it even when it had nothing to do with identifying a vampire, but Elena had a lot of experience.

Pushing it aside so it no longer dominated her senses, she carried on.

And came to a halt at the outline of a door on the right-hand side of the passageway. *Be helpful if you could see through stone walls.*

I can scan mortal minds with ease.

Elena shook her head at the implied offer. *No, we don't cross that line.* Not even if it would make this easier—some lines were bright lines, and this one, the two of them had negotiated during a prior investigation. And while it was important to Elena's sense of honor, it was also important in keeping Raphael "human." *Can you tell if there are mortal minds behind the door without scanning them?*

No. If I search, I'll scan.

Shit. Elena bit down hard on her lower lip. *Ideas?* It was never a good plan to go into a room with unknown threats.

It's highly unlikely that anything this close to the entrance is beyond the expected. Unethical and ugly if the people within are coerced rather than volunteers, but nothing dangerous.

Elena nodded. *Right. It's all about easy access.* Exhaling quietly, she twisted the handle with care and stepped inside, going low so Raphael could see over her.

Her mouth fell open.

She—Raphael, too, when he came in behind her—stood in

a lush living area. It was nice and spacious, the carpet beneath their feet a thick, velvety gray, while what looked to be priceless paintings hung on the walls on either side. The settees—definitely not sofas—were an exquisite, deep burgundy with curved wooden arms and legs.

The furniture was clearly meant to accommodate wings.

A waiting area, Raphael said.

Or one where the sick bastards hang out. Scanning the three doors to their left and seeing no differences between them, Elena decided to go from closest to farthest. She walked in silence to the first door while Raphael stayed slightly back so he could cover her from threats from the other two doors or the one through which they'd entered.

This time when Elena opened the door—after turning the key in the lock—she scented the opulent perfume . . . and came face to face with a small and curvy young woman dressed only in a towel, her hair damp. Her mouth opened, as if to cry out in shock, but Elena was already moving, her hand clamped over the woman's mouth before the sound could escape.

The mirror in front of them reflected their images, Elena's golden-skinned hand covering the woman's mouth—a woman who had her own hands, her skin a rich cream, holding on tight to her towel. Her eyes were huge amber orbs.

Shaking her head in the mirror, Elena lifted her free hand and pressed a finger to her lips. "*Shh.*" A sound and an action understandable in any language.

The woman gave a jerky nod. Releasing her but ready to react at any hint she might scream, Elena watched as the brunette spun around to face her.

40

"Hunter angel." It was an awed statement.

"You speak English."

Another jerky nod. "Do you want . . ." She waved hesitantly at the bed on her right, the sheets still tumbled.

Relieved not to see any bruises or other signs of mistreatment on the woman, Elena put her hands on her hips. "You think you can compete with Raphael?"

The brunette smiled with firefly suddenness, dimples appearing in both cheeks. She was beautiful, Elena realized, but it wasn't the kind of beauty that was intimidating. No, her beauty was soft and sensual and welcoming. "I am glad you do not stray," she whispered. "You and your archangel, it is a storybook come to life." A long sigh. "*C'est tellement romantique.*"

That had definitely not been Moroccan, and this woman's English was accented in a way that wasn't local . . . and that made an ache form in the center of Elena's chest. "You're French?"

"*Oui.*" Still smiling, the woman pointed to a small vanity that held the usual accoutrements—well, usual for most women. Potions and pots and cosmetics. "I will brush my hair, yes?"

"Go ahead. I just wanted to talk to you, promise. Nothing to fear."

"But it is . . ." The woman lifted a finger to her lips.

"Yeah." Arms folded, Elena leaned against the wall after letting Raphael know everything was fine. "How did you come to be here?"

"I came with an angel down the long tunnel." She shivered. "I had to close my eyes or I would've screamed."

"No, not physically. How did you come to be . . ." Elena fought to find words that wouldn't be an insult.

"Providing joy to the Luminata?" A mischievous smile. "I was traveling through this area and I was made an offer." A liquid shrug. "It is a wild thing to do, but they are angels and I have not made promises to any man yet. When I am old and gray, I will have scandalous stories to tell my children, *non*?"

Elena felt her lips curve at that utterly unrepentant and happy statement. "What's your name?"

"Josette."

"Josette, I got to agree with you about angels—though I'm only partial to one particular angel."

The other woman's laugh was half giggle and all delight. "If I had Raphael, I would not look at any other pair of wings, either." Having combed her damp hair smooth, the dark strands showing signs that they might curl as they dried, Josette turned and went to her wardrobe to pull out underwear. Unselfconsciously shrugging off her towel to slip on white lace panties, she then picked up a nightshirt she'd already hung on a chair and pulled it on. "You worry for me?" Josette asked.

At Elena's nod, the other woman smiled again. "I am happy here, and though it is a thing that is a little naughty, I will leave here with many delicious memories."

A hint of wickedness, those dimples just the icing on the cake. "I have asked for nothing, no money, no gifts. Just memories. So I do not think of it as a transaction, more a . . . mutual pleasure, yes? An adventure before I go back to my normal life as a woman who works in an office and who wants to one day have a small house with a husband and babies."

Elena had no problem believing Josette—but she'd heard how Gervais and his friend had spoken about those hidden in this clandestine space. Josette might see this as a little harmless adventure in a life that would be ordinary enough otherwise, but Elena wasn't so sure about her safety. "The other men and women here," she said. "You know them?"

The first hint of trepidation colored Josette's features, the shorter woman twisting her fingers together in front of Elena. "I can't open the door from this side. Only the angels have the key."

Elena looked at the door, saw it had a keyed lock on this side, too. But there was no key in it at present. "Are you sure you're not a prisoner, Josette?"

"I have been here six days," the woman answered. "One more and I am meant to be returned to the town so I can find my way to the nearest big city and fly home." She swallowed. "They said they had to bring me here deep in the night, and that I had to stay in this room, because not all of the angels in this place accept the needs of the flesh. It felt like a fun secret."

Amber eyes stark, she stared at Elena. "Was I wrong to trust them?"

"I'm not sure yet," Elena murmured, wondering exactly how the Luminata had kept this secret for so long if they were picking up not only men and women from the town—people they could control and intimidate—but travelers like Josette who *would* speak of her adventures. The only answer was a deadly one. "I need you to enter the other two rooms so those inside aren't scared as you were when I came in. I want to check if they're here voluntarily, too."

Nodding, Josette padded forward.

"Wait," Elena said, suddenly realizing a rather big fact. "Raphael's outside. Don't scream."

Face paling, Josette swayed on her feet. Elena caught her, held her until the other woman's eyes focused again. "You good?"

"Yes." It was a breathy whisper. "He's here? Really?"

Elena nodded and stepped out first. "Remember, no squeals or sounds."

Peeking out, Josette stared at Raphael for a long moment, seemed to stop breathing for nearly a minute before she pressed both hands to her mouth and sighed. "*Il est magnifique*," she whispered to Elena, then, at her nod, walked out to go to the door next to hers. She turned the key, entered—and returned almost at once. "It's empty."

Elena checked, tasted the scent of disuse in the air. "How many angels come regularly to you?"

Blushing, Josette leaned in close to whisper, "Three come almost every day. Two others have come once each."

Five angels, Elena thought, even as the scent of the sea surrounded her.

There have to be more involved, Raphael said. *The sense of wrongness in Lumia is too deep for it to be only five angels who are breaching the core values on which Lumia is built.*

Agreeing, Elena spoke to Josette again. "I don't think the third room will be empty."

Taking a deep breath, the other woman walked over. She turned the key, stepped in. Elena heard a gasp almost at once, but there was no scream.

Staying out of sight of whoever was in that room, Elena listened as Josette said, "It is all right. I am Josette. I am in the other room."

The response was in broken English, the voice feminine. "Key? You have?"

Elena's heart thudded. The only reason the woman within would ask that question was if she needed that key. Shifting into view, she raised a finger to her lips as the woman sitting on the bed stared at her. Her hair was as black as night, her skin a light brown that looked pale and lifeless, as if it had been deprived of the sun. She was taller than Josette, but more slender. A willow dressed in a gown of pale yellow.

Seeing Elena, she began to hunch into herself, tears pooling in her eyes.

Josette rushed forward, hugged her. "Don't cry. Elena will help us. She is a good angel."

It didn't look like the woman believed her, but she let Josette tug her up to her feet and told them her name was Sahar. Making a command decision, Elena didn't immediately allow Sahar out of the room—things were apt to disintegrate the instant she saw Raphael. "Were you forced here?" she asked point blank.

Sahar went white under the pale brown of her skin. "Family I have," she said. "Baby son. Husband."

"No one will hurt them," Elena promised, her skin hot with an anger that kept growing bigger. "Please answer my question."

Josette murmured encouragement until, finally, the other woman nodded. "They come always," she whispered. "No go, they hurt family." She swallowed. "If go, don't scream, maybe come home."

"Maybe?"

A ragged nod. "Not always. My cousin . . . my neighbor . . . never come home."

The slowly dawning fear in Josette's eyes turned darkly potent. "Will you help us?" she asked, a tremor in her tone.

"Yes." Elena looked at the Frenchwoman. "Explain to her about Raphael."

Leaving the two alone in the room, Josette murmuring to Sahar, she went to Raphael, told him what she'd found. The ice in his eyes was so cold it frosted the air.

"We need to go deeper into this level, find the 'he' Gervais was talking about," she said, "but I'm not leaving them here."

"I think, Consort, we must rely on our friends."

Realizing what he planned to do, Elena went to Josette. "Get dressed," she said. "You'll have to travel through the hallways to a safe room."

Josette didn't delay, Sahar going with her.

It was only a few minutes later that Raphael went back down the corridor and to the paving stones, asking the women to follow. When he told them to come close enough for him to hold them around the waist, they hesitated until Elena said, "Go. He's taking you to freedom."

It was a powerful motivator.

Eyes of mountain sky blue met hers just before Raphael took off, the women clinging to him. *Do not get hurt while I'm gone.*

I'll stay right here. No matter her furious desire to discover the truth, she wasn't going to be stupid. All the Luminata were over ten centuries old; Elena was smart and she was fast, but she was still a whole lot mortal. Going in half assed would get her killed, break Raphael's heart, and not help any other man or woman who might still be a captive.

So she'd wait for her archangel.

He returned in a matter of minutes. "Eli was waiting on the other side of the door, is spiriting the women to his and Hannah's suite under glamour, so we have more time to unearth what lies here."

Cupping his face in her hands, she kissed him hard. "I *love* you." She had to say that, had to get it out before it overwhelmed her.

He touched his hand to her cheek, a warm, possessive caress. "Let's go end this."

Pulling the door shut behind them, he used his angelfire to fuse the iron of it to the walls. "No one will be coming in behind us."

Elena smiled grimly and went on down the corridor ahead of him, her crossbow out. She'd decided the gun was too dangerous in close quarters, could lead to a ricochet. And a bolt embedded in the face would give even a powerful angel pause.

She could feel Raphael gritting his teeth at having her in the line of fire, but he didn't try to push her behind him. In return, and because she knew how damn hard it was to let the person you loved walk into danger in front of you, she hunched down a little so he had a clearer view over her head.

Only there was nothing to see: the corridor came to a dead end on a smooth wall.

This time it was Elena who dropped to the ground and checked the air at the bottom using the feather she'd saved from before. The movement was again, very slight, but it existed. She searched all over for a mechanism to open it, could find nothing. "We can't wait," she whispered, urgency pounding at her.

. . . special chamber to see his pet.

Someone was trapped beyond this wall and awful things were being done to that person. And it was being done by a Luminata who held enough power or control over the others that they obeyed his every word.

"Step back, Guild Hunter."

As she squeezed past him, Raphael pulled one of her thin throwing blades from a wrist sheath. She didn't react except with a confused scowl—he was one of the few people she'd let get that close, do what he'd just done.

Taking her knife, he stared at the wall for a few seconds before reaching up and pushing the tip of the blade into a spot that looked like any other.

The door cracked open in smooth silence.

So did Elena's mouth. "Care to explain?"

"My mother has been around a long time," he said, returning the knife to her. "I asked her if she'd seen such invisible doors before, with no indentations that could be pressure sensors." *Now we go silent.*

Thank your mom for me.

Already done, Elena-mine.

And funny how you're in the front all of a sudden.

A small smile over his shoulder but, to her surprise, he turned to back himself up against the wall. She squeezed past—and stole a kiss on the way. *Thank you.* For understanding that she needed to confront this evil head-on.

This is important to you.

Yes. Elena couldn't tell him why it was so important—maybe because it was near certain that underneath Lumia lay the bones of her grandmother and grandfather. In a strange way, it was a connection to her mother, a chance for Elena to fight another piece of the evil that had destroyed Marguerite's life.

This passageway was clean enough, but nowhere near as pristine as the other section. Cobwebs hung in the corners and the footprints on the floor had been created in new dust that sat over old, pressed-in dust. *Only one set going and coming from what I can see.* She bent down to examine the prints more closely. *Soft shoes with boot soles like what so many of the Luminata wear. Large-ish but not huge.*

Getting up, she followed the footsteps—not that there were any side passages to misdirect or distract her. The deeper they went, the less "finished" the passageway became. Exposed beams, the floor going from stone to wood that was rotten in places and had been inexpertly replaced in other areas. As if someone just patched up the holes when they got too bad.

The person who comes here, Raphael said, *does not permit anyone else within, even to do cleanup and repairs.*

Elena nodded as the passage began to slope downhill. *Whoever he has trapped down here, he must've brought that person in long enough ago that the footprints have faded or been stood over.*

Or he may have carried in his victim, Raphael replied.

And, Elena thought, it was possible that victim had been unconscious at the time, that they'd fought their captor and lost. *I really want to kill someone today.*

People will die. Raphael's words were a chilly promise.

The temperature around them also dropped the deeper they went, until her breath was coming in bursts that seemed like they should be white. From the freshness of the air, it was clearly coming in from somewhere outside; she couldn't see ventilation shafts, however. That didn't mean they didn't exist. As Raphael had just demonstrated with the "invisible" door, angels had been around a long time, had a number of tricks up their sleeves.

Cave system nearby? she asked Raphael. *Natural ventilation channels through stone?*

I know of none in this area, but it's possible they exist. Or it's possible a large pipe has been bored through to the surface some distance from Lumia, and hidden in the vegetation.

They've certainly got the privacy and time to do something like that. It's not like anyone polices them.

That will change. If the Luminata even exist after today.

A harsh pleasure mixing with the anger inside her, Elena suddenly frowned. *Where are they burying the bodies? I thought it'd be through this door, but if only one person is allowed here, that's not likely.*

Raphael took too long to reply. When he did, she realized why.

41

The pavings on which we landed after flying down the shaft aren't sunken into the earth as they should be after hundreds of years of angelic landings. They're being lifted up on a regular basis.

Gut churning, Elena fought back her horror. *We walked over the victims.*

We came with clean hearts. Raphael ran his hand down her back. *The ones who did this, however, chose that location because it is a final insult. Whatever happens, the insult ends tonight.*

Elena went to reply, paused midstep without consciously understanding why, hunkered down . . . and realized she could see. The lights came all the way through here, though they weren't the seamlessly integrated ones she'd seen in the earlier section. These were lightbulbs strung along the side of the passageway, the burned-out ones creating pools of shadow. It was a glimmer of white in one of those shadows that had attracted her attention: a feather.

Picking it up, she passed it back to Raphael.

Many angels have feathers of pure white, even if there are other shades mingled in with the white.

Yes, not exactly a smoking gun. Elena had no white feathers in her wings, but Raphael had the odd few that had no metallic filaments of white gold. Caliane's were the purest white Elena had ever seen, and even Favashi had the odd downy white feather scattered among the sleek ivory of her wings.

Gian, of course, had a lot of white feathers in his wings. But despite the fact Gervais was his best bud, she couldn't assume it was Gian she'd be facing at the end of this journey. If he had been obsessed with her grandmother to the point of writing her love poetry, it didn't make sense to Elena that he'd switch so quickly—in immortal terms—to someone else.

Then again, maybe he was a psychopath who fixated on mortal after mortal. *Feather's not dusty, though, which means he passed through very recently.*

And, Raphael reminded her, *he hasn't come back.*

Elena looked at her crossbow, assessed the increasingly narrow passage, and decided she needed a close combat weapon that wouldn't pose a risk to innocent bystanders. Strapping on the crossbow, she dropped a knife into her hand. *Let's go get the bastard.*

Exactly one hundred steps later, she heard the echo of a scream, but it wasn't one of terror. Frowning, she walked faster, driven by the pounding urgency deep in her gut.

Guild Hunter.

Raphael's tone had her freezing. *I'm not in control.* She wasn't used to this feeling, wasn't used to hunting without a plan.

I will be your control.

Had anyone, even Raphael, made that offer a year ago, Elena might've bristled.

Today, safe in the knowledge he wouldn't allow her to mess this up, she moved on. And when she felt the waves of his mind crashing into hers, she knew to pull back, to slow. The screams got louder the deeper they went, the emotion in those screams easy to identify now.

Someone's having one hell of a tantrum, she said as they came to a narrow door with a padlock that was hanging open on the latch on one side.

Raphael touched her on her shoulder. When she glanced

back, he made a motion. She nodded. She'd go in low, and he'd come up behind her.

". . . going to be mine, too!" It was a male voice yelling, so much twisted emotion in it that it hurt Elena's ears. "Did you hear me? I'm going to own your child as I own you!"

Movement, boots slapping on the floor, then, "Scream! Scream!"

The speaker switched languages on his next words.

You understand that one, Archangel?

It's a mishmash of various languages. Not much sense. He's continuing to demand that someone scream.

Elena smiled grimly. *Which means whoever he has down here, that person is refusing to give him what he wants even though he's threatening to take their child.* Knife held ready in her hand, she unlatched the unlocked door and said, *One, two . . . three!*

Pulling open the door, she rolled in and took in the situation at a single glance. The shock of what she saw might've paralyzed her if she hadn't been so angry and so well trained. Coming up in a fluid strike, she swapped the knife for the blade star at the same time. This brick-lined cell was much bigger than she'd imagined and Gian was way on the other side. Given his age and strength and training, he might be able to move fast enough to avoid a knife thrown at him.

The blade star was whirling from her hand even as those thoughts passed through her head, the calculations done on a subconscious level. It whipped through the air at lightning speed as Gian went to thrust his knife through the eye of a battered and emaciated male chained to the wall, one of his eyes already pulp, blood dripping down his cheek. His hair might've been blond once; it was now dry straw.

The knife fell with a clatter a heartbeat after the blade star embedded itself in Gian's throat, blood spurting out to spray the face of the blond male . . . who lunged forward as Gian crumpled toward him, and sank his fangs into Gian's throat. The blond's throat moved in deep gulps as he drank, while Gian struggled ineffectually.

The sudden blood loss shouldn't have weakened him that much, so the blade star must've done damage to his trachea, too. Angels didn't *need* to breathe to live, but not breathing had an impact on their strength.

Especially if a vampire was feeding right from the artery at the same time.

Elena wasn't about to stop that feeding. The vampire looked like he was starving and had been starving—starved—for a long time. She left Raphael to monitor the situation and to make sure Gian wouldn't escape; she hadn't forgotten what Raphael had told her about exactly how dangerous the leader of the Luminata had once been—but on the flip side, Gian had been ruling this little fiefdom for centuries.

Elena had a feeling his flunkies didn't ever dare challenge him. A ruler as egotistical as Gian wouldn't stand for it. And Gian had cleared the area of all other possible threats. Unlike the angel she'd seen in the hallway, he hadn't let his body go to seed, but he had allowed the razored edge of his self to dull, his instincts no longer as sharp.

"Don't."

The single chilly word had her swiveling back in readiness to fight—to see Gian's hand glowing with a green-gold power. Of course he'd have the ability to utilize energy like Aodhan and Illium, she realized. He'd been an archangel's second once. But he wasn't the biggest predator in the room. And when Gian ignored Raphael's order, began to raise his hand up to the vampire's throat, Raphael seared off half of Gian's left wing using his own violent energy, the wound cauterized as it was made.

The angel convulsed, his hand falling to his side as the green-gold energy fizzled.

Gian, however, wasn't the only threat. If the vampire was insane after his trauma, there wasn't much anyone could do. He'd have to be executed, no matter how unfair that was.

Maddened vampires rarely came back from their murderous urges.

Those thoughts tumbled rapid fire through her brain as she turned to the other captive in the room, her mind trying to catch up with what her eyes were seeing: a woman with hair of moonlight who stared at Elena as if she'd seen a ghost.

Majda had Ari's eyes, Beth's eyes, she found herself thinking. Stunning turquoise, so clear and so painfully familiar.

"Marguerite." The raw whisper was shaped by full lips set in a face that was wrinkled and haggard, those stunning eyes smudged with tears, but it was undoubtedly of the woman in the miniature.

Elena's breath caught.

"Elena," she corrected gently as she broke through her shock to examine the chains that held Majda's wrists and ankles pinned to the wall. "Marguerite was my mother. My *maman*." She didn't know if Majda spoke English, but the word "*maman*" should be understandable to a woman who'd lived in France.

The chains were heavy iron.

"I'll take care of it, Guild Hunter."

Stepping back, Elena let Raphael pulverize the irons and caught Majda in her arms.

Her grandmother's legs were shaky, her arms, too, but those arms came around her with unexpected fierceness. "Marguerite's baby?" Tears in every word. "My granddaughter."

Going down to the floor with Majda in her arms, Elena fought her own tears. "You need blood," she said, recognizing the cinnamon spice and wild raspberry scent of this woman as that of a vampire.

Her grandmother pushed away Elena's wrist when she offered it.

Elena tried again. "You need to drink." Majda wasn't emaciated or starving like the other vampire, but she was weak, as if she hadn't fed for at least a week or longer.

Majda shook her head. "Not from my *bébé*, from my Marguerite."

Realizing her grandmother was still disoriented, Elena went to make a small slit in her forearm, but Raphael was there before her. "Let me, *hbeebti*. I am far stronger and she'll heal faster."

Her grandmother's eyes flicked from Elena to Raphael at the word *hbeebti*, her pupils dilating. When Raphael's wing pressed over Elena's as he crouched down to offer Majda his forearm, she scuttled back . . . and then her gaze seemed to focus on Elena's own wings. Her breath began to come faster.

"I'll explain," Elena said, desperate to help her. "But please drink, Grandmother."

Elena didn't know if it was the "please" or the "Grandmother" that did it, but Majda made her way cautiously closer and, lowering her head, sank her fangs into Raphael's wrist. She jerked back after a single long pull at most, and when her lashes lifted, there was a glow to her eyes that reminded Elena of Raphael's wings.

"Not an angel," Majda said even as her skin smoothed out to flawless beauty, her hair turning glossy and shiny.

In a matter of heartbeats, she looked no older than Elena.

"No." Elena just stared. "He's an archangel."

And her grandmother was astonishingly beautiful.

Her eyes were also no longer locked on Elena. "Jean-Baptiste!" Scrambling to her feet, she ran to the other vampire, the one Gian had been torturing.

He was still feeding—and Gian was the one who was shrinking and shriveling, the vampire growing healthier in a slow motion contrast. His eye had healed first, the crusted blood and ocular fluid around it falling away in flecks when he blinked. His hair was no longer straw but becoming softer blond, his body filling out in a way that told her he was a tall, solidly built man when not starved.

Still, the transformation was nothing close to that with Majda.

Then Raphael got up, pulled Gian away to drop his wasted but still alive form to the floor, and pressed his wrist to the vampire's bloody mouth. The vampire fed, jerking the same way as Majda had done at the punch of power, but he didn't wrench away, his starvation too great. He drank for at least a minute before he lifted his head.

By then, he had starkly handsome features that looked oddly familiar to Elena.

"You have her hair, her skin," Raphael murmured. "But much of the rest, it comes from him."

And it really hit her; she was staring at her grandfather. And Raphael was right—much as she superficially resembled her grandmother, it was her grandfather whose genes had held sway over both Marguerite and Elena, though if anyone had asked her to explain exactly how, she'd have been stumped.

"They're my grandparents," she whispered, trying to make sense of it all.

"Not a single doubt. And both appear to be sane." Having already removed Jean-Baptiste's chains, Raphael turned to Gian while Majda sobbed and kissed her husband at the same time, uncaring of the blood that smeared his lips.

Looking away to give them privacy as they embraced, Elena watched Raphael go to Gian, haul him up with a single hand fisted in his shirt. "Explain yourself."

Gian opened his mouth but nothing came out. Too much damage from the feeding, Elena thought, then, when the Luminata clawed at his throat, she realized the blade star was still lodged in there somewhere. "He needs help to get that blade star out," she said, her tone flat. "I have a hunting knife."

"No, Elena, this we will do in front of the Cadre." A glance at her grandparents. "You will follow us."

It was the male who answered. "Yes, sir." In the light silvery blue of his eyes was understanding of Raphael's identity. And around him hung the same sense of raw power Elena sensed in Ashwini's Janvier. Like Janvier, her grandfather might've been young in immortal terms, but he was strong—else his blood wouldn't have held power enough to linger through his child.

When those eyes turned to Elena, they held incandescent joy. "Marguerite's daughter?" he asked Majda in a chaos of intermingled disbelief and joy. "Our baby's baby?"

Throat thick, Elena touched her hands to theirs. "We'll have centuries to talk, an eternity." She couldn't wrap her mind around the fact that she was looking at her maternal grandparents, but one thing she knew: this woman of her family hadn't been murdered. She'd *survived*. She lived. "But first, we need to take care of this asshole before the storm ends and the Cadre flies away."

They had no context for her statement, but Majda and Jean-Baptiste were willing to follow her lead, their hands interlocked. Both had used the backs of their forearms to wipe the blood off their mouths.

While her grandmother wore a flowing gown of misty blue that looked strangely new, her grandfather was all but naked, the rags that clothed his body having fallen off as he healed. Elena tried not to look that way. It was clear he didn't like being near-naked in front of his granddaughter—and wow, yeah, that was definitely a trip, that these two beautiful, ageless people were her family.

Following Raphael as he hauled Gian up the passageway by the neck, the Luminata's feet and wings dragging on the floor, she asked him to wait when they reached the suite where the women had been kept. She entered with care lest another Luminata had somehow managed to come in, quickly cleared the area, then began to search the wardrobes, hoping some of the Luminata had forgotten clothing.

There was an edge to her grandfather's stance that told her he was a man of quiet pride. She would not take that from him, would not let the Luminata gawk at him when they entered the main part of Lumia.

She found nothing suitable in what had been Josette's room, but when she checked the room that wasn't in use, it was to discover a stack of civilian male clothing. She tried not to think about the fact that some of these clothes could well have belonged to young males who'd been taken and who'd never gone home again. "I'll get vengeance for you," she whispered.

Stepping out, she found Raphael had sent her grandparents into the plush waiting area. Elena kept her eyes resolutely on her grandmother as she said, "I found male clothing in there."

Majda and Jean-Baptiste slipped into the room without further discussion, their linked hands never breaking.

Dropping Gian in one corner after coming into the suite, Raphael brushed away strands of hair stuck to her cheek from perspiration she hadn't even felt in the heat of the moment. "So, *hbeebti.*"

"Yeah." Rubbing her cheek against his palm when he spread it open on her skin, she blew out a breath. "I'm the grandchild of a vampire."

"Two vampires."

She bit down on her lower lip, shook her head. "Majda wasn't a vampire when she had my mother." Riad's great-grandparents had made it clear Jean-Baptiste couldn't find an angel who'd fast-track her application. "I have a feeling she was Made after she left France." As for the how of the latter, and where the bus crash fit in, she'd get the details from her grandmother later.

Raphael considered it, sliding his hand down her arm. When she caught his hand, he smiled, linked his fingers with hers. "You may be right." A dangerously calm glance over at where Gian whimpered and gasped, his eyes bugging out of his head as he continued to dig at his throat. *"Quiet."*

Gian flung his fist at Raphael, but no green-gold energy came from it.

"You have lost half your volume of blood and your body is focusing on healing your throat," Raphael told the other angel in a voice so cold it raised every tiny hair on Elena's body. "You have no resources to muster an attack. Do not attempt it again or I'll forget about a trial in front of the Cadre and turn you to dust where you crawl."

His eyes were deep Prussian blue when he returned his attention to Elena, the otherness of him a heavy presence in the room. *You look a little terrified, Elena-mine.*

In a good way. She wove her fingers even tighter with his, banishing the chill of violent power and long immortality with the love that lived in her, in him, between them. *No matter how scary you get, Archangel, I always want to dance with you.*

Majda and Jean-Baptiste returned from the room right then. To Elena's surprise, both had changed. Her grandfather wore black pants and a simple white shirt that suited his blunt handsomeness. He didn't have the prettiness developed by some vampires. No, he was like Dmitri—he'd retained a harsh edge to his features that said he was a dangerous man, but vampirism had given him unblemished white skin that needed the kiss of the sun, and hair that gleamed with silken health.

As for Majda . . .

Gone was her grandmother's gown, in its place a pair of brown pants that she'd rolled up at the bottom and tied tightly around her waist using a belt Elena remembered seeing in the wardrobe. On top, she wore a woman's shirt, so that must've also been in the wardrobe.

And Elena knew without asking that the gown had been forced on Majda by Gian.

Majda's lips suddenly curved, her eyes bright.

Following the line of her gaze, Elena realized her grandmother had seen Raphael and Elena's linked hands. "Let's go get rid of the garbage," Elena said softly.

42

As Elena slipped out her crossbow in readiness for any possible threats, Raphael grabbed Gian once again, his grip so powerful that Gian couldn't have escaped it even at full strength. When Elena heard angry murmuring behind her just after they reached the paving area onto which she'd stepped with a quiet "Forgive me," she looked back over her shoulder and shook her head at her grandparents. "The angels have *far* more brutal methods of punishment than you could ever imagine."

"But will they punish one of their own when the victims are no one important?" A deep voice, deeper than it had been before, Jean-Baptiste clearly still healing in the wake of the infusion of archangelic blood.

Raphael was the one who answered. "You are family," he said, his wings suddenly afire and cuttingly bright in the gloom of the shaft. "It does not matter what anyone else in the Cadre says or believes, I have the right to punish those who seek to harm my family."

Both Majda and Jean-Baptiste had flinched at the blaze of Raphael's power, but straightened almost immediately and—after a glance at one another—nodded at Raphael. And they held his gaze as they did so. Holding him to account.

It appears stubborn courage runs in the family line.

You better believe it, Archangel. Elena looked at the pathetic form of Gian. "Fly him up first. I'll come with you and keep an eye on him while you bring up Majda and Jean-Baptiste." She didn't want them up there alone and no way was she going to leave Gian alone for even a second.

Snakes had a habit of slithering away.

One hand still gripping Gian, Raphael circled her waist with his other arm and they lifted off. As she looked down, she saw her grandparents heads tilt back, their eyes glowing in the light coming off Raphael's wings and their bodies touching. Then Raphael was releasing her and she was winging her way up to the platform at the top of the shaft.

Raphael waited until she caught up and got on the platform before he threw Gian with enough force that the Luminata ended up at the bottom of the staircase. He dropped without saying a word, the two of them in perfect sync.

Crossbow lifted and aimed at Gian's forehead, Elena didn't take her eye off the staircase or off Gian's mewling form. And when the angel began to crawl forward, she didn't ask what the fuck he was doing. She just shot a crossbow bolt half an inch from the front of his face. "The next one goes through your skull." It wouldn't kill him. He was too old. But it'd hurt like a bitch and put him out for a while.

Pale green eyes looked at her with soft confusion in their depths, as if he couldn't understand why she was so angry at him. Thank God Raphael was the archangel who'd make the call about his punishment—because the bastard knew how to use words, how to use charm, how to twist the world so it was his.

A rush of air behind her, then Majda's voice. "Thank you," she said, the tone holding a tremor that wasn't of fear. "I never thought I would one day fly out of that hellhole."

Her husband chuckled. "Such stories we will have to tell, my love."

It made Elena's heart melt, that even after decades in hell, they spoke to one another that way, touched one another with care. *Will you call me Elena-mine when we've been together two thousand years and you're annoyed by the size of my knife collection?*

The firelight of Raphael's wings brushed hers as he passed. *First, as I would be responsible for having given you the majority of those knives, how could I be annoyed? And second, I will always call you Elena-mine.* Vivid blue eyes holding her own gaze even as he leaned down to grab Gian. *Nothing in this world or the next can change who you are to me.*

He went up the steps first, with Majda and Jean-Baptiste following, Elena in the rear just in case one of those doors to the Gallery hadn't been painted or tiled over from the other side, and was still in use. No way was she allowing anyone to ambush them now.

But the shaft remained silent and they exited into the hallway to find it empty.

Elena was a little disappointed. She'd been ready to shoot bolts into the lying mouths of the Luminata, both the pious bastards who treated mortals as commodities and the ones who'd been aware of what was going on in the deepest recesses of Lumia, yet had done nothing to stop it.

"I'll show them luminescence," she muttered as she stalked down the hallway at Raphael's side, her crossbow held to her left but cocked and ready to fire.

They made no attempt to conceal their presence and the first Luminata they met in the hallway gasped and ran toward them. "Gian!"

"*Silence.*" Power honed to a lethal blade, Raphael's voice commanded absolute obedience. The Luminata, a small man with hair of darkest brown and huge, dark eyes, bowed his head, but Elena had caught the secondary layer of shock in his gaze.

These assholes really weren't used to being given orders by anyone, not even the Cadre.

"Gather your brothers," Raphael said, the words an archangelic decree. "All must be in the Atrium by the time the Cadre gathers or their lives are forfeit. *Go.*"

The now white-faced Luminata ran.

Raphael gave the same order to others, until any "brother" they passed was either running to tell others or hurrying in the direction of the Atrium. Turning to Elena, her archangel spoke but he'd stolen all her breath, her blood such a loud roar in her ears that she couldn't hear him. His eyes were liquid blue flame, the Legion mark on his temple sparking with wildfire, his wings still rippling white flame.

And she knew. "The Cascade changes have rooted." It came out a whisper, terror clutching at her heart—because this being, the one who looked back at her, he was *other* in ways her Raphael wasn't. As if he was growing into a plane of existence where she could not follow.

His responding shrug cut through the sudden fear, it was so natural. "We will test it later. For now, we need Ibrahim in the Atrium. I have told Aodhan and Laric to bring him there. Xander and Valerius will assist."

"How did they know?"

"Xander came to ask you if you would play a blade game with him, stayed when he realized what was happening." A faint smile. "It appears the boy is ever more in love with your skill with sharp objects."

"Figures. Men only ever want me for my weapons."

Raphael's laughter caused the already shocked Luminata around them to stare in disbelief, but when Elena checked behind them to make sure her grandparents were following— *yes, still weird to think that*—she found them both smiling.

It was Majda who said, "Jean-Baptiste has a predilection for knives as well." A soft voice, almost breathy in its husky sexiness, but it was clearly not an affectation, simply the way her vocal cords produced sound. "He had quite a collection."

"My consort has never met a blade she doesn't love." Raphael's contribution had Majda's and Jean-Baptiste's smiles growing even wider.

"Not true," Elena said. "No rusty blades—except, of course, when I want to carve out the eyes of vicious monsters." She locked gazes with Gian, who was already looking better than he had in the torture chamber he'd created.

Bastard was strong.

And this time, he wasn't quick enough to hide his true self: hate foamed in his eyes, though those eyes weren't on Elena but on Jean-Baptiste.

Elena heard movement behind her, followed by a sharp word in a feminine voice, the language the same one she'd heard in the town. Her grandfather held his peace, but she could feel his simmering rage.

The same lived in her.

She carried the crossbow openly in one hand when they walked into the Atrium. It was full of Luminata, all in those hideous robes that were less about conformity for the sake of luminescence and more about hiding evil. At least the bastards weren't arrogant enough to keep up their hoods. Fear twisted too many of their exposed faces, the kind of fear that spoke of guilt, but there were as many faces that held only confusion.

It confirmed Elena's supposition that the ugliness had been perpetrated by a select group. More had known what was happening or had an idea of the wrongness—and were equally guilty in her eyes—but there *were* a few who'd known nothing. People like Ibrahim, who'd innocently come here in a search for enlightenment, and older Luminata who might've been considered too set in their ways to trust with the vicious break in Lumia's traditions.

"Raphael, why do you call us to a meeting?" It was Astaad's voice, an edge to his tone that reminded her that, elegant manners or not, he was an archangel, a power beneath the skin. "All has been decided." The Archangel of the Pacific Isles stood in the center of the Atrium, in a large area that had been left empty by the gathered Luminata.

Disapproval was an open stain on his features when he spied Gian's broken form. "We do not treat the Luminata with such disrespect."

Raphael had come to know his fellow archangel far better since Elena became friends with Mele. So he knew the most important thing of which Astaad needed to be aware. *Do you believe in forcing women to be your concubines, Astaad?*

A look of pure distaste in Astaad's dark eyes. *Where is the pleasure in force?* His gaze landed on Gian again, flicked to Majda, then, with a startled jerk, to Elena. Comprehension sparked. *I see.*

The other man didn't interfere when Raphael threw Gian into the center of the circle. Fresh blood sputtered from his wound to mark the polished stone of the floor. As the leader of the Luminata struggled to speak, clutching at his throat in a futile attempt to remove the blade star, the two archangels stood in a silence that had the gathered Luminata going dead silent as well.

The next to arrive was Michaela. "Really, Raphael, if you wanted to see me, you just had to knock on my door," was her opening salvo, her voice a sensual huskiness. "And are you now building a harem of odd, white-haired women?"

"I will explain," he said, in no mood for games. "The others will be here soon."

Michaela sauntered over to stand next to Astaad, her eyes on Gian. "There appears to be something stuck in his throat," she said conversationally. "Perhaps I should slit it to give him relief."

As the audience flinched, Elena held out a large knife, hilt first.

It might've been the first known occasion where Michaela and Elena had been in agreement.

Taking the blade with a mocking smile, Michaela bent, wrenched back Gian's head with a grip in his hair, and did exactly what she'd said: she slit the man's throat. Choking and with blood bubbling out in a dark red pulse, Gian clawed at the wound while Michaela wiped the blade on his clothing, then threw the blade back at Elena with archangelic speed.

Raphael was just far enough from his consort that he couldn't intercept it, knew it was going to embed itself in Elena's face—because Michaela was far better with knives than most people realized. Then Elena's hand was in the air, gripping the blade by the hilt as the sharp tip hovered a centimeter from her eye.

Michaela's wasn't the only face that reflected stunned surprise.

The female archangel, who kept her territory under control by engendering a careful mix of bone-chilling fear and respect at her icy competence, wiped the expression off her face within a split second but Raphael had spotted it. As he'd spotted Astaad's responsive jerk toward Elena, as if to attempt to intercept the knife himself.

Raphael would forget neither reaction.

The Archangel of the Pacific Isles began to smile an instant later, faint enough that he erased it easily off his face when Michaela spun around to stalk back to stand beside him.

Gian, meanwhile, was still clawing at his throat with his right hand.

As Raphael watched, Gian dug into the wound and came out with fingers sliced off at the tips, the bones showing. He stared at the amputated tips, his face white. When one of the other Luminata made a move as if to help him, Raphael just looked at the tall, thin male who would not survive this night. Gervais froze, swallowed, scuttled back.

Alexander and Caliane walked into the room just as Gian finally got the fingers of his left hand around the blade star and tore it out to throw it across the floor in a spray of blood. His fingers flopped backward a heartbeat later, the blade having cut through bone when he gripped the blade star. The severed fingers fell to the floor even as Gian attempted to hold them to his hand. Which was now nothing but a lump of bloody meat.

Raphael felt more than saw Elena's lips kick upward. "I owe Ash dinner at the flashiest vampire restaurant I can find."

"I am glad your friend is on our side, *hbeebti*." Janvier's lover—and now wife—was extraordinary in many ways, but her ability to glimpse pieces of the future was one that had first put her on immortal radar.

"Me, too."

Movement, Elena's grandfather walking over to retrieve the blade star. Jean-Baptiste Etienne had learned from watching Gian, picked up the weapon with the shield of a doubled-up handkerchief that must've been in the clothing he wore, and utilizing only the very tips of his fingers.

Rising to his full height, he used the handkerchief to clean off the blood, then walked back to pass the blade star to Elena. "An expedient tool. You shouldn't lose it."

Elena grinned. "Thanks."

Stubborn courage indeed, Raphael thought. Not many vampires would have walked into the center of a group of archangels at any point. Who did this vampire belong to?

"Jean-Baptiste?" It was Favashi's voice, the surprise on her face unhidden and so genuine Raphael couldn't doubt it. "You are meant to be dead. The Luminata reported your death to the steward of my court."

"My lady." Jean-Baptiste bowed in deepest respect to his sire. When he straightened from the bow, his voice rang around the Atrium. "As you see, I am not dead." His eyes held those of his archangel. "I have been kept on the brink for decades. It is Raphael's blood that courses through my veins today, that gives me my strength."

A dangerous glance at Gian, who was still gripping his throat but had to be healing behind it now that the blade star was gone. "I took this one's blood, too, but he is weak, nothing."

Bowing again, the vampire returned to stand beside Majda, who herself had come to stand next to Elena. That close, only the blind would miss the family resemblance between the three. Raphael heard a gasp, more than one, as all the remaining members of the Cadre took their places in the circle.

43

Caliane chose to flank Jean-Baptiste in a silent display of family unity.

On Raphael's left stood Alexander.

He and the Ancient parted in silence when Aodhan, Xander, Laric, and Valerius arrived with a makeshift stretcher bearing Ibrahim's broken body. They placed the stretcher in the circle, close to Neha, then backed off. Having witnessed Neha's earlier reaction, Raphael wondered at the placement until Neha sucked in a breath and went down on one knee. She was still in the dark green clothing similar to a fighter's leathers, her hair braided and her face clear of the cosmetics she usually wore.

God, Raphael, Neha is a warrior goddess.

Yes, Raphael said. *She is also a Queen. That is her duality.*

It was the warrior goddess who touched her hand to Ibrahim's bruise-blackened and swollen face. "Who did this?" Her voice was a whip of fury, her wings aglow.

And Raphael realized that Neha hadn't actually seen the beaten man's face until now.

Aodhan, who'd come to stand behind Elena and Raphael, quietly filled them in. "Valerius recognized Ibrahim from

Neha's court. He was a respected scholar, one much in Neha's favor until he came to join the Luminata."

No one answered Neha.

Rising to her feet, the Archangel of India stared at Raphael. "You know the answer."

"I know some of it." He began to speak, starting with the fear that strangled the nearest township.

"They are mortals," Charisemnon interrupted, and for once, his view wasn't an outlier.

Raphael had once been part of that group, believing a life that was over in a firefly flicker had no relevance to him. He'd forgotten that Dmitri had once been mortal, the years having jaded him. Until a hunter faced him down with a foolish courage that dug its way into his heart. As he fell with Elena's broken body in New York, he'd known there would be no one else like Elena in all his existence, her firefly flicker a dazzling light that had marked him, branded him forever.

"It is natural that they should fear their masters," Michaela added with a mocking smile directed at Elena. "Such is the way of the world."

Raphael felt Elena bristle, but his hunter was no green youth; she faced the archangel with expressionless calm. "Yes, they are mortals," he said. "But those mortals are not the Luminata's to rule. Or did you cede them the right to their own fiefdom?" The latter question, he directed to Charisemnon.

The Archangel of Northern Africa narrowed his eyes. "Morocco is mine. Lumia and Lumia alone is theirs."

Leaving the other man to consider that fact, Raphael then spoke about what the Cadre would consider the most egregious crime. "Using the shield of seeking luminescence, the Luminata—at least a certain percentage of them—have been living a life free of all oversight. These men do not consider themselves as having to respect the boundaries we have laid down for all angelkind. They believe themselves above the Cadre."

The wings of every archangel in the circle began to glow.

"The search for luminescence is a mask," he said bluntly. "The ones involved have used it to enslave mortals and slake their carnal lusts without having to answer for their crimes to anyone." Again, he knew crimes against mortals meant nothing to several of the archangels, so he continued. "Jean-Baptiste is not the only vampire who is apt to have 'died' while seconded to serve at Lumia."

"I believe most are truly dead," Jean-Baptiste said when Raphael looked at him. "Gian taunted us during our captivity with stories of all the 'inconvenient' guards he and his cohort had murdered without repercussion." The vampire spoke with clear-eyed focus, his assurance a testament to his spirit. "He meant to frighten us into believing him omnipotent—he told us he was the final law in Lumia and even archangels didn't question his word."

"*Liar.*" The rasp of sound came from Gian, his vocal cords clearly recovering.

Ten archangelic heads turned toward the Luminata. None of the looks were friendly. It was Elijah who spoke. "I have lost three vampires over the past three and a half centuries. Two to an apparent freak accident during combat training when they attacked each other with too much force, one to a disappearance that was never explained except as a desertion of his post."

"Ibrahim is mine," Neha confirmed, crouching down again to touch his hand gently with her own before she rose. "A vampire seconded to Lumia was also said to have deserted out of boredom."

"Two," Michaela snapped. "Two of my most talented young angelic warriors, seconded here as squadron leaders for a short term because Lumia is considered a prestigious position and I wanted them to have that experience on their records."

I keep forgetting she's an actual archangel, Elena said. *One who obviously rules well since her territory is stable. Then she says something like that.*

Never forget no archangel is one-dimensional. It was a lesson that could well save her life one day.

"One," Titus said in his booming voice. "A young vampire who disappeared without a trace and who, it was told to me, had been aggressive before he strode off into the darkness never to be seen again."

In the end, the Cadre confirmed they'd lost a total of at *least* twenty-five vampires as well as ten angels over the centuries since Gian took leadership. Most of the latter had been seconded as squadron leaders.

The number wasn't much in the grand scheme of things, but fighters with enough promise to be sent to Lumia were considered valuable assets and many had personal relationships with their archangels—or with the weapons masters of those archangels. They had been missed. The only reason no one had connected the dots was because the disappearances and deaths had been spread out across many archangelic territories and over centuries.

"Why did they die?" The question came from Alexander, and it was directed not at Gian, but at Jean-Baptiste. "Did Gian boast of his reasons?"

Once more, even in the face of an Ancient's regard, the vampire held his ground.

Any archangel would be proud to have your grandfather in his forces, hbeebti.

Pride tinged the silver-rimmed gray of his consort's eyes when she smiled at him.

"They began to ask questions," Jean-Baptiste said.

"Liar!" Gian's attempt at a yell was only a slightly louder rasp that everyone ignored, their attention on the vampire who was Elena's blood.

"All of the ones who are gone were highly intelligent," the other man said, "and they weren't willing to look the other way when they realized Lumia was breaking the rules that permit it to be a self-governing society."

Shoulder muscles bunched and his feet set firmly apart, he said, "The current squadrons are all privately sourced and paid for with the money the Luminata bring in with them when they pledge to Lumia—it means there is no risk the men will have any loyalty but to Lumia."

Majda spoke into the pause, gripping at the back of her husband's forearm and voice trembling. Yet she would not be silenced. "He calls himself the King of Kings, a man beyond the reach of anyone on this earth."

Michaela would've fried Gian on the spot if Raphael hadn't held up a hand. "I call blood debt."

Everyone froze.

He waited for a challenge, but what he got was an incline of the head from Neha. "It is obvious you have a right to the blood debt." Her eyes flicked to Elena, Majda, and Jean-

Baptiste. "For the sake of formalities, do you claim the two vampires as family?"

"Yes." He turned to Favashi. "Will you dispute?"

A shake of her head. "Jean-Baptiste's term of service at Lumia ended four decades ago. He is free to choose his allegiance."

"The copy of your consort is young, Raphael," Michaela said, hip cocked, one hand placed on that hip. "She remains within her Contract period, will have to serve it out to whoever owns her."

Jean-Baptiste closed his hand tightly over his wife's as Majda's face went white. Jaw rigid, he said, "Gian Made her by force. There is no Contract."

His words were live grenades thrown into the room. The Making of vampires was strictly regulated. Each archangel had his or her own rules, but there *were* rules. Angels couldn't simply go around Making vampires; they needed the permission of at least one of the Cadre, though that permission might be given once and hold for millennia.

There were meant to be *no* vampires in the world who did not trace back to at least one of the Cadre, even if the thread was a nebulous one where the Cadre member would not interfere in the vampire's existence except in very rare circumstances. It had to do with the balance of the world, with blood and with life.

"He lies," Gian said again. "She is Charisemnon's."

This time, Raphael knew they couldn't simply ignore the words.

Unexpectedly, it was Raphael's mortal enemy who handed Majda her freedom. "Do you think me a fool?" Charisemnon said to Gian, his voice full of rage. "I will not be used by a mere angel who wishes to meddle in the affairs of his betters. The woman is yours, Raphael."

Raphael turned to Majda. "Choose your allegiance—you are not under Contract, but you must be under archangelic oversight until you have passed ten decades as a vampire."

Despite the fact Jean-Baptiste was free and clear of his own obligations to serve an archangel, he came immediately to kneel in front of Raphael. He had his hand clasped around his wife's, and though it was apparent she didn't understand the rules, she followed him without hesitation.

"I swear to be loyal. My blood is your blood," Jean-Baptiste said, his wife repeating the words. "My life is yours to command. I will serve no other but you."

Raphael nodded at the two to return to their previous positions. "Gian is mine to punish," he said flatly. "However, the wider question of Lumia remains."

"Raze it," Favashi said, exposing the steel core that lived beneath her soft, elegant surface. "There should've never been a place on earth that wasn't under Cadre control."

Charisemnon nodded. "We are the masters of this world."

"If I may . . ." The hesitant words were spoken by Donael, the eons-old angel having been hovering on the edge of the circle since the beginning.

Neha looked at him with a coldness that spoke of the poison that was her greatest weapon. "Speak, Donael. I give you this opportunity only because I knew you once as a man of great wisdom."

Bowing his head lower than Elena had ever before seen one of the Luminata bow to anyone, Donael said, "The Luminata play an important role in angelic society. We are the seekers of knowledge and the keepers of art, and we are the one group that can call the Cadre to a meeting when things reach a breaking point as they have in Lady Lijuan's territory."

He breathed deep, exhaled. "Ending us will leave a vacuum. And even should we put all that aside, angels need a space where they can come to find their souls, a place where the mind can be free."

Elena felt her lips twist at that pretty little speech, but she kept her silence. Surprisingly, it was Hannah who broke it, the other woman having come in with Elijah. "I would speak," she said quietly. "Not as Elijah's consort, but as an artist."

When no one in the Cadre interrupted, she said, "I have been absorbed in the Gallery since we arrived. I found great joy in this place that safely houses so much of our artistic history."

Elena saw Donael begin to smile. But Hannah wasn't done.

"However," she said, "even as I studied the astonishing array in the Gallery, I was aware that few eyes ever get to see these works of art." A frown lay heavy on her elegant features.

"The Luminata have become a more and more closed sect in the time since I have been Elijah's consort, until ordinary angels do not believe they have the right to come here and interrupt the brothers' contemplation."

No smile on Donael's face now, nothing but an insulted stiffness.

"That is not right," Hannah said. "If the Gallery is a library of the greatest art produced by our people, then angelkind should be able to visit at will, should be *encouraged* to visit. It disturbs me that the Luminata seem to consider these treasures their own and that they, and they alone, are the ones who decide which works will be displayed and which won't."

The other consort's gaze went to beyond Elena. "I would ask that Aodhan also be permitted a voice."

"He is an artist," Caliane murmured. "A respected student of the Hummingbird. I would hear his thoughts."

Aodhan rarely spoke when he was with a larger group, but today, he said, "Lady Hannah speaks true. It is also regretful that the Luminata have discarded artworks without any oversight.

"While I was visiting with the healer who has been helping Ibrahim"—he indicated Laric's small form, the healer almost hiding behind Aodhan—"I discovered a damaged painting by the Hummingbird. Laric saved it from a room that seems to act as a gathering place for things bound for destruction, was told he could have it as it was no longer good enough for the Gallery."

The reaction to his revelation was visible and audible. Even Titus, who Elena hadn't thought was particularly artistically inclined, fisted his hands. *Illium's mother is far more important to angelkind than I understand, isn't she?*

Raphael's response held a gentleness he only ever betrayed when speaking about the Hummingbird. *She is a treasure, broken perhaps beyond repair, but a treasure nonetheless.*

44

"If we have made mistakes," Donael said into the dangerous quiet, "we are happy to mend our ways. If the Cadre says the Gallery should be open to all angelkind, then it will be opened."

"That is the problem, Donael," Astaad said, his fingers stroking his goatee. "The Luminata should have come to that conclusion themselves. What is the goal of luminescence if not wisdom?"

Elena wanted to speak so badly that she could feel the words shoving at her throat, but she'd learned a few things about angelic politics in the time since she'd become Raphael's consort. Her voice could well work against her interests— many of the Cadre still viewed her as too mortal to understand immortal concerns.

She held her silence. For now.

"You set yourself up as rulers in my territory," Charisemnon said, his eyes hot with a rage that had never died down. "How do you excuse this?"

Donael bowed low again. "There is no excuse."

"Pretty words." Michaela's green eyes glowed as if backlit. "You are one of the oldest and most respected men here, and yet you expect us to believe you did not know of your brethren's traitorous actions?"

"I focused too deep on my own luminescence," Donael said, apology in every line of his body. "I let Gian and his coterie run things because it was easier than arguing and because it permitted me to walk the path without distractions."

"As far as I'm concerned," Elena muttered under her breath, "he's as culpable as Gian."

Wildfire blue eyes met hers. "I agree, Guild Hunter. But we must let this run through—there are certain rules to be observed."

"That is akin to a general leaving his troops in the care of a lower-ranked soldier," Titus said, folding his arms across his massive chest, his muscles bulging under the cream-colored linen of his shirt. That color reflected the feathers at the inner curve of his left wing, before they darkened slowly into a golden honey shade at the primaries, the change so gradual that it was impossible to say where one color ended and the other began.

His right wing was the opposite: golden honey at the inner curve, flowing out into pure cream primaries.

"The Gallery is a custom-built construction that has survived countless earth shakes, storms, and rains," Favashi pointed out, dismissing Donael without a word. "Should it survive this storm, there is no need to destroy it even if we erase the Luminata."

"Agreed." That came from every one of the Cadre.

The Luminata, meanwhile, were beginning to turn a little green—and Donael no longer looked so confident in his self-appointed role as speaker for the sect. But he spoke again. "We cannot all be blamed for the actions of the few."

Alexander stirred. "He is correct in one respect. We should separate the ones who truly seek luminescence from the ones who are here only because Lumia provides them a safe haven from angelic law."

"Elijah," Raphael said. "The mortal women we discovered, we need to speak to them."

"I will fetch them," Hannah said and disappeared from the room in a sweep of wings, to return a bare minute later, Josette and Sahar having clearly been stashed nearby.

The two were dressed in simple but exquisite gowns that must've come from Hannah, their hair braided neatly. Fear made their faces stark, their movements ragged as they followed Hannah to stand between her and Elijah.

"Can you identify the Luminata who visited you?" Hannah asked without prompting.

The women trembled.

"No harm will come to you." It was Michaela who spoke. "You have the promise of the Cadre."

Josette's amber eyes met Elena's at that instant. Elena gave her a slight nod.

"Yes," the Frenchwoman whispered. "I know the ones who came to me." She named them one by one. "I was willing," she added in fairness. "They said I could go afterward."

Space appeared around certain Luminata as their brethren drew away in a whisper of robes.

Finishing her list, Josette whispered to Sahar, who nodded and, standing up straight, began to recite her own list. "Two don't give name, say to call him 'Master.'" Her descriptions of those two were very precise.

More spaces opened up.

In the end, the women marked twelve Luminata, not counting Gian—who appeared to have saved his sadism for Majda and Jean-Baptiste.

Faces holding no arrogance now, nothing but terror, the twelve marked men obeyed an order to join their leader, all going down on their knees, heads bowed.

"We strayed off the path," one whispered. "Please forgive us."

Elena recognized that rough voice. *Gervais*. The man who had referred to the Luminata's victims as "sluts and toys." Gritting her teeth, she gripped Raphael's hand hard to keep herself from stabbing the bastard right through his lying mouth.

Blood spurted from his mouth in the next instant.

Elena jerked, wondering if she had thrown the knife. Then his eyes began to bleed, as did his ears. She didn't know which archangel in the circle had done that, but as his body fell twitching to the floor, his brethren began to beg for mercy.

"Silence!" Alexander's voice filled the air, cutting off all other sound. "I do not care for mortal concerns except in my own territory," he said, "but I care that vampires were Made without permission, that immortals were murdered, and that the Luminata believe themselves beyond all oversight. That ends today."

"First," Caliane murmured, "we must dig out every piece of the rot. Thirteen alone could not have done this." She began to sing, a haunting, beautiful song that brought tears to Elena's eyes and had Majda and Jean-Baptiste clinging to each other.

The most interesting affect, however, was on the Luminata.

A number seemed compelled to drag themselves to join their marked brethren, some literally crawling there on their hands and knees as they fought the pull, their faces distorted into a mask of horror as Caliane stripped away their free will.

For the first time, Elena couldn't bring herself to care. These men had stolen others' free will; the punishment suited the crime.

Caliane stopped singing when the group in the center had grown to twenty-seven and no other Luminata crawled forward. "These are the ones who abused and murdered mortals, and who killed the vampires and angels who would not look the other way." She flicked out a hand and twenty-six bodies, including Gervais's yet-twitching form, turned to ash under the searing white of her power.

Gian stared unblinking at where his brethren had knelt.

"You may not care about mortal concerns outside your lands, Alex," Caliane murmured, "but I have always believed that we rule only if we prove ourselves rulers."

Heart thunder in her ears, Elena swallowed to wet a dry throat. *Jesus, Raphael. Your mother doesn't play games.*

She is too old for it. Pure ruthlessness in his tone. *And her song does not lie.*

Oh, I'm not sorry the bastards are dead.

"There is a second layer of rot," Elijah said into the stunned silence.

"Yes. The ones that knew and did nothing, though they did not participate." The Archangel of India looked around at the Cadre. "We must make certain decisions."

Whatever happened next, it wasn't vocalized, but Elena could feel the violent energy in the air as the Cadre spoke mind to mind. It was Caliane who pronounced the judgment. "The Cadre is agreed. Lumia will continue to exist, as will the Luminata."

No one shuddered in relief, well aware the hammer was yet to fall.

"Only Luminata who have joined the sect in the past fifty years are permitted to remain—we judge that these novices are apt to be untainted by corruption and offer the best hope for Lumia's future. The rest are exiled forever from Lumia."

Donael fell to his knees, his face crumpling into near-tears. "Mercy, my lady."

Caliane's eyes held no pity. "If you are a true seeker, you do not need Lumia. You will find luminescence on a rocky mountaintop or on sandy soil or in a ragged hut in the forest. You do not need the comforts of this place."

It was a harsh judgment.

"There is no appeal," Charisemnon added, his tone unbending.

"And," Alexander said, "Lumia will now be under direct Cadre oversight, watched over by a group formed of angels and vampires from each of our territories. The private guard will be disbanded."

"As for the charge given to the Luminata to call the Cadre to meet," Neha said, "you still hold this charge for it is unlikely the issue will come up again in the near future. By the time it does, it is the Cadre's hope that the Luminata will be back on the right path."

Raphael, the townspeople. We made a promise.

Trust me, Elena-mine.

Always. With not just her life, but the lives of all those she loved.

There were a number of other comments by the Cadre. It was as things appeared to be winding down that Raphael spoke. "We cannot leave the situation with the town as it is."

"Not all of us have a soft spot for mortals," Michaela said with silken venomousness.

Thank God, Elena thought to herself. Michaela had been acting a little too likable. Good to know she was still a bitch.

"It is a town only of mortals."

That fact caused several frowns.

"An imbalance that could spread." Alexander looked at Caliane.

His fellow Ancient nodded. "Such an imbalance has led to mass bloodshed in the past. When you isolate a group of prey, it is an invitation to a certain class of vampires."

"You are the one who saw the problem," Astaad said to Raphael. "Do you see a solution?"

"That the vampires and angels who are to guard and oversee Lumia make their homes in town. There is no need for them to stay in the barracks—whatever rules the Luminata created of late, it was never custom that the guards also take vows of celibacy."

Alexander laughed, the sound echoing inside the Atrium. "I know for a fact none of my warriors would've ever volunteered for guard duty had that been a requirement."

"Charisemnon," Raphael said, "do you particularly desire to rule the town? It will mean extra work for you in comparison to the rest of us."

Clever, Raphael. He'd just made it so if Charisemnon took over the town, he'd have his attention divided when Titus was massing on his border.

"No." Charisemnon waved a hand. "The oversight committee can handle the town."

"You must cede your rights to it," Elijah said, picking up the baton with a smoothness that said he'd guessed exactly what Raphael was doing. "Else, we will be accused of stealing your lands."

"Since when did you become such a stickler, Eli?" Charisemnon's tone made Elena blink—because it was clear the two men had been friends once upon a time. "Very well, I cede any ruling rights to the township, as per the borders marked on the map kept in the Refuge."

"It will not be a part of Lumia," Raphael said. "That must be clear. There must *never* be a repeat of an effective fiefdom."

"Agreed." Every single archangelic voice seemed to say that at the same time, their combined power so violent it made Elena's lungs hurt as her body struggled to take in enough oxygen for a couple of seconds.

"Our people will live in and rule the township," Favashi completed. "We will have to come up with a group that we trust." A frown. "It would be better if someone with wisdom and age was at the center."

"Sire." Aodhan's quiet voice. "If I may suggest the Hummingbird."

That, Elena was not expecting. Illium's mother was astonishingly gifted and had a sense of goodness about her that was haunting, but she was also fractured deep within. "Are you sure?" she murmured. "I've always thought she needs routine." The Hummingbird had come more often to New York since the time Illium fell from the sky, but even then, she tended to stick to the people and places she knew.

"She does," Raphael said, a frown on his face. "Why do you suggest this, Aodhan? You know she will not leave the Refuge beyond a certain period."

"The Hummingbird also has a compulsion to help others," Aodhan said. "And she does not need to be always at the township—she can return to the Refuge several times a year. Healing the people of the town will give her a purpose."

Something unspoken passed between Aodhan and Raphael at that instant, and Elena knew she was missing something, but she didn't ask. When Illium wanted her to know, he'd tell her. Until then, she'd keep her counsel. But she wanted to add something. "If you suggest her, make sure she has support staff."

A nod, before Raphael turned to the Cadre. His suggestion was met with shock . . . then slow and thoughtful agreement. In the end, it was decided to offer the task to her, and tell her that she could bring anyone she wished with her. Though she was technically part of Raphael's territory, no one appeared to have any concerns that she'd be partisan.

"The Hummingbird lives in her own world," Neha murmured. "She will not play politics."

That seemed to be it. The Cadre left one by one, after first ordering the exiled Luminata to gather their belongings in readiness for departure as soon as the storm passed. Neha took charge of Ibrahim, asking General Hiran, Valerius, and Xander to bring the injured man to her suite. Laric went with his patient.

Caliane was the last to leave. Touching her hand to Raphael's, she said, "Do not let death define you, my son."

"Gian's crime was against you," Raphael said to Elena's

grandparents after his mother had exited the room, leaving the six of them alone. "You have the right to decide his punishment."

Elena saw rage fill the eyes of her grandfather, saw his fangs flash. But when he would've stalked toward Gian, Majda placed a single hand on his chest and shook her head. "We are not him," she whispered to Jean-Baptiste. "The archangel's advice was not for our grandchild's husband, it was for us. We are *not* him. We do not torture. We do not get drunk on ugliness and violence." Her voice shook. "We love. That is who we are."

Jean-Baptiste trembled, but forced his eyes off Gian's cringing body. "Archangel," he said roughly, his gaze locked with his wife's. "I would ask a great favor. Imprisonment, not death." He shook his head at Majda when she parted her lips. "We are not him, but he also does not deserve to die quickly. That is too much mercy."

"Imprisonment. It is done." Raphael looked at Gian. "You will not fly free for the same amount of time you imprisoned each of your victims, the terms to run consecutively. At which point, they will decide if you deserve the mercy of death."

Gian screamed. "No! I am the Luminata! I am—"

Flicking a faint touch of power toward him, Raphael sent him into unconsciousness. "Aodhan, carry him to an empty room and lock him there for the duration. Stand guard. We will take him with us and he'll serve his imprisonment under the same sky where Majda and Jean-Baptiste's blood flies free."

Thunder boomed above them, but when Elena looked up to the miraculously whole glass dome of the Atrium, she saw no flashes of lightning in the turbulent black sky. The storm was passing. Raphael would leave for China in a matter of hours . . . would fly into the territory of the Archangel of Death.

45

Stay safe, Archangel. Or I'll hunt you down.

The words she'd spoken to Raphael before she got on the plane to New York and he turned to fly back to rejoin the rest of the Cadre.

As always, he'd smiled, kissed her. "I would not dare be hurt. Watch over my city, *hbeebti*."

She would, to the very best of her ability.

Turning from the edge of the high Tower balcony from where she'd watched the skies for him since the instant she landed earlier that morning, Elena looked at the woman who stood in the doorway. Majda and Jean-Baptiste had come with her to New York, would stay for a little while, but Elena guessed they'd be returning to Morocco, to the place that had been their home.

Sadness lay a heavy shroud on Majda's features; it had been that way ever since Elena told her about Marguerite on the plane, about the baby Majda had fled with to safety. "Jean-Baptiste had told me to run if he ever disappeared," Majda had said after the first rush of tears. "Just run and keep going."

"Did you go to France because it was his homeland?"

A smile that held no joy. "No. That would've made it too easy for Gian to track us. My husband, though he has such a French name, was born in the Amazon jungle to scientist parents. I ended up in France by chance, stayed because my baby needed a home."

The two of them hadn't spoken much more about the details behind Majda's flight. They'd had time in Lumia, but Majda and Jean-Baptiste had needed that time to adapt to freedom and to just be with one another after decades of torment. One thing Majda had asked was why Elena was named Elena.

"After you," Elena had told her. "My father chose the name that's on my birth certificate, but I'm fairly certain my mother made sure that name was one that could be shortened to Elena."

It had made Majda cry again. "Sana Alayna," she'd whispered. "That is the name I used in Paris—most people who knew me called me Alayna. To a child, it must've sounded very much like Elena."

Now, Elena forced herself to stop watching the sky for her archangel, knowing it was far too early to see him, and walked to join her grandmother. Like most beings without wings, Majda didn't like to come out onto these railingless balconies where, when the wind was high, it could shove you right off if you weren't careful. "I want you to meet someone, Majda."

The beautiful woman with hair just a shade more golden than Elena's reached out to touch her fingers to Elena's cheek. "I am your grandmother, child."

"I know." Elena gave her a wry smile. "But you look my age. I'm having difficulty getting my head around that." She wasn't sure she'd ever be able to address Majda by anything but her name.

Majda's expression altered, became layered with myriad emotions. "My parents didn't want me to marry Jean-Baptiste," she told Elena as they walked down the hallway. "He was young for a vampire but he was still a vampire. They knew of a woman in a neighboring town who'd been abandoned by her vampire husband after she began to turn gray."

"Unfortunately, that still happens." It was what Elena had worried most about when it came to her sister, Beth, but Bethie had gained an unexpected internal strength with the birth of her daughter. Elena didn't think this new, fiercely protective Beth would break even if Harrison pulled a disappearing act. Not that Beth's vampire husband seemed in any danger of ever doing that—he was terrified of losing her to time, regret in his every action.

Harrison had become a vampire first even though he and Beth had agreed that they'd wait until both of them were accepted. He'd been impatient, cocky. And he would pay for it through eternity. Because Elena's baby sister could never become a vampire—her body would reject the change in a gruesome, painful manner. Elena would one day have to watch her baby sister close her eyes forever, Beth's body no longer able to hold on to life.

It hurt to think about.

"Yet you married Jean-Baptiste anyway," she said to her mother's mother.

"I love him, have loved him from the instant we first bumped into each other in the marketplace." Majda spread her hand over her heart. "It felt as if I'd found a missing part of my soul."

"Did you plan to apply to become a vampire?"

A nod. "But we had no expectation that I'd be accepted—Jean-Baptiste was a young vampire himself, hadn't earned the right to ask the favor of a powerful angel." Majda touched her hand to Elena's wing, a wondering light in her eyes. "And to think we now have an angel in the family."

"More than one," Elena pointed out. "You also have Raphael and Caliane."

Gentle laughter as Majda dropped her hand, but the sadness, it never faded. "We married with the knowledge that I would leave him after a mortal lifetime—I was overjoyed that I would never have to worry about his death. For my husband . . . it was hard."

"It *is* hard," Elena said, thinking of Sara, of Beth, of Zoe, of Maggie, of Deacon, of Ransom . . . So many strong, unique lives that would one day no longer exist. "But my friend, Sara, she pointed out that immortals live dangerous lives. Knowing I could actually die before her helps me deal."

Majda gave her a considering look before her lips kicked up. "Of course, you are right." She shook her head. "My parents are gone, but it's not as if Jean-Baptiste and I have had an easy life for the past six decades." The dry way she said that told Elena a hell of a lot about her grandmother's strength.

"When did Gian become obsessed with you?" she asked, having the feeling her grandmother could talk about this today.

"He tried to court me a month after my wedding." Majda hugged her arms around herself, running her hands up and down her arms. "At first, I was kind. I thought he simply didn't realize that I was married, so I told him I was a new bride and that I honored my husband." An exhale. "I added that last because there are women who do not honor their husbands when angels invite them to their beds."

"Angel groupies."

"Yes, is this what you call them? We used to call them angel-drunk." Majda got into the elevator with her, and Elena pushed the button to take them to the ground floor. It was a floor she rarely visited now that she had wings—but today, she wouldn't be flying across the sky.

"Of course," Majda added, "it wasn't only women who could become drunk on the angels, though we did not talk about that in my time."

"I'm guessing Gian didn't stop his efforts to win you?"

"No, he did," Majda said to her surprise, "and I thought that he was one of the better angels from that place." A twist to her mouth. "Then Jean-Baptiste came home in a fury one day. Gian had called him into his office and offered him money if he would surrender his rights to me." Her body shook. "As if I was a thing to be bought and sold."

"Bastard." The deep, dark hole where Raphael had dropped Gian wasn't a harsh enough punishment as far as Elena was concerned. Maybe rats would get into that hole, start feasting on him. At least he couldn't use his powers to escape. Anything he blasted would just fall on top of him, crushing him to a pulp. Of course, they weren't leaving that to chance. Illium had helped bug the hole with cameras and microphones so the Tower could monitor it, make certain Gian didn't find a way out.

And with each and every breath he took, the former leader of the Luminata had to inhale the bitter knowledge that he was buried in the same place where his victims—and their granddaughter—walked free. Majda and Jean-Baptiste had asked not to be told where exactly in the territory Gian was imprisoned; it was enough for them that he was paying for his crimes—they didn't want to take the chance of obsessing on the location of Gian's prison should they become aware of it.

Majda's voice broke into Elena's thoughts, the other woman continuing her story. "I was young, and I was afraid my husband would blame me for Gian's interest. Many men would have." Her tone was pragmatic, that of a woman who'd seen such unfairness too many times to be surprised by it. "But he didn't. He said he knew I would never dishonor our vows, that the dishonor was Gian's and Gian's alone. And he said the same to Gian's face."

"Grandpa has guts," Elena said, then shook her head as they stepped out of the elevator. "Yeah, I can't call him Grandpa, either. He's way too hot." And *that* thought wigged her out but it was a hard one to avoid when others in the Tower insisted on pointing it out.

Majda's laughter was startled. "He adores you already, you know." A deep smile that reached her sad eyes. "Not simply because you are the child of our child, but because you have so much courage and fire."

"He clearly has a thing for women with courage and fire," Elena said to the woman who must have an incredible well of both to have survived the decades she'd spent as a prisoner.

Majda's eyes lit up even more. "Clearly."

Elena said hello to Suhani as they walked through the lobby, her mind skipping back to their first meeting—on the day her life changed forever. "I can guess the rest," she said after Suhani replied with a wave and a smile, the receptionist proud of the fact that she was the first person to whom Elena had ever spoken in the Tower, not counting Dmitri, who'd been on the door that fateful day. "Gian kept up the pressure—"

"No," Majda interrupted. "He backed off and we thought he'd accepted the rebuke." She drew a deep draught of the New York air as they stepped out into the sunny day, the noise of the city assaulting their senses. "This city you live in, it is extraordinary. So *big* and chaotic and yet with such a vibrant pattern to its chaos."

Elena felt a flicker of hope. "You're thinking of staying?"

"Yes." The clouds returned. "We will visit our town one day soon, but we'll go knowing that most of the people we loved are gone. And our memories of it are forever twined with pain and fear."

She reached out to take Elena's hand. "This place, it is our granddaughter's home, and it is new. We will become new here, too." A smile. "Old in our love—that has never faltered. But new in our paths." She looked curiously at the large vehicle that had just come to a standstill at the end of the path to the Tower.

It was a Hummer SUV that had been gutted so the back was open but for metal bars that provided a handhold. "Wings," Elena said, jerking her thumb back to indicate hers. "I wanted to ride with you and this was the best option." She glanced around. "Where's Jean-Baptiste?"

"He should be here soon," Majda answered. "I told him you'd asked to meet—but he has found a friend in the vampire who sounds like liquid music when he talks. They were with Dmitri when I left."

"Janvier?"

"Yes, Janvier." A sparkle in Majda's eyes. "That one has charm bred into his bones, just like Jean-Baptiste." The sparkle grew. "You have not seen it yet for he is so very angry, but I think when it reappears, you will understand how I stood no chance when he decided I was the woman for him."

Elena grinned at the idea of her grandfather being a smooth-talking charmer. "You two fit." Just like she fit with Raphael, Janvier with Ashwini.

"Yes." Looking back toward the Tower door, as if searching for him, Majda said, "It hurts him to talk about Marguerite, so I will tell you what you should know before he arrives."

"You don't have to—"

"It is part of your history, *azeeztee*—"

Elena didn't hear the rest through the slam of emotion, her heart a tornado in her chest. "No one has called me that for two decades."

"She remembered?" A rasping whisper. "My precious baby remembered?"

Elena nodded. "Her mother's kisses, the way you had such

a soft voice when speaking to her, the words you used most often."

Tears glittered in Majda's eyes. "She didn't believe herself abandoned?"

"No." Elena frowned. "She grew up believing you died in a bus accident where your body was washed away."

"Sister Constance." A shaken whisper. "She did what I asked, must've used the bus crash when it happened at the right time." Sobs broke her words into pieces.

Elena didn't hesitate. She leaned in and took the woman who was her grandmother into her arms. And thought—*she's so small.* Like her own mother had been. It was Jeffrey who'd given Elena her height. Wrapping her wings around Majda to shield her from prying eyes, she held her grandmother as Majda sobbed for her lost child who had grown up knowing she had been deeply loved by her mother.

"Gian left me alone for a year," Majda whispered some time later, her sobs having left a rasp in her throat and her arms still around Elena. "I thought he'd moved on, but he hadn't. And when I became with child, he was enraged, though I didn't discover that until he had me captive. He beat one of the other Luminata so badly that it took him months to recover."

"Hell." All those angels were over a thousand years old, with the attendant healing powers, which meant Gian had turned someone into mincemeat. As he'd nearly done to Ibrahim. The angel remained in *anshara* under Laric's watchful eye, the healer having chosen to stay in Lumia until Ibrahim was healed. He had the Cadre's permission to continue on at Lumia afterward, but he'd decided to head for the Refuge and the Medica, where Keir had already offered him a position.

"I will be brave," he'd told them using the silent tongue. "I will try. I do not want to become like the Luminata, so closed within myself that I cease to see the value of others."

Elena intended to get in touch with Jessamy, give the other woman a heads-up that Laric might need a little of her gentle kindness and guidance. But today, her attention was on the woman who'd survived interminable horror.

"Gian didn't come near me while I was pregnant," her grandmother told her. "He was repulsed by the fact I carried

Jean-Baptiste's child. But two weeks after our baby was born, before we had settled our argument over her name—Jean-Baptiste wanted to call her Marguerite, while I preferred Taliyah—my husband disappeared."

Majda pulled away, her face marked by tears but her eyes clear. "I searched for him, we all did, never thinking the angels would go so far as to hurt a vampire aligned to the Archangel Favashi—until Gian came to my parents' home and made me an offer: that he would take care of me like a princess if I would be his mistress. I just had to leave my daughter behind."

Hands fisting, she gritted out the next words. "He made it a point to say that my husband was no longer a problem. That was when I knew Gian had taken him. At the time, I believed Jean-Baptiste dead. And I knew my baby was another problem Gian would either eventually eliminate . . . or he'd abuse that babe. Simply because she was my husband's child."

Majda's gaze was no longer broken; it held only fury. "Gian, he taunted us that he would have you. He called you my daughter."

"The asshole isn't taunting anyone now."

A hard nod from her grandmother, this soft woman who nonetheless had a core of steel. "No, but back then, he held all the power."

"So you ran." Elena couldn't imagine her fear and pain.

"I wasn't yet fully recovered from the birth, but my parents urged me to go, gave me every last cent they had, did all they could to conceal my departure to give me time to get away." Her body shook. "Gian told me later that he'd beaten them both when they wouldn't tell him where I'd gone, left them so severely injured that they would've died if not for neighbors who nursed them back to health. He said it was a sign of his *devotion*."

Elena's grandmother looked like she wanted to spit. "I learned how to look after my beautiful Marguerite without my own mother nearby and my heart's love presumed dead, managed to make a life for me and my baby in Paris, thought we were safe as she grew into a toddler who spoke so sweetly to me . . . then I saw an angel watching me one day."

A chill of remembered fear drew the blood away from her

face. "I thought I was being foolish, but still, in the depths of the night, I carried Marguerite out of our apartment and I hid in a place where I could watch that apartment. I told Marguerite it was a game."

She smiled. "My baby was so good, played with her toys and never complained even when I realized I'd forgotten to pack her favorite snack. Even when I told her we couldn't go back to our apartment because a bad angel was watching it. Instead, I took my child into a church where I knew the nun was kind."

She rubbed a fist over her heart. "I kissed my *azeeztee* good-bye, and then I ran, my intent to lead the hunters as far from Marguerite as possible. They caught up to me in Turkey."

Squeezing her eyes shut, Majda breathed in and out in a fast rhythm. "I escaped once from Lumia. That was when Gian chained me up underground. It was a horror to see Jean-Baptiste, see how Gian had been taking his jealous rage out on my husband, but seeing that he was alive, it also kept me strong."

"*Why* is Jean-Baptiste still alive?"

"At first, it was so Gian could brutalize him for his own gratification. Later, it was because Gian wanted us to suffer—I by watching my husband being hurt, Jean-Baptiste by having to watch Gian . . ."

Anger scalded Elena's veins at the words her grandmother didn't say, the atrocities she didn't enumerate. "You don't have to tell me. I can guess."

"When I thought I'd break," her grandmother said instead, "I'd speak to my husband, and no matter how emaciated he became, or how much pain he was in, he'd tell me to think of our daughter growing in freedom, in the light. We knew Gian hadn't found her—he would've never been able to keep that to himself. "

A soft hand cupping Elena's cheek. "Now we will think of you. Daughter of our daughter."

"My mother loved to dance," Elena found herself saying just as Jean-Baptiste stepped out of the Tower doors, his hair shining golden. "When I was little, sometimes we'd dance in the rain and play in water pools." It caused her pain to talk about Marguerite, but it was worth it to see the hungry joy in Majda's eyes.

She continued to speak after they got into the SUV.

Her grandparents soaked up her stories, laughed and cried, asked her more and more questions about her mother. Elena answered everything, found herself smiling more than once as she talked about events she'd almost forgotten—like the time she'd found her mother and Beth giggling together as Beth "helped" her bake a cake. "Except most of the mix was on Beth's face," she said with a laugh.

"I would like to meet our other granddaughter," Jean-Baptiste said. "I think we are ready."

"That's where we're going." Ten minutes later, she nodded to the right. "This is her house." It was a home into which Beth had moved without telling Elena until it was done.

"It has big enough doors for you," her sister had said when she finally sent Elena a message asking her to come over. "Harrison picked our other house, and he wouldn't let me renovate. So I moved."

Elena's heart had all but exploded—she'd never expected such stubborn determination from her baby sister. Neither had Harrison. But the vampire had caved and the entire family now lived in the dual-level Lenox Hill home Beth had chosen.

Elena had offered to give Beth any money she needed to clear what she'd assumed was a large mortgage, given the location of the house. She'd already set up a regular transfer to Beth's account so that her sister didn't have to rely financially on her husband. The only reason she hadn't given Beth a big chunk at once was because she knew that while Bethie was a great mom, she wasn't too good with money.

But her sister had shaken her head. "Daddy paid," she'd said, her turquoise eyes dark as they looked into Elena's. "He's not so bad, Ellie. He loves you, too. I told him why I wanted to move and he didn't argue, just wrote the check."

That Elena and Jeffrey had a complicated relationship was an understatement.

"Beth is strong," Elena told her grandparents. "Stronger than I knew for a long time, but she's also the baby of our family." Not Jeffrey's new family, but their original unit of six.

"I understand, Elena," Majda said. "We will treat her with care."

Elena had told her sister they were coming and Beth was waiting for them in the doorway, a wide smile on her face and her body clad in a lovely floral print dress with a big skirt. "Is this them?" she asked excitedly before running over to hug first Majda then Jean-Baptiste with warm exuberance. "I'm so happy to meet you!"

Both grandparents smiled in unabashed delight.

Beth had that effect on people.

"Hello, Bethie." Elena hugged her sister when she came over, kissed her temple.

And heard an excited cry behind Beth. Releasing her sister, she turned just in time to scoop up a gorgeous toddler dressed in a neat blue pinafore and with a ribbon in her air. "Hello, Giggles."

Her niece giggled and kissed her on the mouth. "Aniellie!"

"Yes, Auntie Ellie." Elena rubbed noses with her niece before turning to her stunned grandparents. "Grandmother, Grandfather," she said because this was about family, "I'd like you to meet Marguerite Aribelle, your great-granddaughter." She kissed her niece's soft cheek. "Maggie."

Maggie stared from Elena to Majda as her great-grandparents' eyes shined wet at the knowledge that their family line was another generation strong.

"Aniellie?" Maggie said at last, a frown on her little face as she looked at Majda.

"No, this is Great-grandma Majda," Elena said. "You want to give her a kiss?"

Maggie's smile was shy, but she held out her arms. Majda took her great-granddaughter with gentle care, her entire body trembling. "Hello, *azeeztee*." It was a whisper.

Patting at her wet cheeks, Maggie said, "Gamma have boo-boo?"

Majda shook her head. "I'm happy." She leaned in, accepted Maggie's sweet kiss. "Would you like to meet your great-grandfather?"

Her mother's daughter, Maggie fell head over heels for her handsome great-grandfather, all but batting her lashes as he took her into his arms. He, in turn, was clearly besotted.

Looking at Elena with eyes that held a piercing joy, Majda said, "We will be staying here. Near our family."

Beth, leaning against Elena, clapped her hands as Elena smiled . . . but her heart, it wasn't in this city she loved or with the people who meant so much to her. It was with an archangel with wings of white gold who was in the heart of nightmare.

Bloodlust

The Cadre had been forced to make landfall not once but multiple times when the lightning storm returned three hours after their departure from Lumia, appearing in erratic bursts as if it was formed by the sheer proximity of so many archangels. Avoiding it had put them behind schedule, but they'd finally arrived in China.

As for their specific destination, they headed straight to the area Jason had pinpointed as having fallen to bloodlust. Jason's information, however, was now a week out of date—and things had deteriorated. Smoke rose from burning homes several miles forward of where Jason had marked the then current line of blood red.

The Cadre flew on, past the burning buildings and deeper.

Below them, the movements were jagged. People running, others moving almost like crabs as they scuttled over the landscape and tried to hide from angelic shadows. The same pattern continued for miles, right up to the mountains that acted as a natural barrier.

Turning in silence, they flew back over the bloodlust-drenched lands. Elijah dropped first, to take care of what appeared to be a large village. Favashi took the next kiss of vampires. Then Raphael. He knew the others would continue on to do the same. After he cleaned up the insane vampires in his area, executing them as quickly and as cleanly as possible, he rose up and flew past the areas the other archangels were handling, found another section to clear.

Relatively speaking, it didn't take them long to get things under control: a single day. They were a Cadre of archangels after all. The villagers would put out the fires now that they no longer had to fear a vampiric attack.

"We need to go to Lijuan's stronghold," Raphael said when they landed as a group in a clean section ten minutes from the final nest of blood-maddened vampires. "I have the location." He assumed the others did, too—though they might not have been able to get inside. Most archangels didn't have Jason and Naasir on their side.

No one argued with him and they lifted off. All of them should've rested after the amount of time they'd already spent in the air, but this situation had the potential to be catastrophic. And they were archangels for a reason.

They flew.

And arrived at the stronghold in stygian darkness long past midnight. No lights, no sounds, no hint of habitation, the stronghold offered the chilliest welcome. Throwing power into the sky, Alexander lit up the world for a vital minute so they could confirm that the jewel in Lijuan's crown was indeed deserted.

Landing, they explored the hallways to ensure there could be no misunderstanding.

Those hallways were not only empty of all life, but bare of any signs that anyone had *ever* lived here. No paintings, none of the large vases Naasir's mate had mentioned seeing here, nothing but dusty emptiness. The starkness couldn't take away from the beauty of the stronghold itself, but there was a hollowness here now, a sense of loss.

Meeting back in the courtyard at dawn, they waited for everyone to arrive before Titus said, "Lijuan wouldn't strip her stronghold if she planned to return."

"It is clear that she's gone," Astaad said. "She wouldn't have permitted our interference elsewise."

Not even Charisemnon raised an objection to that summation.

Neha spoke next. "We are agreed that Favashi will take over, with Caliane's assistance until such time as Favashi has developed enough power to rule alone. Are there any new objections?"

"Then," Michaela said when no one spoke, "Favashi is now Archangel of China, and Alexander regains control of all of Persia."

"That is the will of the Cadre," they stated as one.

Their work complete, they took off into the air one by one. Favashi would return with her people as fast as possible. Since the Cadre had already cleaned up the bloodlust, she'd have a territory that was ragged at the edges, but not one in the process of destroying itself. With Caliane watching, Raphael was confident Favashi could take and maintain control.

As part of that, she'd not only bring in her own people, she'd retain those of Lijuan's people who would work with her. Those who didn't want to serve her would be permitted to scatter after being given any payments they were due. Raphael didn't think Favashi would find any signs of Xi or the tight squadron that reported to him. Wherever it was that Lijuan had made her place of Sleep, that was where they'd find Xi.

Hours of flight later, he wasn't the least surprised to hit the water border of his territory and see wings of midnight and dawn on the horizon. The weight of the world fell away as he closed the distance to his consort. She flew right into his arms and he took them into the sea, protecting them with a bubble of power. He was tired after the sustained time in the air, but the instant he touched Elena, life burst inside him in a scatter of wildfire.

Her kiss held the same fire. "Did you miss me, *hbeebti*?" he asked quietly when they came up for air, his forehead pressed to her own.

"'Missing' isn't a strong enough word." Silver eyes held his own. "Is she dead?"

"No," Raphael said. "The death of someone as powerful as Lijuan would mark the world, as when an archangel rises to power." He shook his head. "No, I am very much afraid she Sleeps to grow to full strength." Lijuan had made mistakes, sought to act the goddess too quickly. It appeared she had learned from her mistakes at long last.

Elena hissed out a breath. "So the next time she rises . . ."

"Yes, Elena-mine. The next time Lijuan rises, she will be a monster to end all monsters."

Author's Note

I visited Morocco knowing I'd be returning to it in spirit when it was time to explore this part of Elena's past, but I never expected to find my inspiration for Lumia right there, perched on a hilltop with astonishing views in every direction and wildflowers dotting the landscape.

Once a grand city, Volubilis now lies in ruins, but it is magnificent nonetheless. Lumia sits in a different location within Morocco and ended up being designed far differently from Volubilis, but Volubilis was the spark from which it grew. If you'd like to see the pictures I took there, please visit the Travel Diary section of my website (you can find it under the "About Nalini" link): www.nalinisingh.com.

While there, I invite you to join my newsletter, which goes out monthly and includes exclusives like free Guild Hunter short stories and deleted scenes. The Welcome newsletter includes several stories sent out in previous newsletters, so you can catch up on any you've missed.

I also want to take this opportunity to thank all the generous people online who so often come to the rescue of writers needing answers to last-minute research questions. I'd particularly like to thank Sonja, Lexxie, Sarah, and Maya, who helped me out on Twitter with my questions about the French language.

Any errors are mine. These people are awesome. And so are all of you!

Turn the page for an excerpt from the

Wild Embrace Anthology

part of Nalini Singh's incredible
Psy-Changeling series!

Author's Note:
This scene takes place on the
deep-sea station Alaris.

Next mail drop, Tazia ensured she was fixing a hydraulic lift on the lowest floor of the station, where no one would come looking for her and where she didn't have to hear the excited cries and see the beaming smiles of her colleagues as they received care packages or unexpected gifts, or letters that made them shed tears of joy.

"Great," she muttered when the relay tube turned out to have a hole in it.

"A problem?"

Her back stiffening where she crouched in front of the exposed inner machinery of the lift, she glanced up at Stefan. "Can't you wear a bell or something?"

"No."

Of course he didn't have a sense of humor. Psy never did. She still couldn't get her mind around the fact that two powerful cardinal Psy, including a gifted foreseer, had recently defected into a changeling pack. How could that possibly work? Changelings were as primal as Psy were cerebral. Like Stefan with his remote gaze and cool words.

"The tube is busted," she told him. "I missed the last equipment request, so we'll have to wait till next month."

"Is it urgent?"

She considered it, aware Stefan was a teleport-capable tele-kinetic. He could bring in emergency equipment in the space of mere minutes if not seconds, his mind reaching across vast distances in a way she could barely comprehend, but the unspoken rule was that the rest of the station personnel didn't ask him for anything that wasn't critical. Everyone knew that if Alaris sprang a fatal pressure leak, they'd need every last ounce of Stefan's abilities to get them to the surface.

"The other lift is still functional," she said, hooking her spanner into her tool belt and tapping in the code that meant the computer would bypass this lift until she recorded it as being back online. "We can survive a month."

He nodded, his dark brown hair military short. Since he wasn't part of the Psy race's armed forces, she thought it was because he had curls; Psy hated anything that was out of control. When he continued to loom over her, she rubbed her hands on her thighs and stood up. That didn't exactly even things out since he was so much taller, but it made her feel better.

He reached out and gripped a lock of hair that had escaped her ponytail. "Grease."

Rolling her eyes, she pulled it out of his grasp. "Was there anything else you wanted?"

"It appears I made a mistake last month in telling you no letter or package would come."

Pain in her heart, her throat. "No, I needed to hear that."

"However, instead of having you snap at everyone for two days a month, you're now so quiet that people are becoming concerned."

Tazia remembered how Andres had been poking at her this morning, trying to make her smile with those silly jokes of his. But he was her friend. Stefan was nothing. "I'm not Psy," she said point-blank. "I can't ignore hurt or forget that my family hates me."

He didn't flinch. "You knew that before. What changed?"

"You took away my hope."

There was a small silence that seemed to reverberate with a thousand unspoken things. For a single instant captured in time, she thought she saw a fracture in his icy composure, a hint of something unexpected in those eyes she'd always thought were beautiful despite their coldness.

Then a tool fell off Tazia's belt and she bent to grab it off the floor. By the time she rose, Stefan was gone. Just as well, she thought, though there was a strange hollowness in her stomach. She wasn't some bug under a microscope for him to study. She was a flesh-and-blood human being with hopes and dreams and emotions. Maybe those emotions made her heart heavy with sorrow and her soul hurt, but she would never choose to erase them in the way of Stefan's people.

What use was it to have such power if you saw no beauty in a child's smile or in the sea's turbulent moods? If you didn't understand friendship or laughter? No, she'd rather feel, even if it hurt so much she could hardly breathe through it at times.

ABOUT GOLLANCZ

Gollancz is the oldest SF publishing imprint in the world. Since being founded in 1927 Gollancz has continued to publish a focused selection of bestselling and award-winning authors. The front-list includes **Ben Aaronovitch**, **Joe Abercrombie**, **Charlaine Harris**, **Joanne Harris**, **Joe Hill**, **Alastair Reynolds**, **Patrick Rothfuss**, **Nalini Singh** and **Brandon Sanderson**.

As one of the largest Science Fiction and Fantasy imprints in the UK it is no surprise we have one of the most extensive backlists in the world. Find high quality SF on Gateway written by such authors as **Philip K. Dick**, **Ursula Le Guin**, **Connie Willis**, **Sir Arthur C. Clarke**, **Pat Cadigan**, **Michael Moorcock** and **George R.R. Martin**.

We also have a strand of publishing in translation, which includes French, Polish and Russian authors. Gollancz is home to more award-winning authors than any other imprint, with names including **Aliette de Bodard**, **M. John Harrison**, **Paul McAuley**, **Sarah Pinborough**, **Pierre Pevel**, **Justina Robson** and many more.

The SF Gateway
More than 3,000 classic, rare and previously out-of-print SF novels at your fingertips.
www.sfgateway.com

The Gollancz Blog
Bringing you news from our worlds to yours. Stories, interviews, articles and exclusive extracts just for you!
www.gollancz.co.uk

GOLLANCZ
LONDON

BRINGING NEWS FROM OUR WORLDS TO YOURS . . .

Want your news daily?

The Gollancz blog has instant updates
on the hottest SF and Fantasy books.

Prefer your updates monthly?

Sign up for our
in-depth newsletter.

www.gollancz.co.uk

Follow us  @gollancz

Find us facebook.com/GollanczPublishing

Classic SF as you've never read it before.

Visit the SF Gateway to find out more!

www.sfgateway.com